OXFORD WORLD'S CLASSICS

AGAINST NATURE
(A rebours)

JORIS-KARL HUYSMANS was born in Paris in the revolutionary year of 1848 into a family of Dutch origins with an artistic pedigree (a background reflected in his own art criticism collected in *L'Art moderne* of 1883 and *Certains* of 1889). The pattern of a life shared between bureaucratic drudgery and literary creativity was set in 1866 when Huysmans was employed by the Ministry of the Interior. Interrupted by conscription in the army in 1870, this pattern was continued when he took up a position in the Versailles Ministry of War during the Commune. His literary career only took off with the publication of *Le Drageoir à épices* in 1874, and for much of the remaining decade he was to be associated with Naturalism, the sociologically engaged literary project which revolved around Émile Zola. The publication of the Decadent 'bible' *Against Nature* (*A rebours*) in 1884 marked a turning-point not only in the creative life of Huysmans but also in the history of *fin de siècle* literary and artistic movements, with which he was intimately connected through his friendships with such writers and critics as Gide, Valéry, Barbey d'Aurevilly, Arthur Symons, and Havelock Ellis. He never married, but maintained an intermittent relationship with a seamstress, Anna Meunier, from 1872 until her death in 1895. The antagonism expressed towards contemporary society and the exploration of a narcissistic and hyperaesthetic subjectivity in *Against Nature* set Huysmans on the path from Symbolism to the Catholicism evident in *La Cathédrale* (1898) and *Sainte Lydwine de Schiedam* (1901). By the time of his death in 1907 he had been made an Officer of the *Légion d'honneur*.

MARGARET MAULDON was born in Buenos Aires, read French and Spanish at Cambridge University, and now lives in the United States. She has taught French in several universities, most recently in Amherst at the University of Massachusetts, and she has worked as a translator since 1987. Her translations of Zola's *L'Assommoir* and Stendhal's *The Charterhouse of Parma* are published in Oxford World's Classics.

NICHOLAS WHITE is a Lecturer in French at Royal Holloway, University of London. In addition to writing a series of articles on the representation of the family in late-nineteenth-century French fiction, he has edited Émile Zola's *L'Assommoir* (Everyman, 1995) and, with Naomi Segal, a collection of essays entitled *Scarlet Letters: Fictions of Adultery from Antiquity to the 1990s* (Macmillan, 1997).

OXFORD WORLD'S CLASSICS

For over 100 years Oxford World's Classics have brought readers closer to the world's great literature. Now with over 700 titles—from the 4,000-year-old myths of Mesopotamia to the twentieth century's greatest novels—the series makes available lesser-known as well as celebrated writing.

The pocket-sized hardbacks of the early years contained introductions by Virginia Woolf, T. S. Eliot, Graham Greene, and other literary figures which enriched the experience of reading. Today the series is recognized for its fine scholarship and reliability in texts that span world literature, drama and poetry, religion, philosophy and politics. Each edition includes perceptive commentary and essential background information to meet the changing needs of readers.

OXFORD WORLD'S CLASSICS

JORIS-KARL HUYSMANS

Against Nature
(À rebours)

Translated by
MARGARET MAULDON

Edited with an Introduction and Notes by
NICHOLAS WHITE

OXFORD
UNIVERSITY PRESS

OXFORD
UNIVERSITY PRESS

Great Clarendon Street, Oxford OX2 6DP

Oxford University Press is a department of the University of Oxford.
It furthers the University's objective of excellence in research, scholarship,
and education by publishing worldwide in

Oxford New York

Athens Auckland Bangkok Bogotá Buenos Aires Calcutta
Cape Town Chennai Dar es Salaam Delhi Florence Hong Kong Istanbul
Karachi Kuala Lumpur Madrid Melbourne Mexico City Mumbai
Nairobi Paris São Paulo Singapore Taipei Tokyo Toronto Warsaw

with associated companies in Berlin Ibadan

Oxford is a registered trade mark of Oxford University Press
in the UK and in certain other countries

Published in the United States
by Oxford University Press Inc., New York

British Library Cataloguing in Publication Data

Data available

Library of Congress Cataloging in Publication Data

Huysmans, J.-K. (Joris-Karl), 1848–1907.
[A rebours. English]
Against nature—A rebours/Joris-Karl Huysmans; translated by
Margaret Mauldon; edited with an introduction and notes by
Nicholas White.
(Oxford world's classics)
Includes bibliographical references.
I. Mauldon, Margaret. II. White, Nicholas, 1967– . III. Title.
IV. Series: Oxford world's classics (Oxford University Press)
PQ2309.H4A6213 1998 843′.8—dc21 97–47774

ISBN–13: 978–0–19–282367–0
ISBN–10: 0–19–282367–1

6

Typeset by Best-set Typesetter Ltd., Hong Kong
Printed in Great Britain by
Clays Ltd, St Ives plc

CONTENTS

INTRODUCTION

If, in a cosy fantasy of cultural influence, one were to present one's young niece or nephew with their first nineteenth-century novel, only the most wicked amongst us would choose Joris-Karl Huysmans's *Against Nature* (in the original French, *A rebours*). Indeed, it is no surprise that Stéphane Mallarmé, the object of Malcolm Bowie's study *The Art of Being Difficult*,[1] should be one of the artists most favoured by Des Esseintes, the hero of *Against Nature*. For the concept of difficulty aptly describes the experience of any reader of Huysmans's farewell to the classic forms of nineteenth-century fiction: difficult, as it is, in its challenge to the received novelistic modes of romantic and realist prose, in its abundance of apparently obscure references which test the reader's cultural knowledge, and quite simply in the linguistic challenge which it presented even to late-nineteenth-century native speakers. Even its hero could be described as difficult, just as a petulant but precocious niece or nephew might be said to be a 'difficult' child. So when *Against Nature* is said to be a 'challenging' novel, this description carries its full potential for euphemistic irony. However, such an epithet also articulates the intellectual excitement of a work which very quickly obtained the status of a cult classic after its publication in 1884.

Huysmans's previous writing did little to prepare his contemporary readership for the shock of a text in which he seemed to turn his back on many of the concerns and themes of his writing career up to that point. Born in the revolutionary year of 1848 to a family of Dutch origins (hence the decidedly un-Gallic name), Huysmans grew up during the Second Empire and became a part of its system of administration in his career as a minor civil servant. At the same time, the background of artistic creativity in the Huysmans family reappeared in the literary talents of this avaricious reader which were to bear fruit in the early years of the Third Republic with the publication of *Le Drageoir à épices* (*The Spice Dish*) in 1874. Until the publication of *Against Nature* a decade later Huysmans was

[1] See Malcolm Bowie, *The Art of Being Difficult* (Cambridge: Cambridge University Press, 1978).

associated (more closely in the public's mind than in actuality) with the project of Naturalist fiction which found its most garrulous French exponent in Émile Zola (born in 1840). In turn quirky, humorous, acerbic, and stubborn, Huysmans would never sit easily within the confines of a literary school, but his early fiction includes some of the most interesting contributions to Naturalism's vast mapping of the modern social universe in all its extremes. In this fiction we see many of Naturalism's cherished themes: *Marthe* (1876), subtitled 'Story of a Prostitute', allowed him to probe the moral hypocrisy of bourgeois society which unofficially condoned forms of behaviour which publicly it chastised, and *En ménage* (*Living Together*, 1881) explored the infelicities of domestic life. Huysmans himself never married but maintained an intermittent relationship with a seamstress, Anna Meunier. The most public assertion of a collective Naturalist method were the short stories published to mark the anniversary of the Franco-Prussian War as *Les Soirées de Médan* (1880), to which Huysmans contributed his *Sac au dos* (*Packs On!*). It is only against the background of this commitment to an engaged account of recognizable social types and experiences that the shock created by the publication of *Against Nature* can be gauged.

Though the beginnings of Zola's enormous *Rougon-Macquart* series, subtitled 'A Natural and Social History of a Family under the Second Empire', dated back to the turbulent year of 1871, it was only with the publication of *L'Assommoir* (*The Drunkard*) in 1877 that he achieved a notoriety which was to be transmuted by the alchemy of critical posterity into canonical status. As the series's subtitle implies, Zola's bid for authenticity was strategically authorized by borrowing from the methods and knowledge of those new sciences, genetics and sociology, particularly evident in the after-the-fact theoretical justifications of his collection of essays *The Experimental Novel*, published at the end of 1881 in the wake of another scandalous success, Zola's novel of prostitution, *Nana*. Zola, fêted by his acolytes as the Master of Médan (where he had used his new-found wealth to buy a house at some distance from the grim metropolis which he had evoked so potently), took as a personal affront Huysmans's account in *Against Nature* of an aristocratic dandy who turns his back on the realities of mass consumption, mass oppression, and mass manipulation in a quest for a truly aestheticized existence in a suburban retreat at Fontenay-aux-Roses. In a letter to Mallarmé, Huysmans explained this 'strange story, the subject of which is as follows: The last representative of an illustrious race, appalled by the invasion of American manners and the growth of an aristocracy of wealth, takes refuge in absolute solitude. He is well-read, cultured, and refined. In his comfortable retreat he substitutes the pleasures of artifice for the banalities of Nature.'[2] The history of this 'illustrious race' is condensed in the Prologue, which also explains how the neurosis of Des Esseintes has driven him to the point where he feels he must experiment with a solitary existence cut off from the horrors of the bourgeois century and create a museum dedicated to the life of the educated senses. The novel charts Des Esseintes's attempt to live out his life in such a 'museum'. Though other characters appear either in memories, dreams, or in the service of the hero's project, Des Esseintes is the only major character in the novel. Each chapter presents the reader with different aspects of his refined taste in sensory and aesthetic pleasure, interspersed with memories of the sordid metropolitan world he has left and with the perverse dreamscapes of his neurotic imagination. To focus on such an untypical and antisocial figure who chooses to turn his back on the social universe embraced, however critically, by Naturalism was almost bound to invite the censure of its leading figure, Zola.

Ever since his entry into Zola's circle in the later months of 1876, Huysmans seemed to have followed zealously the Master's principles of literary engagement with the socio-economic problems of modern France. In 1877 his article on 'Émile Zola et *L'Assommoir*' had proved his loyalty by defending openly the author of such a controversial confrontation with injustice and inequality in the impoverished quarters of Paris. It may well be this earlier public support (as well as the private bonds of friendship) which made it particularly difficult for Zola to stomach the *volte-face* of 1884, not least as he prepared for yet another landmark in his series, the writing of *Germinal*. The contemporary Catholic writer and critic Léon Bloy described Huysmans as 'formerly a Naturalist, but now an Idealist capable of the most exalted mysticism, and as far removed from the crapulous Zola as if all the interplanetary spaces had suddenly accumulated between them'.[3] However misguided Zola felt Huysmans to

[2] Letter dated 27 October 1882.
[3] Léon Bloy, 'Les Représailles du Sphinx', *Le Chat Noir*, 14 June 1884.

be in his choice of subject and style, it would have been hard for him not to sense that it was his long-time acolyte who now embodied the paradoxically vigorous forces of a seemingly exhausted modern aesthetic sensibility (an aesthetic which Symbolism was starting to voice and which was to flourish in the modernist explosion of the new century). As Huysmans told fellow writer and critic Francis Enne as he prepared the novel: 'It will be the biggest fiasco of the year—but I don't care a damn! It will be something nobody has ever done before, and I shall have said what I had to say.'[4]

The publication of *Against Nature* is one of a series of symptomatic cultural moments which usher in the *fin de siècle*, that culturally defined historical moment in which the ubiquitous self-awareness of artistic activity developed into a particularly acute self-consciousness as the nineteenth century drew to a close (a self-consciousness echoed in the *fin de siècle* and the *fin de millénaire* at the end of the twentieth century). The French model of a terminal historical crisis in the 1880s and 1890s was evidently the political cataclysm of the French Revolution and its aftermath, the Terror, which had marked the previous *fin de siècle* in such an apocalyptic fashion. The sense of national decline underpinned by the military defeat of 1870–1 at the hands of the Prussians and the scandals of a republican regime which in many ways seemed no better than its imperial predecessor both made for an atmosphere of cultural cynicism. Moreover, that culture felt saturated with the massive expansion of print media throughout the century, so that by its end writers felt, as La Bruyère once had, that all had been said and that nothing original was possible.[5] Though Harold Bloom's oft-used concept of the 'anxiety of influence' may describe a general state to which writers and artists are prone, in *fin-de-siècle* France such an anxiety was heightened to a point of acute, and in some cases almost debilitating, paralysis.

If the publication of *Against Nature* represents one of the *faux débuts* of the *fin de siècle*, then the following year another *faux début*, the death of Victor Hugo and his carnivalesque burial in the Panthéon in June 1885, only confirmed that sense of liberation which

---

[4] Francis Enne, *Le Réveil*, 22 May 1884.

[5] See Henri-Jean Martin and Roger Chartier (eds.), *Histoire de l'édition française*, 4 vols. (Paris: Promodis, 1983–6), vol. III: *Le Temps des éditeurs: du Romantisme à la Belle Époque* (1985).

Des Esseintes's private 'counter canon' of writing and art had already affirmed in the face of such constraints and influences. In the wake of this unburdening of young poetic voices, Stéphane Mallarmé (already discreetly enthroned by Des Esseintes) explained in 'Crise de vers' the degree of influence which this literary colossus had exerted: 'Hugo, in his mysterious task, boiled all prose, philosophy, eloquence, history down to verse, and, since he *was* verse, personally, he confiscated from anyone who thinks, discourses, or narrates almost the right to speak.'[6] The achievement of *Against Nature* is to have imagined an alternative literary history in which the hitherto apparently esoteric Baudelaire and Mallarmé, rather than a literary colossus such as Hugo, might become the dominant voices. This symbolic 'murder' of Victor Hugo in 1884 provided a 'cultural coffin' into which the biological cadaver could, so to speak, be lowered the following year. But as far as Des Esseintes was concerned, Hugo the writer was already dead and buried.

One characteristic of the Decadent movement (notoriously pathologized by a widely disseminated German account, Max Nordau's *Entartung* of 1892, which associates this literary and artistic movement with the rabid influence of Latin, and particularly Gallic, culture) is precisely an awareness of the unbearable weight of cultural models, and one effect of the density of reference in *Against Nature* is to highlight the unliveable pressure of such a heavily mediated existence. As the contemporary critic Jules Lemaître noted in his review of *Against Nature*: 'A man of letters, a mandarin, has too full a memory; impressions no longer reach him except through a layer of literary memories.'[7] Such a resistance to forgetfulness inevitably presents a threat to an individual identity grounded in a sense of one's own novelty. Yet Des Esseintes's individuality stems precisely from his willingness to embrace a paradoxical selection of cultural models which were at once highly idiosyncratic and uncannily prophetic, and to allow himself to be saturated by them. What the Decadent movement achieves is a sublimation of the alienation of industrial man by revelling in the symptoms of his modern malady, finding in his neuroses the hypersensitivity habitually associated with artistic responsiveness.

[6] Stéphane Mallarmé, *Œuvres*, ed. Yves-Alain Favre (Paris: Bordas, 1992), 270.

[7] Cited in Lucien Descaves's Note on *Against Nature*, in Joris-Karl Huysmans, *Œuvres complètes* (Geneva: Slatkine, 1972), vii. 349.

(We use the term 'man' advisedly here, for Decadent authors and heroes are only too keen to indulge in misogynist fantasies in their archly 'unreconstructed' evocation of female cupidity and sensuality. Indeed, not only is the development of female characters conspicuously absent from Huysmans's novel; so is any attempt to absorb women writers and artists into the library of references which feeds the novel. According to the classic critical position of Huysmans's major biographer, Robert Baldick, 'Huysmans . . . found that he had given *expression to the aspirations of all* those who scorned accepted aesthetic standards, who delighted in the perverse and the artificial, and who sought to extend the boundaries of emotional and spiritual experience'.[8] But modern feminist readings of Decadent writing show us to what extent female points of view are excluded from the 'aspirations' of such texts.)

In a sense *Against Nature* articulates a reactionary nostalgia, as the remoteness of the aristocracy is taken to an extreme by Des Esseintes's flight from sociability to narcissism. As such, the novel may also be seen as a reaction against the public world of political conflict, for Des Esseintes tries to retreat from the network of interpersonal relations which define social experience. Such encounters only return in the novel at the level of anecdote. In particular, a perverse sexuality is echoed as a textual memory in the tales of d'Aigurande, Langlois, Miss Urania, and the unnamed young man mentioned at the end of Chapter 9. In the first case, Des Esseintes recalls how he encouraged his friend to get married, safe in the ironic knowledge that conjugal happiness was virtually unattainable, and sure enough adultery and separation follow. In the case of the young urchin, Auguste Langlois, whom Des Esseintes had picked up in the street, he subsidizes this young man's immersion into the world of the brothel only to remove such financial help after a few months and thereby condemn the sexually dependent Langlois to a life of crime, perhaps even murder. Unfortunately Des Esseintes loses touch with Langlois and does not know how this tale ended. But in both cases the novelistic hero is no longer at the centre of sexual adventure, and is instead the agent who facilitates disaster. Like a pimp, or a director of the drama of sexual mores, the hero stands at an ironic dis-

[8] Robert Baldick, *The Life of J.-K. Huysmans* (Oxford: Clarendon Press, 1955), 87 (emphasis added).

tance from the stupidity of human drives which he stages. His own propensity for sexual inversion is recalled in his affair with the American acrobat Miss Urania, whose robust muscular frame overpowers the frail degeneracy of the pale aristocrat. But in the present of the narrative, however, there are no sexual or family relations. Desire is reformulated in the private sphere of cultural consumption, and consequently so is the desire which animates our reading of traditional Aristotelian plot structures which habitually propel the curious mind from beginning to resolution via the crisis of the middle. As we read *Against Nature*, we realize that family life (and its narratives) are elsewhere.

It is fitting therefore that the working title of the novel was *Seul* (*Alone*), though this was rejected in favour of the far more perplexing *A rebours*. This notoriously untranslatable title (variously 'Against the Grain' or 'Against Nature') refers to a contrary and paradoxical motion. Much can be gleaned from its multiple connotations if we cite the dictionary's inventory of some of its French contexts: *caresser un chat à rebours*, to stroke a cat the wrong way (perverse sexual overtones aside, Huysmans was a great cat-lover, was famously photographed with one of his feline friends, and described himself in a thinly disguised autobiographical text as 'a courteous cat, very polite, almost likeable, but nervous, ready to reveal his claws at the slightest word'[9]); *prendre quelqu'un à rebours*, to rub someone up the wrong way, and *aller à rebours de la tendance générale*, to run counter to the general trend (like the solitary and eccentric Des Esseintes); *prendre l'ennemi à rebours*, to surprise the enemy from behind (indicative of the aggression and anality of our hero); *faire un trajet à rebours*, to make a journey the other way round, and *prendre une rue en sens unique à rebours*, to go the wrong way up a one-way street (like the literal and narratological journeys denied or rerouted in a text which manages, as Huysmans's personal literary hero Flaubert would have it, to 'dérouter le lecteur' or disconcert the reader); and finally, even though the reconditeness of the novel does seem to invite in Stendhalian fashion the élite readership of the Happy Few, there is ironic solace for Huysmans's readers, who are in fact not so Happy and not so Few, in the connotations of *feuilleter un magazine à rebours*,

[9] A. Meunier [pseudonym of Joris–Karl Huysmans], 'J.-K. Huysmans', *Les Hommes d'Aujourd'hui*, No. 263 (Paris: Vanier [1885]).

to flick through a magazine from back to front, and *comprendre à rebours*, to get the wrong end of the stick! As with the lists articulated in the novel itself, such inventories are skipped over at the reader's peril.

This notion of *writing against* allows us to situate the novel in the movements and counter-movements which characterize the cultural turbulence of the *fin de siècle*. We are told in the 'Notice' which accompanied the original publication of the novel in 1884 (and which is translated as the Prologue in this edition) that Des Esseintes is the last in a long line of consanguineously degenerating aristocrats. He sports his sterility as a badge of honour, knowing that he will not add to what he sees as the inanity of biological perpetuation. So as we have seen, *Against Nature* can be read as a goodbye to the family fictions in which Realist and Naturalist writers continued to indulge. Whereas Zola's cycle, *Les Rougon-Macquart*, expands with the logic of the family tree from which it takes its shape (from the initial transgressions of *La Fortune des Rougon* to the procreative incest of its final novel, *Le Docteur Pascal*), Huysmans's novel ironically eschews such a concern for the crises of family life. It provides a novelistic response to the following dilemma: what type of narrative can we tell after the conclusion of the plot of family procreation? As such Huysmans exposes the delusion which dictates the association between the mimetic readability of Realist-Naturalist texts, family fictions, and the traditional Aristotelian plot. In its aversion to such a plot's presuppositions about the advance of (family) history, Huysmans's adopts the ironically abortive narrative pattern championed by Flaubert's *L'Éducation sentimentale* (*Sentimental Education*, 1869) and borrowed by Henry Céard's novel of adultery *manqué*, *Une Belle Journée* (*A Lovely Day*, 1881). As such, description threatens to overwhelm the imperative of plotting and story-telling.

In one of the most famous opening lines in nineteenth-century fiction, Tolstoy's *Anna Karenina* tells us that all happy families are the same and all unhappy families different; in *Against Nature* it seems as if all families—happy or unhappy—are equally pathetic and as if their happiness is merely a matter of collective self-delusion. One of Des Esseintes's most nauseous experiences is to feel the pain (metaphysical as much as bodily) of a pram crashing into his legs as he walks down the street, and as we have stressed, his retreat from the human carnival of Parisian life involves a denial not only of the public world of politics but also of the private world of individual (and particularly sexual) encounters. The archetypal gourmand at such a feast, who had been famously depicted by Baudelaire, is the *flâneur* who strolls the streets of the city in search of those momentary aesthetic experiences afforded by urban modernity. *Against Nature* is in a sense the tale of the *flâneur*'s last stand (or at least of his attempt to stand still). No longer willing to bear the ennui of walking the city's streets in search of the unexpected and the impromptu, Des Esseintes leaves the modern realm of the *ad hoc* for the inner sanctum of selected, and thus predetermined, delights. His is a private museum of mediated pleasures where the primacy of the body's sensory gratifications is relativized by an awareness of how our own representational strategies operate. Des Esseintes learns that desire does not precede cultural practice but enjoys a relationship of reciprocal influence with it. For cultural practice reflects and expresses, but also helps to inflect and define our desires. Once this notion has been established, Des Esseintes can refuse to behave as a largely passive subject upon whom desires may exert their tyranny; for he prefers to stage (and stage-manage) desire in an active manner. So reliably bizarre pleasures are condensed and refracted in that experimental chamber which is his new home at Fontenay-aux-Roses.

This home does not simply lock Des Esseintes *in*; it also attempts to lock the rest of the world *out*. As such we may think of Des Esseintes as excluding his compatriots and imprisoning them in a savage modernity rather than merely hiding himself away. As a Frenchman of Dutch origins who had known the humiliation and suffering of the Franco-Prussian War and the Siege of Paris (1870–1), Huysmans's cynicism about family life also threatened to unpick the ideology of fertility which characterized a Gallic spirit of revenge fostered in the wake of national defeat. In a tone which General de Gaulle was later to adopt, right-wing politicians of the Third Republic called for rapid repopulation in order to fill the ranks of an anti-German force which might recapture Alsace and Lorraine. At the same time, the novels of a liberal such as Zola also indulged paternalist fantasies of reproduction, which culminated in the aptly titled *Fécondité* (*Fertility*) of 1899. Zola supported both the 'Alliance nationale pour le relèvement de la population française' (National Alliance for the Recovery of the French Population) and the 'Société

maternelle parisienne' (Society of Parisian Motherhood). Huysmans's hero (or rather anti-hero) represents a repudiation of collective identities such as nationhood.

This relocation of heroic endeavour outside of the *polis* not only
represents an inversion of the bourgeois tale of the parvenu who tries
to make his way in Parisian society (most notably Balzac's Rastignac,
whose rise to a position of power and influence is charted in the
Comédie humaine); it also reflects a philosophical position most elo-
quently voiced by the German thinker Arthur Schopenhauer. Made
accessible in France not only by translations of his work but also by
the analysis of Elme-Marie Caro, he laments the poverty of imagination which finds generation after generation compelled to repro-
duce its own image in its progeny.[10] From a pessimistic perspective
which finds echoes in the twentieth century in the work of Samuel
Beckett, Huysmans adopts Schopenhauer's suspicion of life's
promises, a suspicion which had already been parodied in Zola's *La
Joie de vivre* (serialized from November 1883). This pessimism was
pronounced in the first novel of the triptych to which *Against Nature*
and *En rade* (*Becalmed*, 1886) belong. The chief protagonist of *A
vau-l'eau* (*Downstream*, 1881), Folantin, claims that 'Only the worst
things happen', but does not have the means to escape the banality
of his social world and the irritating presence of those around him.
In a manner which Beckett's devotees would recognize, *Against
Nature* nevertheless achieves a stoical and at times outrageously
funny sense of the absurdity of Des Esseintes's endeavours, in incidents such as the funereal dinner, the episode of the extracted molar,
and his enema 'menu'. Des Esseintes shares the sense of Baudelairean 'spleen' but also enjoys the means to fight back against modernity, for he is the sole heir of the château de Lourps and sells this
noble patrimony in order to set up his aesthetic palace in Fontenay-
aux-Roses, which is isolated (but not totally cut off) from the city
proper by poor transport links. Though this image of the stoical
hermit isolated in his bejewelled lair has significant distant prece-
dents, Huysmans echoes in particular the influence of Edmond de
Goncourt's *La Maison d'un artiste* (*An Artist's House*, 1881) which
fictionalizes the latter's remarkable home in Auteuil.

---

[10] See Elme-Marie Caro, *Le Pessimisme au XIXᵉ siècle: Léopardi, Schopenhauer, Hartmann* (Paris: Hachette, 1878).

For all of this reaction against Zola's Naturalist account of a social universe, it would nevertheless be quite wrong to depict *Against Nature* as a wholly anti-mimetic venture. Though Des Esseintes is an improbable character, he does have traceable models, including not only the eccentric Ludwig II of Bavaria and writers such as Baudelaire, Barbey d'Aurevilly, Edmond de Goncourt, and Francis Poictevin, but in particular the aesthete Count Robert de Montesquiou-Fezensac—as was revealed by the publication in 1892 of the latter's *Les Hortensias bleus* (*The Blue Hortensias*). Montesquiou, who was to be the model for Proust's Charlus, had a house on the Rue Franklin, many of whose bizarre features (which seem to have been relayed to Huysmans by Mallarmé) also appear in Des Esseintes's lair. More significantly, if Des Esseintes disdains the logic of everyday life, his antithetical reaction to it is framed in contradistinction to its recognizable scenarios. The social universe of Naturalist family fiction is the binary 'other' which *Against Nature* acknowledges by its own dissent from that model. The mimetic order of space and time is not upset by the narrative. By trying to escape the real, Des Esseintes also underlines its stubborn self-affirmation. For what is conspicuous in the novel is the absent material which Huysmans avoids (or perhaps remodulates in another key). Just as the political history of 1848 haunts Flaubert's *L'Éducation sentimentale* (that ideal novel as far as Huysmans is concerned), so more generally the harsh realities of nineteenth-century social history are studiously circumscribed in this depiction of an alienated heroism which feels no longer willing nor able to act upon the world. Indeed, the effects of the novel might usefully be described in terms of a principle of inverse complementarity, such that Realist and Naturalist fiction of familial and social contexts is inferred rather than imitated. It is little surprise that Des Esseintes finds contemporary politics absolutely banal, and if he is a reactionary figure, it is precisely because of his refusal to react to his surroundings. What *Against Nature* therefore dramatizes is the apparent incompatibility of élite aesthetic taste, on the one hand, and social and political engagement on the other, and this is a question to which the avant-garde movements of the twentieth century have continually turned, not surprisingly without an ultimate resolution.

Two of the most famous possessions of Des Esseintes are paintings by Gustave Moreau which are described in Chapter 5: the oil painting, *Salomé dansant devant Hérode* (*Salomé dancing before Herod*), in front of which he sits at night and dreams, and a water-colour which is apparently even more perturbing, *L'Apparition* (*The Apparition*). These represent the biblical tale of the dancing girl seducing King Herod with her exotic dance and, at her mother's behest, thereby obtaining with her self-exhibition the head of John the Baptist on a platter. Pregnant with psychosexual reverberations of decapitation and symbolic castration by the all-powerful phallic females, this tale ultimately articulates an interior drama of psychic tension which sits persuasively with Huysmans's other dream narra-tives in fictions such as *En rade*. Certainly psychoanalytical critics have found in Huysmans fertile analytical terrain. The Huysmans–Freud connection is not, however, just another case of literary text meeting critical model, for we might venture the hypothesis that both provide vastly differing articulations of the same concern for the interiority of the individual human subject which is common to so much turn-of-the-century European culture. Counter to the mass effects and experiences of the urban crowd,[11] the inflections of the individual psyche became an object of a radical new intellectual endeavour which had its roots in France in the neuropsychiatry of Charcot and Bernheim. What *Against Nature* manages is to ennoble, via aestheticism, the necessarily pathologized patient, taking its readers into a strange domestic universe and showing them—amidst accounts of Des Esseintes's bodily and psychological discomfort—a mental design and furniture which is as alluring as it is alien . . . in spite of the fact that the doctor does have the final say at the end of the novel.

Even if we were naïve enough to assume that Des Esseintes's posi-tions are shared unambiguously by Huysmans, we should still note the stubborn ambiguities of the author's own attitudes. In a reflection of his own predilections in painting, for instance, he hesitated in his choice of ideal artist for his anti-hero. In the manuscript of *Against Nature* it is clear that Huysmans initially conceived of another version of Des Esseintes's artistic obsessions in which Degas's impressionism of modern life (and not the academic, mytho-

---

[11] Charted in fairly recent times by Susanna Barrows, *Distorting Mirrors: Visions of the Crowd in Late Nineteenth-Century France* (New Haven: Yale University Press, 1981), but also studied at the time by, among others, Gustave Le Bon, *Psychologie des foules* (*Psychology of Crowds*) (Paris: Alcan, 1895).

historical work of Moreau) is favoured. Though Huysmans stuck
with Moreau, it is clear that both Degas's insight into the horrors of
contemporary society and Moreau's sublime exile from contemporary images represent two sides of Huysmans's bitter distaste for
modernity. This is thus a novel which by its very withdrawal from
the social and political domains of contemporary society forces the
reader to confront the question of their genuine value. Perhaps
Huysmans dropped the working title, *Seul*, because Des Esseintes is
not actually alone at Fontenay. Beyond the figurative presence of
artists in the form of their work, the servant couple whose living
quarters are soundproofed and segregated from Des Esseintes's
provide some personal interaction. We might see their role in the
household as a residual Naturalist fragment. What they show is the
impossibility of absolute solitude for the aristocratic dandy, for Des
Esseintes needs to be served by others. He is also in regular contact
with suppliers who sell him the *objets d'art* which turn his home into
a private museum, most memorably in Chapter 4 when his bejewelled tortoise is delivered. These essentially economic relations reveal
the interdependence of the class structure: the aristocrat requires
both the bourgeois supplier and the working-class servants. Thus the
novel inscribes sociology *à rebours*, in the shadow of its explicit
agenda, because of as well as in spite of its penchant for what
Edmond de Goncourt termed 'cultured beings and exquisite things'.

Indeed, by the end of the novel Paris, that capital of politics and
of desire, draws this hero back from the brink of a neurosis diag-
nosed by another outsider, the doctor, that figure of modern science
who enjoys a singular right and invitation in nineteenth-century
fiction to invade the privacy of the individual. In a denouement
which is persuasively glossed by a comparison with Zola's *Le Docteur
Pascal* in Christopher Lloyd's exemplary account of *fin-de-siècle*
fiction,[12] Des Esseintes's physician insists that only this resocializa-
tion of the solipsist will cure his psychological and physiological ills.
So the whole novel is framed by an exit from and a return to the irresistible hurly-burly of Paris, as if it were a pair of brackets from
which a heightened sense of the aesthetic has tried in vain to escape.
As Barbey d'Aurevilly notes, the author behind Des Esseintes is so

---

[12] See Christopher Lloyd, *J.-K. Huysmans and the* Fin-de-siècle *Novel* (Edinburgh:
Edinburgh University Press, 1990).

sickened by modernity that he will be forced to choose between the mouth of a gun and the foot of the Cross (in other words, suicide or faith). The authority of this prediction is underwritten by Huysmans's Preface composed for the de luxe limited edition of the novel which appeared in 1903, illustrated by the coloured wood engravings of Auguste Lepère. Bound in Moroccan leather and housed in its own casing, such a rare objet d'art would doubtlessly have attracted a collector such as its own hero, Des Esseintes. The Preface (which is reprinted here as an Appendix) allows Huysmans the benefit of hindsight as he glances back twenty years to this turning point in his career. By 1903 the world appears changed: the new century has arrived and Zola is now dead, and Huysmans's own beliefs have shifted in line with Barbey's warning. He offers a personal version of the breakdown in his relationship with Zola at the time of the novel's publication, and twists the knife by explaining how, in any case, Flaubert's *L'Éducation sentimentale*, and not *L'Assommoir*, was the true model for Naturalist novelists of his generation.

This Flaubertian model is particularly influential in its unstitching of the narrative thread of the traditional Aristotelian plot. For it circumvents the potential for conclusive action in its own narrative situation by highlighting the final reminiscence of Frédéric Arnoux and his friend, Deslauriers, who recall an abortive adolescent trip to a brothel as 'the best that we have known'. (This reminiscence is echoed in Des Esseintes's sadistic provision and subsequent removal of funding for Auguste Langlois's trips to the brothel which are intended to lead to a tale of theft and perhaps even murder. As we have seen though, once again the plot fails to unfold as Des Esseintes loses touch with Langlois.) Even more radically than *L'Éducation sentimentale*, *Against Nature* resists the developmental plot structure of traditional fiction by removing its hero from the sphere of human interaction. Plots (like sexual encounters) only exist as a memory for these problematic bachelor figures who sit on the edge of the grand family narrative of bourgeois society. Ironically, though, in the novel itself Huysmans's protagonist favours Flaubert's *La Tentation de saint Antoine* (*The Temptation of St Anthony*) (final version, 1874) above *L'Éducation sentimentale*, and this is symptomatic of the gap not only between author and hero, but also between modulated versions of an authorial self at different moments in Huysmans's cultural odyssey. The whole issue of cultural models which Huysmans's

Preface raises is, to say the least, paradoxical, for what Des Esseintes and Huysmans both privilege are models which are beyond imitation (see the latter's proud observation to Enne quoted above). It is this which makes both Moreau and Flaubert so eye-catching. Unlike Zola, who sits proudly at the head of a genealogy of Naturalist novelists, Flaubert's innovations are so equivocal as to make the matter of influence and allegiance anything but straightforward. So the notion of cultural as well as biological paternity is undermined by a novel which disavows the notion of the family in both contexts. Retrospectively, Moreau's genius lies for Des Esseintes in his resistance to the categorizations of artistic schools (or cultural families); and prospectively, there is, it seems, simply no point in trying to 'out-Flaubert' Flaubert.

As we have already noted, the Preface of 1903 ends by quoting Barbey's definition of Huysmans's alternatives and asserts the reactionary (and bizarre) Catholicism to which later works such as *En route* bear witness. By resisting suicide, Huysmans worked through his Schopenhauerian moment and lived to embody in his perversely paradoxical manner the resurgence of Catholicism in the final years of the century (known in France as the *ralliement*). Indeed, it is hard to find a literary figure whose aesthetic shifts embodied more completely the succession of movements and concerns which characterized the cultural life of the Third Republic. First a Realist-Naturalist, then via Des Esseintes a voice of Decadent aestheticism, and finally in the wake of *Against Nature* a Catholic reactionary, Huysmans's multiple artistic personality provided a conduit for the strongest currents of the age. Many attempts have been made to impose a unifying coherence on this career, not least by the eminent Pierre Cogny.[13] At their worst such attempts involve a psychologizing reductivism (hence the conclusion of H.-M. Gallot's analysis of his maternal fixations: 'so Huysmans holds no enigma'[14]). This conspicuous desire to fix Huysmans's subjective centre is a reaction both to this shifting artistic focus and to the obsessive self-concern which his array of anti-heroic fictional *alter egos* reveals. Des Esseintes is one such version of the writing self, but it would be an error to assume that the novel is strictly autobiographical. At the level of

[13] See Pierre Cogny, *J.-K. Huysmans à la recherche de l'unité* (Paris: Nizet, 1953).

[14] H.-M. Gallot, *Explication de J.-K. Huysmans* (Paris: Agence Parisienne de Distribution, 1954), 195.

economic independence Des Esseintes represents a fantasy for this author who led a double life as both a minor civil servant and an avant-garde writer. In this sense, Folantin would be a far more convincing double, as Des Esseintes can afford to purchase the freedom of insularity at one remove (or one removal) from niggling interactions with others. The identification between an author and a hero, otherwise held at a distance by the narrator's incursions and objectifications, is to be found in the manic collecting of texts and images which colour this insular space. Though there are sleights of hand and moments of self-conscious perversity in Des Esseintes's choice of his favourite writers and artists, they do in many cases reflect the esoteric eclecticism of the author (though, as Marc Fumaroli suggests, the hero should be seen as a myth rather than an example).

As Fumaroli notes in his French edition of the novel, it would require the vast scholarly apparatus of an edition such as Rose Fortassier's to attend to the nooks and crannies of this labyrinth of intertextuality (a practice defined by critics as the implicit as well as explicit invocation of other texts).[15] (Even the latter edition by no means explains everything, and what the present volume intends to provide is an annotation which simply facilitates the act of reading and suggests further fruitful lines of enquiry.) It is in the face of this citational barrage that the reader undergoes one of his or her greatest challenges. Which reader can claim to feel truly at home in this strange treasure trove which is in no sense of the term a commonplace? Another way of putting this question is to ask which reader can truly identify with Des Esseintes who enjoys such a vast range of images (including the sadistic Luyken and Bresdin), objects (such as jewels, and the flowers studied in Chapter 8), perfumes (in Chapter 9), and texts (which range from Latin theology via medieval esotericism to modern French fiction)? For his possession of such a museum of abstruse beauty is intellectual as well as economic. His return to Paris on doctor's orders at the end of the novel is, however, the sign that ultimately he cannot *afford* to live such a life. He must choose between the inhumanity of art and the artfulness of people.

---

[15] See Marc Fumaroli's edition (Paris: Folio, 1977) and Rose Fortassier's (Paris: L'Imprimerie Nationale, 1981).

In the English-speaking world it is the identification of *Against Nature* with the yellow book so prized by Oscar Wilde's Dorian Gray which underpins the cult status of Huysmans's awkward master-piece. As Dorian turns its pages, 'it seemed to him that in exquisite raiment, and to the delicate sound of flutes, the sins of the world were passing in dumb show before him. Things that he had dimly dreamed of were suddenly made real to him. Things of which he had never dreamed were gradually revealed.'[16] Indeed, Wilde will doubtless be the route by which many readers of this translation will have reached Huysmans's 'breviary of the Decadence' (as Arthur Symons called it). The self-regard of readers is seduced by Huysmans's offer of membership of that most élite of clubs, a readership no longer defined by a regressive nostalgia for the natural but by an immersion from within the inner space of personal experience and taste into the confected world of a distasteful modernity in need of radical refashioning. Like Groucho Marx, the novel's implied readers are not interested in joining any club so undistinguished as to accept them as members. (In other words they would only be keen to join a club that derided their very audacity in confronting the text.) Such playful seduction drew the wrath of contemporary critics such as the bad-tempered Lemaître, who laments that 'this book's mis-fortune is that it looks too much like a wager and you are afraid of being duped by taking it too seriously'. But such insecurity on the part of critics, surely tempted by the detective game offered by the novel's apparently obscure references, merely underlines unwittingly the modernity of an artist who poses as con-artist (not unlike a Queneau or a Robbe-Grillet). To read *Against Nature* is either to accept the rules of its cultural game or to face absolute disorienta-tion. At a time when educators confront challenges to the written word and—so we are told—see, in the immediate cultural experience of their students, seductively accessible rivals to the act of reading itself, brave is the teacher who prescribes such a challenge for his or her students . . . unless the text is presented as a way into a remark-ably rich cultural landscape and not just a testing ground intended to exalt the literary pedant. For *Against Nature* does not simply offer the *richesse nécessaire* defined by Moreau; within this pruned plot

---

[16] Oscar Wilde, *The Picture of Dorian Gray*, ed. Isobel Murray (London: Oxford University Press, 1974), 125.

there is at the level of description and reference a wealth (in an economic as well as an aesthetic sense) of texts and images which can inspire and motivate. The novel is one way of clocking on in the factory of cultural production, and not just a way of clocking, or nodding, off (though Des Esseintes would of course be horrified by such a metaphor, which threatens to demystify the process of artistic labour).

Modernity's analytical dissection of the individual (be it by Charcot, Gide, Freud, or Proust) highlights the inner mental drama of subjectivity and always carries with it the risk of narcissistic self-indulgence. As Des Esseintes retreats from the social world into a realm he can master and fashion in his own fractured self-image, the novel threatens to dissolve into an unknowable domain that is not unnameable but, on the contrary, excessively well labelled. The immediacy of 'natural' perception is postponed and filtered by this welter of cultural references which lies like an orientational grid over the objects which populate Des Esseintes's domain. On his personal map of experience it is not merely better to travel than to arrive, but actually better to look at the signposts than to travel (in semiotic terms, signs displace veritable objects of reference). At one point Des Esseintes plans to visit London, and travels to Paris in order to catch the boat train. Once inside an English-style pub in Paris, however, he realizes in archly Baudelairean fashion the futility of such a journey across the Channel, now that he has discovered this Dickensian confection of the metropolis, and so he chooses to miss his train and retreat to his home. For his is a virtual reality and his journeys are voyages of the mind in which the tools of perception might be said to be the vital factor, and not just empirical experience.

It is not only at the level of its references but also from a stylistic perspective that *Against Nature* sits on the very edge of readability. Its highly mannered prose offers very particular challenges to the reader (as it does to the translator), especially given its debt to the baroque embellishments of *l'écriture artiste*, habitually associated with the Goncourt brothers. In contrast to classical simplicity or Naturalist immediacy, Huysmans's writing is characterized by what Lemaître terms 'useless neologisms, improprieties, solecisms, and barbarisms'. Certainly Huysmans's writing sits on the difficult boundary between illumination and alienation. For as much as it offers the reader access to a brave new world of cultural consumption, so it also threatens to disorientate and alienate the 'common reader' (whoever that might actually be). Des Esseintes, on the other hand, is alienated by common experience and as such anticipates the salient role of the outsider in twentieth-century fiction. In one particular sense the novel may prove less resistant to modern readers because Huysmans was so forward looking in his selection of proto-modernist icons, such as the *poètes maudits*, Baudelaire, Mallarmé, and, subsequently, Rimbaud, who have now entered the literary pantheon. Des Esseintes's literary tastes also helped to assert the significance of a range of related authors, such as Verlaine, Corbière, Barbey d'Aurevilly, and Villiers de l'Isle-Adam. Precisely because of the influence of his aesthetic choices, the readability of Huysmans's novel has grown, so at certain moments we are in the strange position of being closer to the original than were his contemporaries. If this reversal of defamiliarization is testament to the insight of Huysmans's tastes, it also means that it is virtually impossible for us to reconstruct a sense of the shock which these contemporaries would have felt on their initial encounter with the novel, or a sense of the perversity of the project's insistence on operating *à rebours*. No wonder Huysmans could take such delight in the scandal and debate which the publication of his novel had triggered.

This extravaganza of aesthetic appreciation characterizes Des Esseintes as a privileged reader and, in another prefiguration of twentieth-century thinking, allows the novel to break down the potentially artificial barrier between critical writing and creative writing. It might be from this angle that those students of literature interested in questions of a theoretical nature might most usefully enter this text. Even so, this artful reader, Des Esseintes, never manages to become a writer himself; he consumes but does not produce. In effect, the writing of the novel itself is the measure of the gap between author and hero (or between writing and reading). By the end of *A la recherche du temps perdu*, Proust's Marcel has learnt to become the narrator of the novel he has just lived, but the circularity of *Against Nature* merely takes Des Esseintes back to the Parisian encounters already retold in his recollections. This proto-modernist interest in the artist as both a young and not such a young man defines a new marginal 'hero' whose worries are symptomatic rather than simply typical. When we see the fascination exerted in modern popular culture by stylized figures of alienation (James

Dean, Kurt Cobain, *et al.*), it becomes clearer how this Greta Garbo of the fictional universe fits into a longer cultural history of marginals and misfits suddenly recentred as apropos icons, who conform by their very marginality to the ideals of a youth culture which might itself be charted back to the turn of the century. If the apparent intellectual immodesty of Huysmans's 'difficult' hero is approached in this spirit, then there should be little to fear and much to enjoy in this narrative journey tracked backwards and inwards via the signposts of a culturally saturated imagination, through forms of a self experienced as at once inescapable and unavoidable—indeed like this novel.

NOTE ON THE TRANSLATION

This English translation of Huysmans's *A rebours* is based on Rose Fortassier's critical edition, published in the series Lettres françaises (Paris, L'Imprimerie Nationale, 1981). I have also referred to the Folio edition by Marc Fumaroli (Paris, Gallimard, 1977); I found Fumaroli's notes and especially those of Rose Fortassier extremely valuable. They do, however, leave some questions unanswered, some avenues unpursued, some literary echoes unidentified. I am greatly indebted to Nicholas White, whose daunting task it has been to annotate this text. His help in resolving many of the countless puzzles it presents to the translator has been invaluable.

If some obscurities still persist in my English version—as they surely must—this is a measure of the encyclopaedic cultural baggage and the idiosyncratic intellectual pursuits of Huysmans's solitary hero, Des Esseintes; it is also a consequence of the dense, convoluted style in which his strange history is narrated. I have done my best to achieve a balance between readability, accuracy, and fidelity to the author's style. Time and again this has entailed deciding between a comprehensible, but unremarkable, expression and one which would more faithfully reflect Huysmans's penchant for fashioning neologisms, and for using esoteric or technical terminology, specialized slang, and unexpected, even bizarre, imagery.

Against Nature is a difficult, unsettling, thought-provoking novel. Many of the questions it poses are astonishingly modern, and I have tried to ensure that these questions are not obscured for the English reader by problems of comprehensibility. Not everyone has a crossword puzzle mentality, so I have limited my use of 'dictionary' words, aiming at a rendition which would be as accessible as possible without, I hope, sacrificing the richness and uniqueness of the original. In the interests of clarity I have enclosed Des Esseintes's interior monologues, as well as his (very few) actual utterances, inside quotation marks, and I have attempted to rationalize the paragraphing.

In this translation Huysmans's 1903 Preface, 'written twenty years after the novel', appears as an Appendix.

My grateful thanks go to Peter Marshall, the Zephaniah Swift Moore Professor of Latin at Amherst College, for his kind and expert help with the chapter on Latin literature (Chapter 3). And, as always, my special thanks go to my most meticulous and discerning reader, Jim Mauldon. I could never have completed this translation without his devoted support and practical assistance.

Margaret Mauldon

SELECT BIBLIOGRAPHY

Editions of the Novel

First edition (Paris: Charpentier, 1884).

De luxe edition illustrated by the coloured wood engravings of Auguste Lepère, whose press produced a limited run of 130 copies (1903). First appearance of Huysmans's Preface, which is translated in our edition.

Printed in Volume VII of the *Œuvres complètes*, ed. by Huysmans's associate, Lucien Descaves (Paris: Crès, 1929). Reprinted by Slatkine (Geneva, 1972). Most of Huysmans's output can be found in the volumes of this edition.

Amongst numerous subsequent French editions of the novel, two stand out: Marc Fumaroli's (Paris: Folio, 1977) and Rose Fortassier's (Paris: L'Imprimerie Nationale, 1981).

Penguin edition (1959), translated into English with an Introduction by Robert Baldick.

Bibliography

Michael Issacharoff, *J.-K. Huysmans devant la critique en France* (1874–1960) (Paris: Klincksieck, 1970).

G. A. Cevasco, *J.-K. Huysmans: A Reference Guide* (Boston: G. K. Hall, c.1980).

Critical Biography

Robert Baldick, *The Life of J.-K. Huysmans* (Oxford: Clarendon Press, 1955).

James Laver, *The First Decadent, Being the Strange Life of J.-K. Huysmans* (London: Faber & Faber, 1954).

Alain Vircondolet, *Joris-Karl Huysmans* (Paris: Plon, 1990).

Books on the Writing of Huysmans and His Contemporaries

Jennifer Birkett, *The Sins of the Fathers: Decadence in France, 1870–1914* (London and New York: Quartet, 1986).

Jean Borie, *Huysmans: Le Diable, le célibataire et Dieu* (Paris: Grasset, 1991).

Victor Brombert, *The Romantic Prison: The French Tradition* (Princeton: Princeton University Press, 1978).

Pierre Cogny, *J.-K. Huysmans à la recherche de l'unité* (Paris: Nizet, 1953).

Pierre Cogny, *J.-K. Huysmans: de l'écriture à l'écriture* (Paris: Téqui, 1987).

Richard Griffiths, *The Reactionary Revolution: The Catholic Revival in French Literature, 1870–1914* (London: Constable, 1966).

Christopher Lloyd, *J.-K. Huysmans and the Fin-de-siècle Novel* (Edinburgh: Edinburgh University Press, 1990).

Jean-Pierre Vilcot, *Huysmans et l'intimité protégée* (Paris: Lettres modernes, 1988).

Fernande Zayed, *Huysmans peintre de son époque* (Paris: Nizet, 1973).

Books on Against Nature

Nathalie Limat-Letellier, *Le Désir d'emprise dans «A Rebours» de Huysmans* (Paris: Archives des lettres modernes, 1990).

François Livi, *«A Rebours» et l'esprit décadent* (Paris: Nizet, 1972).

P. Besnier, R. Besshde, J. Borie, and others, *J.-K. Huysmans: «A Rebours»* (Paris: SEDES, 1990).

Articles and Chapters on Against Nature

Two journals focus on the work of Huysmans in particular, namely the *Bulletin de la Société J.-K. Huysmans* and *A Rebours* (named after this novel, of course). They include many scholarly (as well as anecdotal) pieces on all aspects of his life and writing. Another important source is to be found in Robert Brunel and André Guyaux (eds.), *Les Cahiers de l'Herne: Huysmans* (Paris: Herne, 1985). Other articles and chapters include:

Françoise Carmagnani-Dupont, 'Fonction romanesque du récit de rêve: l'exemple d'*A Rebours*', *Littérature*, 43 (1981), 57–74.

Natalie Doyle, 'Against Modernity: The Decadent Voyage in Huysmans's *A Rebours*', *Romance Studies*, 21 (1992–3), 15–24.

Joseph Halpern, 'Decadent Narrative: *A Rebours*', *Stanford French Review*, 2 (1978), 91–102.

Leonard Koos, 'Fictitious History: From Decadence to Modernism' in Christian Berg, Frank Durieux, and Geert Lernout (eds.), *The Turn of the Century: Modernism and Modernity in Literature and the Arts* (Berlin: Walter de Gruyter, 1995), 119–31.

J. H. Matthews, 'André Breton, J.-K. Huysmans, «ces abominables Zola et autres»', *Nineteenth-Century French Studies*, 17 (1988–9), 98–113.

Julia Przybos, 'De la poétique décadente: la Bibliothèque de Des Esseintes', *L'Esprit Créateur*, 28/1 (1988), 67–74.

Nicholas White, 'Narcissism, Reading and History: Freud, Huysmans and Other Europeans', *Paragraph*, 16 (1993), 261–73.

——'*A Rebours* et la "Préface écrite vingt ans après le roman": écoles, influences, intertextes', in K. Cameron and J. Kearns (eds.), *Le Champ littéraire: 1860–1900* (Amsterdam: Rodopi, 1996), 105–11.

Robert Ziegler, 'From Body Magic to Divine Alchemy: Anality and Sublimation in J.-K. Huysmans', *Orbis Litterarum*, 44 (1989), 312–26.

A CHRONOLOGY OF JORIS-KARL HUYSMANS

1848 (5 February) Birth of Charles-Marie-Georges (who would write under the name Joris-Karl) in a house in the Rue Suger, Paris, to Elizabeth-Malvina Badin and Victor-Gottfried Huysmans, a lithographer and miniaturist.

1856 Death of his father.

1857 Mother marries again, this time to Jules Og, by whom she will have two daughters, Juliette and Blanche.

1865 Leaves the lycée Saint-Louis and takes private lessons.

1866 (7 March) Passes the first part of the baccalaureat.
     (1 April) Employed in a minor administrative post at the Ministry of the Interior.

1867 (8 August) Death of his stepfather.

1870 (30 July) Returns to the 6th Battalion of the National Guard of the Seine. Moved between Châlons, Arras, Rouen, and finally Paris which is under siege from the Prussians, before moving to Versailles with the Ministry of War under the Commune.

1871 Though still employed in Versailles, he takes up rooms at 114 Rue de Vaugirard, Paris, then 73 Rue du Cherche-Midi, where every Wednesday evening he entertains friends such as Henry Céard, Albert Pinard, and Maurice du Seigneur.

1872 Start of intermittent liaison with the seamstress, Anna Meunier.

1874 (10 October) Dentu publishes his *Drageoir à épices*, which is praised in *L'Illustration* and *L'Événement*.

1875 Completes a brief autobiographical account of his military endeavours, *Sac au dos*.

1876 (May) Death of Huysmans's mother. Now responsible for family affairs and the well-being of his stepsisters, Huysmans moves to 11 Rue de Sèvres, where his artistic circle expands to include Villiers de l'Isle-Adam and Lucien Descaves.
     (12 September) Fearing censorship, he has *Marthe, histoire d'une fille* published in Brussels, only to have it seized on the border as 'pornography'. (October) Though Edmond de Goncourt is tepid in his response to the book, Zola invites Huysmans to join his Naturalist circle, which includes Paul Alexis, Léon Hennique, Henry Céard, and Guy de Maupassant.

1877 (April–May) Publishes a series of articles in Brussels under the title 'Émile Zola et *L'Assommoir*'.

(19 August) *Sac au dos* starts to appear in serialized form in *L'Artiste*.

1879 (26 February) Charpentier publishes his *Les Sœurs Vatard*, with a Preface by Zola.

1880 (17 April) *Sac au dos* reprinted by Charpentier in the *Soirées de Médan* collection.

(11 May) Follows Flaubert's funeral cortège in Rouen, alongside Zola, Daudet, and de Goncourt.

(22 May) *Croquis parisiens* published in Paris by Henri Vaton, with illustrations by Forain and Raffaëlli.

1881 (February) Publication of *En ménage*.

1882 (26 January) Publication of *A vau-l'eau* in Brussels.

1883 (May) Publication of his first collection of essays on the visual arts, *L'Art moderne*.

1884 (May) *Against Nature* published, to the delight of many artists and writers, including the Catholics Bloy and Barbey, but not Zola.

(July) Zola and Huysmans meet at Médan, but the relationship of master and disciple is effectively over.

(September–October) Publication of the novella, *Un Dilemme*, in *La Revue indépendante*.

1886 (November) *La Revue indépendante* serializes *En rade*.

1888 (July) Admires in Cassel the *Crucifixion* by Grünewald.

1889 (19 August) Death of his friend, Villiers de l'Isle-Adam. Huysmans and Mallarmé are to be the executors of his will.

(September) Visits Gilles de Rais's château at Tiffauges in the Vendée with Francis de Poictevin.

(November) Publication by Stock of *Certains*, a collection of articles on art and architecture.

1890 (7 February) Meets Stanislas de Guaita, who tries to warn him about the ex-priest, Boullan. However, Berthe Courrière introduces him to Boullan and informs him of the 'satanic' activities of one abbé Van Haeke.

(July) Publication of *La Bièvre*.

1891 (15 February) Serialization of *Là-bas* begins in *L'Écho de Paris*.

(April) Replies to Huret's inquiry into the evolution of contemporary literature.

1892 (12 July) Retreats to the Trappist monastery of Notre-Dame d'Igny.

(25 July) Visits Boullan in Lyons. On his return asks abbé Ferret to become his *directeur de conscience*.

1893 (12 April) Anna Meunier's long-term illness leads to general paralysis and Huysmans must take her to the Sainte-Anne hospital.

(5–10 August) Returns to the Trappe d'Igny.

(3 September) Made a chevalier de la Légion d'honneur for twenty-seven years of loyal bureaucratic service.

1895 (12 February) Death of Anna Meunier at Sainte-Anne.

(23 February) Stock publishes *En route*.

1898 (February) Publication of *La Cathédrale*. Retires from the civil service.

1900 (18 March) Enters the noviciate of oblation at the Abbey of Saint-Martin in Ligugé.

(6 April) Presides over the inaugural meeting of the Académie Goncourt.

1901 (January) De luxe edition of *La Bièvre, les Gobelins, Saint-Séverin*.

(8 June) Publication of *Sainte Lydwine de Schiedam*.

(23 September) Returns to Paris, to 20 Rue Monsieur, in the annex of the Benedictine convent.

(November) Publication of *De tout*.

1902 (August) Publication of an *Esquisse biographique de Don Bosco*.

1903 (March) Publication of *L'Oblat*.

Trip to Lourdes.

1906 (October) Publication of *Les Foules de Lourdes*.

(24 November) Undergoes an operation which reveals the first signs of cancer.

1907 (13 January) Made an officer of the Légion d'honneur.

(11 May) Death of Huysmans.

(15 May) Funeral at Notre-Dame-des-Champs.

1908 Posthumous publication of *Trois églises et trois primitifs* by the executor of his will, Lucien Descaves.

AGAINST NATURE

I must rejoice beyond the confines of time . . . though the world be repelled by my joy, and in its coarseness know not what I mean.

(Ruysbroeck the Admirable)*

PROLOGUE

Judging by the few portraits that have been preserved in the Château de Lourps,* the line of the Floressas des Esseintes consisted, in bygone days, of muscular warriors and grim-looking mercenaries. Cramped and confined within those old frames where their great shoulders stretched across from side to side, they startled you with their staring eyes, their handlebar moustaches, and their swelling chests that curved outward to fit the enormous shell of the breast-plate.

Those were the ancestors: the portraits of their descendants were missing; a gap existed in the series of faces of that family line; one canvas only served as intermediary, providing a link between past and present, an inscrutable, wily face, its features lifeless and drawn, with cheekbones accentuated by a dash of rouge, thickly pomaded hair intertwined with pearls, and a taut, white-painted neck emerging from the goffers of a highly starched ruff.

In this painting of one of the closest friends of the Duc d'Épernon and the Marquis d'O,* the defects of a debilitated constitution and the excess of lymph in the blood were already apparent.

It was obvious that the decline of this ancient house had followed an inevitable course; the males had grown progressively more effeminate; as if to perfect the work of time, for two centuries the Des Esseintes intermarried their children, thus exhausting, through inbreeding, what little strength they yet possessed.

Of this family, which had once been so numerous that it occupied almost all the lands of the Île-de-France and the Brie, there now remained but one solitary descendant, the Duc Jean, a frail young man of thirty, nervous and anaemic, with hollow cheeks and cold, steel-blue eyes, a straight nose with flaring nostrils, and dry, slender hands.

By an odd atavistic coincidence, the last descendant resembled his early forebear the court favourite, for he had the same extraordinarily pale blond pointed beard, and the same cryptic expression, at once weary and cunning.

His had been a dismal childhood. Susceptible to scrofula and burdened by persistent fevers, he nevertheless succeeded, thanks to fresh air and careful nursing, in safely weathering the rough waters of puberty, and then his nervous system regained control, checking the languour and apathy of chlorosis and bringing to full completion the process of maturation.

The mother, a tall woman, silent and wan, died of extreme debility; then the father, in his turn, succumbed to some indeterminate malady; this occurred when Des Esseintes was almost seventeen.

The only memory of his parents that he retained was one of fear; he knew no feeling of gratitude or of affection. His father, who as a rule resided in Paris, he scarcely knew; his mother he remembered as lying motionless in a dark room in the Château de Lourps. Only rarely did husband and wife meet, and of those occasions he recalled lacklustre encounters, with the father and the mother seated opposite one another before a table lit only by a lamp with a large, very deep shade, because bright lights and noise brought on the attacks of nerves to which the Duchess was subject; they would exchange barely a couple of words in the semi-darkness, then the Duke would coldly take his leave, and hurry to catch the first available train.

At the Jesuit College where Jean was sent to be educated, he found life kinder and sweeter. The Fathers pampered this child whose intelligence amazed them; but, despite their efforts, they could not make him settle down to any systematic programme of study; he did well at certain subjects, excelling at Latin while still very young, but he was, by contrast, quite unable to construe two words of Greek, he revealed no aptitude for modern languages, and seemed irremediably obtuse the moment they tried to teach him the basic principles of science.

His family hardly paid him any attention; sometimes his father would visit him at his boarding school: 'Hallo, goodbye, be a good boy, work hard.' He spent the summer holidays at the Château de Lourps; his presence did not disturb his mother's reveries; she seemed barely conscious of his presence, or else might watch him for a few seconds with an almost painful smile on her face, then disappear once again into the artificial night with which the thick casement curtains shrouded the room.

The servants were tedious and old. The child, left to his own devices, rummaged about among the books on rainy days; on fine afternoons he wandered round the countryside. What he really delighted in was to go down to the little valley and head for Jutigny, a village which lay at the foot of the hills, a tiny huddle of cottages whose thatched caps were speckled with tufts of houseleek, and patches of moss. He would lie in a meadow, in the shade of the tall haystacks, listening to the muffled sound of the watermills and breathing in the cool air of the Voulzie.* Sometimes he would go as far as the peat-bogs and the green, dark hamlet of Longueville, or he might climb up the wind-swept hillsides from where the view was immense. There, below him on one side, he could see the valley of the Seine, receding as far as the eye could reach and merging with the blue of the confining distance; on the other side, high up on the horizon, the churches and tower of Provins seemed to tremble in the powdery gold of the sun-filled air.

Reading or dreaming, he would soak himself in solitude until nightfall; by dint of always mulling over the same thoughts his mind became more concentrated and his as yet indeterminate ideas matured. After every holiday he went back to his teachers more thoughtful and more stubborn; these changes did not escape them; perspicacious and astute, trained by their calling to probe the deepest levels of the soul, they were not taken in by this lively but intractable intelligence; they realized that this pupil would never enhance the glory of their school, and since his family was rich and appeared indifferent to his future, they immediately gave up their attempts to steer him towards the colleges that prepare students for lucrative professional careers; and although he would readily debate with them any theological doctrine that interested him by its subtlety and fine distinctions, they did not even consider encouraging him to enter their Order, because despite their efforts his faith remained weak; in the last resort, out of prudence and fear of the unknown, they allowed him to study those subjects that appealed to him and to ignore the others, not wishing to alienate this independent spirit by subjecting him to the nagging demands of lay assistant-instructors.

In this manner he lived perfectly happily, hardly conscious of the fatherly yoke of the priests; he continued his studies in Latin and French, in his own fashion, and although theology did not figure in his curriculum, he completed the grounding in this science which he had begun at the Château de Lourps, in the library left by his great-great-uncle Dom Prosper, a former Prior of the Canons Regular of Saint-Ruf.*

The day dawned, however, when he had to leave the Jesuit college; he was about to come of age and acquire control of his fortune; his cousin and guardian the Comte de Montchevrel gave him a reckoning of his stewardship. The relationship between these two was of short duration, for there could be no point of contact between them, one being old, the other young. Out of curiosity, and idleness, and politeness, Des Esseintes did visit the Count's family, and on several occasions sat through grimly boring evenings in their mansion in the Rue de la Chaise,* while relatives of his, women older than time, conversed about quarterings, and heraldic crescents, and obsolete ceremonial.

Even more so than these dowagers, the men who gathered round the whist table revealed themselves as fossilized nonentities; these descendants of valiant knights of yore, these scions of feudal families seemed to Des Esseintes's eyes a group of asthmatic, finicky old men, endlessly repeating the same pointless remarks, the same age-old phrases. As happens in the snapped-off stem of a fern, a fleur-de-lis seemed the only thing imprinted in the decaying pulp of those ancient brain-pans.

The young man was filled with inexpressible pity for those mummies buried in their elaborately panelled Pompadour-style hypogea, for those morose sluggards who lived with their gaze permanently fixed on a nebulous Canaan, an imaginary Palestine.

After several visits to those circles he decided, invitations and reproaches notwithstanding, never again to set foot there. He then began to consort with young men of his own age and his own class. Some, who like him had attended Catholic boarding schools, still bore the special stamp of that education. They went to church, took communion at Easter, frequented Catholic clubs, and, avoiding one another's eyes, kept their encounters with prostitutes as secret from each other as if they had committed a crime. They were, for the most part, obtuse, obsequious dandies, successful dunces who had tried the patience of their teachers but had, nevertheless, fulfilled the latter's aim of peopling society with submissive believers.

Others, educated in the state colleges or at lycées, were less hypocritical and more free and easy, but they were neither more interesting nor less narrow in their views. These men were libertines, devotees of musical comedy and of horse-racing, who played lansquenet and baccarat, and bet fortunes on horses, on cards, on every diversion dear to the empty-headed. After a year's trial of these companions, Des Esseintes was filled with an immense weariness by their excesses, which struck him as petty and facile, pursued with no discrimination, with no feverish involvement, with no genuine, intense excitement of blood and nerves.

Little by little he dissociated himself from them, and sought the company of men of letters with whom his mind would surely find more common ground and feel more at ease. This was yet another delusion: he was revolted by their spiteful, mean-spirited opinions, by their conversation which was as trite as a weekday sermon, by their sickening discussions which measured the value of a work by the number of editions and the profit on the sales. Meanwhile he also observed the free-thinkers, the doctrinarians of the bourgeoisie, people who claimed the right to every freedom in order to stifle the opinions of others, rapacious and insolent puritans whose breeding he considered inferior to that of the neighbourhood bootmaker.

His contempt for humanity increased: at length he realized that, for the most part, the world is made up of scoundrels and half-wits. There was absolutely no hope of his finding, in another person, the same yearnings and aversions that he felt, no hope of his joining forces with another intellect which would take pleasure, as he did, in a life of studious ineffectiveness, no hope of associating a sensitive, devious mind such as his with that of a writer or a man of letters.

In a state of irritable unease, filled with indignation by the triviality of the ideas he heard exchanged and accepted, he became like those people described by Nicole,* who hurt all over; he began incessantly excoriating his too-thin skin, he began to suffer from the jingoistic and social nonsense asseverated each morning in the newspapers, and to exaggerate, in his own mind, the extent of the success that an all-powerful public invariably and inevitably accords works written without either ideas or style. Already he was dreaming of a peaceful, civilized retreat, a comfortable desert, a snug, immovable ark where he could take refuge, far from the incessant deluge of human folly.

One passion only, the passion for women, might have restrained him in this universal contempt that was gnawing at him, but that passion too was spent. He had tasted the feasts of the flesh, with the appetite of a capricious man who suffers from malacia, who is beset by pangs of desire yet whose palate rapidly grows dull and surfeited;

in the days when he consorted with so-called country gentlemen, he
had attended those long-drawn-out suppers where, at the dessert
stage, drunken women unhook their gowns and bang their heads on
the table; he had also frequented theatrical dressing-rooms, sampled
actresses and singers, and had to endure, over and above the innate
stupidity of woman, the frenzied vanity of third-rate performers;
then he had kept women who were already celebrated whores, con-
tributing to the prosperity of those agencies which provide questionable pleasures in exchange for money; in the end, sated and weary
of this unvarying profusion, of these identical caresses, he had
plunged down in among the dregs of society, hoping to revive his
desires by contrast, and thinking to arouse his dormant senses with
the provocative squalor of extreme poverty.

No matter what he tried, he was oppressed by an overpowering
sense of ennui. He grew desperate, and resorted to the dangerous
caresses of virtuoso professionals, but then his health began to
fail and his nervous system became hypersensitive; the nape of his
neck was already painful to the touch and he could not keep his hand
still: if he grasped a heavy object he could hold it straight, but if he
held something light such as a small glass, his hand jerked limply
about.

The doctors he consulted frightened him. It was time to call a halt
to this life-style, to give up these practices which were exhausting his
vitality. For a while he lived quietly, but before long inflammation of
the cerebellum set in and once again goaded him to action. In the
same way that pubescent girls hanker after tainted or revolting food,
he began to dream of, then to indulge in, bizarre sexual practices and
deviant pleasures; this marked the end; as though satisfied at having
exhausted every possibility, as though worn out with the strain, his
senses were overpowered by inertia, and impotence was close at
hand.

When his sanity returned, he found himself alone, sober, abom-
inably tired, craving an end that the cowardice of his body prevented
his attaining. His idea of hiding himself away, far from the world, of
burrowing down into some nest, of muffling the never-ending racket
of relentless existence in the way straw muffles the street-noises
outside the homes of the sick, grew more intense.

In any case it was now time to take action: the reckoning he made
of his assets appalled him: he had consumed the greater part of his

inheritance in wild and extravagant living and the remainder, which was invested in property, brought in only derisory returns.

He decided to sell the Château de Lourps, which he no longer ever visited, and which for him held no tender memories, no sense of loss; he also liquidated his other assets and bought government stocks and bonds; in this manner he provided himself with an annual income of fifty thousand francs, and he also put aside a lump sum with which to buy and furnish the small house where he planned to steep himself in eternal quietude.

He ransacked the outskirts of the capital and found a small property for sale above Fontenay-aux-Roses,* in an out-of-the-way spot, with no neighbours, near the fort; his dream was fulfilled: in that neighbourhood, which was relatively free from the depredations of the Parisians, he was certain of being safe: the difficulty and unreliability of communications, which depended on an absurd train service from the other end of the town, and on little trams that seemed to determine their own routes and times of departure, reassured him. Picturing this new life he hoped to establish filled him with a joy that was all the greater, because he saw himself as cast away on the shore at a sufficient distance for the tide of Paris to no longer reach him, yet still close enough to the capital to ensure his solitude. And, indeed, since it only has to be impossible to get to a particular place, for one instantly to feel the urge to go there, there was a good chance that, by not cutting himself off irrevocably, he would not be tormented by any return of a need for society, by any regrets.

He set masons to work on the house he had acquired, and suddenly, one day, without telling anyone of his plans, sold off his old furniture, dismissed his servants, and disappeared, leaving no address with the concierge.

1

More than two months elapsed before Des Esseintes was able to immerse himself in the silent tranquillity of his house at Fontenay; purchases of every kind still kept him roaming the Paris streets and scouring the city from end to end.

And yet how thorough had been the researches he had undertaken, how deeply had he reflected, before entrusting his home to the decorators!

He had long been expert at distinguishing between genuine and deceptive shades of colour. In the past, in the days when he received women in his apartments, he had designed a bedroom where, amid the small pieces of furniture carved in pale Japanese camphor wood, beneath a sort of canopy of pink Indian satin, women's bodies took on a soft blush under the artfully prepared lighting that filtered through the fabric.

This bedroom, where mirrors mirrored one another and reflected an infinite series of pink boudoirs on the walls, had been celebrated among the prostitutes, who loved to soak their nakedness in this bath of rosy warmth, perfumed by the minty aroma coming from the wood of the furniture.

But, even aside from the benefits of that artificial atmosphere, which seemed to transfuse fresh blood into complexions faded and worn from constant use of makeup and from misspent nights, he felt, in that languorous environment, special pleasures on his own account, pleasures made keener and in a sense energized by memories of past afflictions, of vanished troubles.

Thus, out of loathing and contempt for his childhood, he had hung from the ceiling of this room a little cage of silver wire, in which a captive cricket sang, just as crickets had sung among the cinders on the hearths of the Château de Lourps; listening to that song he had heard so often, all the constrained, silent evenings he had spent with his mother, all the neglect he had experienced during his sickly, repressed youth surged up within him, and then, aware of the paroxysms of the woman he was mechanically caressing, whose words or laughter broke into his vision and brought him abruptly back to reality, to the bedroom, to earth, his soul would be filled with turmoil, with a need for revenge for the miseries he had endured, with a fierce urge to defile the family mementoes, with a furious desire to lie, panting, upon cushions of human flesh, to explore to the last drop the fiercest and the bitterest of carnal excesses.

And there were other times when he was gripped by an irritable moroseness, when, on rainy autumn days, he would be filled with abhorrence for the streets, for his own home, for the muddy yellow sky, for the dirty grey clouds, and he would seek refuge in this retreat, gently shaking the cage and watching the infinite play of its reflections in the mirror, until his intoxicated eyes noticed that the cage was not moving at all, but that the entire bedroom was swinging and gyrating, filling the house with a rose-coloured waltz.

And then, during that period when Des Esseintes had felt the need to draw attention to himself, he had devised sumptuous, peculiar schemes of decoration, dividing his salon into a series of variously carpeted alcoves, which could be related by subtle analogies, by indeterminate correlations of tone, either cheerful or gloomy, delicate or flamboyant, to the character of the Latin or French works he loved. He would then settle himself in that alcove whose furnishings seemed to him to correspond most closely to the essential nature of the work which the whim of the moment induced him to read.

Lastly, he had had a high-ceilinged room prepared for the reception of his tradesmen; they would enter and seat themselves side by side in church stalls, and then he would climb up into an imposing pulpit and preach to them on dandyism,* exhorting his bootmakers and tailors to comply in the most scrupulous manner with his briefs on the cut of his garments, and threatening them with pecuniary excommunication if they did not follow to the letter the instructions contained in his monitories and his bulls.

He acquired a reputation for eccentricity, to which he gave the crowning touch by dressing in suits of white velvet and gold-embroidered waistcoats, with, in place of a cravat, a bunch of Parma violets set low in the open neck of the shirt. He used also to host dinners for writers which caused quite a stir, one in particular, a copy of an eighteenth-century feast when, to celebrate the most trifling of misadventures, he organized a funerary collation.

The black-draped dining-room where he gave this dinner opened on to the garden, which had been transformed overnight, its paths sprinkled with charcoal, its little pond now rimmed with basalt and filled with ink, its shrubbery planted with cypresses and pines. The meal was served on a black tablecloth decorated with baskets of scabias and violets, and lit by green-flaming candelabras and by chandeliers in which wax tapers burned. While a concealed orchestra played funeral marches, the guests were waited on by naked black women, wearing stockings and slippers of silver cloth sprinkled with tears.

From black-rimmed plates they ate turtle soup, Russian rye bread, ripe Turkish olives, caviar, salted mullet roe, smoked Frankfurt black puddings, game in gravies the colour of liquorice and boot-blacking, truffled sauces, chocolate caramel creams, plum puddings, nectarines, preserved fruits, mulberries, and heart-cherries; from dark-coloured glasses they drank the wines of Limagne and Rousillon, of Tenedos, Val de Peñas, and Oporto, and, after the coffee and the walnut cordial, they enjoyed kvass, porters, and stouts. The invitations to this dinner to mark the temporary demise of the host's virility* were written out in a form similar to that used to announce a funeral.

But these extravagances in which he had once taken such pride had burnt themselves out; now he was filled with contempt for those childish, outmoded displays, for that eccentric clothing, for that bizarre ornamentation of his apartments. Now he simply wanted to arrange, for his own enjoyment rather than for the amazement of others, a domestic interior that was comfortable yet appointed in an exceptional manner, to fashion for himself a unique and tranquil setting suited to the requirements of his future solitude.

When the Fontenay house was ready, and the alterations had been carried out by an architect in accordance with his plans and wishes, when all that remained was to decide on details of the furniture and décor, he again, and at considerable length, examined the whole range of colours and their gradations.

What he sought were colours that increased in intensity by lamplight; little did he care if they appeared insipid or harsh by daylight, for it was at night that he really lived, believing that you were more completely at home, more truly alone, that the mind was only aroused and kindled into life as darkness drew near; he found too that there was a particular pleasure in being in a well-lit room, in being the only person up and about amid the shadowy, sleeping houses, a kind of pleasure which perhaps included a touch of vanity, a most unusual kind of satisfaction, like that experienced by people working late at night when, drawing aside the window curtains, they realize that round about them everything is dark, everything is silent, everything is dead.

Slowly, one by one, he sorted through the shades of colour. By candlelight, blue is almost an artificial green; a dark shade of blue, like cobalt or indigo, turns black; a pale shade turns grey; a true and gentle blue, like turquoise, looks faded and lifeless. So unless it was coupled with another colour, as a helper, blue could not possibly be used as the predominant shade in a room. On the other hand, iron greys grow still gloomier and heavier; pearl greys lose their azure tints and mutate into a dirty white; browns turn lethargic and cold; as for dark greens, such as emperor green and myrtle green, they behave like bright blues and merge into shades of black; that left the paler greens, like peacock green, the vermilions, and the reddish-brown laquers, but light washes out their blue tones, leaving behind only the yellow ones, which themselves then appear spurious and murky.

Tints of salmon, maize, and rose were also out of the question, for their effeminizing character would interfere with thoughts inspired by solitude; nor, lastly, could violets be considered, since they lose their colour; only red survives at night, and what a red! A viscous, winy, vulgar red; in any case he thought it quite pointless to make use of this colour, since by ingesting santonin* in the appropriate dosage, everything looks violet and it is then easy to change the hue of one's wall hangings without so much as touching them.

When these colours were set aside, only three remained: red, orange, and yellow. The colour he preferred to all others was orange, thus confirming by his own example the truth of a theory which he asserted was almost mathematically exact: to wit, that there exists a harmony between the sensual nature of a truly artistic individual, and the colour that his eyes perceive as most significant and most vivid.

If, in fact, you disregard the majority of ordinary mortals whose coarse retinas can discern neither the peculiar cadence of each colour nor the mysterious charms of their gradations and their subtleties; if you also ignore those bourgeois eyes which are insensible to the ceremonial and triumph of strong, vibrant colours; if you then consider none but those whose discriminating vision has been refined through contact with literature and art, he was convinced that the eye of that individual who dreams of ideal beauty, who craves illusions, who seeks some mystery in his women, is as a rule attracted to blue and its derivatives—mauve, lilac, and pearl grey—always provided these remain soft in tone, and do not cross that boundary where they lose their identity and are transformed into pure violets and forthright greys.

By contrast, those men who affect the military style, who are full-blooded, handsome, and brash, who scorn society's restraints, fling themselves into things, and promptly lose their heads, those men, for the most part, take pleasure in the dazzling brightness of yellows and reds, in the blinding, intoxicating clang of bright reds and chrome-yellows.

Lastly we have those weak and nervous people whose sensual appetite demands foods enhanced by smoking and pickling, and those with over-stimulated or consumptive constitutions; their eyes, almost without exception, are drawn to that irritating, morbid colour, with its deceptive splendours, its febrile sourness: orange.*

Des Esseintes's choice, therefore, did not admit of the smallest doubt; but very real difficulties still remained. If red and yellow are made more glorious by candle-light, the same is not always true of their compound, orange, which can flare up angrily, often turning a fiery nasturtium red.

He studied all its nuances by candle-light, and discovered one shade which he felt would not lose its stability and disappoint his expectations; when these preliminaries were completed, he decided, at least as far as his own study was concerned, to try to avoid Oriental fabrics and carpets, which, now that wealthy businessmen can buy them at a discount in the latest department stores, have become so boring and so commonplace.

In the end he decided to have his walls bound like books, in heavy smooth Morocco leather, using skins from the Cape glazed by huge plaques of steel under a powerful press.

Once the panelling had been decorated, he had the mouldings and the tall skirting-boards painted with a dark indigo blue enamel, similar to that used by coach-builders on the panels of carriages; the slightly domed ceiling, also covered in Morocco leather, displayed, like a vast sky-light framed in its orange mounting, a circle of sky of royal blue silk, in whose centre silver seraphims—embroidered long ago, for an ancient cope, by the Weavers' Guild of Cologne*—winged their way swiftly upward.

When all this was in place, the entire effect, at night, blended together, becoming tempered and settled; the blues of the panelling, now stabilized, were sustained and as though warmed by the oranges, while these in their turn maintained their integrity, being supported and, in a sense, enlivened by the compelling proximity of the blues.*

As for the furniture, Des Esseintes did not have to undertake any lengthy researches, inasmuch as books and rare flowers were to be that room's only luxury; later he planned to decorate the still-bare panelling with a few drawings or paintings, but for now he contented himself with installing shelving and bookcases of ebony on most of the walls; he scattered wild-animal skins and blue fox pelts on the parquet and, alongside a massive fifteenth-century money-changer's table, he placed some deep, winged armchairs, and an old wrought-iron stand taken from a chapel, one of those antique lecterns on which, in the past, the deacon placed the Antiphonary, and which now held one of the weighty in-folios of the *Glossarium mediae et infimae latinitatis* of Du Cange.*

The casement windows, whose bluish, crackled panes, studded with the bulging, gold-flecked irregularities of bottle glass, cut off the view of the countryside and allowed only a deceptive light to penetrate, were in their turn hung with draperies made out of antique stoles, whose darkened, smoky gold threadwork was quenched by the almost lifeless russet of the weave.

Lastly, upon the mantelpiece which was likewise draped in fabric cut from the sumptuous folds of a Florentine dalmatic, between two gilded copper Byzantine ostensories which came from the former Abbaye-au-Bois of Bièvre,* stood a marvellous ecclesiastical canon with three separate compartments, as intricately fashioned as a piece of lace, containing, beneath the glass of its frame, three works by Baudelaire, copied on genuine vellum in exquisite lettering like that of a missal and splendidly illuminated: to left and right the sonnets on 'La Mort des amants' and 'L'Ennemi',* and in the centre the prose poem with the English title: 'Anywhere out of the World.'*

2

After the sale of his possessions, Des Esseintes kept on the two old servants who had looked after his mother and between them had served as steward and concierge of the Château de Lourps, which remained untenanted and empty until it was put up for auction.

This couple he brought to Fontenay; they were accustomed to caring for the sick, to the regular, hourly dispensing of doses of draughts and tisanes, to the unvarying silence of the cloistered monk who lives without communication to the outside world, in apartments where the windows and doors are kept permanently closed.

The husband was responsible for cleaning the rooms and buying food, the wife did the cooking. He let them have the first floor of the house, made them wear thick felt slippers, ordered double doors installed with well-oiled hinges, and thick carpeting to pad their floors so that he would never hear the sound of their footsteps overhead.

He came to an understanding with them as to the meaning of different rings on the bell, depending on how many peals and whether they were short or long; he indicated, on his desk, the spot where each month they were to place the household account book while he was asleep; in fact he so arranged matters that he would not often have to speak to them or see them.

Nevertheless, as the wife had sometimes to walk round the side of the house to reach a shed where the wood was stored, he wanted her silhouette, as she passed his windows, not to seem inimical, and he had made for her a costume of Flemish faille, with a white cap and a large black cowl pulled down over it, such as the lay sisters of the *Béguinages* still wear today in Ghent.* The outline of this head-dress slipping past him in the dusk gave him the feeling of being in a convent, reminding him of those silent, God-fearing communities, those dead neighbourhoods shut away and buried in a corner of a busy and lively town.

He also established unvarying times for his meals; these were in any case uncomplicated and quite frugal, the weakness of his digestion no longer permitting him to assimilate elaborate or rich dishes.

At five o'clock, in the winter, after night had fallen, he breakfasted lightly on two boiled eggs, toast, and tea; then he dined at about eleven o'clock; drank coffee, sometimes tea and wine, during the night; and finally picked at a bit of supper towards five in the morning, before going to bed. He ate these meals, the times and the menus of which were definitively fixed at the start of each season, on a table in the centre of a small room which was separated from his study by a passage-way that was hermetically sealed and also padded, allowing neither odours nor sounds to penetrate the two rooms it served to connect.

This dining-room resembled a ship's cabin with its vaulted ceiling, its semicircular beams, its bulkheads and floorboards of pitch-pine, its tiny casement cut into the panelling like a porthole. Like those Japanese boxes which fit one inside the other, this room was inserted into another, larger room, the actual dining-room built by the architect.

The latter had two windows; one was now invisible, concealed by the bulkhead which could, however, be slid aside at will by pressing on a spring, in order to renew the air which, entering through this opening, could then circulate around the pitch-pine box and penetrate within it; the other, directly opposite the porthole in the panelling, was visible but no longer served as a real window; in fact, a large aquarium filled all the space between the porthole and the genuine window, housed in the actual wall. Thus, in order to light the cabin, the daylight had to pass, first, through the window, where the panes had been replaced by a sheet of plate glass, then through the water, and finally through the permanent glass pane of the porthole.

In autumn, at the moment when the samovar stood steaming on the table and the sun had nearly set, the water in the aquarium, which during the morning hours had looked vitreous and cloudy, turned red, dappling the golden panelling with the glowing radiance of blazing embers.

Sometimes of an afternoon, when Des Esseintes happened to be up and about, he would set in operation the various pipes and ducts that permitted the aquarium to be emptied and refilled with clean water, and then pour in some drops of coloured essences, thus creating for himself, at his own pleasure, the various shades displayed by real rivers, green or greyish, opaline or silvery, depending on the colour of the sky, the greater or lesser intensity of the sun, the

more or less imminent threat of rain, depending, in a word, on the
stage of the season and the state of the atmosphere. He would
then imagine he was between-decks in a brig, and would watch with
great interest as marvellous mechanical fish, driven by clockwork,
swam past the porthole window and became entangled in imitation
seaweed; or, while inhaling the smell of tar which had been pumped
into the room before he came in, he would examine some coloured
engravings hanging on the walls that depicted—like those in the
agencies for steamship lines and for Lloyd's—vessels bound for
Valparaiso and the River Plate, and framed notices listing the itiner-
aries of the Royal Mail packet steamers, the Lopez and Valéry
Companies,* and the freight charges and ports of call of the Atlantic
mail-boats.

Then, when he tired of consulting these timetables, he would rest
his eyes by contemplating the chronometers and compasses, sextants
and dividers, binoculars and maps that were scattered over a table
upon which was displayed only one book, bound in sealskin, *The
Adventures of Arthur Gordon Pym*,* printed specially for him on pure
linen-laid paper, selected by hand, bearing a seagull as its watermark.
Finally, he could examine a heap of fishing rods, nets browned with
tannin, rolled up russet-coloured sails, and a tiny anchor made of
cork and painted black, piled up near the door that communicated
with the kitchen via a passage with padded walls which, like the cor-
ridor between the dining-room and study, absorbed every odour and
every sound.

In this manner, without ever leaving his home, he was able to enjoy
the rapidly succeeding, indeed almost simultaneous, sensations of a
long voyage; the pleasure of travel—existing as it largely does only
in recollection and almost never in the present, at the actual moment
when it is taking place—this pleasure he could savour fully, at his
ease, without fatigue or worry, in this cabin whose contrived disorder, whose transient character and as it were temporary furnishings
corresponded almost exactly with his brief sojourns in it, with the
limited time spent on his meals, and which provided a complete contrast with his study, a permanent, orderly, well-established room,
fitted out for the solid sustainment of a domestic existence.

Besides, he considered travel to be pointless, believing that the
imagination could easily compensate for the vulgar reality of actual
experience. In his view, it was possible to fulfil those desires reputed

to be the most difficult to satisfy in normal life, by means of a trifling subterfuge, an approximate simulation of the object of those very desires. Thus, nowadays it is widely known that, in restaurants celebrated for the excellence of their cellars, gourmets enjoy drinking fine vintages made out of inferior wines which have been treated by the method of M. Pasteur.* Now, whether genuine or fake, these wines have the same aroma, the same colour, the same bouquet, so therefore the enjoyment experienced in tasting these adulterated imitations is absolutely identical with the pleasure one would take in savouring the pure, natural wine which is unobtainable today, even at an astronomical price.

By applying this devious kind of sophistry, this adroit duplicity, to the world of the intellect, there is no doubt that you can enjoy, just as easily as in the physical world, imaginary pleasures in every respect similar to the real ones; no doubt, for example, that you can embark on long explorations by your own fireside, stimulating, if need be, a reluctant or lethargic mind by reading a suggestive account of distant travels; nor is there any doubt that you can—without stirring from Paris—obtain the beneficial sensations of sea-bathing; you would simply have to go to the Vigier baths which are located on a boat in the middle of the Seine.*

There, by salting your bathwater and mixing into it, according to the formula given in the Pharmacopœia, sodium sulphate, hydrochlorate of magnesium, and lime; by taking from a tightly closed, screw-topped box, a ball of twine or a tiny piece of rope specially purchased in one of those huge ship's chandlers whose enormous warehouses and basements reek of sea-tides and sea-ports; by sniffing those fragrances which will still cling to the twine or piece of rope; by perusing a really good photograph of the casino and zealously studying, in the *Guide Joanne*,* a description of the beauties of the seaside resort where you would like to be; by letting yourself be rocked in your bath-tub by the waves made by the *bateaux-mouches*,* as they pass close beside the pontoon; finally, by listening to the moaning of the wind gusting under the arches of the bridge, and the rumbling of the omnibuses as they cross the Pont Royal just a few feet above you, the illusion of being near the sea is undeniable, overpowering, absolute.

The secret is to know how to go about it, to know how to concentrate the mind on one single detail, to know how to dissociate

oneself sufficiently to produce the hallucination and thus substitute
the vision of reality for reality itself. Des Esseintes considered, furthermore, that artifice was the distinguishing characteristic of human
genius. As he was wont to remark, Nature has had her day; she has
finally exhausted, through the nauseating uniformity of her landscapes and her skies, the sedulous patience of men of refined taste.
Essentially, what triteness Nature displays, like a specialist who
confines himself to his own single sphere; what small-mindedness,
like a shopkeeper who stocks only this one article to the exclusion of
any other; what monotony she exhibits with her stores of meadows
and trees, what banality with her arrangements of mountains and
seas!

Moreover, there is not one single invention of hers, however subtle
or impressive it may be thought to be, that the human spirit cannot
create; no forest of Fontainebleau or moonlit scene that cannot be
produced with a floodlit stage set; no waterfall that hydraulics cannot
imitate so perfectly as to be indistinguishable from the original;
no rock that papier-mâché cannot copy; no flower that specious taffetas and delicately painted papers cannot rival! There is no doubt
whatever that this eternally self-replicating old fool has now
exhausted the good-natured admiration of all true artists, and the
moment has come to replace her, as far as that can be achieved, with
artifice.

And then, if one carefully considers that work of Nature's generally deemed to be her most exquisite, that creation of hers whose
beauty is, everyone agrees, the most original and the most perfect,
namely woman: has not man, for his part, made, entirely on his own,
an animate yet artificial being that is, from the point of view of plastic
beauty, fully her equal? Does there, in this world, exist a being conceived in the joys of fornication and born of the birth pangs of a
womb, of which the model and type is more dazzling or more splendid than those of the two locomotives now in service on the railroad
of Northern France?

One of these, the *Crampton*,* an adorable blonde with a shrill
voice, a long slender body encased in a gleaming brass corset and the
supple, nervous resilience of a cat, is a stylish golden blonde whose
extraordinary grace is almost frightening as, stiffening her muscles
of steel and breaking into a sweat that streams down her warm flanks,
she sets in motion the immense rosaces of her elegant wheels and

leaps forward, a living thing, at the head of an express or a train bearing the day's catch!

The other, the *Engerth*,* is an enormous, gloomy brunette with a hoarse, harsh voice and thick-set hips squeezed into armour-plating of cast iron, a monstrous creature with a tousled mane of black smoke and six wheels coupled together low on the ground; what overwhelming power is hers when, setting the earth atremble, she slowly and ponderously pulls along behind her her heavily laden train of merchandise!

Comparable types of delicate slenderness or terrifying strength are most certainly not to be found among the frail, golden-haired beauties and handsome majestic brunettes of our human race; one can definitely assert that man has done as well, in his own sphere, as the God in whom he believes.

These thoughts came to Des Esseintes when he heard, carried on the breeze, the faint whistle of the toy trains that spin about between Paris and Sceaux; his house was some twenty minutes from the Fontenay station, but because of the height and isolation of its position, the hubbub made by the disgusting crowds that invariably haunt the neighbourhood of a station on Sundays could not reach as far as that.

As for the village itself, he scarcely knew it. One night he had gazed through his window at the silent landscape which slopes down to the foot of a hillside, on whose summit stand the batteries of the Verrières woods.* In the shadows, to left and right, indistinct shapes rose up one behind the other, while above them, far away, loomed other batteries and other fortifications, whose high supporting-walls seemed in the moonlight to have been washed over with silver gouache, against a background of dark sky.

Its size diminished by the shadow of the hills, the plain looked as if its centre had been powdered with dry starch and daubed with white cold-cream; in the balmy air that fanned the faded grasses, generating cheap, spicy scents, the trees, chalk-white in the moonlight, fluffed out their pale foliage, replicating their trunks with black shadows that striped the limy soil, on which pebbles sparkled, like shards of broken china.

Because of its painted and powdered appearance and its air of artifice, this landscape was not displeasing to Des Esseintes; but, ever since the afternoon spent looking for a house in the village of

Fontenay, he had never walked on the roads during the day; the verdancy of the area did not, in any case, interest him at all, for it did not even afford the delicate and plaintive charm of the pathetic, sickly vegetation that barely manages to cling to life on the suburban rubble-heaps near the ramparts. And then, in the village that day, he had seen corpulent middle-class worthies with side-whiskers, and well-dressed individuals with moustaches, who flaunted their magistrate's features or military mien as if they were parading the holy sacrament; since these encounters, his horror of the human countenance had increased.

During the final months of his stay in Paris, when, having lost faith in everything, he was oppressed by hypochondria and ravaged by spleen, he had reached such a pitch of nervous sensibility that the sight of a disagreeable object or person would etch itself into his brain so deeply as to require several days for its imprint to be even slightly dulled; during that period the touch of a human form, brushed against in the street, had been one of his most excruciating torments.

The sight of certain physiognomies caused him actual suffering, and he saw almost as insults the benevolent or peevish expressions on certain faces, feeling an urge to box the ears of, for example, this gentleman who strolled along half-closing his eyes in a learned manner, or of that one who rocked back and forth on his heels while gazing admiringly at his own reflection, or of yet a third who seemed prey to a thousand concerns, as with furrowed brow he pored over the long-winded articles and the news reports in a daily paper.

He could smell the presence of such ingrained stupidity, of such loathing for what he himself believed in, of such scorn for literature, for art, for everything that he himself adored, implanted and firmly rooted in these shallow tradesmen's brains—brains preoccupied exclusively with swindles and money and accessible only to that ignoble distraction of mediocre minds, politics—that he would return home in a fury and lock himself in with his books.

Lastly, he loathed with all the intensity of which he was capable the rising generations, those new classes of dreadful louts who feel the need to talk and laugh loudly in restaurants and coffee houses, who jostle you without apology on the pavements, and who without even a word of excuse or so much as a slight bow, ram you in the legs with the wheels of a baby carriage.

3

One section of the bookshelves lining the walls of his orange and blue study was filled exclusively with works in Latin, works which are classified under the generic term 'The Decadent Period'* by those intellects which have been tamed into conformity by the deplorable, endlessly reiterated lectures of the colleges of the Sorbonne.*

In actual fact, the Latin language, as it was practised during the period which professors still persist in calling the 'Golden Age', did not appeal to him in the least. That limited language, whose constructions, so few in number, are almost entirely without variation, syntactical flexibility, colour, or nuances, whose seams have been smoothed over and trimmed of the rugged but sometimes picturesque expressions of earlier ages, was capable, at a pinch, of expressing the pompous nothings, the vague platitudes rehashed by orators and poets, but it exuded such a lack of curiosity, such a list-lessness, that one had to go right back, in linguistic studies, to the French of Louis XIV's reign, to encounter another style as wilfully enervated, as solemnly wearisome and lacklustre.

Among writers, the dulcet Virgil, he whom schoolmasters call the swan of Mantua,* doubtless because he was not born in that city, struck him as not only one of the most terrible pedants but also one of the dullest bores that Antiquity ever produced; his well-washed, powdered shepherds, spewing out, turn by turn, vast quantities of cold and sententious verses, his Orpheus whom he likens to a tearful nightingale, his Aristaeus snivelling over some bees,* his Aeneas, that irresolute, indeterminate character who struts about gesturing woodenly, like a silhouette in a shadow box, behind the ill-fitting, obtrusive transparency of the poem, infuriated him. He might well have put up with the tiresome twaddle that these puppets proclaim to the wings in their unnaturally contrived dialogues, he might also have put up with the brazen borrowings from Homer, from Theocritus, from Ennius, from Lucretius, the outright theft, revealed by Macrobius, of the Second Book of the *Aeneid* which he lifted almost word for word from a poem of Pisander's, in brief, all the indescribable inanity of that bunch of cantos; but what he found

even more unbearable was the style of these hexameters, with their
tinny, hollow ring, spinning out their carefully measured quantities
of words in accordance with the rigid requirements of a pedantic and
sterile prosody; nor could he tolerate any better the structure of these
strident, studied verses, with their officially formal appearance, their
contemptible deference to grammar, their mechanical bisection by an
invariable caesura, their flow always staunched in the same way by a
dactyl colliding with a concluding spondee.

That humdrum, inflexible metrical scheme, copied from the
unvarying prosody hammered into perfection by Catullus, and which
was crammed with useless vocabulary, with padding, with pre-
dictable, identical words added to satisfy metrical requirements,
those pitiful Homeric epithets that reappear incessantly, without ever
designating or describing anything, that entire poverty-stricken
vocabulary with its flat, unevocative tones, were to him a form of
torture.

It is fair to add that, while he felt only the most lukewarm admiration for Virgil, and only the most guarded, muted liking for the
limpid utterances of Ovid, his loathing for the elephantine charms
of Horace, for the prattling of that insufferable bungler as he archly
tells off-colour stories worthy of a senescent, white-plastered clown,
was unbounded.

In prose, the verbose style, tautological metaphors and rambling
digressions of 'Chick-pea'* give him no pleasure either; the arrogance of his apostrophes, the wordy repetitiveness of his appeals
to patriotism, the bombast of his harangues, the ponderous density
of his style, fleshy, rich, but run to fat and lacking pith and bones,
the insupportable mediocrity of his long introductory adverbs, the
unvarying formulae of his adipose phrases, poorly linked by the
thread of his conjunctions, and finally his tedious habit of redundancy, did not appeal to him at all; nor did Caesar, famed for his suc-
cinctness, appeal to him much more than Cicero; for he embodied
the opposite extreme—a martinet's aridity, a sterile log-book style,
an incredible, uncalled-for costiveness.

In brief, he could find no sustenance either among these writers
or even among those in whom literary dabblers delight: Sallust,
admittedly less dreary than the rest; Livy, sentimental and pompous;
Seneca, turgid and lack-lustre; Suetonius, lethargic and spineless;
Tacitus, who in his calculated concision is the most virile, the most

biting, the most vigorous of them all. In poetry Juvenal, despite some very sprightly lines, and Persius, despite his mysterious insinuations, left him cold. Passing over Tibullus and Propertius, Quintilian and the two Plinys, Statius, Martial of Bilbilis, even Terence, and Plautus, whose diction, with its many neologisms, compound words, and diminutives, might have appealed had his vulgar humour and coarse wit not disgusted him, Des Esseintes only began to feel an interest in the Latin language* with Lucan, whose pen enlarged its scope, making it more expressive and less harsh; his brightly enamelled, gem-studded verses with their well-crafted structure captivated him, but that exclusive preoccupation with form, those sonorous reverberations, those metallic bursts of sound did not completely blind him to the intellectual vacuity, to the bloating of the stylistic blisters that mar the surface of the *Pharsalia*.

The author whom he really loved and who made him forever banish Lucan's ringing tones from his reading, was Petronius.

Petronius was an acute observer, a sensitive analyst, a superb painter; calmly, without bias, without rancour, he described the daily life of Rome and recounted the manners and morals of his time in the lively little chapters of the *Satyricon*. Noting down facts as he went along and recording them in permanent form, he laid out before the reader the everyday existence of the common people, with its incidents, its savagery, its lusts.

Here, we see the Inspector of Lodgings asking for the names of newly arrived travellers; there, we see brothels, where men prowl among the naked women who stand beside advertising placards, while through partly open doors couples can be glimpsed disporting themselves; elsewhere, both in the villas with their brazen luxury, their senseless wealth and ostentation, and in the wretched inns with their dishevelled, flea-ridden pallet beds that we find throughout the book, the society of the time goes about its business; foul pickpockets like Ascyltus and Eumolpus, hoping for a windfall; elderly aberrants with their gowns tucked up and their cheeks plastered with white lead and acacia rouge; catamites of sixteen, plump and curly-headed; women ravaged by hysteria; legacy-hunters offering their sons and daughters to the lusts of rich old men; they all race through the pages, argue in the streets, paw one another in the baths, and bash one another about like characters in a pantomime.

And all this is told in an extraordinarily vigorous style, precise in coloration, a style that draws from every dialect, that borrows expressions from every language Rome has known, that pushes back all the boundaries, that ignores all the trammels of the so-called Golden Age, letting each man speak in his own tongue: uneducated freedmen in vulgar Latin, the argot of the streets; foreigners in their cacophonous idiom, a hybrid of African, Syrian, and Greek elements; half-witted pedants, like the Agamemnon of the *Satyricon*, in a rhetoric full of spurious expressions. These folk are drawn with a single stroke of the pen, sprawled round a table, exchanging drunken inanities, delivering themselves of senile maxims and pointless bromides, their mugs turned towards Trimalchio* who picks his teeth, offers the company a piss-pot, describes the state of his bowels and farts, urging his guests to make themselves comfortable.

This realistic work, this slice carved from the flesh of Roman daily life, without—whatever anyone may say—any thought of reform or satire or any need for a specific goal or moralizing purpose; this story, without any plot or any action, which sets before us the sexual encounters of sodomites, analysing with shrewd placidity the pleasures and the pains of those amours and those couples; this story depicting, in splendidly wrought language, without the author ever showing himself or passing a single comment, or approving or condemning the actions and the thoughts of his characters, the vices of a decayed civilization, a splintering empire; this work of Petronius excited and gripped Des Esseintes's attention. In its highly polished style, its astute observation, its solid structure, he could discern curious parallels and strange analogies with the handful of modern French novels he was able to tolerate.

Doubtless he bitterly regretted the disappearance of the *Eustion* and the *Albutia*, those two works by Petronius that Planciades Fulgentius mentions and that have completely vanished, but the bibliophile in him consoled the scholar, as with reverent fingers he leafed through the superb copy of the *Satyricon* in his possession—the 1585 octavo edition bearing the name of J. Dousa, of Leyden.

After Petronius, his Latin collection included works from the second century of the Christian era,* omitting the bombastic Fronto who had unsuccessfully tried to refurbish and recondition his old-fashioned vocabulary, skipping over the *Attic Nights* of Fronto's disciple and friend Aulius Gellius, a shrewd and enquiring intellect but one whose writing was bogged down in a glutinous stylistic sludge,

and stopping at Apuleius, whose works Des Esseintes possessed in
the folio *editio princeps*, printed in Rome in 1469.

This African writer delighted him; in his *Metamorphoses*,* the
Latin language was flowing at full tide, carrying along with it the
sediment and waters of different tributaries from every province; all
this, blended together and intermingled, created a tone that was
strange, exotic, almost novel; new mannerisms and new details of
Latin society were given linguistic form in neologisms coined for the
conversational needs of a tiny corner of Roman Africa. Moreover,
Des Esseintes found Apuleius' hearty good humour—the joviality of
an unquestionably fat man—and his southern exuberance entertaining. He seemed like a bawdy, high-spirited companion when compared with the Christian apologists of the same period—for example
the soporific Minucius Felix,* a pseudo-classic, who poured into his
Octavius the emulsions of Cicero in a yet more gluey form, or even
Tertullian, whom perhaps Des Esseintes kept for the Aldine edition
of his works rather than for the works themselves.

Even though he was reasonably well informed on theology, the
Montanist quarrels with the Catholic Church and the polemics
against Gnosticism left him cold; also, and despite the intriguing
quality of Tertullian's style (a style that was succinct, full of ambi-
guity, heavily dependent on participles, jostled by antitheses,
bristling with puns and epigrams, riddled with terms taken from
jurisprudence and from the language of the Fathers of the Greek
Orthodox Church), he now hardly ever opened the *Apologeticus* or
the *De patientia*, and read at most a few pages of the *De cultu femi-
narum* in which Tertullian exhorts women not to adorn their persons
with jewels and precious materials, and forbids them the use of cosmetics, this practice being an attempt to correct and embellish
Nature.

These ideas, the exact opposite of his own, made him smile; and
then he found that the part played by Tertullian as Bishop of
Carthage evoked pleasant reveries in him; in reality what attracted
Des Esseintes was not so much Tertullian's works as the man himself.

He certainly lived in tempestuous times, times rent by appalling
disturbances, under Caracalla, under Macrinus, under that astonishing high-priest of Emesa, Elagabalus, and he calmly went on
composing his sermons, his dogmatic treatises, his apologias, and
his homilies while the Roman empire was being shaken to its

foundations, while the madness of Asia and the filth of paganism
were running rampant. With the most admirable self-possession, he
continued to advocate carnal abstinence, frugality at table, sobriety
of dress, during the very time when Elagabalus, his feet treading on
powdered silver and sand of gold, his head encircled by a tiara, his
garments studded with precious stones, spent his time, surrounded
by his eunuchs, at women's work, giving himself the title of Empress,
and every night bedding a different Emperor, preferably chosen from
among his barbers, kitchen boys, and charioteers.

This sharp contrast enchanted Des Esseintes; furthermore, the
Latin language, having attained its greatest perfection with Petronius, was on the point of dissolution; the literature of Christianity was
now establishing itself, bringing, along with new ideas, fresh words,
innovative constructions, unknown verbs, adjectives with over-subtle
meanings, and abstract terms, which had hitherto been rare in the
Roman tongue, and which Tertullian was one of the first to use.

However, this linguistic deliquescence, which continued after Tertullian's death with his pupil St Cyprian, with Arnobius, and with
the ponderous Lactantius, was an unappealing process. An incomplete and sluggish decay, it was marked by awkward regressions to
Ciceronian grandiloquence, and as yet lacked that special gamey
redolence which during the fourth century, and more particularly
during the centuries that followed, the odour of Christianity was to
impart to the language of pagan Rome, which decomposed like
venison, falling apart at the same time as the civilization of the
Ancient World crumbled into dust, at the same time as Empires,
rotted by the putrefaction of centuries, collapsed under the onslaught of the Barbarians.

The art of the third century* was represented in his library by a
solitary Christian poet, Commodian of Gaza, with his *Carmen apologeticum*, written in 259, and a compendium of moral maxims that
he had twisted into acrostics, couched in unpolished hexameters
divided, as in heroic verse, by caesuras, composed with no attention
to quantity or to the rules of hiatus, and repeatedly rounded out with
the kind of rhymes of which Church Latin was subsequently to
provide abundant examples.

Those stilted, gloomy verses, with their whiff of the feral, full
of everyday terms, of words with their original sense distorted,
appealed to him and interested him even more than the style (for all

that it was over-ripe and already green with rot) of the historians
Ammianus Marcellinus and Aurelius Victor, of the letter-writer
Symmachus or of the compiler and grammarian Macrobius; he
even preferred them to the genuinely scanned lines and the many-
faceted, magnificent language that came from the pens of Claudian,
of Rutilius, and of Ausonius.

These last three were, at that time, the masters of the art; they
filled the dying Empire with their cries; the Christian Ausonius with
his *Cento nuptialis* and his rich, elaborate poem *The Moselle*; Rutilius, with his hymns to the glory of Rome, his imprecations against
Jews and monks, his journey from Italy into Gaul, in which he
manages to convey certain impressions of what he sees, the indistinct quality of landscapes reflected in water, the mirages of mist,
the swirling of fog about the mountain tops.

For his part, Claudian—a kind of avatar of Lucan—dominates the
entire fourth century with the mighty clarion of his verse; a poet
forging dazzling, sonorous hexameters, and amid showers of sparks
beating out his epithets with staccato blows of his hammer; attaining a certain greatness, and breathing life into his work with the force
of his inspiration. Amid the ever-growing decay of the Western
Empire, with the chaos of endless massacres reigning on every side,
and the perpetual threat of the Barbarians now pushing in their mul-
titudes against the straining hinges of the gates to the Empire, he
brings Antiquity back to life, sings of the Rape of Proserpina, daubs
on his vibrant colours and moves past with all his lights brightly
shining into the darkness that is encroaching upon the world.

Paganism lives again in him, sounding its final fanfare, raising up
its last great poet high above Christianity which will from then on
engulf the language in its entirety, which will become, and forever
remain, sole master of the poetic art, with Paulinus, the pupil of
Ausonius; with the Spanish priest Juvencus, who paraphrases the
Gospels in verse; with Victorinus, the author of the *Machabaei*; with
Sanctus Burdigalensis who, in an eclogue imitated from Virgil, shows
the shepherds Aegon and Buculus lamenting the ailments that plague
their flocks. Then there follows a whole series of saints: Hilary of
Poitiers, Defender of the Faith of Nicaea, called the Athanasius of
the West; Ambrosius, the author of indigestible sermons, the boring
Christian Cicero; Damasus, coiner of lapidary epigrams; Jerome,
the translator of the Vulgate, and his adversary Vigilantius of

Comminges who inveighs against the worship of saints, the exploita-
tion of miracles, the practice of fasting, and, even in those days,
invoking arguments which will be repeated down the ages, preaches
against monastic vows and the celibacy of the priesthood.

Finally, in the fifth century, we have Augustine, Bishop of Hippo.
Him Des Esseintes knew only too well, for he was the most revered
of the writers of the Catholic Church, the founder of Christian
orthodoxy, the theologian seen by Catholics as an oracle, as a supreme
authority. The consequence was that he no longer ever opened St
Augustine's works, even though, in his *Confessions*, he had proclaimed his loathing of this world, and though his sorrowing piety
had, in his book *De civitate dei*, attempted to alleviate the appalling
misery of the century with soothing promises of a better life to come.
In the days when Des Esseintes used to study theology, he was
already weary of, already surfeited by, St Augustine's sermons and
jeremiads, his theories on predestination and on grace, his fights
against the schisms.

He much preferred browsing through the *Psychomachia* of Prudentius, the inventor of the allegorical poem, a form which was
to enjoy such a long run of popularity in the Middle Ages, and
he enjoyed dipping into the works of Sidonius Apollinaris, whose
correspondence, studded with witticisms, conceits, archaisms, and
enigmas, he found enticing. He was fond of rereading the panegyrics
in which that Bishop invokes, in support of his self-satisfied encomia,
the deities of the pagan world, and, in spite of everything, he had to
admit to a weakness for the affectations and innuendos of these
poems, constructed by an ingenious mechanic who takes good care
of his machine, keeping its working parts well oiled, and who if
required can devise new ones which are both complicated and
useless.

After Sidonius there was also the panegyrist, Merobaudes, whom
he frequently read; Sedulius, the composer of rhymed poems and
alphabetical hymns, certain parts of which the Church has appropriated for use in her services; Marius Victor, whose obscure treatise
De perversis moribus is lit up in places by verses that glow like phosphorus; Paulinus of Pella, author of that trepid work, the *Eucharisticon*; Orientius, Bishop of Auch, who in the distichs of his
Commonitorium denounces the licentiousness of women whose faces,
he claims, bring ruin upon the nations of the world.

Des Esseintes's interest in the Latin language remained undiminished, now that it hung like a completely rotted corpse, its limbs falling off, dripping with pus, and preserving, in the total corruption of its body, barely a few firm parts, which the Christians took away to steep in the brine of their new idiom.

The second half of the fifth century had arrived, that horrifying period when the world was convulsed by appalling cataclysms. The Barbarians were ravaging Gaul; Rome, paralysed, sacked by the Visigoths, felt herself grow chill as her life ebbed away, and saw her distant limbs—the East and the West—thrashing about in blood and growing weaker day by day.

Amid the general dissolution, amid the assassinations of the Caesars that follow one another in quick succession, amid the uproar of the carnage that engulfs Europe from end to end, a terrifying hurrah rings out, stifling the clamour, silencing the voices. On the banks of the Danube thousands of men, wrapped in cloaks made from rat pelts and mounted on little horses—horrific-looking Tartars, with enormous heads, flat noses, chins furrowed by gashes and scars, and jaundiced, hairless faces—swoop down at lightning speed, enveloping in their whirlwind the provinces of the Lower Empire.

Everything vanished in the dust from those galloping horses, in the smoke from those fires. Darkness covered the earth and the nations trembled in consternation, as they listened to the dreadful whirlwind passing by with a thunderous roar. The horde of Huns razed Europe, hurled itself upon Gaul, and then broke apart on the plains of Chalons where Aetius routed it in a terrible charge. The plain, surfeited with blood, frothed like a sea of purple, two hundred thousand corpses blocked the way and broke the impetus of this avalanche which, deflected, fell like an exploding thunderbolt upon Italy, where the devastated cities flamed up like hay-ricks.

The Western Empire crumbled under the impact; the failing life it was dragging out in imbecility and infamy was extinguished; the end of the universe seemed to be at hand; the cities forgotten by Attila were decimated by famine and by plague, and Latin in its turn appeared to be collapsing beneath the ruins of the world.

Years went by; the Barbarian tongues began to systematize themselves, to emerge from their sclerosis, to develop into true languages; Latin, saved from the cataclysm by the cloister, remained confined to the convents* and the presbyteries; here and there a handful of poets sparkled, cold and deliberate: the African Dracontius with his *Hexameron*, Claudius Mamertus with his liturgical verses, Avitus of Vienne; then the biographers, such as Ennodius, the astute, venerated diplomat and upright, vigilant pastor, who relates the miracles of St Epiphanes, or Eugippus who has recorded for us the incomparable life of St Severinus, that mysterious hermit and humble ascetic who, like an angel of mercy, appeared to the weeping masses that were frantic with suffering and fear; writers such as Veranius of Gevaudan who composed a little treatise on continence, or Aurelian and Ferreolus who compiled Church canons, or historians such as Rotherius of Agde, famed for a chronicle of the Huns, now lost.

The centuries that followed were represented on Des Esseintes's shelves by just a scattering of works. Nevertheless he did have, for the sixth century, Fortunatus, Bishop of Poitiers, whose hymns and whose *Vexilla regis*, carved out of the old carcass of the Latin language and seasoned with the aromatic spices of the Church, haunted him on particular days; Boethius, old Gregory of Tours, and Jornandes. Then because, during the seventh and eighth centuries, apart from the Low Latin of the chroniclers such as Fredegarius and Paul the Deacon, and the poems of the Bangor Antiphonary (in which he would occasionally glance at the alphabetical, mono-rhyming hymn sung in honour of St Comgall), literature consisted almost exclusively of the biographies of saints—the legend of St Columba by the cenobite Jonas and that of the blessed Cuthbert, composed by the Venerable Bede from the notes of an anonymous monk of Lindisfarne—he confined himself to leafing through, in his idle moments, the works of these hagiographers, and to rereading a few extracts from the Lives of St Rusticula and St Radegunde, the first related by Defensor, Synodite of Ligugé, the second by the modest and artless Baudonivia, a nun of Poitiers.

There were, however, a number of singular works of Anglo-Saxon literature, written in Latin, that he found more enticing: the entire series of enigmas by Aldhelm, Tatwine, and Eusebius, those disciples of Symphosius, and above all the enigmas composed by St Boniface in the form of versified acrostics, with the solution given by the initial letters of each line.

His enjoyment lessened as these two centuries drew to a close; by and large he took little pleasure in the ponderous works of the

Carolingian Latinists, the Alcuins and the Einhards, being content, as far as examples of ninth-century Latin were concerned, with chronicles by the anonymous writer of Saint-Gall, by Fréculf and by Regino, with the poem on the siege of Paris composed by Abbo le Courbé, and with the *Hortulus*, the didactic poem written by the Benedictine Walafrid Strabo, in which the chapter in honour of the pumpkin, symbol of fruitfulness, filled him with delight. He also took pleasure in the poem by Ermold le Noir celebrating the exploits of Louis le Débonnaire, its regular hexameters couched in an austere, almost grim, style, an iron-clad Latin toughened in monastic waters with specks of sentiment embedded here and there in the hard metal; and in Macer Floridus' poem *De viribus herbarum*, which particularly appealed to him because of its poetic recipes and the extremely strange qualities he attributes to certain plants and flowers; to the aristolochia, for example, which, mixed with beef and plastered on the belly of a pregnant woman, infallibly ensures that she will bear a male child; to borage which, made into an infusion and sprinkled round a dining-hall, fills all the guests with good cheer; to the peony, the powdered root of which cures epilepsy once and for all; and to fennel which, if laid upon a woman's breast, clarifies her urine and regulates her periods.

Apart from a handful of special, unclassified volumes that were modern or undated;* a few works on cabbala, medicine, and botany; a few odd tomes of Migne's *Patrology* containing some Christian poetry that was unobtainable elsewhere, and Wernsdorf's anthology of minor Latin poets; apart from Meursius, and Forberg's *Manual of Classical Erotology*, the *Moechialogy* and the *Diaconals* for the use of confessors, which he would very occasionally dust off, his Latin library stopped at the beginning of the tenth century.

For in fact the quaintness, the complicated artlessness of Christian Latin had likewise come to an end. The rubbish produced by philosophers and scholiasts, the logomachy of the Middle Ages would henceforth hold undisputed sway. The sooty piles of chronicles and historical works, of crude, ponderous chartularies would grow ever greater, while the faltering grace, the sometimes exquisite ineptitude of the monks as they mixed the poetic leftovers of Antiquity into a pious mish-mash, were no more; the makers of verbs of highly concentrated meaning, of nouns smelling of incense, of eccentric adjectives, roughly shaped out of gold after the uncouth and charming style of Gothic jewellery, were destroyed. The old editions, so cherished by Des Esseintes, ended, and, with a prodigious leap over the centuries, the books that now covered the remaining shelves, heedless of the passage of the years, led directly to the French of the present day.

4

Late one afternoon a carriage drew up in front of the house at Fontenay. Since Des Esseintes received no visitors, since the postman dared not even set foot within those unfrequented precincts, having neither newspaper, nor journal, nor letter to deliver there, the servants hesitated, uncertain whether or not to open the door; then, on hearing the ringing of the bell as it clanged vigorously against the wall, they ventured to uncover the spy-hole cut into the door and saw a gentleman whose entire chest, from neck to waist, was concealed by a huge golden shield.

They informed their master, who was breakfasting. 'Certainly, show him in,' he said, recollecting that he had once given his address to a lapidary, so that he could deliver an order.

The gentleman bowed and placed his shield upon the pitchpine parquet of the dining-room. Rocking itself and rising up a trifle from the floor, it stretched forth a tortoise's serpentine head; then, suddenly taking fright, retreated into its shell.

This tortoise* was the consequence of a whim of Des Esseintes's, which antedated his departure from Paris. One day, while gazing at a shimmering Oriental carpet and following the sheen of the silvery lights darting about on the woven woollen threads, plummy purple and golden yellow in colour, he had thought: it would be a good idea to place upon this carpet something that moves, and is dark enough in hue to set off the brilliance of these tones.

Wandering haphazardly through the city streets in the grip of this idea, he had reached the Palais-Royal, and in front of Chevet's shop-window had struck himself upon the forehead: an enormous tortoise was there, in a tank. He had bought it; then, once it was let loose on the carpet, he had sat down in front of it and watched it for a long time, screwing up his eyes. Unquestionably, the dark brown and raw Sienna shades of that shell dimmed the play of colours in the carpet without bringing them to life; the overwhelmingly silvery lights now barely even gleamed, deferring to the chill tones of unpolished zinc that edged the hard, dull carapace.

He gnawed at his fingernails, searching for ways to reconcile these ill-matched partners and to avoid the absolute divorce of these tints;

he finally saw that his first idea, of trying to enhance the fire of the carpet's colours by the movement of an object placed upon it, was mistaken; in brief, that carpet was still too garish, too undisciplined, too new. The colours had not become sufficiently muted and faded; it was a matter of inverting the idea, of tempering and deadening the tones by contrasting them with a brilliant object which would subdue everything around it, which would cast its golden light over the pallid silver. Put like that, the problem became easier to resolve. He decided, therefore, to have his tortoise's shell gilded.

Once back from the gilder's where it had been lodging, the creature blazed like a sun, shining triumphantly over the subjugated tones of the carpet, radiant as a Visigoth's shield inlaid with scales by an artist of barbaric tastes.

At first, Des Esseintes was enchanted with this effect; then it struck him that this gigantic jewel was still unfinished, and would not be truly complete until it had been encrusted with precious stones.

He chose, from a Japanese collection, a design depicting a cluster of flowers showering out from a slender stalk; he took this to a jeweller, sketched in an oval frame round the bouquet, and informed the stupefied lapidary that the leaves and petals of each of these flowers were to be made of gem stones and set in the actual shell of the tortoise.

Choosing the stones took some time; diamonds have become extraordinarily commonplace now that every tradesman sports one on his little finger; Oriental emeralds and rubies are less degraded, and they do emit a glowing fiery radiance, but they look too much like the green and red eyes of certain omnibuses which display head-lamps in those two colours; as for topazes, whether burnt or raw, they are cheap stones, dear to the hearts of the lower middle classes who revel in stowing away their jewel-cases in their mirrored wardrobes; then again, although the Church has perpetuated the hieratic character—both unctuous and solemn—of the amethyst, that stone too has been debased on the blood-red earlobes and tubulous fingers of butcher's wives who seek to adorn themselves, for a modest outlay, with genuine, weighty jewels; of those stones only the sapphire has managed to keep its fires inviolate from industrial and financial absurdity. Its scintillations, flashing out over clear and icy waters have, one might say, preserved the purity of its discreet and haughty lineage. Unfortunately, in artificial light, its clear flame no longer sparkles; its blue waters sink low and seem to slumber, only awakening to glittering life at break of day.

None of these gems at all satisfied Des Esseintes; they were, in any case, too civilized and too well known. He ran some stones that were more unusual, more bizarre, through his fingers, finally selecting a series of both real and artificial gems, which in combination would produce a harmony at once fascinating and unsettling.

He fashioned his bouquet of flowers in the following manner: the leaves were set with stones of an intense, unequivocal green: with asparagus-green chrysoberyls; with leek-green peridots; with olive-green olivines; and they stood out against branches made of purplish-red almandine* and ouvarovite,* sparkling with a dry brilliance like those flakes of scale that shine on the inside of wine-casks.

For those flowers which were isolated from the stem and well separated from the base of the spray, he employed azurite, but he rejected out of hand that Oriental turquoise which is used on brooches and rings and which, along with the humdrum pearl and the odious coral, delights the hearts of the humbler classes; he chose only Western turquoises, stones which are, strictly speaking, simply a fossil ivory impregnated with coppery substances and whose blue-green is clogged, opaque, sulphurous, as though yellowed with bile.

That done, he could now set the petals of the flowers blooming in the centre of the bouquet, those flowers closest to the trunk, using stones that were transparent, glinting with vitreous, morbid lights, with feverish, piercing flashes of fire.

He formed them using only cat's eyes from Ceylon, cymophanes and sapphirines.* These three stones did indeed emit mysterious and perverse scintillations, painfully wrested from their icy, murky depths. The cat's eye is a greenish grey, striped with concentric veins that constantly appear to shift and change position, depending on the way the light falls. The cymophane has azure moirés running across the milky tints floating within it. The sapphirine glows with bluish phosphorus flames on a ground of dull chocolate brown.

The jeweller successively noted down the places where the stones were to be set, 'And what about the edge of the shell?' he asked Des Esseintes.

Initially, the latter had thought of using a few opals and hydrophanes; but these stones, which are interesting because of their indeterminate colouring and fitful radiance, are much too intractable and unreliable; the opal has a truly rheumatic sensitivity, the play of its rays being affected by the degree of damp, of heat, or of cold, whereas the hydrophane will glow only in water, being loath to set its grey embers afire unless it is first wetted.

He finally chose stones whose tones would contrast with one another: the mahogany-red of the hyacinth of Compostella and the blue-green of the aquamarine; the vinegar pink of the balas ruby and the pale slate-grey of the Sudermanie ruby. Their feeble iridescence was enough to light the shadows of the shell without distracting the eye from the blossoming of the jewels, which they encircled with a narrow wreath of indeterminate flames.

Des Esseintes gazed now at the tortoise as, cowering in a corner of his dining-room, it glittered in the semi-darkness. He felt perfectly happy; his eyes were intoxicated by those resplendent corollas blazing on a golden ground; and then, being, for him, unusually hungry, he dipped his toast—spread with a quite unique butter—in a cup of tea, brewed from a flawless blend of Si-a-Fayoune, Moyou-tann, and de Khansky,* green teas which had come by very special caravans from China by way of Russia.

He drank this liquid perfume from cups of that Chinese porcelain which is called eggshell because it is so translucent and light, and, just as he would use nothing but those enchanting cups, he would also use, for cutlery, nothing but genuine silver-gilt that was a trifle shabby, so that the silver, barely visible through the faintly eroded layer of the gold, gives it a suggestion of something sweetly old-fashioned, a vague hint of something utterly weary and close to death.

After swallowing his last mouthful of tea, he returned to his study and had his servant bring in the tortoise, which still obstinately refused to move.

It was snowing. In the lamplight, blades of ice were growing on the outside of the blue-tinged window-panes and the hoarfrost, like melted sugar, glittered on the gold-spangled bottle-glass of the windows. Absolute silence enveloped the little house as it slumbered in the shadows.

Des Esseintes let his mind wander: the big log fire filled the room with scorching exhalations; he set the window slightly ajar. Like some great hanging of reversed ermine, the sky rose before him, black and dappled with white. An icy wind gusted, intensifying the wild scudding of the snow, inverting the proportions of black and white. The heraldic hanging of the sky turned itself over, becoming true white ermine, itself dappled with black by the tiny patches of night strewn among the snowflakes.

He reclosed the casement; this sudden change, without transition, from scorching heat to the chill of midwinter had given him a shock; huddling by the fire, he thought he might drink something alcoholic to warm himself.

He went into the dining-room, where a cupboard built into one of the bulkheads contained a series of little barrels set side by side on minute stands of sandalwood, each pierced by a silver spigot low down in its belly. He called this collection of casks of liqueur his mouth organ.*

A rod linked all the spigots and controlled them with a single action, so that once the apparatus was set up, it only required the touch of a button concealed in the panelling for every tap to be turned on simultaneously and fill the minuscule goblets which stood beneath them. The organ could then be played. The stops labelled 'flute, horn, vox angelica' were pulled out, ready for use. Des Esseintes would drink a drop of this or that, playing interior symphonies to himself, and thus providing his gullet with sensations analogous to those which music affords the ear.

Furthermore, the flavour of each cordial corresponded, Des Esseintes believed, to the sound of an instrument. For example, dry curaçao matched the clarinet whose note is penetrating and velvety; kummel, the oboe with its sonorous, nasal resonance; crème de menthe and anisette, the flute, at once honeyed and pungent, whining and sweet; on the other hand kirsch, to complete the orchestra, resonates in a way extraordinarily like the trumpet; gin and whisky overpower the palate with the strident blasts of their cornets and trombones; liqueur brandy booms forth with the deafening racket of the tubas, to the accompaniment of the rolling thunder of the cymbals and the drum as the rakis of Chios and the mastics strike with all their might upon the skin of the mouth!

He was also of the opinion that the correlation could be extended and that string quartets could perform under the palatal vault, with the violin represented by fine old liqueur brandy, smoky, pungent and delicate; rum, being more robust, more sonorous and rumbling, took the part of the viola; vespetro, heart-rendingly long-drawn-out, melancholy and caressing, was the cello; while an old, pure bitter stood in for the double-bass, vigorous, solid, and black. One could even, if one wanted to form a quintet, add a fifth instrument, the harp, which was very closely imitated by the vibrant flavour and aloof, high-pitched, silvery note of dry cumin.

The correlation could be extended even further: there were tonal relationships in the music of the liqueurs: to cite only one example, Benedictine stands, so to speak, for the minor key of that major key made up of those cordials which commercial specifications designate by the label of green Chartreuse.

Once he had grasped these principles he was able, after some erudite experimentation, to play himself silent melodies on his tongue, soundless funeral marches of great pomp and circumstance, and to hear, in his mouth, solos of crème de menthe, duets of vespetro and of rum. He even succeeded in transferring actual pieces of music to his jaw, following the composer step by step and rendering his thoughts, his effects, and his subtleties, through close associations or contrasts, through roughly estimated or carefully calculated blends of liqueurs.

At other times he himself would compose melodies, performing pastorals with the gentle blackcurrant cordial which filled his throat with the warbling trills of the nightingale's song, or with the sweet cacaochouva which hummed sickly-sweet bergerettes like the 'Ballads of Estelle'* and the 'Ah! mother, shall I tell you?'* of bygone days.

But, that evening, Des Esseintes felt no urge to listen to the taste of music; he confined himself to taking one note from the keyboard of his organ, carrying away a little cup which he had filled with a genuine Irish whiskey. He settled down again into his armchair and slowly sipped the fermented juice of oats and barley; a powerful, unpleasant flavour of creosote filled his mouth.

Little by little, as he drank, his thoughts followed the impression that had been evoked on his palate, closely pursuing the taste of the whiskey and awakening, by a fatal conjunction of odours, memories that had long since vanished. That bitter carbolic aroma inevitably reminded him of the identical savour which had saturated his palate on those occasions when dentists had worked on his gums.

Once embarked on that train of thought, his musings, which had at first encompassed all the practitioners he had known, became more concentrated, focusing on one in particular, stirring a bizarre recollection which had engraved itself on his memory with special intensity.

It was three years ago; beset by a raging toothache in the middle of the night, he had plugged his cheek with cotton wool and, stumbling against the furniture, had paced up and down his room like a madman. The molar had already been filled; there was no hope of saving it; the only remedy lay in the dentist's forceps. Feverishly awaiting the dawn, he determined to endure the most agonizing of operations so long as it put an end to his suffering.

Nursing his jaw, he debated what to do. The dentists he patronized were well-to-do practitioners whom one could not visit at will; the times of appointments had to be arranged in advance. 'That's out of the question,' he thought, 'I can't wait any longer'; he made up his mind to go to any dentist he could find, some poor man's toothpuller, one of those men with a grip of iron who, though untutored in the (in any case useless) art of treating caries and filling cavities, are skilled at extracting, with unparalleled speed, the most tenacious of stumps; such people open their doors at dawn and there is no waiting. Seven o'clock struck at last. He raced out of his house, and, recollecting the name of an operator who called himself a dentist of the people and lived on a corner by the river, he rushed down the streets, biting his handkerchief and blinking back his tears.

On reaching the house, recognizable by a huge black wooden sign with the name 'Gatonax' spread across it in enormous pumpkin-coloured letters, and by two little glassed-in display cases in which plaster teeth were carefully aligned on pink wax gums and connected in pairs by brass wire springs, he gasped for breath, his forehead drenched in sweat; a horrible panic overtook him, a cold shiver ran over his skin, his pain subsided, his suffering ceased, the tooth fell silent.

He stood there, in a daze, on the pavement; steeling himself, finally, to face the pain, he had climbed up a dark staircase, mounting four steps at a time to the third floor. There, he had found himself before a door on which, in sky-blue letters, an enamel plate repeated the name on the sign. He had pulled the bell, then, terror-struck by the big blood-red gobs of spittle he saw plastering the stairs, he had turned round, determined to suffer toothache all his life, when a harrowing cry pierced the dividing wall, filling the stairwell and riveting him to the spot in horror, just as a door opened and an old woman invited him to enter.

Shame had prevailed over fear; he was ushered into a dining-room; another door had crashed open, admitting a terrible grenadier-like figure dressed in a frock coat and black trousers rigid as wood; Des Esseintes followed him into another room.

From that moment on his feelings became confused. He vaguely recalled sinking into an armchair in front of a window, and stammering, as he touched his tooth with a finger: 'It's already been filled; I'm afraid there's nothing can be done.'

The man had immediately put a stop to his explanations by sticking a colossal forefinger into his mouth; then, muttering into his curly waxed moustaches, he had taken an instrument from a table.

It was then that the drama really began. Clutching the arms of his chair, Des Esseintes had felt a cold sensation in his cheek, stars had swum before his eyes and, in the grip of unbelievable agony, he had started stamping his feet and bellowing like an animal being slaughtered.

A cracking sound was heard: the molar broke in two as it came out; he felt then as if his head was being wrenched off, as if his skull was being shattered; losing all control, he screamed at the top of his voice, frantically fighting off the man who was setting upon him once more as if he meant to shove his arm right down into his belly, but then, suddenly, taking a step back, lifted up the body that was attached to the jaw, and brutally let it fall back into the armchair on its buttocks, while he stood there filling the window-frame, breathing heavily, and brandishing on the end of his forceps a purple tooth dripping with red!

Utterly exhausted, Des Esseintes had spat out a bowlful of blood, waved aside the old woman who, coming in again, offered to wrap his stump in a newspaper for him, and had fled, paying two francs and in his turn expelling bloody spittle on to the stairs, and then found himself once again outside in the street, full of joy and ten years younger, feeling an interest in the most trivial little things.

'Brrrr!' he muttered, depressed by the onslaught of these recollections. To free himself from the vision's horrifying spell he rose to his feet and, returning to the present, began to worry about the tortoise.

It was still quite motionless and he felt it with his fingers; it was dead. Accustomed, no doubt, to an uneventful existence, to a humble life spent beneath its poor carapace, it had not been able to bear the dazzling splendour thrust upon it, the glittering cope in which it had been garbed, the gems with which its back had been encrusted, like a ciborium.

5

As his urge to sequester himself from a loathsome age of shameful duplicity intensified, the need to see no longer pictures representing the human figure toiling away in Paris between four walls, or roaming the streets in quest of money, grew more overpowering.

After dissociating himself from contemporary life, he had resolved to introduce into his retreat no larvae of aversions or regrets; he had therefore wanted paintings that were subtle, exquisite, steeped in an ancient vision, in an antique corruption, remote from our ways, remote from our time.

He had wanted, to satisfy his intellect and give pleasure to his eyes, a few evocative works which would project him into an unfamiliar world, revealing to him evidence of fresh possibilities, and stimulating his nervous system with learned depictions of frenzy, with complicated phantasmagoria and dispassionate, horrific visions.

There was one artist above all others whose talent filled him with never-ending ecstasy: Gustave Moreau.* He had acquired Moreau's two masterpieces, and spent night after night pondering over one of these, the painting of Salome.* This work portrayed a throne, set up like the high altar of a cathedral, beneath a ceiling where innumerable arches, arising out of squat, Romanesque-style columns, were studded with multi-coloured bricks, set with mosaics, and encrusted with lapis lazuli and sard; all this within a palace that resembled a basilica, in an architectural style at once Islamic and Byzantine.

In the centre of the tabernacle surmounting the altar, which was approached by a flight of crescent-shaped steps, sat Herod the Tetrarch, his head encircled by a tiara, his legs together and his hands upon his knees. His face was yellow, parchment-like, deeply lined, thinned by age; his long beard floated like a white cloud over the jewelled constellations that shone on the gold-embroidered robe stretched across his breast. Around this immobile, statue-like figure, fixed in the hieratic pose of a Hindu god, burned incense, disgorging a vaporous mass through which—like phosphorescent eyes of wild animals—shone fiery brilliants set into the sides of the throne;

then, rising higher, the vapours unravelled beneath the arcades, where the blue smoke mingled with the golden dust of the great beams of daylight coming from the domes.

In the perverse odour of these perfumes, in the overheated atmosphere of this church, Salome, her left arm extended in an imperious gesture and her right arm bent, holding a large lotus blossom in front of her face, moves slowly forward on tiptoe to the strains of a guitar, whose cords are strummed by a crouching woman.

A pensive, solemn, almost august expression on her face, she begins the lubricious dance which is to awaken the slumbering senses of the ageing Herod; her breasts rise and fall, their nipples hardening under the friction of her whirling necklaces; the diamonds adhering to her moist skin glitter; her bracelets, her belts, her rings, flash and sparkle; on her triumphal gown—pearl-seamed, silver-flowered, gold-spangled—the breastplate of jewellery, each of its links a precious stone, bursts into flame, sending out sinuous, intersecting jets of fire, moving over the lustreless flesh, the tea-rose skin, like a swarm of splendid insects whose dazzling wing-sheaths are marbled with carmine, spotted with saffron yellow, dappled with steely blue, striped with peacock green.

Totally absorbed, with the staring eyes of a sleep-walker, she sees neither the trembling Tetrarch nor her mother, the implacable Herodias, who watches over her, nor the hermaphrodite or eunuch who stands, a terrifying figure, sabre in hand, at the foot of the throne, the lower part of his face veiled, with his eunuch's breasts dangling like gourds beneath his orange-striped tunic.

The image of Salome, which so haunted the imagination of poets and artists, had obsessed Des Esseintes for many years now. Time without number had he read, in Pierre Variquet's old Bible, translated by the doctors of theology of the University of Louvain,* in the Gospel according to St Matthew, the naïve, short sentences that relate the beheading of the Baptist; time without number had he pondered over these verses:

'But when Herod's birthday was kept, the daughter of Herodias danced before them, and pleased Herod.

'Whereupon he promised with an oath to give her whatsoever she would ask.

'And she, being before instructed of her mother, said: "Give me here John Baptist's head on a charger."

'And the king was sorry; nevertheless, for the oath's sake, and them which sat with him at meat, he commanded it to be given her.

'And he sent, and beheaded John in the prison.

'And his head was brought in a charger, and given to the damsel: and she brought it to her mother.'

But neither St Matthew, nor St Mark, nor St Luke, nor the other Evangelists dwelt upon the frenzied charms, the purposeful depravity of the dancer. Her indistinct presence faded away, mysterious and faint, into the far-off mists of the ages, imperceptible to those of a precise, pedestrian cast of mind, accessible only to sensibilities that had been unsettled and sharpened, rendered almost visionary by neurosis; resistant to artists who portrayed flesh—to Rubens, who painted her disguised as a Flemish butcher's wife; incomprehensible to all the writers who were never capable of depicting the disturbing exaltation of the dancer, the subtle majesty of the murderess.

In Gustave Moreau's painting, which was conceived without any reference to the facts of the Gospel story, Des Esseintes could at last see realized that superhuman, strange Salome of whom he had dreamt. No longer was she just the dancer who by a shameless gyration of her hips wrests a lustful, ruttish cry from an old man, who destroys the resoluteness and breaks the will of a king with thrusts of her breasts, undulations of her belly, and quiverings of her thighs; there she became, in a sense, the symbolic deity of indestructible Lechery, the goddess of immortal Hysteria, the accursed Beauty singled out from among all others by the cataleptic paroxysm that stiffens her flesh and hardens her muscles; the monstrous, indiscriminate, irresponsible, unfeeling Beast who, like the Helen of Antiquity, poisons everything that comes near her, everything that sees her, everything that she touches.

Perceived in that light, she belonged to Far Eastern theogonies; she could no longer be associated with biblical tradition, could no longer even be likened to the living symbol of Babylon, the royal Harlot of the Apocalypse who, like her, is draped in jewels and purple, who, like her, is powdered and rouged; for the latter was not impelled by a fateful force, by a supreme power, into the alluring degradations of debauchery.

Besides, the artist seemed to have wanted to assert his intention of remaining outside the passing centuries, of not specifying either race, country, or period, by placing his Salome within this extraordinary

palace built in a grandiose mixture of styles, by dressing her in sumptuous, fanciful garments, by crowning her with a kind of diadem
shaped like a Phoenician tower, like that worn by Salammbô,* and
finally by placing in her hand the sceptre of Isis, the sacred flower of
Egypt and India, the great lotus.

Des Esseintes speculated about the meaning of this emblem. Did
it have the phallic significance with which it is endowed by the
primeval religions of India; did it promise the ageing Herod an oblation of virginity, an exchange of blood, an impure penetration
solicited and tendered under the express condition of a murder; or
did it represent the allegory of fertility, the Hindu myth of life, an
existence held between a woman's palms whence it is torn and
crushed by the quivering grasp of men overpowered by madness,
deranged by a frenzy of the flesh?

Perhaps, also, by arming his enigmatic goddess with the venerated
lotus, the artist had thought of the dancer, the mortal woman, the
sullied Vessel, the source of every sin and every crime; perhaps he
had called to mind the rites of ancient Egypt, the funereal cere-
monies of embalmment, when the chemists and the priests lay out
the corpse of the deceased on a bench of jasper, use curved needles
to extract her brains through her nasal fossae, her entrails through
an incision made in her left side, then, before gilding her nails and
her teeth, before anointing her with tars and essences, insert into her
genitals, to purify them, the chaste petals of the divine flower.

Be that as it may, this canvas held an irresistible fascination, but
the watercolour entitled *The Apparition** was perhaps even more disturbing. In that picture, Herod's palace soared up, like an Alhambra,
on slender columns iridescent with Moorish tiles that seemed to be
embedded in silver and cemented in gold; arabesques, beginning at
diamonds of lapis lazuli, swooped along the length of the cupolas
whose surfaces of mother-of-pearl marquetry were criss-crossed by
iridescent lights, by flashes of prismatic colour.

The murder had been carried out; now the executioner stood
impassive, his hands on the hilt of his long, bloodstained sword.

The decapitated head of the saint had risen from the charger lying
upon the flagstones, and he was staring, his countenance livid, his
open mouth waxen, his neck scarlet and dripping tears of blood.
Mosaics framed the face, from which emanated a halo radiating out
into shafts of light beneath the porticos, illuminating the horrifying

levitation of the head, igniting the glassy orbs of the pupils which remained fixed, almost riveted, on the dancer.

With a terror-stricken gesture, Salome wards off the ghastly vision which keeps her standing there, motionless, on tiptoe; her eyes widen, her hand clutches convulsively at her throat. She is almost naked; in the heat of the dance, the veils have come undone, the brocaded draperies have fallen; now she is clad only in the creations of goldsmiths and silversmiths, and in pellucid precious stones; a gorgerin encircles her waist as would a corselet, and, like some magnificent fastener, a marvellous jewel flashes with light in the cleft of her breasts; further down, round her hips, a girdle embraces her, concealing the upper part of her thighs where a gigantic pendant hangs, spilling over with rubies and emeralds; finally, on the now bare flesh between the gorgerin and the girdle, her belly swells, dimpled by a navel whose hollow resembles a medallion carved in onyx, a navel that is milky white, tinted with shades of fingernail pink.

In the blazing shafts of light emanating from the head of the Baptist, all the facets of the jewels catch fire; the stones come to life, tracing out in incandescent contours the body of the woman; catching her at the neck, the legs, the arms, with sparks of fire, bright red like glowing coals, violet like jets of vapour, blue like flaming alcohol, white like starlight. The dreadful head blazes with light and continues to drip with blood, which forms clots of deep purple on the ends of the beard and hair. Visible to Salome alone, it embraces in its bleak gaze neither Herodias who sits brooding over her hatred, now finally appeased, nor the Tetrarch who, leaning forward slightly with his hands upon his knees, still pants with desire, driven wild by this woman's nakedness which has been soaked in musky scents, drenched in sweet-smelling balms, and steeped in the fumes of incense and of myrrh.

Des Esseintes, like the old king, was overwhelmed, stunned, unhinged by this dancer, who was less majestic, less haughty, but more unsettling than the Salome of the oil painting. In the unfeeling, ruthless figure, in the naïve yet dangerous idol, the sexual excitement and the terror of the human being were apparent; the great lotus-blossom had disappeared, the goddess had vanished; a fearful nightmare now held in its grip both the performer, intoxicated by the whirling dance, and the courtesan, frozen, mesmerized by horror.

In this picture she was truly a whore, obedient to her temperament of a cruel and passionate woman; she lived again, more polished and more barbaric, more hateful and more exquisite; arousing the languorous senses of man more vigorously, she bewitched and subjugated his will more surely, with her charms as of some great venereal flower that had burgeoned in a sacrilegeous seedbed, and grown to maturity in a hothouse of impiety.

Des Esseintes maintained that never again, at any period, had watercolours been capable of achieving that same brilliancy of hue; never had the limitations of chemical colour been able to produce, on paper, such scintillations of precious stones, such gleaming colours as of stained glass struck by sunlight, such fabulous, blinding displays of fabrics and of flesh.

And, deep in reverie, he sought to understand the origins of this great artist, of this pagan mystic, of this Illuminatus who could sufficiently dissociate himself from the world to see blazing gloriously, in the very heart of Paris, the cruel visions and magical apotheoses of an earlier age.

Des Esseintes found it hard to determine what influences might have shaped him; here and there were vague recollections of Mantegna* and Jacopo di Barbarino;* here and there, confused suggestions of Da Vinci and feverish colours in the style of Delacroix;* but on the whole the influence of those masters was scarcely discernible: the fact was that Gustave Moreau was not derivative of anyone. With no true forebears and no possible descendants, he remained a unique figure in contemporary art. Going back to ethnographic sources, to the origins of mythologies whose blood-stained enigmas he compared and unravelled; uniting and melding into a single entity legends of Far Eastern origin which had been transformed by the beliefs of other peoples, he justified by these means his architectonic fusions, his sumptuous, unexpected combinations of fabrics, his hieratic, sinister allegories to which the disturbing insights of a profoundly modern nervous disorder lent added trenchancy; he remained an eternally painful artist, haunted by the symbols of superhuman depravities and passions, of divine abominations perpetrated without abandon and without hope.

There was a singular enchantment in his erudite, despairing paintings, a magic which stirred you to the depths of your soul, like that of certain poems of Baudelaire's, and left you astounded, bemused, disconcerted, by this art which went beyond the confines

of painting, borrowing from the art of writing its most subtle evocations, from the art of the enameller* its most marvellous brilliancy,
from the art of the lapidary and the engraver its most exquisite
delicacy. These two pictures of Salome, pictures for which Des
Esseintes's admiration knew no bounds, were, to his eyes, living
things, as they hung on the walls of his study on special panels
reserved for them between the shelves of books.

However, these were by no means the only pictures he had purchased for the adornment of his solitude. Although he himself did
not use the first—and only other—floor of his house, having given
it over to his servants, the ground floor alone had needed several
series of pictures to dress its walls.

This ground floor was laid out as follows: a dressing-room, which
connected with the bedroom, occupied one of the corners of the
building; the bedroom led into the library, and the library into the
dining-room, which formed the other corner. These rooms comprised one side of the building and extended in a straight line that
was pierced by windows looking out over the valley of Aunay. The
other side of the building contained four rooms which, as far as their
arrangement was concerned, were exactly similar to the first. Thus
the kitchen formed a corner which corresponded to the dining-room;
a large hall, serving as an entrance to the house, corresponded to the
library; a small sitting-room counterbalanced the bedroom, and the
water-closet the dressing-room. All these rooms looked on to the side
opposite the valley of Aunay, in the direction of the Tour du Croy
and Châtillon. As for the staircase, it was outside, built on to one of
the exterior walls of the house; for this reason the noise made by the
servants' feet as they tramped up the stairs reached Des Esseintes's
ears in a less distinct, more muffled form.

He had had the sitting-room papered in bright red and on each of
its walls had hung, framed in ebony, engravings by Jan Luyken,* an
old Dutch engraver, who was almost unknown in France.

He owned the series entitled *Religious Persecutions* by this strange,
gloomy, violent, savage artist; these were horrifying engravings that
depicted every torture ever invented by religious mania, engravings
that screamed forth the spectacle of human suffering, bodies roasted
on blazing coals, craniums scalped with sabres, trepanned with nails,
hacked at with saws, intestines drawn from the belly and wound
round bobbins, fingernails slowly pulled out with pincers, eyes put

out, eyelids turned up and pinned back, limbs dislocated, meticulously broken, bones bared of flesh and scraped, very slowly, with a blade. These pictures, replete with abominable imaginings, stinking of scorched flesh, oozing with blood, filled with shrieks of horror and with curses, made Des Esseintes's skin crawl, keeping him riveted to the spot, unable to breathe, when he entered that red room.

But, quite apart from the shudders they occasioned, quite apart from this man's terrible talent and the extraordinary life that animated his figures, one could observe, in his astonishing, swarming crowd scenes, in the waves of humanity captured with a skill reminiscent of Callot's* but with a power never attained by that entertaining dauber, meticulous re-creations of places and of periods; architecture, costumes, and customs from Rome, in the days of the Maccabees when the Christians were being persecuted; from Spain, under the Inquisition; from France, in the Middle Ages and at the time of the St Bartholomew Massacres and the dragonnades;* all observed with scrupulous care and depicted with consummate skill.

These engravings were mines of information; one could gaze at them for hours without wearying; profoundly thought-provoking, they frequently helped Des Esseintes to while away those days when books held no charm for him.

The life of Luyken was for him an added attraction; it explained, moreover, the hallucinating power of his works. A fervent Calvinist, an obdurate sectarian, obsessed with hymns and prayers, he wrote religious poems which he illustrated, he paraphrased the Psalms in verse, and could become so deeply engrossed in reading the Bible that he would emerge ecstatic, hollow-eyed, his mind possessed by gory subjects, his mouth distorted by the curses of the Reformation, by its songs of terror and of rage.

In addition, he despised this world and gave all his possessions to the poor, existing on crusts of bread; eventually he set sail, in the company of an old servant whom he had infected with his fanaticism, going from place to place at random, depending on where his boat came ashore, preaching the Gospel everywhere, trying to live without eating, on the verge of insanity, almost of brutishness.

The adjoining apartment, the entrance hall, was larger, and panelled in cedar the colour of cigar boxes; it was hung with row upon row of other engravings, other weird drawings. Bresdin's *Comedy of Death*★ depicts an improbable landscape bristling with trees and bushes and tufts of vegetation that are shaped like demons and phantoms, and covered with birds with rat heads and vegetable tails, on a ground strewn with vertebrae and ribs and skulls, on which grow gnarled and cracked willows, surmounted by skeletons waving bouquets of flowers in the air as they intone a song of victory. A Christ figure is fleeing across a cloud-dappled sky while a hermit meditates, head in hands, deep in a grotto, and a miserable wretch lies dying, exhausted by privations, prostrated by hunger, stretched out on his back with his feet by a pool of stagnant water.

The same artist's *Good Samaritan*,* a lithograph of an immense pen-and-ink drawing, portrays a fantastic jumble of palms, rowans, and oaks, growing all together in defiance of seasons and of climates, a patch of virgin forest crammed with monkeys, owls, and screech-owls, nodulated with old tree-stumps as misshapen as mandrake roots, a magic wood with a clearing in its centre through which you can glimpse, beyond a camel and the group formed by the Samaritan and the wounded man, a river, then a fairy-like city scaling the horizon, climbing up into a strange sky that is bird-stippled, foam-flecked with rolling billows, as though swollen with close-packed clouds. One might have supposed it to be a drawing by an early master, perhaps someone after the style of Albert Dürer, dreamt up by an opium-befuddled mind; but, although he enjoyed the delicacy of detail and the impressive style of this lithograph, Des Esseintes found himself more particularly drawn to the other works which decorated the room.

Those were pictures bearing the signature: Odilon Redon.* They held, between their gold-edged frames of unpolished pearwood, undreamed-of images: a Merovingian-type head, resting upon a cup; a bearded man, reminiscent both of a Buddhist priest and a public orator, touching an enormous cannon-ball with his finger; a dreadful spider with a human face lodged in the centre of its body. Then there were charcoal sketches which delved even deeper into the terrors of fever-ridden dreams. Here, on an enormous die, a melancholy eyelid winked; over there stretched dry and arid landscapes, calcinated plains, heaving and quaking ground, where volcanos erupted into rebellious clouds, under foul and murky skies; sometimes the subjects seemed to have been taken from the nightmarish dreams of science, and hark back to prehistoric times; monstrous flora bloomed on the rocks; everywhere, in among the erratic blocks and glacial mud, were figures whose simian appearance—heavy jawbone, protruding brows, receding forehead, and flattened skull top—recalled the ancestral head, the head of the first Quaternary Period, the head of man when he was still fructivorous and without speech, the contemporary of the mammoth, of the rhinoceros with septate nostrils, and of the giant bear. These drawings defied classification; unheeding, for the most part, of the limitations of painting, they ushered in a very special type of the fantastic, one born of sickness and delirium.

And, indeed, some of those countenances, in which gigantic, insane eyes dominated all other features; some of those bodies—inordinately magnified or else distended, as though viewed through a carafe of water—recalled for Des Esseintes memories of typhoid fever, memories that he had somehow never cast off, of the delirious nights and terrifying fantasies of his childhood.

Filled with an indefinable sense of unease by these drawings, just as he was by certain of Goya's *Proverbs** which they recalled, and just as he also was by reading Edgar Allan Poe,* whose hallucinatory phantasms and terror-inducing effects Odilon Redon seemed to have transposed into a different art form, Des Esseintes would rub his eyes and rest them upon a radiant figure which arose, serene and calm, from among these disquieting prints, a figure of Melancholy seated on some rocks before the disk of the sun, in an attitude of despondency and gloom.

The shadows would vanish by magic; a delightful sadness, an as it were languorous dejection would wash over his thoughts, and he would pass hours meditating on this work which, with its touches of gouache stippling the heavy crayon, introduced a luminosity of aquamarine and pale gold into the unrelieved blackness of those charcoals and those prints.

In addition to this series of Redon's works which decorated almost the whole of the panelling in the hall, he had hung, in his bedroom, a confused sketch by Théotocopuli,* a Christ in extraordinary tones, drawn in an exaggerated style, violently coloured, filled with a frenetic energy, a picture from that painter's second period, when he was tormented by the overriding desire to no longer resemble Titian.

This sinister painting, with its shades of boot-polish black and cadaver green, was in keeping with certain theories of Des Esseintes's on the subject of interior decoration. In his view there were only two ways to arrange a bedroom: either make it into an exciting bed-chamber, a setting for nocturnal pleasures; or else devise a place of solitude and repose, a retreat for meditation, a kind of private chapel.

In the one case, the Louis XV style was the obvious choice of the discerning, and particularly of those exhausted by extreme cerebral irritability; indeed, the eighteenth century is the only period which has known how to envelop woman in an atmosphere of depravity, modelling its furniture after the curves of her charms, mimicking her spasms of pleasure, her spiralling convulsions, with the undu-lating and twisting intricacies of wood and of copper, adding spice to the sugary languor of the blonde with its light, bright décor, moderating the salty piquancy of the brunette with tapestries in cloying, bland, almost insipid tones.

Such a bedroom had once formed part of his lodgings in Paris, including the broad white-enamelled bed which is an additional tit-illation, a depravity of the seasoned voluptuary who is aroused by the specious chastity, the hypocritical modesty of Greuze's* tender virgins, by the contrived artlessness of a licentious bed that seems destined for a child or a young girl.

In the second case—and now that he intended to leave behind him the disturbing memories of his past life, this was the only possible choice—the bedroom must be contrived so as to resemble a monas-tic cell; but this gave rise to endless difficulties, since he refused to accept, for his own use, the ugly austerity characteristic of places of penitence and prayer.

By dint of considering and reconsidering every aspect of the problem, he concluded that the effect for which he was striving could be summed up in the following way: to furnish a depressing space with joyous objects, or rather, without sacrificing the ugly character of the room, imprint upon it, by this treatment, a kind of overall ele-gance and distinction; reverse the approach of a theatrical décor in which tawdry fabrics mimic luxurious, expensive cloths; achieve precisely the opposite effect, by using magnificent materials to create the impression of rags; in a word, to fit out a monastic cell which appeared to be genuine without, of course, actually being so.

He set about it in this way: to imitate that dark yellow paint favoured by administrators and clerics, he had his walls hung with saffron silk; to imitate the chocolate brown wainscoting customary in that kind of room, he covered those lower areas with thin strips of dark purple kingwood. The effect was enchanting, and suggested, though only very remotely, the displeasing rigidity of the model he was transforming as he copied it; in its turn the ceiling, hung with white holland, could mimic plaster, but without its crude, obtrusive effect; as to the chilly stone floor of the cell, he succeeded in imitating it quite well, thanks to a carpet made in a design of red tiles, with some whitish areas in the wool that simulated places worn by sandals and rubbed thin by boots.

He furnished this room with a little iron bedstead, a fake monastic bed, constructed from very old pieces of polished wrought iron, set off, at its head and foot, by some close-worked ornamentation, of fully opened tulips intertwined with vine branches, taken from the banister of a magnificent staircase in an old mansion.

As a bedside table, he installed an antique prayer-stool which could accommodate a chamber pot inside and a prayer-book on top; against the opposite wall he placed a church-warden's pew, surmounted by a large openwork screen equipped with misericords carved out of the solid wood; he set, in his pair of altar candle-sticks, tapers of genuine wax which he bought in an establishment which specialized in supplying the needs of the Church, for he professed an undisguised aversion to petrol, shale-oil, gas, and stearin candles, to all of modern lighting, which is so garish, so crude.

In bed, in the morning, lying with his head on his pillow before going to sleep, he would gaze at his Théotocopuli, the hideous tones of which tended to play down the smiling yellow of the draperies and reduce it to a deeper shade, and he could then easily imagine that he was a hundred leagues from Paris, far from the world, buried in the depths of a monastery.

And, on the whole, the illusion was easy to maintain, since he led a life almost analogous to that of a monk. He thus enjoyed the advantages of the cloister while avoiding its drawbacks: the barrack-room discipline, the lack of attentive service, the filth, the promiscuity, the monotony of idleness. Just as he had made his cell into a warm and comfortable bedroom, so too had he made himself a life that was normal, pleasant, full of well-being and of occupation, and free.

Like a hermit, he was ripe for seclusion, worn out by life and expecting nothing more of it; and also like a monk, he was overcome by a tremendous lassitude, by a need for contemplation, by a longing no longer to have anything in common with the heathen—which was what he called Utilitarians and fools.

In short, although he experienced no vocation for the state of grace, he felt a genuine sympathy for those who are confined in monasteries and persecuted by a vindictive society, which cannot forgive them either for the well-merited scorn that they feel for the world, nor the intention they profess of redeeming, of expiating, by a protracted silence, the ever-increasing shamelessness of its preposterous or inane conversations.

6

Sunk into a huge wing chair, his feet resting on the gilded, bulbous ends of the andirons, his slippers scorched by the logs which crackled and shot forth bright darts of flame as though whipped by a blowpipe's fierce blast, Des Esseintes laid down upon a table the old quarto volume he was reading, stretched, lit a cigarette, and abandoned himself to a delightful reverie, racing headlong in pursuit of memories forgotten for many months and now suddenly revived by the recollection of a name which, for no apparent reason, was stirring in his memory.

He saw again, with surprising clearness, the embarrassment of his friend d'Aigurande, when, at a gathering of confirmed bachelors, he had been forced to admit he was making final preparations for marriage. The company expostulated, evoking the horrors of sleeping in a shared bed; all in vain; he had lost his head, and believed his future wife to be intelligent, claiming that in her he had detected exceptional qualities of devotion and tenderness.

Des Esseintes alone, of all those young men, encouraged him in his resolutions, as soon as he discovered that d'Aigurande's fiancée wanted to live on the corner of a new boulevard, in one of those modern apartments built in the shape of a rotunda.

Convinced of the inexorable power of petty vexations—more disastrous than great ones to the well-tempered mind—and depending on the fact that d'Aigurande had no money of his own and that his wife's dowry was virtually non-existent, he perceived, in this simple desire, a never-ending prospect of ludicrous misfortunes.

D'Aigurande did indeed buy furniture built on the round—pier tables with their backs hollowed out in semi-circles, curved curtain rods, carpets cut into crescent shapes, a complete set of furniture made to order. He spent twice the amount that others spend, and then when his wife, finding herself short of money for her dresses, grew tired of living in this rotunda and moved into a square apartment that was less expensive, not a single piece of furniture either suited or fitted it. Little by little, this cumbersome furniture became a source of untold annoyances to the couple; their relationship, already undermined by their shared existence, disintegrated further with each passing week; they lost their tempers, upbraiding one another for being unable to remain in that drawing-room where the sofas and the tables did not touch the walls and shook, in spite of being wedged, the moment anyone brushed against them. They lacked the resources for remedying the problem, which would in any case be almost impossible. Everything was grounds for bitterness and quarrels, everything from the drawers, which had warped in the wobbly furniture, to the thefts of the maid who, profiting from the inattention resulting from the quarrels, robbed the till; in a word, their life became intolerable; he found amusement elsewhere while she sought, among the resources offered by adultery, a way to forget her grey, monotonous life. With one accord they terminated their lease and petitioned for a separation.

'My battle plan was absolutely correct,' Des Esseintes had told himself then, experiencing the satisfaction of strategists whose manœuvres, thought out far in advance, are crowned with success. Now, seated before his fire, reflecting upon the breakup of that couple whom he had helped, with his sensible advice, to marry, he threw a fresh load of logs into the fireplace and once more launched headlong into his dreams.

Other memories of the same general kind were now thronging into his mind. One evening, some years earlier, in the Rue de Rivoli, he had passed an errand boy of about sixteen, a peaky, sly-looking child, as tempting as a girl. He was laboriously sucking at a cigarette, the paper of which was splitting, punctured by the sharp fragments of tobacco. Cursing, the boy was striking against his thigh kitchen matches which would not light; he used them all up. Noticing that Des Esseintes was watching him, he approached him, his hand on the peak of his cap, and politely asked him for a light. Des Esseintes gave him some scented Dubèque cigarettes, then engaged him in conversation, encouraging the lad to tell him his story.

This was simplicity itself; his name was Auguste Langlois, he worked for a cardboard-maker, his mother was dead, and his father beat him mercilessly.

Des Esseintes listened to him thoughtfully. 'Come and have a drink,' he said. And he took him into a café where he ordered him some very potent punch. The child drank, without saying a word. 'Look,' said Des Esseintes suddenly, 'would you like to have some fun tonight? I'm paying.' And he took the boy to visit Madame

Laure. This lady ran an establishment on a third floor in the Rue Mosnier; she employed an assortment of girls, in a series of red rooms decorated with round mirrors and furnished with couches and wash-basins.

There, crumpling up the cloth of his cap, Auguste had gazed in utter amazement at a troop of women whose painted mouths all opened simultaneously:

'Oh, the little rascal! Isn't he sweet!'

'But see here, dearie, you aren't old enough,' added a big dark woman with bulging eyes and a hooked nose; her role at Madame Laure's was the indispensable one of the beautiful Jewess.

Comfortably settled, almost at home there, Des Esseintes chatted quietly with the manageress.

'Don't be scared, you noodle,' he went on, addressing the child. 'Come on, make your choice, it's my treat.' And he gently pushed the boy on to a couch between two women. At a sign from Madame they squeezed up to him a little, covering Auguste's knees with their wrappers, pushing into his face shoulders frosted with warm, intoxicating powder, while he sat motionless, his cheeks scarlet, his mouth hard, his eyes under lowered lids venturing curious glances, which lingered persistently on the women's thighs.

Vanda, the beautiful Jewess, kissed him, giving him good advice, admonishing him to obey his father and mother, while at the same time her hands strayed slowly over the child, whose rapturous face, transfigured, buried itself in her neck.

'So it isn't on your own account that you've come tonight,' said Madame Laure to Des Esseintes. 'But where the devil did you pick up that kid?' she went on, when Auguste had vanished in the wake of the beautiful Jewess.

'In the street, my dear.'

'But you're not drunk,' murmured the old woman. Then, after a moment's reflection, she added with a motherly smile: 'I understand: but my goodness, you certainly have to have them young, don't you!'

Des Esseintes shrugged: 'You're not with me; no, far from it,' he said; 'the truth is that I'm simply trying to produce a murderer. Now pay close attention to my reasoning. This boy's a virgin, and he's reached the age where the blood begins to seethe; he could chase the girls in his neighbourhood, he could have some fun but go on behaving decently, he could, in a word, enjoy his little share of the humdrum happiness which is the lot of the poor. On the other hand, by bringing him here, by showing him a luxury which he didn't even suspect existed and which will necessarily imprint itself on his mind; by giving him such a windfall every couple of weeks, he'll become accustomed to these pleasures which his means do not permit him to enjoy; let's suppose that he'll need three months for them to become absolutely essential—and by spacing them out as I shall do, I do not run the risk of sating him—so, at the end of the three months, I shall put a stop to the little income which I'm going to advance you for this good deed, and then he'll steal, to be able to come here; he'll do something quite desperate, so that he can tumble about on this couch, under these gas-lights!

'To take an extreme case, Auguste will—I hope—kill the man who turns up at the wrong moment while the lad's trying to break into his desk; in that event I'll have achieved my purpose, I'll have contributed, as far as lies within my power, to creating a scoundrel, one more enemy of this hideous society which is holding us to ransom.'

The women stared at him, wide-eyed.

'There you are!' he went on, seeing a blushing and sheepish Auguste skulking behind the beautiful Jewess as he came back into the room. 'Come on, boy, it's getting late, say goodnight to these ladies.' And, on the stairs, he explained to him that he could return, every fortnight, to Madame Laure's, without it costing him a penny; then, down in the street, on the pavement, gazing at the bewildered boy:

'We shall not meet again;' he said; 'go straight home to your father, whose idle hand is itching for something to do, and keep in mind this quasi-biblical saying: "Do unto others as you would not have them do unto you"; you'll go far with that precept. Goodnight. Above all don't be ungrateful, let me hear word of you as soon as possible, in the law reports in the newspapers.'

'The little Judas!' Des Esseintes was muttering now as he poked the embers, 'to think I've never seen his name mentioned in the paper! It's true, I wasn't able to cover every eventuality, there were certain risks I could foresee but not preclude, such as Mother Laure cheating, and pocketing the money without delivering the goods, or one of those women becoming infatuated with Auguste, who may perhaps have got it for free when his three months were up; or even the lovely Jewess's vicious proclivities which may have frightened the boy, too impatient and too young to submit to the long-drawn-out preliminaries and electrifying climaxes achieved through artifice. Unless he's been in trouble with the law since I came to Fontenay and am no longer reading newspapers, I've been swindled.'

He stood up and took several turns about his room.

'Still, that would be a shame,' he reflected, 'for by behaving in that way, I was putting into practice the layman's parable, the allegory of universal education which aims at nothing less than transforming all men into Langloises, by—instead of permanently and mercifully putting out the eyes of the poor—by striving to force them to open their eyes wide, so that they may notice that some of their neighbours have destinies that are quite undeservedly more merciful, and enjoy pleasures that are keener and more multi-faceted and, consequently, more desirable and more precious.

'And the fact is,' continued Des Esseintes, following his train of thought, 'the fact is that since pain is an effect of education, since it deepens and sharpens in proportion as ideas spring up, the more one tries to polish the intelligence and to refine the nervous system of those poor devils, the more one will develop in them those fiercely long-lasting seeds of moral suffering and of hatred.'

The lamps were smoking. He trimmed them, and looked at his watch. Three in the morning. Lighting a cigarette, he immersed himself afresh in his reading, which his reverie had interrupted, of the old Latin poem *De laude castitatis*,* written during the reign of Gondebald, by Avitus, Metropolitan Bishop of Vienne.

7

After that night on which, for no apparent reason, he had conjured up the depressing memory of Auguste Langlois, he lived his entire life over again.

He was incapable, now, of understanding one word of the books he consulted; his very eyes would no longer read; he felt as though his mind, saturated with literature and art, was refusing to absorb anything further from them.

He lived on himself, feeding on his own substance, like those torpid creatures that bury themselves away in a hole all winter long; solitude had affected his brain like an opiate. After first making him feel edgy and strained, it had brought on a lethargy haunted by vague reveries; it annihilated his plans and nullified his desires, marshalling a parade of dreams to which he submitted passively, not even attempting to escape from them.

The chaotic mass of readings and meditations on art that he had stored up during his solitude, like a dam built to stem the flow of former memories, had been suddenly swept away, and the flood-tide was on the move, buffeting the present, the future, drowning everything beneath the waters of the past, filling his mind with an immense expanse of sadness upon which floated, like ridiculous bits of wreckage, meaningless episodes from his life, absurd trivialities.

The book that he was holding in his hand would fall into his lap; he would give himself up and watch, filled with distaste and alarm, as the years of his dead life passed before him; they swirled about, flowing now round the memory of Madame Laure and Auguste, which remained embedded in these fluctuating waters like a well-driven pile, like an indisputable fact. What a period that had been! A time of evening parties, of excursions, of card games, of loves ordered in advance and punctually served up, at the stroke of midnight, in his rose-coloured bedroom! He recalled faces, appearances, pointless remarks which obsessed him with the persistence of a hackneyed tune which you cannot stop yourself humming, but which finally dies away, quite suddenly, when you are thinking of something else.

That period was of short duration; his memory took a brief siesta, and he immersed himself anew in his Latin studies so as to expunge even the last traces of these recollections. But the impetus had been given; almost immediately a second phase followed upon the first, bringing memories of his childhood, above all of the years spent with the Jesuit Fathers.

These memories were more distant and more definitive, etched in a bolder, surer manner; the wooded grounds, the long paths, the flower-beds, the benches, all the physical details materialized in his room. Then the gardens filled up, he heard the shouts of the pupils reverberating and the laughter of the teachers as they joined in the activities at recreation, playing tennis with their hitched-up cassocks tucked between their knees, or else chatting with the boys under the trees, without affectation or self-importance, as if they were friends of the same age.

He recalled that paternal yoke which was ill-adapted to punishing, which resisted imposing penalties of five hundred or a thousand lines but was satisfied with having the badly done lesson 'made up' while the other pupils enjoyed themselves, or even more often resorted to a simple reprimand, surrounding the child with an active but gentle vigilance, seeking to please him, agreeing to whatever expedition he might propose on a Wednesday, seizing the opportunity of every minor Church feast day to include cakes and wine in the bill of fare or to organize a picnic as a treat; a paternal yoke which consisted in not bullying the child, in reasoning with him, in treating him as a grown man while still pampering him like a spoilt little boy.

In this way they succeeded in acquiring a real ascendancy over the child, in shaping, to a certain degree, the minds they were nurturing, in controlling them in a sense, in implanting particular ideas in them, in ensuring the development of their thoughts through an insinuating, smooth-tongued technique which they later maintained by trying to keep abreast of their lives and to support them in their careers, by writing them affectionate letters, like those that the Dominican Lacordaire* was so skilled at composing to his former pupils in Sorrèze.*

Des Esseintes was fully aware of this process, which he believed he had undergone to no effect; his character, resistant to advice, touchy, probing, argumentative, had prevented his being moulded by their discipline or subjugated by their teaching; once he had left the College his scepticism had grown; his encounters with an intolerant, monarchical, and narrow-minded society, his conversations with unintelligent lay Church officials and mean-spirited priests, whose blunders destroyed the illusion so deftly created by the Jesuits, had further strengthened his spirit of independence and increased his distrust of any kind of faith.

In a word, he considered himself free of any bond, of any constraint: it was simply that, by contrast with all those men educated in lycées or secular boarding schools, the recollections he had retained of his school and his teachers were excellent ones, and now here he was examining his own feelings, and going so far as to wonder if the seeds which until the present had lain on barren ground, were not beginning to germinate.

Indeed for the past several days his state of mind had been indescribable. For a brief instant he would believe, and instinctively turn towards religion, then in the face of the slightest argument this longing for faith he was experiencing would evaporate; but he remained, in spite of everything, profoundly troubled.

Nevertheless, he was well aware, in the depths of his soul, that a truly Christian spirit of humility and penitence would never be his; he knew, beyond any doubt, that the moment Lacordaire speaks of, that moment of grace 'when the final ray of light penetrates the soul and connects to a common centre the truths that lie scattered there', would never come for him; he did not feel that need for mortification and prayer without which, according to the majority of priests, no conversion is possible; he did not experience any desire to implore a God whose mercy seemed to him to be questionable in the extreme; and yet the sympathy which he still retained for his former teachers was such as to make him interested in their work and their doctrines; those inimitable accents of conviction, those ardent voices of men of superior intellect came back to him, leading him to doubt his own intelligence and strength. In the midst of this solitude in which he lived, without new sustenance, without fresh experiences, without any renewal of his thoughts or that interchange of sensations that comes from the world outside, through life in society, through shared experiences, in that unnatural confinement to which he obstinately clung, all those questions which he had forgotten during his time in Paris presented themselves anew as vexatious problems.

The reading of the Latin works he loved, works almost all composed by bishops and by monks, had undoubtedly played a part in bringing on this crisis. Enveloped in a convent-like atmosphere that was scented with the heady, intoxicating perfume of incense, his nerves had become overwrought and, through associations of ideas, these books had, in the end, repressed the memories of his life as a young man, and brought back into the limelight these memories of his childhood years with the Jesuit Fathers.

'There's no denying it,' thought Des Esseintes, trying to be reasonable, trying to trace the course this assimilation of the Jesuit influence had taken at Fontenay; 'ever since my childhood, and without my ever being aware of it, I've carried this unfermented leaven within me; even the predilection I have always felt for religious artefacts may perhaps be proof of it.'

But he tried to convince himself of the contrary, displeased at no longer being absolute master in his own house; he found motives for his behaviour; surely his turning towards the Church had been forced on him, since the Church, alone, has collected together the art, the lost configurations of past centuries; the Church has established in permanent form (even in cheap modern reproductions) the outlines of the goldsmiths' work, preserved the charm of chalices as tall and slender as petunias, of purely contoured ciboria; preserved, even in aluminium copies, in imitation enamels and in coloured glass, the enchanting workmanship of earlier times. In brief, the majority of the precious objects catalogued at the Cluny Museum* and which had miraculously escaped the vile savagery of the Republican extremists, come from the former monasteries of France; just as the Church, during the Middle Ages, saved philosophy, history, and literature from Barbarism, it also rescued the plastic arts, preserving right up to the present day those marvellous examples of fabric and jewellery which the manufacturers of holy artefacts do their best to debase, without, however, being able to mar their fundamental, exquisite shapes. There was nothing, therefore, surprising about the fact that he had hunted down these antique knick-knacks and that he, along with a number of other collectors, had wrested these treasures from the Paris antique sellers and the second-hand dealers in the provinces.

But it was in vain that he invoked all these reasons; he could not manage to convince himself completely. Certainly, when he summarized his thoughts, he continued to think of religion as a superb legend, as a magnificent imposture, and yet, in spite of all his reasoning, his scepticism was beginning to be eroded.

Obviously, this extraordinary fact existed: he was less certain now than during his childhood, when he had been directly under the Jesuits' attentive care, when their teaching was unavoidable, when he was in their hands, belonging to them body and soul, without family connections or external influences to counterbalance them. They had, furthermore, inculcated in him a certain taste for the supernatural which had slowly and obscurely ramified in his soul, and which today, in his solitude, was blossoming, which despite everything was influencing his mind, working in silent confinement within the restricted interplay of his obsessions.

In examining the workings of his thought, in trying to connect together its different threads and discover its origins and causes, he eventually came to the conclusion that his behaviour, during his life in society, had sprung from the education he had received. Thus, were not his propensities towards artifice, his need for eccentricity, the result, in short, of the specious subjects he had studied, of otherworldly subtle distinctions, of quasi-theological speculations? They were, essentially, outbursts of feeling, impulses towards an ideal, towards an unknown universe, towards a far-off blessedness as desirable as that which we are promised by the Holy Scripture.

He stopped short, breaking off the thread of his reflections. 'Come on,' he told himself, annoyed, 'I'm still more affected than I thought; here I am arguing with myself like a casuist.'

But he continued to ponder, troubled by deep-seated misgivings; to be sure, if Lacordaire's theory was correct, he had nothing to fear, since the magic of conversion does not take effect instantaneously; in order for the explosion to occur the ground must be slowly and systematically mined; but if novelists speak of love at first sight, a certain number of theologians speak of religious conversion in similar terms; if one believed that doctrine to be true, then no one was certain of not succumbing. There was no point in engaging in further self-analyses, nor in paying heed to forebodings, nor in seeking out preventive measures; the psychology of mysticism was non-existent. It was so because it was so, and that was the long and short of it.

'Hey! What an idiot I am,' thought Des Esseintes; 'if I go on like this, in the end my dread of the disease will bring on the disease itself.'

He succeeded, in some small degree, in shaking off these pressures; his recollections faded away, but other morbid symptoms made their appearance; now it was solely the subjects of theological discussion that haunted him; the school grounds, the lessons, the Jesuits were far away; he was wholly dominated by abstractions; in spite of himself his thoughts focused on contradictory interpretations of dogmas and forgotten apostasies, that were recorded in Father Labbé's work on the Synods.* Snippets of those schisms, bits and pieces of those heresies which had, for centuries, divided the Western from the Eastern Church, were coming back to him. Here it was Nestorius disputing the right of the Virgin to the title 'Mother of God', because, in the Mystery of the Incarnation, it was not the God but the human creature that she had borne in her womb; there it was Eutyches, declaring that Christ's appearance could not have resembled that of other men, because the Divinity had elected to inhabit his body and had therefore totally transformed it; then there were other quibblers maintaining that the Saviour had had no body at all, and that the expressions used in the Holy Writ should be taken in a figurative sense; while Tertullian pronounced that famous quasi-materialistic axiom: 'Nothing is incorporeal except that which is not; everything that is, had a body of its own';* and, finally, he considered this old, old question, debated for centuries: was Christ nailed to the cross alone or did the Trinity—one in three persons—suffer, in its triple hypostasis, on the cross at Calvary? These problems troubled and disquieted him, and mechanically, like some lesson long since assimilated, he asked himself the questions and told himself the answers.

For several successive days his brain teemed with paradoxes, with fine distinctions, with a mass of petty quibbles, a tangle of rules as complicated as articles in a legal code, open to every interpretation, to every play upon words, resulting in a body of celestial law of the most subtle and the most elaborate kind; then in their turn the abstractions faded away, giving place to the visual, under the influence of the Gustave Moreaus hanging on his walls.

He saw a whole procession of prelates walking past: archimandrates and patriarchs raising their golden arms to bless the kneeling crowds, their white beards moving up and down as they read or prayed; he saw silent columns of penitents descending into gloomy crypts; he saw vast cathedrals rising up, where white-robed monks thundered from the pulpit. Just as De Quincey,* after smoking a little opium, would, on hearing the words 'Consul Romanus,' conjure up entire pages of Livy, would watch the consuls solemnly processing and the stately array of the Roman armies beginning their march, he, upon hearing some theological expression, would be left gasping, seeing surging crowds, and priestly presences silhouetted against a background of golden basilicas; these visions held him spellbound, extending through the ages right up to present-day religious cere-monies, cocooning him in infinite swathes of mournful, tender music.

There, he had no more arguments with himself to engage in, no more debates to endure; he experienced an indefinable impression of respect and fear; his artistic sense was subordinated to those care-fully orchestrated Catholic scenes; these memories sent a shiver through his nerves but then, in a sudden rebellion, in a rapid rever-sal, monstrous ideas sprang up in him, ideas of those sacrileges pro-vided for in the confessor's manual, shameful and impure abuses of the holy water and the holy oil. In the face of an omnipotent God there now arose a rival full of vigour, the Devil, and it seemed to him that a dreadful grandeur must result from a crime carried out, within the very walls of a church, by a believer who, filled with horrible delight and sadistic joy, was desperately determined to blaspheme, to commit outrages upon revered objects, to cover them with shame; then cabbalistic excesses, black masses, witches' sabbaths, fears about possession, thoughts of exorcism, all these came into play; he went so far as to wonder whether he was committing a sacrilege by owning objects consecrated in earlier times: altar cards, chasubles, and cus-todials; and this thought, of being in a state of sin, filled him with a kind of pride and relief; in it he detected a sacrilegious pleasure, but these sacrileges were debatable, or at any rate not very grave, since in fact he loved these objects and did not debase their function; in this manner he beguiled himself with cautious, cowardly thoughts, the wariness of his soul denying him overt crimes, and robbing him of the courage needed for committing horrifying, intentional, genuine sins.

At last, little by little, these quibbles disappeared. He saw, as it were from the higher reaches of his soul, the panorama of the

Church, its hereditary influence on humanity over centuries of time; he imagined her, imposing in her grief, proclaiming to mankind the horror of life and the harshness of fate; preaching patience, contrition, and the spirit of sacrifice; attempting to heal injuries by pointing to the bleeding wounds of Christ; guaranteeing privileges in heaven and the best share of everything in paradise to those in affliction; exhorting the human creature to suffer, to offer up to God, as a sacrifice, his tribulations and his transgressions, his vicissitudes and his troubles. The Church became truly eloquent, maternal to the unfortunate, compassionate to the oppressed, threatening to oppressors and to despots.

Here, Des Esseintes found his footing again. To be sure, he was in accord with this acknowledgement of the vileness of the social order, but then he rebelled against that vague remedy of hope in another life. Schopenhauer* was closer to the truth: his teaching and that of the Church started from a common viewpoint: he too took as his basis the iniquity and turpitude of the world, he too uttered—echoing the *Imitation of Christ**—this tormented cry: 'Life here on earth is truly a bed of sorrows!' He too preached the nothingness of existence, the benefits of solitude, warned humanity that no matter what it did, no matter where it turned, it would still be unhappy; if poor, because of the suffering born of privation, if rich, because of the relentless tedium engendered by abundance; but he did not extol any panacea nor lull you with any sham enticement as a remedy for inevitable evils.

He did not defend the validity of the revolting doctrine of original sin; did not attempt to prove to you that the God who protects scoundrels, assists imbeciles, oppresses children, brutalizes old age, and punishes the innocent is a supremely good God; he did not extol the blessings of a Providence which invented that useless, incomprehensible, unjust, idiotic depravity, physical suffering; far from attempting to justify, as does the Church, the necessity of pain and tribulation, he cried out, filled with compassion and indignation: 'If a God did make this world, I should not like to be that God; the misery of the world would break my heart.'

Ah, he alone was right! What were all those evangelical pharmacopoeias compared to his treatises on spiritual health? He did not claim to cure anything, did not offer the sick any redress, any hope; but his 'Theory of Pessimism' was, when all was said and done, the great consoler of exceptional minds, of lofty souls; it revealed society as it actually is, stressing the innate stupidity of women, drawing your attention to the pitfalls, saving you from disillusion by advising you to restrict your hopes as much as possible, or, if you felt sufficiently strong, not to let yourself conceive any at all; in a word, to deem yourself happy if huge roofing tiles did not come clattering down, when you least expected it, upon your head.

Branching off from the same path as the *Imitation*, this theory likewise led—but without losing its way in mysterious mazes and improbable side-roads—to the same destination, to resignation, to inaction.

Only, if this resignation—the simple consequence of acknowledging that a deplorable state of affairs existed which it was impossible to change in any way—was accessible to those with strong minds, it was only the more difficult of comprehension to the poor in spirit, whose demands and whose anger were all the more readily soothed by their compassionate religion.

These reflections relieved Des Esseintes of a heavy burden; the great German thinker's aphorisms calmed the agitation of his thoughts, although, the points of contact between these two doctrines making it easier for each of them to remind him of the other, he was unable to forget that Catholicism—so poetic, so poignant—in which he had been steeped, and whose essence he had, in the past, absorbed through every pore.

These renewals of belief, these stirrings of faith tormented him, especially now that his health was deteriorating; they coincided with certain nervous disorders which had recently manifested themselves.

Ever since his early youth, he had been tormented by inexplicable feelings of revulsion, by shuddering spasms which left him chilled to the marrow, his teeth on edge, whenever, for instance, he saw wet laundry being wrung out by a servant; these reactions still persisted; even today it actually made him suffer to hear someone tearing up a cloth, or to rub his finger over a bit of chalk or run his hand over a piece of watered silk.

The excesses of his bachelor days, and the enormous strain to which his brain had been subjected, had aggravated his original neurosis to an extraordinary degree and further weakened the already exhausted blood of his stock; in Paris, he had had to undergo a course of hydrotherapy* for tremors of the fingers, for terrible neuralgic pains which cut his face in two, hammering unremittingly at his temples, lancinating his eyelids, bringing on attacks of nausea which he was unable to control except by lying on his back in the dark.

These troubles had slowly disappeared, thanks to his quieter, more regulated life; now they were manifesting themselves afresh, taking different forms and travelling all over his body; abandoning his skull, the pains moved to his rigid, swollen belly, to his bowels pierced by a red-hot knife of pain, to his urgent, useless straining; then the nervous, rasping, dry cough, beginning punctually at a particular time and always lasting the same number of minutes, would wake him, half-suffocating him in his bed; finally his appetite vanished, and his stomach was beset by hot and flatulent acidity, by dry, burning sensations; after every attempted meal he would be swollen and breathless and could no longer endure wearing his trousers buttoned or his waistcoat tightly fastened.

He gave up alcohol, coffee, tea, drank milk products, tried affusions of cold water, stuffed himself with asafoetida, with valerian,* with quinine: he even made an effort to leave the house, and go out a little into the countryside when rainy weather made it silent and empty; he forced himself to walk, to take some exercise; as a last resort, he temporarily gave up reading and, consumed with boredom, decided, as a way of filling his now idle existence, to carry out a project which, out of laziness and dislike of upsets, he had constantly deferred since settling at Fontenay.

No longer able to intoxicate himself afresh with all the magic of style, to excite himself over the delicious sorcery of the exceptional epithet which, while yet retaining its precision, nevertheless opens up to the imagination of the initiated an infinity of possibilities beyond itself, he resolved to put the finishing touches to the furnishing of the house, and obtain some very special hothouse flowers, thus providing himself with a material occupation which would distract him, relax his nerves, rest his brain, and, as he also hoped, would, with their strange and splendid hues, compensate him somewhat for the colours of style—both imaginary and real—which his present literary diet would make him, for a brief time, either forget about or forfeit altogether.

8

He had always adored flowers, but this passion which, during his visits to Jutigny, had at first included all flowers without distinction of species or genera, had eventually narrowed itself down, fixing on one single family.

For many years now he had despised the common plants which bloom on the display tables of Parisian markets, in dripping-wet pots, beneath green awnings or reddish sunshades. At the same time as his literary tastes and his artistic interests had matured, no longer focusing on anything but meticulously selected works distilled from tormented and subtle intellects, at the same time also as his weariness with generally received opinions had grown more acute, his love of flowers had cleansed itself of all residue, of all impurities, and had, in a sense, clarified and corrected itself.

He liked to compare a horticulturist's shop to a microcosm in which all categories of society were represented: the flowers that are poor and coarse, the flowers of the slum, which are not truly at home unless reposing on a garret window-sill, their roots jammed into a milk bottle or an old pot, the sunflower for example; the pretentious, conformist, stupid flowers, like the rose, which belong exclusively in porcelain holders painted by young girls; finally the flowers of high lineage such as orchids, delicate and charming and quiveringly sensitive to cold, exotic flowers exiled in Paris to the warmth of glass palaces, princesses of the vegetable kingdom, living a segregated life, having no longer anything in common with the plants of the street or the flora of the middle classes.

In short, he did still feel a certain interest in, a certain pity for, plebeian flowers which are debilitated, in poor neighbourhoods, by the vapours from sewers and drains; but, by contrast, he detested flower arrangements designed to harmonize with the cream and gold drawing-rooms of the newly erected houses; and, lastly, he set apart, for the unalloyed pleasure of his eyes, plants that were elegant, rare, and of exotic origin,* preserved with cunning skill in artificial equatorial zones produced by the carefully measured warmth of stoves.

But this definitive choice of the hothouse bloom had itself been modified under the influence of his general ideas, of his now fixed opinions about everything; in the past, in Paris, his natural inclination towards artifice had led him to forsake the real flower for its replica, faithfully imitated thanks to the miracles of gums and threads, percalines and taffetas, papers and velvets.

He consequently possessed a marvellous collection of tropical plants, worked by the fingers of true artists who copied nature step by step, creating it afresh, taking the flower from its birth, guiding it to maturity, mimicking it right up to its decline; successfully noting the most infinitesimal shadings, the most fleeting details of its awakening or its repose; observing the way its petals lie, when bent back by the wind or puckered by the rain; strewing dew-drops of gum upon its matutinal corollas; fashioning it in full bloom, with its branches bending beneath the weight of the sap, or else when it stretches forth its dried-out stem and shrivelled cupule, as the calyxes shed their petals and the leaves fall.

He had long been fascinated by this wonderful art-form; but now he dreamt of planning a different kind of flora. After having artificial flowers that imitated real ones, he now wanted real flowers that mimicked artificial ones.

This was the direction his ideas took; he did not have to search for long, since his house was situated right in the heart of the area of the great horticulturalists. He simply went and visited the greenhouses of the Avenue de Châtillon and the Aunay valley, returning exhausted, his purse empty, filled with wonder at the vegetative follies he had seen, his mind fixed exclusively, now, on the species he had acquired, and haunted by incessant memories of magnificent and outlandish beds of flowers.

Two days later, the carts arrived. List in hand, Des Esseintes identified and verified his purchases, one by one.

The gardeners took down from their carts a collection of Caladiums, whose turgid, hairy stalks supported enormous heart-shaped leaves; while they all bore an air of kinship, no single one exactly resembled any other. Some were extraordinary, pinkish in colour, like the Virginal which looked as if it had been made out of oilcloth or court plaster; some were entirely white, like the Albany which could have been cut from the transparent pleura of an ox or the translucent bladder of a pig; a few, particularly the Madame Mame, mimicked zinc, parodying pieces of punched metal that had been dyed Emperor green and stained with drops of oil-paint and splashes of red and white lead; the plants before him—the Bosphorus, for example—gave the impression of a starched calico pebbled with crimson and myrtle green, while those further away—such as the Aurora Borealis—displayed a leaf the colour of raw meat, striated with purple ribs and purplish-blue fibrils, a distended leaf that sweated dark red wine and blood.

Between them, the Albany and the Aurora exemplified the two extremes of a plant's constitution, the apoplectic and the chlorotic.

The gardeners were bringing in yet more new varieties; this time they simulated the appearance of fake skin scored by artificial veins; and the majority, as though eaten away by syphilis and leprosy, exhibited livid flesh marbled with roseola and damasked with dartres; others were the bright pink of scars that are healing, or the brownish tint of scabs in the process of forming; others were blistering from cautery or puffing up from burns; still others revealed hairy skins pitted by ulcers and embossed with chancres; and then, finally, there were some which looked as though they were covered with dressings, plastered with black mercury ointment, with green unguents made from atropine, or sprinkled with the glittery-yellow dust of iodoform powder.

Grouped together, these flowers dazzled Des Esseintes, more extraordinary than when he had unexpectedly come upon them, mingled in with others as if in some hospital, within the glassed-in wards of the hothouses.

'My God!' he exclaimed fervently.

A new plant, of a similar kind to the Caladiums, the *Alocacia metallica*, excited him afresh. This one was coated with a layer of bronzish green shot with silvery glints; it was a masterpiece of the artificial; one might have thought it a part of a stove-pipe, cut into a point by a stove-setter.

Next the men unloaded sheafs of diamond-shaped, bottle-green leaves; from the centre of each a cane emerged, on the end of which quivered a large ace of hearts as shiny as a capsicum; as if in defiance of all the normal visual qualities of plants, from the middle of this deep red ace there erupted a white and yellow brush, plump and feathery; in some cases it came out straight, in others in a corkscrew, like a pig's tail, from the very top of the heart. This was the Anthurium, an aroid recently imported into France from Colombia; it was part of a group of that family which also comprised the

Amorphophallus, a plant from Cochin China, with a leaf shaped like a fish slice, and long black stalks ridged with scars like the scourged limbs of negro slaves.

Des Esseintes was filled with exultation.

A fresh lot of monstrosities* was being unloaded from the carriages; the Echinopsis, its flowers—the vile pink of amputated stumps—emerging from compresses of cotton wool; the Nidularium, its sabre-shaped leaves opening to reveal flayed, gaping flesh; the *Tillandsia lindeni*, projecting jagged blades the colour of unfermented wine; the Cypripediums, intricate and irrational in shape, born of the imagination of some demented inventor. They resembled a clog, or a small oval bowl, with a human tongue curled back above it, its tendon stretched tight just as one sees tongues drawn in the illustrations to works dealing with diseases of the throat and mouth; two little wings, gumdrop red, which might have been taken from a child's toy windmill, completed this weird assemblage made up of the underside of a tongue, the colour of wine-lees and slate, and of a shiny pouch, its lining oozing with a viscous glue.

He could not tear his eyes away from this improbable orchid from India; the gardeners, annoyed at these delays, themselves began to read aloud the labels stuck in the pots they were carrying in.

Des Esseintes watched apprehensively, listening to the repellent sound of the names of these green plants: the *Encephalartos horridus*, a gigantic iron artichoke, covered with rust, such as one sees placed on top of chateau gates to hinder intruders; the *Cocos micania*, a kind of palm, serrated and slender, covered all over by tall leaves that resembled paddles and oars; the *Zamia lehmanni*, an immense pineapple, a vast Cheshire cheese, planted in heath-mould, its top bristling with barbed javelins and ferocious arrows; the *Cibotium spectabile*, which by its capricious structure went one better than its congeners, challenging visions seen in dreams, thrusting forth from its palmate greenery an enormous orang-outang tail, a hairy brown tail with a crooked tip like a bishop's crozier.

But he barely glanced at them, impatiently awaiting the group of plants that fascinated him most of all, the vegetable ghouls, the carnivorous plants such as the velvety-rimmed Antilles Fly-trap, which secretes a digestive liquid, and is furnished with curved spines which fold over one another so as to form a web above the imprisoned insect; the Drosera of the peat-bogs, equipped with glandular hairs;

the Sarracena, the Cephalothus, opening voracious trumpets capable of digesting and absorbing actual meat; and lastly the Nepenthes, whose freakishness of form transcends the acknowledged boundaries of eccentricity.

He never wearied of turning round and round in his hands the pot in which this floral extravaganza was stirring. It mimicked the indiarubber plant, with its long leaves of a dark metallic green, but from the end of each leaf a green thread hung down, an umbilical cord supporting a greenish container stippled with violet, a sort of German porcelain pipe, a singular bird's nest which calmly swayed to and fro, revealing an interior thickly matted with hairs.

'That one is truly amazing,' murmured Des Esseintes.

But he had to tear himself away from his enjoyment, for the gardeners, in a hurry to leave, were emptying out the bottoms of their carts, setting down in a jumble tuberous Begonias, and black Crotons flecked with spots of red lead like rusty iron.

Then he noticed that there still remained one name on his list. The Cattleya* of New Granada; they showed him a small winged bell-flower in a muted shade of lilac, an almost colourless mauve; going up close, he put his nose to it and hastily shrank back; it gave off a smell of varnished deal, like a toy chest, evoking the horrors of presents on New Year's Day.

He thought he would do well to treat it warily, and was almost sorry to have included, among the scentless plants in his possession, this orchid whose perfume recalled the most disagreeable of memories.

Alone once more, he gazed at this flood-tide of vegetation spreading across his vestibule; the plants, mingling with one another, crossed swords, kris, spear-heads, making a pile of green weapons above which floated, like so many barbaric pennants, flowers in dazzling, strident hues.

The air of the room was becoming depleted; soon, in a shadowy corner, near the floor, a soft white light appeared. He went up to it and realized that it came from some Rhizomorphes, which were emitting, as they breathed, these dim night-light glimmers.

'These plants are indeed astounding,' he said to himself; then, stepping back, he took in the whole collection at a glance; his object had been achieved; not one appeared real; cloth, paper, porcelain, metal, seemed to have been lent by man to Nature to enable her to create her monstrosities. When she had not been capable of imitating human handiwork, she had been reduced to refashioning the internal membranes of animals, to borrowing the long-lasting colours of their rotting flesh, the magnificent horrors of their gangrened limbs.

'It all comes down to syphilis,'* thought Des Esseintes, his eye drawn towards, mesmerized by, the dreadful striations of the Caladiums, upon which a shaft of daylight was resting. And he was struck by a sudden vision of a humanity eternally tormented by the virus of bygone days. Since the beginning of the world, from father to son, all creatures passed on to one another the everlasting legacy, the eternal disease which ravaged the ancestors of man, which actually hollowed out the bones of the old fossils now being exhumed.

This virus had raced through the centuries without ever exhausting itself; even today it still raged, in the guise of carefully concealed pain, hiding under the symptoms of migraine headaches and bronchitis, fits of dizziness and gout; now and again it made its way to the surface, choosing to attack those who were ill-cared-for and ill-nourished, breaking out in a display of spots like gold pieces and ironically adorning the poor devils' brows with a dancing-girl's circlet of golden coins, engraving on their skin, as a crowning affliction, the symbol of wealth and well-being! And here it was appearing once more, in all its primal splendour, on the bright-hued leaves of plants!

'It's true,' went on Des Esseintes, reverting to the point at which his reasoning had begun, 'it's true that most of the time Nature is incapable of creating, all on her own, such noxious, degenerate species; she provides the raw material, the seed and the soil, the nurturing womb and the elements of the plant which man then grows, fashions, paints, sculpts as he chooses. Obstinate, complicated and limited though she be, Nature has finally surrendered and her master has succeeded in altering, by means of chemical reactions, the components of the soil, in effecting unhurriedly thought-out combinations and systematically prepared cross-pollinations, in using ingenious cuttings, and methodically planned grafts, so that now he makes her produce flowers of different colours on the same bough, he invents new tints for her, changes at will the age-old shape of her plants, smooths over and cleans her unfinished blocks of stone, completes her sketches, marks them with his stamp, and imprints upon them his artistic hallmark.

'There's no doubt about it,' he said to himself, summing up his thoughts, 'man is able to bring about in a few years a range of choice that slothful Nature can only produce after several centuries; unquestionably, as matters stand today, the only artists, the real artists, are the horticulturalists.'

He felt somewhat weary, and found this atmosphere of hothouse plants suffocatingly oppressive; the errands he had undertaken over the last few days had exhausted him; the transition between the open air and the warmth of the house, between the immobility of seclusion and the activity of freedom had been too abrupt; he left the vestibule and went and lay down on his bed; but his mind, although it was asleep, was obsessed by a single idea, and continued—as if wound up by a spring—to tell its tale; and soon he was absorbed in the sombre irrationalities of a nightmare.

He was walking along an avenue, in the heart of a wood, at twilight, beside a woman whom he had never seen or known; she was skinny, with pale yellow hair, a face like a bulldog, freckled cheeks, irregular teeth that jutted out beneath a snub nose. She wore a servant's white apron, a long kerchief crossed over her breast, Prussian military half-boots, and a black bonnet trimmed with ruching and a rosette. She had the appearance of a stall-keeper at a fair, or of a member of a travelling circus.

He wondered who this woman was who, he felt, had long since entered into and become part of his intimate circle and of his existence; in vain he sought to determine her nationality, her name, her trade, her reason for existing; he could call to mind no memory of this inexplicable yet indubitable relationship.

He was still searching his memory when suddenly a strange figure appeared in front of them, on horseback, trotted for a moment, then turned round in the saddle. His blood froze; he remained rooted to the spot in horror. That equivocal, sexless face was green, with terrible eyes of an icy light blue beneath purple lids; pustules encircled its mouth; extraordinarily thin arms, skeletal arms, bare from the elbows down and shaking with fever, emerged from ragged sleeves, and the fleshless thighs shivered in high boots which were far too large.

The dreadful gaze was fixed on Des Esseintes, boring into him, chilling him to the marrow, while the bulldog woman, now in even greater panic, clung to him with her head thrown back on her rigid neck, screaming blue murder. And instantly he grasped the meaning of the horrifying vision. He was looking at the figure of the Pox.

Spurred on by terror, quite beside himself, he turned into a side path and ran as fast as he could to a shooting-lodge standing to his left, among some laburnums; there, in a passageway, he collapsed on to a chair.

A few minutes later, when he was getting his breath back, the sound of sobs made him raise his head; the bulldog woman stood before him; pitiful and grotesque, she was weeping bitterly, saying that she had lost her teeth during their escape, pulling clay pipes out of the pockets of her servant's apron, breaking them, and ramming pieces of white stem into the holes in her gums.

'My goodness, she's quite absurd,' thought Des Esseintes; 'those stems will never stay in'; and, indeed, they were all pouring out of her mouth, one after another.

Just then came the sound of a horse's gallop approaching. Dreadful terror seized Des Esseintes; his legs gave way beneath him; the galloping grew faster; despair, like the lash of a whip, forced him to his feet; he flung himself upon the woman who now was stamping on the pipe bowls, and begged her to be quiet, not to betray their presence with the sound of her boots. He dragged her, struggling, to the far end of the passage, throttling her to prevent her crying out; suddenly he noticed a bar-room door with green-painted, slatted shutters but no latch; pushing it, he leapt inside, and came to a sudden halt.

Before him, in the middle of a vast clearing, enormous white clowns were jumping about like rabbits in the moonlight.

Tears of discouragement filled his eyes; never, no never would he be able to cross the threshold—'I shall be crushed,' he thought—and, as if to justify his fears, the series of enormous clowns was proliferating; now their somersaults were filling the entire horizon, the entire sky which they were knocking into with their feet and their heads, alternately.

Then the sound of the hoof-beats stopped. He was there, the other side of a circular skylight in the passage: more dead than alive, Des Esseintes turned around, and saw through the little window two pricked-up ears, some yellow teeth, and two nostrils breathing jets of steam which stank of carbolic.

He sank down, abandoning any idea of resistance or flight; he closed his eyes so as not to see the terrible gaze of Syphilis pressing down upon him through the wall, a gaze his own eyes encountered even from beneath closed lids, and which he felt sliding down his damp backbone, over his body where the hair was standing on end in pools of cold sweat. He was prepared for anything, even hoping for a death-blow that would end it; a century, that was probably merely a minute, passed; shivering, he reopened his eyes. Everything had vanished; without transition, as if in a transformation scene, by a trick effect of décor, a dreadful mineral landscape stretched on and on into the distance, a bleached, dead landscape of ravines and desert; a light illumined this desolate place, a tranquil white light that called to mind the glow of phosphorus dissolved in oil.

Something stirred on the ground, something which took on the form of a very pale, naked woman, her legs sheathed in green silk stockings.

He gazed at her curiously; her hair, like horse-hair crimped by over-hot irons, was frizzled, with broken ends; Nepenthes pitchers hung from her ears; tints of baked veal glistened in her flaring nostrils. Her eyes were rapturous as she called softly to him.

He did not have time to reply, for already the woman was changing; her pupils blazed with colour; her lips were turning the angry scarlet of the Anthuriums; the nipples of her breasts flashed, as shiny as two red capsicum pods.

A sudden insight came to him: 'It's the Flower,' he told himself; and his compulsive urge to reason persisted in his nightmare, shifting, just as it had done during the day, from plants on to the Virus.

Then he observed the frightening inflammation of the breasts and of the mouth, noticed the blackish-brown and copper-coloured blotches on the skin of her body, and recoiled in alarm; but he was fascinated by the woman's eyes and slowly moved forward, attempting to dig his heels into the earth to stop himself walking, letting himself fall to the ground, but nevertheless getting to his feet again to advance nearer her; he was almost touching her when black Amorphophallus shot up on all sides, thrusting towards that belly which rose and fell like a sea. He had forced them aside and pushed them back, feeling an unbounded disgust at seeing these warm, firm stalks massing together beneath his fingers; then suddenly the odious plants had vanished and two arms were trying to embrace him; an unendurable feeling of anguish made his heart beat with great thuds, for the eyes, the dreadful eyes of that woman were now a pale, cold blue, terrifying to see. He made a superhuman effort to free himself from her embrace, but with an irresistible gesture she held him in her arms, seizing hold of him, and he saw, his face haggard, the wild Nidularium blossoming between her upraised thighs, opening wide its sword-shaped petals above the bloody interior.

His body lightly brushed the plant's hideous wound; he felt himself dying, and awoke with a start, choking, ice-cold, crazed with fear, moaning:

'Ah! Thank God, it was only a dream.'

9

The nightmares returned; he was afraid to go to sleep. He lay for hours on end stretched out on his bed, sometimes in a state of persistent insomnia and feverish agitation, at other times in appalling dreams from which he awoke with a start, convinced he was losing his footing, falling from top to bottom of a staircase, or plunging, unable to stop himself, into the depths of an abyss.

His neurosis, lulled into quiescence for several days, was now regaining control, showing itself to be fiercer and more tenacious in its new forms.

Now he found the bedclothes uncomfortable; the sheets stifled him; his entire body tingled, his blood felt burning hot, he itched as if from flea bites all down his legs; soon to these symptoms were added a dull pain in his jaws and the sensation that his temples were being squeezed in a vice.

His apprehension increased; unfortunately no way of curing this inexorable malady was to be found. He had without success tried to install equipment for hydrotherapy in his dressing-room. He was prevented by the impossibility of arranging for water to be transported up to the lofty height at which his house was perched, and the difficulty of even obtaining the water in sufficient quantity in a village where the supply only ran parsimoniously at certain times; since he could not be scourged by jets of water which, smacking and drumming directly at his dorsal vertebrae, were the only thing powerful enough to quell his insomnia and restore his tranquillity, he was reduced to brief aspersions in his bath-tub or sitz bath, to simple cold affusions followed by vigorous rub-downs by his manservant with a horsehair glove.

But these imitation showers in no way checked the progress of his neurosis; the most he experienced was a few hours' relief, and these moreover were dearly paid for by fresh bouts which returned to the attack with increased violence and intensity.

His boredom became immeasurable; the joy of possessing astounding blooms had run its course; he had already grown indifferent to their composition and their delicate variations; and then, despite the care he lavished on them, most of his plants withered and died; he had them removed from his rooms and, because he was now in a condition of extreme excitability, he became vexed at no longer seeing them and his eyes were offended by the empty spaces which they had occupied.

To amuse himself and fill the interminable hours, he turned to his boxes of prints and sorted his Goyas;* some early versions of certain etchings from the *Caprices*, which were proofs (identifiable by their reddish tints) bought at sales long ago for exorbitant prices, raised his spirits; he immersed himself in them, following the artist's flights of fancy, enthralled by his dizzying scenes, by his witches riding on cats, by his women trying to pull out a hanged man's teeth, by his bandits, his succubi, his devils and his dwarfs.

Then he went through all the other series of Goya's etchings and aquatints, his *Proverbs*, which are so macabre in their horror, his war scenes which are so ferocious in their rage, and finally his etching entitled *The Garrotted Man*, of which he treasured a wonderful trial proof, printed on heavy paper, unmounted, with visible wire-marks criss-crossing the surface of the paper.

He was captivated by Goya's savage exuberance, by his corrosive, frenzied talent, although the universal admiration which his works commanded today did tend to dampen somewhat his enthusiasm, and it was now many years since he had stopped framing them, for fear that if he were to display them, the first imbecile who happened to see them would deem it necessary to proffer some idiotic remarks and to go into carefully studied ecstasies before them.

The same was true of his Rembrandts, which from time to time he would examine on the quiet; and, indeed, just as the most charming tune in the world becomes vulgar, intolerable, as soon as the general public is humming it, as soon as the street-organs have taken it up, the work to which charlatan art fanciers do not remain indifferent, the work which nitwits do not challenge, which is not satisfied with arousing the enthusiasm of the few, also becomes, by virtue of that very fact, corrupted, banal, almost repellent to the initiated.

Indeed, this promiscuity of admiration was one of the greatest trials of his life; incomprehensible successes had ruined forever, in his eyes, pictures and books which he had formerly held dear; in the face of the approbation of the masses, he would eventually discover imperceptible flaws in these works, would reject them, wondering if his own taste was not becoming less discriminating, if he was not being duped.

He reclosed his portfolios and, once again at a loss, relapsed into depression. So as to give fresh direction to his ideas, he then embarked on some soothing reading and, hoping to cool his brain with literary opiates,* tried those books which hold such charm for convalescents and invalids, who would be fatigued by more tetanic or phosphate-rich material: the novels of Dickens.

But these volumes produced an effect quite different from what he expected; those chaste lovers, those Protestant heroines in their high-necked gowns, loved on an astral plane, content with downcast glances, and blushes, and tears of joy, and clasped hands. This exaggerated purity promptly thrust him into the opposite excess; by virtue of the law of contrasts he leapt from one extreme to the other, recalling vibrant, earthy scenes, thinking of what human couples did, of their intermingled kisses, of their 'dove' kisses as ecclesiastical prudery terms them, kisses which penetrate beyond the lips.

He laid aside his reading and let his mind wander far from straitlaced England, to the licentious peccadilloes and salacious practices of which the Church disapproves; he was filled with erotic excitement; his mental and physical sexual frigidity, which he had supposed permanent, vanished; once again, solitude affected his disordered nerves, and once again he became obsessed, not by religion itself, but by the wickedness of the actions and sins which the Church condemns; the eternal subject of its obsecrations and threats became his exclusive preoccupation; the carnal side of his nature, which, torpid for months, had at first been stirred by the irritant of reading pious works, then awakened and fully aroused in a paroxysm of nerves brought on by the cant of the English writer, manifested itself fully, and, his stimulated senses carrying him back to the past, he wallowed in the mire of his former iniquities.

He stood up and gloomily opened a little silver-gilt box, its lid studded with aventurines. It was full of violet sweetmeats; he took one, feeling it with his fingers as he reflected upon the strange properties of this bonbon whose sugar-coating looked like hoar-frost; in the past, when he had first become impotent, when he used to dream of woman without bitterness or regrets or renewed desire, he would place one of these bonbons on his tongue, let it melt, and suddenly, with infinite sweetness, there would arise very faint and languid recollections of his earlier debaucheries.

These sweets, invented by Siraudin* and known by the idiotic name of 'Pearls of the Pyrenees', were a drop of sarcanthus scent or female essence crystallized in a lump of sugar; they penetrated the papillae of the mouth, awakening memories of water opalescent with rare aromatic vinegars and deep, intimate kisses, steeped in perfumes.

As a rule he would smile as he breathed in this amorous aroma, these phantom caresses which evoked glimpses of nudity in his brain and for a second rekindled his once passionate appetite for certain women; now, the effect of the bonbons was no longer half suppressed, no longer content with reviving images of remote, dimly remembered carousals; on the contrary, it tore aside the veils and projected before his eyes the urgent, brutal, corporeal reality.

At the head of this parade of mistresses which the taste of the bonbon helped to portray in precise detail, there was one who paused, displaying large white teeth, satiny rose-pink skin, an uptilted nose, silver-grey eyes, and blond hair worn in a fringe.

This was Miss Urania,* an American, with a sturdy body, sinewy legs, muscles of steel, and arms of cast iron. She had been one of the most famous acrobats of the circus.

Des Esseintes had spent long evenings watching her attentively; the first few times, he had seen her as she actually was, that is, well built and beautiful, but he had felt no urgent desire to make her acquaintance; she had nothing to recommend her to the lusts of a jaded debauchee, yet he returned to the circus, enticed by he knew not what, driven by a feeling that was difficult to define.

Little by little, as he watched her, strange notions came to him; while he was admiring her suppleness and her strength, he began to discern an unnatural change of sex taking place in her; her graceful little ways, her feminine affectations became less and less apparent, while their place was taken by the agile, vigorous graces of a man; in a word, after having first been a woman, she then, after wavering, after toying with androgyny, seemed to make up her mind, to define herself, to become a man completely.

'Therefore,' thought Des Esseintes, 'just as a strapping young fellow will fall in love with a frail girl, this female clown must instinctively be attracted to a weak, hollow-chested, short-winded creature like myself'; and on his part he even actually experienced, while taking stock of himself and giving rein to his spirit of comparison, a sense that he himself was becoming feminine, and he positively coveted the possession of this woman, yearning in the way an anaemic young girl would for the vulgar muscle-man whose arms could crush her in an embrace.

This exchange of sex between Miss Urania and himself had greatly excited him; 'We are meant for one another,' he declared; to this sudden admiration for brute force which, until then, he had detested, was added the monstrous appeal of self-abasement, the pleasure of a common prostitute who eagerly pays a high price for the boorish caresses of a pimp.

Before making the decision to seduce the acrobat, and turn his dreams into reality if that were possible, he confirmed those dreams by putting those thoughts of his own into the unwitting lips of the woman, by reading his own designs afresh in the fixed and unchanging smile of the performer, as she spun on her trapeze.

One fine evening he resolved to send a message via the attendants. Miss Urania deemed it requisite not to yield without a preliminary courtship; nevertheless she did not play too hard to get, knowing, from the gossip she heard, that Des Esseintes was rich, and that his name helped to launch a woman. But, as soon as his desires were fulfilled, he experienced the most inordinate disappointment. He had imagined the American woman to be as stupid and brutish as a wrestler at a fair, yet her stupidity, unfortunately, was entirely feminine. She unquestionably lacked education and tact, had neither good sense nor wit, and revealed a brutish avidity at table, but she still had all the childish emotions of womankind; she was as inclined to chatter and flirt as girls whose minds were filled with nonsense; the transmutation of masculine ideas into her woman's body had simply not occurred.

Furthermore, in bed she displayed a puritanical restraint, and none of those rough, athletic propensities which he both desired and feared; she was not subject, as he had for a moment hoped she would be, to the disordered passions of his sex. Had he thoroughly fathomed the depths of her greedy desires, he would, however, perhaps have detected a leaning towards a delicate, slender creature, towards a temperament diametrically opposite to her own, but then he would have discovered that her preference was not for a young girl, but for a cheerful little shrimp of a fellow, for a skinny, comical clown.

Inevitably, Des Esseintes resumed the male role he had momentarily abandoned; his feelings of femininity, of weakness, of having bought himself a kind of protection, of fear even, vanished; self-deception was no longer possible; Miss Urania was an ordinary mistress, who did not in any way justify the intellectual curiosity she had inspired.

Although the charms of her fresh body, of her magnificent beauty, did at first astonish and captivate Des Esseintes, he very soon sought to escape from the relationship and precipitated the breakup, for his premature impotence was further aggravated by the icy caresses and prudish depravity of this woman.

And yet she was the first to halt before him, in this uninterrupted review of his libidinous past; but, essentially, if she was more strongly imprinted on his memory than a host of others whose charms had been less misleading and who had afforded him less limited pleasures, that was because of her smell—the smell of a healthy, vigorous animal; her superabundant good health was at the opposite pole from the anaemic, highly wrought perfumes of which he recognized faint traces in Siraudin's delicate bonbon.

Miss Urania, like some antithetical fragrance, forced herself inexorably upon his memory, but almost immediately Des Esseintes, jarred by the unexpectedness of this natural and crude aroma, reverted to civilized perfumes, and, inevitably, began thinking about other mistresses; they were crowding in on his thoughts, but now, above all the others, arose the woman whose unnatural gift had satisfied him so completely over a period of several months.

That one was a brunette, small, skinny, and black-eyed, whose pomaded hair, plastered to her head as if painted on with a brush, was parted like a boy's near one temple. He had made her acquaintance at a *café-concert*, where she was performing as a ventriloquist.

To the stupefaction of the crowded spectators, who found these feats disturbing, she made cardboard figures of children, arranged on chairs in a row like Pandean pipe reeds, speak in turn; she conversed with dummies that seemed almost alive and, in the hall itself, one could hear the buzzing of flies round the candelabra and the rustling made by the silent audience as—astonished to find themselves still seated—they instinctively drew back in their chairs, believing imaginary carriages to be grazing them as they drove by between the café entrance and the stage.

Des Esseintes had been fascinated; a mass of ideas sprang up in his mind; first of all he made haste, using his arsenal of banknotes, to conquer the ventriloquist, who appealed to him by the very contrast she provided with the American. This brunette reeked of concocted, noisome, heady perfumes and she burned like the crater of a volcano; despite all his stratagems, Des Esseintes was exhausted after a few hours; but he nevertheless gladly persisted in allowing himself to be fleeced by her, for it was the phenomenon, rather than the mistress, that enticed him.

Besides, the plans he had formulated had matured. He made up his mind to carry out certain projects which until then had been unrealizable.

One evening he had a little sphinx of black marble brought in; it lay couched in the classic pose with outstretched paws and rigidly upright head; he also obtained a polychrome clay chimera with a bristling, spiky mane, that flashed its ferocious eyes and with its ridged tail fanned flanks as puffed-up as a pair of blacksmith's bellows. He placed one of these creatures at each end of the room and put out the lamps, leaving the reddening embers in the hearth to cast an uncertain light round the chamber, and magnify the objects which were almost engulfed in shadow. Then he lay down on a sofa, beside the woman whose motionless face was lit by the glow from a half-burnt log, and waited.

Using strange intonations which he had slowly and patiently made her rehearse beforehand, she, without so much as moving her lips or looking at the mythical creatures, brought the pair of them to life. And in the silence of the night, the wonderful dialogue of the Chimera and the Sphinx* began, recited by guttural, deep voices, now raucous, now shrill, almost supernatural.

'Here, Chimera, stop.'

'No, never.'

Lulled by Flaubert's splendid prose, he listened avidly to the terrible duet; shivers ran down him from head to foot when the Chimera uttered the solemn and magical line:

'I seek fresh perfumes, larger blossoms, pleasures as yet untried.'

Ah! It was to him that this voice, as mysterious as an incantation, was speaking; it was to him that it was describing its feverish craving after the unknown, its unattained ideal, its need to escape the horrible reality of existence, to pass beyond the confines of thought, to cast about, without ever arriving at a certainty, in the misty reaches that lie beyond art! All the miserable inadequacy of his own efforts chilled his heart. Gently he embraced the silent woman by his side, taking refuge in her like a disconsolate child, not even seeing the sulky expression of the ventriloquist who had to play a part and ply her trade, at home, in her leisure hours, far from the footlights.

Their relationship continued, but soon Des Esseintes's sexual inadequacy became worse; no longer could the effervescence of his mind thaw the ice in his veins; no longer did his nerves obey his will; he was obsessed by lewd fantasies typical of dotards. Conscious that he was becoming more and more hesitant with this mistress, he turned for assistance to that most reliable adjuvant of aged and unpredictable lechers—fear.

While he was holding this woman in his arms, a rough drunken voice would suddenly shout from outside the door: 'Open up! I know you're in there with your gigolo, jus' you wait, jus' you wait, you slut!' Instantly, like those rakes who are excited by the terror of being caught *in flagrante delicto*, in the open air—on the river bank, in the Tuileries Gardens, in a shelter or on a park bench—his virility was fleetingly restored and he fell upon the ventriloquist, whose voice went on clamouring outside the room; and he experienced unbelievable transports in the course of this turmoil, this panicky alarm of a man who is in danger, who is interrupted and forced to make haste in his lechery.

Unfortunately these sessions were of brief duration; despite the exorbitant prices he was paying her, the ventriloquist dismissed him and that very same evening gave herself to a likely fellow with less complicated requirements and more reliable loins.

He had been sorry to see that one go; when he recalled her ingenuity, other women seemed without savour; even the corrupt graces of childhood struck him as insipid; the contempt he felt for their monotonous affectations grew so intense that he could no longer bring himself to endure them.

One day as, ruminating on his disgust, he was taking a solitary walk along the Avenue de Latour-Maubourg, he was approached near the Invalides by a very young man who asked to be shown the quickest way to the Rue de Babylone. Des Esseintes pointed it out and, since he too was crossing the esplanade, they walked together.

The young man's voice was insistent, unexpectedly so, asking for more detailed directions, saying: 'So you think that if I took the left turning that would be longer; however I was assured that by cutting across the avenue I'd get there faster'—a voice that was at once beseeching and timid, very low and sweet.

Des Esseintes examined him. He looked as if he should be in school, and was wretchedly dressed in a little cheviot jacket too tight round the hips and barely covering the small of his back, close-fitting black trousers, a low-cut turn-down collar over a ballooning dark-blue cravat striped in white and tied in a loose bow. In his hand he carried a hard-backed school book, and he wore a brown bowler with a flat brim.

His face was disquieting; pale and drawn, with quite regular features under long black hair, it was lit up by great liquid eyes, their blue-shadowed lids close to a nose stippled in gold by a few freckles; the mouth that opened beneath, though small, was bordered by thick lips divided down the centre with a groove, like a cherry.

Face to face, they stared at one another for a moment, then the young man lowered his eyes and came nearer; soon his arm brushed that of Des Esseintes, who slowed his pace as he thoughtfully considered the young man's mincing walk.

And, from this chance encounter, was born a mistrustful relationship which lasted for months; Des Esseintes could no longer think of it without a shudder; never had he submitted to a more seductive, more compelling servitude, never had he experienced such dangers, yet never had he felt more painfully fulfilled.

Among the recollections haunting him in his solitude, the memory of this mutual attachment dominated every other. All the leaven of frenzied passion that a brain over-excited by neurosis could contain was in a ferment; and, in this pleasure he found in memory, in this morose delectation, as theologians call the recollecting of former infamy, he interwove spiritual ardours with the physical visions, ardours sparked by his earlier readings of such casuists as Busembaum, Diana, Liguori, and Sanchez* on the topic of sins committed against the Sixth and Ninth Commandments of the Decalogue.

Religion, by engendering a divine ideal in that soul it had permeated, and which may have been predisposed to her influence by a heredity dating back to the reign of Henri III,* had also aroused in it the illegitimate ideal of sensual pleasure; obsessions both libertine and mystical mingled together, preying on a brain which was tormented by the obstinate desire to escape the crass pleasures of the world, to lose itself, at the opposite extreme from what custom consecrated, in original modes of ecstasy, in celestial or infernal excesses, both equally devastating because of the squandering of phosphorus they entailed.

Emerging, now, from these reveries, feeling drained, exhausted, half dead, he immediately lit the candles and the lamps, flooding himself with light, in the belief that then he would not hear, as clearly as he did in the dark, the muffled, persistent, intolerable sound of his arteries beating faster and faster beneath the skin of his neck.

10

In the course of that singular malady which wreaks havoc on exhausted family blood lines, the crises are followed by periods of sudden calm; without being able to understand why, one fine morning Des Esseintes woke up in excellent health; no more gut-wrenching cough, no more wedges being hammered into the back of his neck, but instead an ineffable feeling of well-being, a lightness in his brain where his thoughts were growing clearer and, instead of being glaucous and opaque, were becoming liquid and iridescent, like delicately tinted soap bubbles.

This state lasted several days; then suddenly, one afternoon, he began to experience hallucinations of his sense of smell.

The fragrance of frangipani filled his room; he checked to see whether a scent bottle might be lying about, unstoppered; there was no scent bottle in the room; he went into his study, into his dining-room: the smell persisted.

He rang for his servant: 'Can't you smell anything?' he asked. The man sniffed the air and declared he could not smell any kind of flower; there could be no doubt about it, the neurosis was returning once again, in the guise of a fresh delusion of the senses.

Wearied by the tenacity of this imaginary fragrance, he resolved to immerse himself in genuine perfumes, hoping that this nasal homeopathy would cure him or at any rate moderate the persistence of the intrusive frangipani.

He went into his dressing-room. There, beside an old font which now served him as a wash-basin, beneath a long mirror with a wrought-iron frame which imprisoned the green, lifeless waters of the glass like the stone rim of a well silvered by the moonlight, bottles of all sizes and shapes were arranged on ivory shelves.

Putting them on a table, he divided them into two groups; the simple perfumes, in other words extracts or essences, and the blends, known by the generic term bouquets. Then he sank into an armchair and collected his thoughts.

For many years now he had been expert in everything relating to olfactory science; he believed that the sense of smell could experience pleasures equal to those of hearing and sight, since every sense was capable, through natural aptitude and expert cultivation, of apprehending new impressions, multiplying them many times over, co-ordinating them, and with them composing that whole which constitutes a work of art; and, in a word, it was no more abnormal that an art of selecting aromatic fluids should exist, than other forms which separate out sound waves, or strike the retina of the eye with variously coloured rays of light; only, just as no one without a special intuitive gift, which has been developed through study, can distinguish a painting by a great master from a daub, a Beethoven melody from a tune of Clapisson's,* so no one can, without some preliminary instruction, avoid confusing, at first, a bouquet created by a true artist with a pot-pourri produced by a manufacturer for sale in grocery shops and bazaars.

There was one aspect of this art of perfumery which, more than any other, had always fascinated him: that of absolute accuracy in imitation.

Actually, perfumes are almost never produced from the flowers whose names they bear; the artist rash enough to borrow his raw material from nature alone would produce nothing but a spurious creation, without authenticity or style, since the essence obtained by distilling the flowers can furnish only a very remote, very coarse analogy with the authentic fragrance given off by the living flower growing in the ground.

Therefore, except for the inimitable jasmine, which does not admit of any counterfeit, any copy, any approximation even, all flowers are represented exactly by blends of alcohols and spirits, which usurp the very personality of the model, endowing it with that elusive something, that extra quality, that heady bouquet, that rare touch which is the stamp of a work of art.

In perfumery, in short, the artist perfects the original natural aroma by refashioning the scent and providing it with a setting, just as a jeweller improves a stone's transparency and lustre, and provides it with a mount to reveal its beauty.

Little by little, Des Esseintes had mastered the arcana of this, the most neglected of all arts, and he could now interpret its language, which was as rich and devious as that of literature, and which, beneath its fluctuating and ambiguous surface, was so incredibly concise in style.

To do this he had first had to study the grammar, master the syntax of aromas, fully assimilate the rules that control them, and once he was familiar with this dialect, compare one with another the works of the masters, the Atkinsons and the Lubins, the Chardins and the Violets, the Legrands and the Piesses,* analyse the construction of their sentences, weigh the proportions of their words and the structure of their periods.

Then, in this idiom of fluids, it was vital that theories—all too often trite and incomplete—be confirmed by experimentation.

Actually there was very little diversity, very little colour in classical perfumery, which had invariably been cast in moulds shaped by chemists in earlier times; it was in its dotage, confined to the old alembics of the past, when Romanticism dawned, bringing changes in perfumery as in other spheres, rejuvenating it, making it more flexible and more supple.

Its history paralleled, at every step, the history of our language. The Louis XIII fashion in perfumery, composed of elements the period held dear: orris-powder, musk, civet, and myrtle-water (already known as angel-water), barely sufficed to express the rakish graces, the somewhat crude colours of that age, which certain sonnets of Saint-Amand's* have preserved for us. Later, myrrh and frankincense, fragrances which are mystical, potent, and austere, could very nearly be seen as symbols of the oratorical language and the bold, stately, well-balanced style of Bossuet* and other masters of the pulpit; later still, the languid and erudite graces of French society under Louis XV found their representatives more easily, in frangipani and *maréchale*, which in a sense constitute the very synthesis of that period; after that, following the tedium and apathy of the First Empire, with its excessive use of eau-de-Cologne and rosemary, perfumery turned eagerly—in the wake of Victor Hugo and Gautier*—towards sun-drenched lands; it created its own Oriental poems, its pungent, spicy salaams, discovering fresh tonalities and antitheses of unexampled boldness, sifting through and selecting delicate variations from earlier times, rendering them more complex, more subtle, more varied; and finally it resolutely repudiated that wilful caducity to which it had been reduced by those vile poetasters the Malherbes, the Boileaus, the Andrieux, and the Baour-Lormians.*

But this language of perfumes had not remained stationary since the 1830s. It had evolved further and, following the march of the century, its progress had been similar to that of the other arts; this language too had listened to the pleas of artists and connoisseurs, immersing itself in Chinese and Japanese culture, devising scented albums, imitating the flower posies of Takeoka, obtaining, by a combination of lavender and clove, the aroma of the Rondeletia; by a marriage of patchouli and camphor, the singular aroma of China ink; by a blend of lemon, clove, and neroli, the emanations of the Hovenia of Japan.

Des Esseintes studied and analysed the soul of these fluids and elucidated these texts; he enjoyed and found personal satisfaction in playing the role of a psychologist, taking apart and reassembling the mechanism of a work, unscrewing the pieces that formed the structure of a composite aroma, and in so doing he had developed an almost infallibly accurate sense of smell.

Just as a wine merchant can recognize a vintage by the nose of a single drop; just as a hop-dealer can judge, by the smell of a sack, the exact value of its contents; just as a Chinese merchant can immediately name the place of origin of every tea he sniffs, can say in which plantations on the Bohea hills, in which Buddhist monasteries, it was grown, can give the date when its leaves were harvested, specify the degree of torrefaction to which the tea was subjected and the effect on it of contact with plum blossom, with the Aglaia, with the *Olea fragrans*, with all those perfumes used to modify its essence, to give an unexpected lift to its flavour, introducing into its rather dry bouquet a faintly musty hint of fresh, exotic flowers; in similar fashion Des Esseintes could, upon breathing in the merest trace of a scent, immediately tell you the proportions used in its composition, explain the psychology of its blending, practically name the artist who had created it and had imprinted upon it the characteristic stamp of his personal style.

It goes without saying that he possessed a collection of every single product used by professional perfumers; he even owned some genuine balsam of Mecca, that exceedingly rare balsam obtainable only in certain parts of Arabia Petraea, the monopoly of which is held by the Grand Turk.

Seated now at his table in his dressing-room, contemplating the creation of a new scent, he was overtaken by that momentary hesitation so familiar to writers who, after months of inactivity, prepare to embark once again upon a new work. Like Balzac, who was obsessed by a fierce need to blacken page after page simply in order to get his hand in, Des Esseintes felt an urge to brush up his expertise with a few trivial tasks: intending to make heliotrope, he weighed flasks of almond and vanilla, then, changing his mind, decided to tackle sweet pea.

Unable to recall the formula or the procedure, he experimented; the dominant element in the fragrance of this flower was unquestionably orange-blossom, so he tried various combinations, eventually achieving the exact tone by mixing the orange-blossom with some tuberose and some rose, and adding a drop of vanilla as a binding agent.

All his uncertainties disappeared; a little fever of excitement ran through him, and he felt ready for work; first he blended some more tea by combining cassia and iris and then, filled with confidence, he resolved to forge ahead, to strike a thunderous chord whose disdainful crash would drown the whispering of that wily frangipani, which was still sneaking stealthily into his room.

He worked with amber, Tonquin musk with its terrifying potency, and patchouli, the bitterest of the vegetable perfumes whose flower, in its natural state, gives off a mouldy, mildewy odour. No matter what he did, haunting visions of the eighteenth century obsessed him; panniered and flounced skirts whirled before his eyes; remembered visions of Boucher's* Venuses, all plump, boneless flesh, padded with rosy cotton-wool, installed themselves on his walls; recollections of the novel *Thémidore** with the exquisite Rosette, her skirts pulled high, fiery-red with blushing despair, pursued him. Furious, he rose to his feet, and to free himself breathed in, with all his might, that pure essence of spikenard which Orientals prize so highly and Europeans find so disagreeable because of its rather too-pronounced smell of valerian. The violence of this shock left him dazed. As if pounded by a hammer, the delicate filigree of the fragrance disappeared; he took advantage of this respite to escape from vanished centuries and outdated aromas and embark, just as he had been accustomed to do in earlier days, on less limited or more novel enterprises.

Long ago he had taken pleasure in lulling himself with perfumed harmonies; he used effects analogous to those employed by poets, imitating, in a sense, the admirable ordering of certain works of Baudelaire's, for example *L'Irréparable* and *Le Balcon*, in which the last of the five lines that make up the verse echoes the first and, returning like a refrain, drowns the soul in a measureless ocean of melancholy and languor. Lost in the dreams that these fragrant stanzas evoked for him, he was suddenly recalled to his point of departure, to the reason for his musings, by the return of the opening theme, which reappeared at carefully determined intervals in the aromatic orchestration of the poem.

His present desire was to wander at will in an unpredictable, ever-changing landscape, and he began with a phrase that was sonorous and full, and afforded him a sudden glimpse of an immense stretch of countryside.

With his vaporizers, he injected into the room an essence composed of ambrosia, Mitcham lavender, sweet pea, and a mixed bouquet, an essence which, when distilled by an artist, does deserve the name it has been given—'extract of meadow flowers'; next, he introduced into this meadow a precisely measured blend of tuberose, orange blossom, and almond blossom, whereupon artificial lilacs instantly appeared, while linden trees swayed in the breeze, shedding their pale efflorescence (mimicked by the London extract of tilia) on to the ground.

With this setting roughed out in a few bold strokes, and stretching, beneath his closed eyelids, far into the distance, he sprayed his room with a light mist of human, half-feline essences, redolent of skirts, heralding the appearance of powdered and rouged womankind: stephanotis, ayapana, opopanax, chypre, champaka, sarcanthus, which he overlaid with a trace of syringa, so as to add to the suggestion they exuded of a life of artifice and make-up, a natural fragrance of sweat-drenched laughter and joyful sunlit revelries.

Next he let these waves of fragrance escape through a ventilator, retaining only the country scents which he renewed, increasing the dose to ensure that they would return again like the verses of a ritornello.

Little by little the women had vanished; the countryside had grown deserted; then, on the magic horizon, factories with enormous chimneys rose up, their tops flaming like bowls of punch.

Now, on the breeze which he was creating by means of fans, there came a breath of factories and chemical products, while nature continued to emit her sweet exhalations into this pestilential atmosphere.

In his hand Des Esseintes held a pellet of styrax and, as he warmed it between his fingers, a very strange odour filled the room, an odour which was both nauseating and exquisite, evoking the delicious scent of the jonquil and the foul stench of gutta-percha and coal tar. He cleansed his hands, placed the resin in a hermetically sealed box, and the factories, in their turn, disappeared. He then squirted a few drops of 'New-mown Hay' perfume among the now revived fragrances of lime-trees and meadows, and in the middle of the magic landscape—temporarily divested of its lilacs—haystacks appeared, ushering in a new season, releasing their exquisite emanations into the scented summer air.

Finally, when he had sufficiently savoured this spectacle, he quickly scattered some exotic perfumes about, used up what remained in his vaporizers, intensified his concentrated essences, and gave free rein to all his balms, so that a demented, sublimated nature exploded into the intolerably hot and stuffy room, a nature whose ever more powerful exhalations loaded the artificial breeze with frenetic alcoholates, a fraudulent, charming nature, utterly paradoxical, combining the spices of the tropics and the peppery whiffs of Chinese sandalwood and Jamaican hediosmia with the French fragrances of jasmine, hawthorn, and verbena and producing, in defiance of seasons and of climates, trees with different aromas and flowers of totally contrasting colours and fragrances, creating by the fusion and the opposition of all these tones, a collective perfume, nameless, unexpected, and strange, in which there reappeared, like a persistent refrain, the ornamental opening phrase, the scent of the great meadow fanned by the lilacs and the lime trees.

Suddenly he felt a sharp stabbing pain, as though a drill were boring into his temples. Opening his eyes, he found himself back in his dressing-room, seated at his table; he staggered in bewilderment over to the window which he set ajar. A gust of air cleared the stifling atmosphere that enveloped him; he walked around the room to steady his legs, gazing, as he went back and forth, at the ceiling where crabs and salt-encrusted seaweed stood out in relief against a grainy background as golden as the sand on a beach; a similar décor covered the skirting-boards below the panelling, which was hung with Japanese crêpe of a watery green, faintly crumpled to simulate the rippled surface of a wind-blown river; floating in this light current was a single rose petal, round which swam a swarm of tiny fishes, sketched with a couple of strokes of the pen.

But his eyelids were still heavy; he stopped pacing up and down the narrow space between the font and the bath-tub, and leaned upon the window-sill; his giddiness disappeared; he carefully replaced the stoppers in the scent-bottles, then grasped the opportunity to remedy the disorder in his supply of cosmetics. He had not touched this since his arrival at Fontenay, and he felt something akin to astonishment on again seeing this collection which had once been examined by so many women. Flasks and jars were piled up one upon the other. Here was a *famille verte* porcelain container of schnouda, that marvellous white cream which, once it is spread on the cheeks, changes, through exposure to the air, to a soft pink then to a rosiness so real that it creates a totally convincing illusion of flushed cheeks; there, laquered jars encrusted with mother of pearl held Japanese gold or Athens green, the colours of the cantharides' wing, golds and greens which transmute to a deep purple as soon as they are wetted; next to pots full of filbert paste, of cold cream, of Kashmir-lily emulsions, of strawberry and elder-flower lotions for the complexion, and alongside little bottles filled with solutions of China ink and rose-water for the eyes, lay an assortment of instruments in ivory, mother-of-pearl, steel, and silver, mixed up with alfalfa brushes for the gums: tweezers, scissors, strigils, stumps, crimpers, powder-puffs, back-scratchers, beauty spots, and files.

He fingered all these gadgets, bought long ago at the urging of a mistress who would go into raptures over particular aromatics and balms; an unbalanced, nervous woman who liked to have her nipples soaked in perfume, but who in actuality only experienced exquisite, overpowering ecstasy when her scalp was being scraped with a comb or when she could inhale, while they were making love, the smell of soot, or of the rain-soaked plaster of unfinished new houses, or of dust spattered by heavy raindrops during summer storms.

As he pondered these memories, he recalled an afternoon spent— out of idleness and curiosity—at Pantin, in the company of this woman, at the home of one of her sisters; this recollection stirred up within him a forgotten world of old ideas and ancient perfumes; while the two women were chattering and showing each other their gowns, he had gone over to the window and, through its dusty panes, had seen the muddy road stretching away into the distance, and heard the paving stones resound under the incessant impact of galoshes splashing through the puddles.

This scene from the distant past came to him suddenly, with extraordinary vividness. Pantin lay before him, bustling with activity and life, in the green, dead-seeming waters of his moonlight-framed mirror into which his unconscious gaze plunged: a hallucination carried him far from Fontenay; the mirror gave him back not only the reflection of the street but also of the thoughts which that street had once evoked and, sunk in a dream, he repeated to himself that ingenious antiphon—melancholy yet consoling—which he had immediately written down upon returning to Paris.

'Yes, the season of heavy rains is here: under the pavements, the down-spouts spew forth their melodious burdens; horse-dung steeps in the bowls of milky coffee that hollow the macadam; foot-baths are available everywhere for the use of the lowly passer-by.

'Beneath the lowering sky, in the clammy air, the walls of the houses sweat black filth, their air-shafts stink; the disgust of existing is ever more acute, the spleen more overpowering; the seeds of vice which lie in every man germinate; cravings for gross pleasures torment the abstinent and the minds of well-regarded citizens beget criminal desires.

'And yet I am warming myself at a good fire, while a basket of flowers blooming on the table fills the room with the scent of benzoin, geranium, and vetiver. In the middle of November, in Pantin, in the Rue de Paris, it is still spring, and privately I enjoy a laugh, thinking of the faint-hearted families who, to avoid the approach of winter, scurry away at top speed to Antibes or to Cannes.

'Harsh nature has no part in this extraordinary phenomenon; it must be clearly understood that it is to industry alone that Pantin* owes this artificial spring.

'In fact, these flowers are made of taffeta and mounted on brass wire, while the spring fragrance comes filtering in through the joints in the window-frame, emitted by local factories where the Pinaud and Saint-James perfumes are manufactured.

'For the craftsman worn out by the hard labours of the workshops, for the lowly clerk burdened by too many offspring, the illusion of breathing a little good clean air is, thanks to these manufacturers, a possibility.

'Moreover, this fabulous counterfeit countryside can yield an intelligent medical treatment: those consumptive libertines who are exiled to the South die there, killed off by the break with their habits, by nostalgia for the Parisian excesses which destroyed them. Here, in an artificial climate maintained by open stoves, licentious memories will reappear in a sweetly attenuated form, thanks to the languid feminine emanations issuing from the perfume factories. In place of the deadly boredom of life in the provinces, the doctor, by this deception, can provide his patient with a Platonic substitute, the atmosphere of the Paris brothels and their prostitutes. In most cases, in order to effect a complete cure, it will suffice if the patient has a fairly fertile imagination.

'Since, the way things are today, nothing remains that is pure and authentic, since the wine we drink and the liberty we proclaim are both adulterated and derisory, since, in short, it requires an uncommonly large dose of goodwill to believe that the ruling classes are worthy of respect and the lower classes worthy of succour and compassion, I do not', concluded Des Esseintes, 'consider it either more ridiculous or more insane to ask of my fellow men a degree of illusion barely as great as that which he expends each day for absurd purposes, to imagine that the town of Pantin is an artificial Nice, an imitation Menton.

'That's all well and good,' he said, interrupted in these reflections by an overwhelming sensation of bodily weakness, 'but I'm going to have to be very wary of these delicious, detestable activities which utterly drain me.' He sighed: 'Well, that means more pleasures to curtail, more precautions to take'; and he sought refuge in his study, thinking that by so doing he would more easily escape the haunting presence of those perfumes.

He pushed the window wide open, glad of the cleansing gusts of fresh air; but, suddenly, it seemed to him that the breeze was wafting in a rising wave of oil of bergamot, blended with essence of jasmine, cassia, and rose-water. He gave a gasp, wondering whether he might not be in the power of one of those evil spirits which, in the Middle Ages, people had exorcised. The odour changed, transforming itself, but persisting. An indeterminate aroma of tincture of tolu, of Peruvian balsam, of saffron, bound by a few drops of amber and of musk, was rising, now, from the village which lay at the bottom of the hill, and then suddenly the metamorphosis took place, those disparate traces blended together and once again frangipani, the elements of which his sense of smell had discerned and analysed, spread from the valley of Fontenay up to the fort, assaulting his over-taxed nostrils, discomposing afresh his ruined nerves, and throwing him into such a state of prostration that he collapsed in a faint, close to death, on to the wooden sill of the window.

11

The servants hurried off in alarm to fetch the Fontenay doctor, who could make nothing whatever of Des Esseintes's condition. He stammered out a few medical terms, felt the patient's pulse, examined his tongue, tried in vain to make him speak, prescribed sedatives and rest, promised to return on the morrow, and then, at a sign of refusal from Des Esseintes (now sufficiently restored to reprove his servants for their zeal and to dismiss this intruder), the doctor departed, to report to the entire village on the eccentricities of this house, whose furnishings had left him dumbfounded, paralysed with shock.

To the great astonishment of his servants who now did not dare stir from their pantry, their master recovered in a few days; and, encountering him unexpectedly, they found him drumming his fingers on the windowpanes and gazing uneasily at the sky.

One afternoon Des Esseintes rang the bell sharply and ordered that his trunks be packed for a long journey.

While the husband and wife were selecting, under his instructions, the appropriate items to pack, he was pacing feverishly up and down his dining cabin, consulting the times of the packet boats, and then striding into his study, where he continued to scrutinize the clouds with an air at once impatient and pleased. For a week now the weather had been atrocious. Across the grey plains of the sky, rivers of soot were endlessly rolling mass upon mass of clouds, like so many boulders torn up from the earth. From time to time a heavy downpour would break out, submerging the valley in torrents of rain.

On that particular day the appearance of the sky had changed. The ink-black floods had vaporized and dried up, the jagged edges of the clouds had melted away; the sky, under a nubilous film, was completely flat. Little by little this film seemed to be moving nearer, and a watery mist enveloped the countryside; the rain was no longer crashing down in cascades as on the preceding day, but instead was falling incessantly, fine, penetrating, stinging, liquefying the garden paths, turning the roads into a swamp, linking earth to sky with its innumerable threads; the light was growing murky; a livid glow lit up the village which was transformed, now, into a lake of mud stippled by the needle-sharp raindrops which pitted the muddy liquid of the puddles with drops of quicksilver; in this desolation of nature, all the colours had faded, so that only the roofs were glistening above the lack-lustre tones of the walls.

'What weather!' sighed the old manservant, putting on to a chair the clothes his master had asked for, a suit made for him in London some time ago.

Des Esseintes's sole response was to rub his hands together, and settle down before a glass-fronted bookcase where a fan-shaped assortment of silk socks was displayed; he hesitated over the shade and then, observing the gloom of the day, the drab monochrome of his outfit, thinking of the object of this enterprise, he quickly chose a pair in dingy green silk, hurriedly slipped them on, put on a pair of buckled high-lows,* then the suit—a mousy grey checked in a darker grey and flecked with brown—placed a small bowler on his head, enveloped himself in a flax-blue Inverness cape, and, followed by his servant bent double under the weight of a trunk, an expanding suitcase, a carpet-bag, a hat box, and various umbrellas and walking-sticks wrapped in a travelling rug, made his way to the station. There he informed his servant that he could not specify the date of his return, that he would be back in a year, in a month, in a week, perhaps sooner, ordered that nothing in the house should be disturbed, handed over the approximate sum of money needed to run the household during his absence, and climbed into a carriage, leaving the old man standing behind the barrier in bewilderment, his arms dangling and his mouth agape, as the train moved off.

He was alone in his compartment; a blurred and dirty countryside, seen as though through an aquarium filled with murky water, raced away at top speed behind the string of rain-lashed carriages. Sunk in thought, Des Esseintes closed his eyes.

Once again, this solitude, which he had desired so ardently and finally obtained, had resulted in dreadful anguish; this silence which he used to think of as compensation for the inanities he had listened to for years, now weighed him down like an intolerable burden. He had awakened one morning feeling as agitated as a prisoner who has been locked in a cell; his trembling lips attempted to articulate sounds, his eyes filled with tears, and he had difficulty breathing, like someone who had been sobbing for hours on end.

Consumed by a longing to walk about, to gaze upon a human face, to talk to another human being, to be part of ordinary life, he went so far as to try to detain his servants, having summoned them on some pretext; but conversation was impossible, for not only had these old people been rendered almost mute by years of silence and sick-room routines, but the distance at which Des Esseintes had always kept them was such as to discourage them from opening their mouths. Besides, they were slow-witted and incapable of giving anything but monosyllabic answers to questions they were asked.

He could not, therefore, find any kind of help or relief with them; but now a new phenomenon was manifesting itself. The novels of Dickens which he had recently read to calm his nerves, and whose sole effect had been the opposite of that improvement in health he had been hoping for, began slowly to act upon him in an unexpected manner, evoking visions of English life which he would mull over for hours; little by little, into these imaginary musings, there crept ideas of a specific reality, of a journey accomplished, of dreams confirmed, and these were joined by a longing to experience fresh impressions and thus escape from the exhausting extravagances of a mind that was growing dazed with operating in a vacuum.

This appallingly foggy and rainy weather further encouraged these thoughts, by intensifying the memories of his reading, by constantly placing before his eyes the image of a land of mist and mud, by preventing his desires from deviating from their point of origin, from straying from their source.

Suddenly, one day, he could stand it no longer, and made up his mind. His haste was such that he made his getaway far too early, longing to escape from the present, to feel himself jostled about in the hurly-burly of the streets, in the din of the crowds and the railway station.

'Now I can breathe,' he told himself as the train waltzed to a halt under the dome of the terminus at Sceaux, timing its final pirouettes by the staccato racket of the turntables.

Once out in the street, on the Boulevard d'Enfer, he hailed a cab, revelling in the way he was encumbered by his trunks and rugs. By promising a generous tip, he came to an understanding with the cabby, who was sporting nut-brown trousers and red waistcoat: 'I'll pay by the hour,' he said; 'stop in the Rue de Rivoli, in front of *Galignani's Messenger*';* for he planned to buy, before departing, a Baedeker or Murray* guide to London.

The cab lumbered off, its wheels sending up arcs of muddy spray;

they were driving straight through a swamp; beneath the grey sky, which seemed to be resting on the roofs of the houses, water was streaming down the walls from top to bottom, the gutters were overflowing, the paving stones were coated with mud the colour of gingerbread, in which passers-by were sliding about; as the omnibuses swept closely by, the people crowding the pavements came to a halt, and women, bending low under their umbrellas and pulling their skirts up to their knees, flattened themselves against the shop-fronts to avoid being splashed.

The rain came slanting in through the windows; Des Esseintes had to pull up the panes which were streaked by the streaming water, while spatters of mire radiated out like fireworks from every side of the cab. To the accompaniment of the monotonous sound of the rain drumming on the trunks and on the vehicle's roof, like so many bags of peas being shaken about above his head, Des Esseintes pondered over his trip; this dreadful weather was already an instalment of England that he was being paid in Paris; a rain-swept, gigantic, measureless London, stinking of heated metal and soot, smoking everlastingly in the fog, was unfolding now before his gaze; then a succession of docks stretched out as far as the eye could see, filled with cranes, and winches, and bales, swarming with men perched on masts and sitting astride spars, while down on the wharfs countless others, heads down and bottoms in the air, bent low over barrels that they were rolling into the cellars.

All this activity was taking place on the waterfront, and in vast warehouses washed by the dark, scummy waters of an imaginary Thames, amid a forest of masts, a thicket of beams which pierced the sky's leaden clouds; high up, on the skyline, trains were racing along at full speed, and down below, in the sewers, other trains were running, emitting hideous shrieks and belching forth clouds of smoke through the shaft openings, while along all the boulevards and streets—where, in an eternal twilight, blazed the monstrous, garish depravities of advertising—streams of carriages flowed between two columns of silent, preoccupied pedestrians who stared straight ahead as they walked, their elbows pressed to their sides.

Des Esseintes shivered with pleasure at feeling himself part of this terrible world of commerce, isolated by this fog, caught up in this incessant activity, in this pitiless machinery which ground down millions of hapless wretches, whom philanthropists, by way of consolation, encouraged to recite verses from the Scriptures and sing psalms.

Then, the vision vanished suddenly as the cab gave a jolt that bumped him about on the seat. He looked out of the windows; night had fallen; the gas lamps, ringed by yellowish haloes, flickered in the thick of the fog; strings of lights swam in the puddles and seemed to encircle the wheels of the carriages as they bounced along through the filthy liquid fire; he tried to see where he was, caught a glimpse of the Arc du Carrousel, and suddenly, for no apparent reason, perhaps as a simple reaction to returning to earth from those imaginary places, his thoughts travelled back in time, to the memory of a trivial incident; he recalled that his servant, whom he had watched packing the trunks, had failed to include a toothbrush among the utensils in his toilet case; so then he mentally checked through the list of what had been packed; everything had been put into his case, but the annoyance of having left this toothbrush out remained with him until the driver stopped the cab, and interrupted the sequence of these reminiscences and regrets.

He was in the Rue de Rivoli, outside *Galignani's Messenger*. Separated by a door of frosted glass covered with notices, and laden with passepartout-framed newspaper cuttings and blue telegraph forms, two huge shop-windows were filled to overflowing with picture-albums and books. He drew closer, attracted by the sight of those paper-board bindings in bright blue or cabbage-green, embossed, along all the seams, with silver and gold arabesques, and of those cloth covers in light brown, leek-green, pale yellowish green, and currant-red, stamped with black fillets on the back and sides. There was something anti-Parisian to all this, a commercial character that was brasher yet somehow not as contemptible as that of cheaply produced French bindings; here and there, among the open albums displaying copies of comic scenes by du Maurier or John Leech,* or catapulting Caldecott's* unruly cavalcades across badly coloured plains, a few French novels could be seen, blending their benign, self-satisfied vulgarity with this verjuice of hues.

Tearing himself away, eventually, from this sight, he pushed open the door and entered a vast bookshop, full of people; foreign ladies sat unfolding maps and chattering away in strange tongues. An assistant brought him a whole collection of guides. He too sat down, turning over these books whose flexible bindings bent in his hands.

He leafed through them, stopping at a page in Baedeker that described the museums of London. He found the brief, precise details given in the guide interesting, but then his attention shifted from the early English painting to the modern, which appealed to him more. He recalled several examples he had seen in international exhibitions and thought that he might see them again in London: paintings by Millais, such as *The Eve of St Agnes*,* with its moon-silvered green tones; some oddly coloured works by Watts,* speckled with gamboge and indigo, pictures that had been sketched by the hand of an ailing Gustave Moreau, painted in by an anaemic Michaelangelo, and then touched up by a blue-obsessed Raphael; among other canvases, he remembered a *Curse of Cain*, an *Ida*, and several versions of *Eve*, where, in the peculiar, mysterious amalgam of those three masters, one could sense the personality—at once sublimated and crude—of a learned, dreamy Englishman, tormented by a fixation on hideous colours.

All these pictures crowded together, battering at his memory. The assistant, startled to see this customer sitting lost in thought at a table, asked him which guide he had selected. Des Esseintes looked at him in bewilderment, then apologized, purchased a Baedeker, and left the shop. Outside it was wet and icy cold; the wind was blowing from the side, whipping the arcades with its stinging rain. 'Drive over there,' he told the cabby, pointing to a shop at the end of an arcade, on the corner of the Rue de Rivoli and the Rue Castiglione. Its whitish panes were lit from inside so that it resembled a gigantic nightlight burning in the sickliness of that fog, in the misery of that pestilential weather.

This was the 'Bodega'. Des Esseintes wandered into a huge room which stretched on and on like a passage, supported by pillars of cast iron, its walls lined along both sides with tall, upright casks on stands.

Girdled by iron hoops, the belly of each cask was encircled with a notched wooden band like a pipe-rack, from which hung tulip-shaped glasses, stem in air. The casks, their lower sections pierced by openings with stoneware spigots connected to them, were emblazoned with the royal arms and bore coloured labels displaying the name of their vineyard, the amount of wine they contained, and its price, whether bought by the cask or by the bottle, or drunk by the glass.

In the space left vacant between these rows of casks, under the hissing gas-jets of a hideous chandelier painted iron-grey, stood a succession of tables laden with baskets of Palmers' biscuits and stale, salty cakes, and with heaped-up plates of mince-pies and sandwiches that concealed, beneath their bland exteriors, fiery mustard poultices; beside them was a hedge of chairs reaching right to the rear of this cellar where yet more hogsheads were visible, bearing on their lids small barrels which lay on their sides and were stamped with names branded into the oak.

A smell of alcohol smote Des Esseintes as he took a seat in this room where strong wines lay slumbering. He looked around: near him stood a row of tuns, with labels naming the entire range of ports: harsh or fruity wines, mahogany or amaranthine in colour, distinguished by laudatory designations: 'Old Port', 'Light Delicate', 'Cockburn's Very Fine', 'Magnificent Old Regina'; over there, thrusting out their formidable bellies, enormous casks stood shoulder to shoulder, containing the martial wines of Spain, sherry and its derivatives, the colour of pale or dark topaz, wines both sweet and dry: San Lucar, Vino de Pasto, Pale Dry, Oloroso, Amontillado.

The cellar was packed; leaning on the corner of a table, Des Esseintes waited for the glass of port he had ordered from an English barman busy opening explosive bottles of soda, whose oval shape recalled, though on a much bigger scale, those gelatin and gluten capsules pharmacists use to mask the taste of certain medicines.

Englishmen swarmed around him: ungainly, pasty-faced clergymen, dressed from head to foot in black, with soft hats, laced-up shoes, interminably long overcoats studded with tiny buttons down the chest, clean-shaven chins, round spectacles, and lank greasy locks; men with coarse, pork-butcher faces, others with bulldog snouts, apoplectic necks, tomato-like ears, bibulous cheeks, bloodshot, moronic eyes and fringe-like whiskers such as one sees on some large apes; further away, at the far end of the wine-cellar, a tall, lanky, tow-headed idler, his chin sprouting white hairs like an artichoke heart, was using a magnifying glass to decipher the minute print of an English newspaper; opposite him some kind of American naval officer, squat and stout, with swarthy skin and bulbous nose and a cigar stuck in the hairy orifice of his mouth, was nodding off while gazing at the framed advertisements hanging on the walls for the wines of Champagne—the labels of Perrier and Roederer, Heidsieck and Mumm, and (adorned with the hooded head of a monk) the name in Gothic script of Dom Pérignon, of Reims.

Overcome by a kind of languor in this guardroom atmosphere, and dazed by the chatter of the Englishmen as they conversed, Des Esseintes let his mind drift, picturing, under the influence of the crimson tints of the port wine filling the glasses, the Dickensian characters who so enjoyed drinking it, and in his imagination populating the cellar with quite different beings, seeing here the white hair and fiery complexion of Mr Wickfield,* there, the cold, cunning expression and implacable eye of Mr Tulkinghorn,* the lugubrious solicitor of *Bleak House*. These characters were actually emerging from his memory and installing themselves, complete with all their exploits, in the Bodega; for his recollections, revived by his recent reading, were uncannily exact. The city of the novels, the well-lit, well-heated, well-cared-for, well-ordered houses of the novels, where bottles of wine were being unhurriedly poured out by Little Dorrit, by Dora Copperfield, by Tom Pinch's sister,* appeared to him in the form of a cosy ark sailing through a flood of mud and soot. He settled down comfortably in this fictional London, happy to be indoors, listening to the sepulchral hooting of the tugs travelling down the Thames, behind the Tuileries, near the bridge. His glass was empty; despite the warm fug that filled this cellar, which the fumes of cigars and pipes made still stuffier, he gave, as he suddenly returned to the reality of this foul-smelling wet weather, a little shiver.

He asked for a glass of Amontillado, but then, in the presence of this dry, pale wine, the gentle lenitives, the soothing stories of the English author vanished and in their place appeared the harsh revulsives, the painful skin irritants of Edgar Allan Poe; the chilling nightmare of the cask of Amontillado,* of a man walled up in an underground vault, gripped hold of his mind; the kindly, commonplace faces of the American and English drinkers filling the room seemed to him to mirror involuntary, monstrous thoughts, and unconscious, abominable designs; then he noticed that people were leaving and that the dinner hour was at hand; he paid, dragged himself from his chair, and, his head swimming, made for the door.

The instant he set foot outside, the rain smacked him in the face; the gas lamps, inundated by the drenching, gusting rain, fluttered their tiny fans of flame without casting any light; the clouds had moved down even lower and now hung round the bellies of the houses. Des Esseintes gazed at the arcades of the Rue de Rivoli, sunk in shadows and submerged in water, and it seemed to him that he was standing in the dismal tunnel dug under the Thames; hunger pangs in his stomach brought him back to reality; he returned to his cab, tossed the driver the address of the tavern in the Rue d'Amsterdam,* near the station, and consulted his watch: it was seven o'clock. He had just enough time for dinner; the train did not leave until 8:50 and, counting on his fingers, he calculated the hours the crossing from Dieppe to Newhaven would take, telling himself: 'If the times given in the guide are correct, I shall be in London at exactly half-past twelve tomorrow.'

The cab drew up outside the tavern; once again Des Esseintes got out and entered a long hall decorated in brown paint without any gilding, and divided by waist-high partitions into a series of compartments like the loose boxes in a stable. This room, which widened out near the door, had a large number of beer pumps set up on a counter, alongside some hams as well-seasoned as the wood of an old violin, lobsters the colour of red lead, and soused mackerel which, with slices of onion and raw carrot, pieces of lemon, bunches of bay leaves and thyme, juniper berries and peppercorns, were swimming in a murky-looking sauce.

One of the stalls was empty. He took possession of it and hailed a young man in a black suit, who bowed and jabbered at him in an incomprehensible tongue. While his place was being laid, Des Esseintes studied his neighbours; just as in the Bodega, islanders with china-blue eyes, purple faces, and pensive or arrogant expressions were glancing through foreign newspapers, only here there were some pairs of unaccompanied women dining on their own, sturdy Englishwomen with boyish faces, oversized teeth, apple-red cheeks, long hands and long feet. They were attacking a beefsteak pie with unfeigned zest; this is a hot dish of meat cooked in a mushroom sauce and then covered, like a pie, by a pastry crust.

After having had no appetite for so long, he was disconcerted by the sight of these strapping females whose voracity whetted his own hunger. He ordered oxtail soup, and really relished this concoction which is at one and the same time rich, smooth, greasy, and substantial; then he studied the list of fish and asked for smoked haddock, which is like smoked cod, and he thought looked good;

then, his appetite sharpened by watching others gorge, he ate some sirloin with potatoes, and downed two pints of ale, spurred on by that faint musky flavour of the byre exuded by this fine pale beer.

His appetite now almost satisfied, he picked at a piece of sweetly-sharp blue Stilton, nibbled on some rhubarb tart, and, for a change, quenched his thirst with porter, that black beer which tastes of sugarless liquorice.

He drew breath; it was years since he had stuffed himself like that or drunk so much; this change in his habits, this choice of unfamiliar, filling food had awakened his stomach from its slumber. He settled back in his chair, lit a cigarette and prepared to enjoy his coffee which he laced with gin.

The rain was still falling; he could hear it pattering on the glass roof at the back of the room and pouring in cascades down the water-spouts; inside, no one was stirring; they were all pampering themselves, just as he was, sitting in the dry with little glasses of spirits before them.

Tongues were loosening; as almost all the English were casting their eyes up as they talked, Des Esseintes concluded that they were discussing the bad weather; not one of them was laughing, and they were all dressed in grey cheviot striped in nankeen yellow and blotting-paper pink. He cast a delighted glance at his own clothes, the colour and cut of which did not differ in any obvious way from those of his neighbours, and he knew the satisfaction of not looking out of place in these surroundings, of being, as it were, in a superficial way, a naturalized Londoner; then he gave a start: 'Is it time for the train?' he wondered. He looked at his watch: 'Ten minutes to eight; I can stay here for almost another half-hour'; and, once again, his thoughts returned to the plan he had formed.

In the course of his sedentary life only two countries had ever appealed to him: Holland and England.

He had satisfied the first of these desires; one fine day, unable to resist any longer, he had left Paris and visited, one after another, the cities of the Netherlands. On the whole, this trip had left him bitterly disillusioned. He had imagined a Holland like that painted by Teniers and Jan Steen, Rembrandt and Van Ostade, picturing in advance, for his own personal enjoyment, ghettoes of superb-looking Jews as sun-tanned as cordovan leather; visualizing prodigious fairs and perpetual drunken revelries in the country villages, expecting to find the patriarchal geniality, the jovial over-indulgence celebrated by the Old Masters.

True, he had indeed found Haarlem and Amsterdam captivating; the peasants, seen in all their crude rusticity out in the actual countryside, undoubtedly resembled those painted by Van Ostade, with their coarse, rough-hewn brats and their monstrously fat old women, all bulging breasts and bellies; but of unbridled merriment or domestic tippling, not a sign; in a word, as he was obliged to admit, the Dutch School* of the Louvre had misled him; it had simply provided him with a springboard for his dreams; he had cast himself off, bounding forward along a false trail and wandering off into unattainable dreams, not finding anywhere on earth that magical, genuine countryside he had hoped for, never ever seeing, on meadows strewn with wine casks, village men and women dancing, their faces streaming with happy tears as they jumped for joy, and laughing so much that they wet their skirts and breeches.

No, certainly, there was nothing like that to be seen; Holland was a country like any other and, furthermore, a country that was not in the least primitive or artlessly good-natured, for in Holland the prevailing religion was Protestantism, with its rigid hypocrisy and solemn inflexibility.

He recalled his disillusionment; again he consulted his watch; he still had ten minutes before the train departed. 'It's high time to ask for the bill and leave,' he told himself. His stomach felt heavy and his whole body was filled with the most extreme lethargy. 'Come on,' he said to get up his courage, 'I'll have one for the road', and, calling for his account, he filled a glass with brandy. An individual dressed in black carrying a napkin over his arm, a kind of major-domo with a bald, pointed head, a greying, wiry beard, no moustache, and with a pencil behind his ear, came up and, standing with one leg forward like a singer, drew a notebook from his pocket; then, without looking at the paper, but gazing at a spot on the ceiling beside a chandelier, he wrote out and added up the cost of the meal. 'Here you are, sir,' he said, tearing the page from his notebook, and handing it to Des Esseintes who was staring at him curiously, as if he were some rare animal. What an unexpected John Bull, he thought, as he contemplated this phlegmatic creature whose clean-shaven mouth made him look vaguely like a signalman in the American navy.

At that moment the door of the tavern opened; some people came in bringing with them a smell of wet dog mingled with coal fumes which the wind blew back into the kitchen as its unlatched door banged; Des Esseintes felt incapable of moving his legs; a gentle, warm languor was flowing through his limbs, and even preventing him from stretching out his hand to light a cigar. He kept telling himself: 'Come on now, on your feet, you must hurry'; but instantly there would be objections to gainsay his commands. What was the point of moving, when one could travel so splendidly just sitting in a chair? Wasn't he in London now, surrounded by London's smells, atmosphere, inhabitants, food, utensils? What therefore could he expect, other than fresh disappointments, as in Holland?

He had just time to hurry to the station, and an immense distaste for the journey, a pressing need to remain quietly where he was, were making themselves felt with ever greater urgency, ever greater persistence. Lost in thought, he let the minutes slip past, thus cutting off his retreat, telling himself: 'Now I'd have to dash to the barrier, deal with the luggage in a great rush; what a bore! What a business that would be!' Then he told himself once again: 'In fact, I've experienced and I've seen what I wanted to experience and see. Ever since leaving home I've been steeped in English life;* I would be insane to risk losing, by an ill-advised journey, these unforgettable impressions. After all, what kind of aberration was this, that I should be tempted to renounce long-held convictions, and disdain the compliant fantasies of my mind, that I should, like some complete simpleton, have believed that a journey was necessary, or could hold novelty or interest?' He looked at his watch; 'It's time I went home,' he said, and this time he got to his feet, went outside, and ordered the cab driver to drive him back to the station at Sceaux, and he returned to Fontenay with his trunks, packages, suitcases, rugs, umbrellas, and walking sticks, feeling as physically exhausted and morally spent as a man who comes home after a long and hazardous journey.

12

During the days following his return home, Des Esseintes turned his attention to his books, and, at the thought that he might have been separated from them for a long period, he experienced a satisfaction as real as what he would have felt had he come back to them after a genuine absence. Under the influence of this feeling, his books seemed new to him, for he discovered beauties in them which he had forgotten about during the years since he had first acquired them.

Everything—books, knick-knacks, furniture—held a special charm in his eyes; his bed seemed softer, compared with the bed he would have occupied in London; he found the discreet and silent attentions of his servants delightful, exhausted as he was by the mere thought of the noisy loquacity of hotel waiters; the methodical organization of his life seemed all the more desirable, now that the randomness of travel was a possibility.

He steeped himself afresh in this bath of habit, to which artificial regrets added a more bracing, more invigorating quality.

But what principally engaged his attention was his books. He examined them, then replaced them on the shelves, checking to make sure that, since his arrival at Fontenay, heat and rain had not damaged their bindings or spotted their priceless paper.

He began by going through his entire Latin library, then rearranged the specialist treatises by Archelaüs, Albertus Magnus, Raymond Lull, and Arnaud de Villanova,* which dealt with the cabbala and the occult sciences; next he inspected his modern books, one at a time, and discovered to his joy that they were all in perfect, dry condition.

This collection had cost him considerable sums of money: for in actuality he could not bear to see, on his own shelves, those authors he treasured represented by editions similar to those he saw in other men's libraries, printed on rag paper, in clumsy, hobnailed lettering.

In Paris, in the past, he had had certain books typeset for him personally, hiring special workers to print them on hand-presses; sometimes he would call on the services of Perrin of Lyons,* whose slender, pure lettering was suited to reprinting old texts in the original archaic form; sometimes he would have new type sent from

England or America for printing books of the current century; sometimes be would turn to a company in Lille which for hundreds of
years had owned a complete font of Gothic characters; sometimes,
indeed, he would commandeer the old Enschedé printing-works at
Haarlem, whose foundry still possesses the stamps and matrices of
the type known as *lettres de civilité*.

And he had obtained his paper by similar methods. Realizing, one
fine day, that he was tired of the available varieties—glazed from
China, pearly gold from Japan, white from Whatmans, unbleached
from Holland, or dyed buff from Turkey and the Seychal mills, and
disgusted with the machine-made product, he had ordered special
hand-made papers from the old mills at Vire, where they still used
the pestles that had once served to beat the hemp. In order to introduce a little variety into his collection he had on several occasions
had paper with special finishes—flocked or rep—sent from London,
and, to underscore his contempt for bibliophiles, a merchant in
Lübeck made him a superior kind of candle-spill paper, bluish,
crackly, rather stiff, in which the straw fibres were replaced by pail-
lettes of gold like the flecks one finds in Danzig brandy.

By these means he had obtained some unique editions, selecting
unusual formats which he had had bound by Lortic, by Trautz-
Bauzonnet, by Chambolle, by the disciples of Capé, in impeccable
bindings made from antique silk, from embossed cowhide, from
Cape goatskin—full bindings, patterned and inlaid, lined with tabby
or watered silk, ornamented with ecclesiastical-style clasps and
corners, and even, upon occasion, decorated by Gruel-Engelmann*
in silver oxide and lucent enamels.

He had had the works of Baudelaire printed in this manner, using
the fine episcopal type of the old Le Clerc house, in a large format
resembling that of a missal, on a very light, absorbent Japanese
felt paper which was as soft as elder-pith, its milky whiteness
faintly tinged with pink. This edition of one single copy, printed
in velvety black China ink, had been covered on the outside and
lined on the inside in a marvellous flesh-coloured piece of genuine
pigskin selected from among many hundreds, punctated all over
where the bristles had been, and delicately ornamented with miraculously appropriate designs tooled in black and chosen by a great
artist.

On that particular day, Des Esseintes took this incomparable volume down from his shelves, caressing it with reverent fingers and rereading certain pieces which, in this simple but incomparable format, he found more than usually profound.

His admiration for this writer was boundless. In his opinion, literature had, until then, restricted itself to exploring the superficial areas of the soul, or searching into those of its subterranean depths which were accessible and well lit, now and again pointing out the lodes of the seven deadly sins, studying their seams, their development, noting, as did Balzac, for example, the stratification of the soul that is possessed by a monomaniacal passion, by ambition, by avarice, by paternal infatuation, by senile lust.

In a work, literature dealt with perfectly healthy manifestations of virtues and vices, orderly operations of brains that conformed to the common mould, practical exemplifications of accepted ideas, without any belief in morbid depravity, any sense of what might lie beyond; in brief, the discoveries of analysts went no further than the speculations about good or evil classified by the Church; their research was a simple investigation, the ordinary observation of a botanist who follows with close attention the expected development of normal flowers planted in natural soil.

Baudelaire had gone further; he had descended to the very bottom of the inexhaustible mine, had journeyed along abandoned or uncharted tunnels, eventually reaching those regions of the soul in which the nightmare growths of human thought flourish.

There, close to those frontiers which are the dwelling-place of aberrations and diseases of the mind—the tetanus of mysticism, the delirious fevers of lechery, the typhoid and yellow fevers of crime—he had found, incubating beneath the dreary bell-glass of Ennui, the terrifying climacteric of emotions and of ideas.

He had exposed the morbid psychology of the soul which has reached the autumn of its capacity to feel; had told of the symptoms of the soul that has been recruited by suffering and singled out by spleen;* had shown the ever-increasing erosion of impressions when the enthusiasms and convictions of youth are exhausted, when nothing remains but the arid recollection of hardships endured, intolerance encountered, and slights borne, by intelligent men whom an absurd destiny holds in bondage.

He had followed each phase of this pitiable autumn, watching the human creature—quick to take umbrage, adroit at self-deception—

forcing his own thoughts to follow a self-destructive pattern so as to suffer the more acutely, and wrecking in advance, thanks to his talent for analysis and observation, every possibility of joy.

Then, in this irritable sensitivity of the soul, in this savage state of mind which rejects the embarrassing warmth of friendship, the well-meaning insults of charity, he had watched the very gradual emergence of those horrifying passions that come with age, of those mature affairs where one partner is still in love while the other is already on his guard, where lassitude forces couples to resort to filial caresses whose apparent childishness seems to offer novelty, and to artlessly maternal embraces whose tenderness is restful and affords, so to speak, interesting feelings of remorse inspired by some vague notion of incest.

He had exposed, in some magnificent pages, those hybrid love affairs which are exacerbated by the impossibility of finding true fulfilment, and those dangerous subterfuges of the narcotic and toxic drugs which people call upon in order to deaden suffering and defeat boredom. At a time when literature attributed the pain of living almost exclusively to the misfortunes of unrequited love or the jealousies inherent in adultery, he had paid no attention to those infantile maladies but had probed wounds that are less easily healed, more lasting, deeper, that are inflicted by satiation, by disillusionment, by contempt, in blighted souls tortured by the present and repelled by the past, whom the future fills with terror and despair.

And the more Des Esseintes reread Baudelaire, the more he became conscious of an indefinable charm in this writer who, at a time when poetry no longer served any purpose save to depict the external appearance of beings and things, had succeeded in expressing the inexpressible, thanks to a style that was muscular and dense, that, more than any other style, possessed that marvellous power of defining, in curiously wholesome terms, the most evanescent, the most fluctuating, of the morbid conditions that afflict exhausted minds and despairing souls.

After Baudelaire, the number of French books displayed on his shelves was relatively small. He was most certainly indifferent to those works over which it is considered socially correct to wax enthusiastic. Rabelais's* 'broad humour,' Molière's* 'enduring comedy' never succeeded in making him smile, and in fact his dislike of those farces was so intense that he did not hesitate to compare them, from the artistic point of view, to those comic parades of clowns which enliven country fairs.

As far as early poetry was concerned, he read nobody but Villon,* whose melancholy ballads he found moving, and an occasional work by d'Aubigné,* in which the incredible virulence of invective and anathema made his blood tingle.

In prose, he had no great opinion of Voltaire or Rousseau,* or even of Diderot, whose highly praised *Salons** he considered extraordinarily full of moralizing nonsense and naïve aspirations; greatly disliking all that stuff, he confined himself almost exclusively to the field of Christian oratory, to reading Bourdaloue and Bossuet,* whose sonorous, highly wrought periods impressed him; but in preference even to them he relished those pithy truths condensed into stark and powerful expressions such as were fashioned by Nicole* in his meditations, and above all by Pascal,* whose austere pessimism and anguished attrition went straight to his heart.

Apart from this handful of books, French literature began, on his bookshelves, with the nineteenth century. It fell into two classes, the first comprising ordinary profane literature, the other the literature of Catholicism;* this specialist literature, largely unknown to the general public, is nevertheless disseminated to the four corners of the earth by huge, long-established publishing houses.

He had been sufficiently determined to explore those literary vaults and—as in the sphere of secular art—he had discovered, beneath a vast accumulation of banalities, a few works written by genuine masters.

The distinctive characteristic of this literature was the eternal immutability of its ideas and its language; just as the Church had perpetuated the original shape of its sacred objects, so it had preserved the relics of its dogmas and piously cherished the reliquary that housed them, the oratorical style of the age of Louis XIV. As one of its own writers, Ozanam,* went so far as to declare, the Christian style had no need of the language of Rousseau; it should use only the style wielded by Bourdaloue and Bossuet.

Despite this declaration, the Church, with greater tolerance, shut its eyes to certain expressions, to certain turns of phrase borrowed from the lay language of that same century, so that the Catholic style had—to some extent—purged itself of its massive, heavy periods, which are especially typical of Bossuet, due to the length of his parenthetical clauses and the distressing redundancy of his pronouns; but that was as far as the concessions went, and others would probably have been unproductive, for, freed of its heavy cargo, this prose style was perfectly adequate for the limited range of subjects to which the Church chose to confine itself.

Incapable of grappling with contemporary life, of representing the simplest aspects of beings and things in a visible, palpable manner, ill-suited to explaining the complicated ruses of a brain indifferent to the state of grace, this style did none the less excel at dealing with abstract subjects; useful for discussing a controversy, for demonstrating a theory, for clarifying an ambiguous commentary, it also possessed, more than any other, the authority necessary for affirming, without discussion, the merit of a doctrine.

Unfortunately, in this as in every case, a myriad of pedants had invaded the sanctuary, defiling, with their ignorance and lack of talent, its uncompromising, noble dignity; as a crowning misfortune, a number of pious females had elected to take up this kind of writing, and maladroit little groups of the faithful had joined forces with foolish salons to extol, as works of genius, the wretched babbling of these women.

Des Esseintes had been curious enough to read some of these writings, in particular those of Madame Swetchine,* the Russian General's wife whose house in Paris was frequented by the most fervent Catholics; her works had filled him with unremitting, overwhelming boredom; they were worse than bad, they were utterly commonplace; they reminded one of an echo repeated back and forth inside a tiny chapel where a number of sanctimonious, affected people were mumbling their prayers, asking one another in whispers for news, repeating to one another—their manner weighty and mysterious—a few platitudes about politics, about the predictions of the barometer, about the current state of the weather.

But there was worse to come: an accredited laureate of the Institute, Madame Augustus Craven,* the author of the *Récit d'une sœur*, of *Éliane*, of *Fleurange*, which had been acclaimed with blaring serpents and organ by the entire apostolic press. Never, no never, had Des Esseintes imagined that anyone could write such inanities. The ideas on which these books were based were so stupid, and the style in which they were written was so nauseating, that they thereby acquired a kind of individuality, a kind of rarity.

In any case, it was not among women writers that Des Esseintes, with his far from unsullied soul and his unsentimental nature, could find a literary sanctum that accorded with his tastes.

Nevertheless he persevered in his efforts and, with an application unaffected by impatience, attempted to derive enjoyment from the work of the young girl-genius, the virgin blue-stocking of the group; but his efforts came to naught; he was incapable of appreciating that *Journal* and those *Lettres* in which Eugénie de Guérin* celebrates, with a total absence of restraint, the prodigious talent of a brother who wrote verses of such ingenuity and such grace that undoubtedly one would have had to go back to the works of M. de Jouy and M. Écouchard Lebrun,* to find any of comparable boldness or originality!

He had also tried without success to fathom the appeal of works where one finds reports of this nature: 'This morning I hung, beside Papa's bed, a crucifix a little girl gave him yesterday.' 'Tomorrow Mimi and I are invited to attend the blessing of a bell at M. Roquiers'; I am not averse to this outing'; or where important events such as these are noted: 'I have just hung round my neck a medal of the Holy Virgin that Louise sent me as a protection against cholera'; or one reads poetry of this type: 'Oh, what a beautiful moonbeam has just fallen on the Gospel I was reading!' or, finally, observations as acute and penetrating as the following: 'When I see a man crossing himself or removing his hat as he passes a crucifix, I think: "There goes a Christian."'

And this went on in similar vein, without pause or respite, until Maurice de Guérin died and his sister mourned him in further pages of lachrymose prose dotted, here and there, with fragments of verse of such embarrassing inadequacy that Des Esseintes was eventually moved to pity.

Alas, there was no denying it, the Catholic party was not very fastidious in its choice of protégés, not very discriminating! Those colourless creatures they had cherished so dearly, on whose behalf they had exhausted the goodwill of their periodicals, all wrote like convent schoolgirls, their anaemic language pouring out in a verbal flux unchecked by any binding astringency!

From these works, therefore, Des Esseintes turned away in

disgust; but neither did he find, among the contemporary masters of the priesthood, any who might compensate him adequately for his disappointment. The latter were impeccably correct preachers or polemicists, but in their sermons and books the Christian idiom had ended up by becoming impersonal, frozen into a rhetoric of which every movement and every pause could be foreseen, expressed in a string of sentences constructed after a single model. And indeed, all the ecclesiastics wrote alike, with a trifle more or a trifle less verve or emphasis, and there was no appreciable difference between the grisailles turned out by Messignors Dupanloup or Landriot, La Bouillerie or Gaume, by Dom Guéranger or Father Ratisbonne, by Monsignor Freppel or Monsignor Perraud, by the Reverend Fathers Ravignan or Gratry, by the Jesuit Olivaint, the Carmelite Dosithée, the Dominican Didon, or by the Reverend Father Chocarne,* sometime Prior of Saint-Maximin.

Des Esseintes had frequently reflected that it required a truly authentic talent, a truly profound originality, a truly firm conviction to thaw out that icy language, to give life to that public style which was not capable of supporting any unusual idea, any daring argument.

Yet there did exist some writers whose fiery eloquence melted and recast that style, Lacordaire* in particular, one of the few genuine writers that the Church has produced in a very long time.

Imprisoned, like all his colleagues, within the narrow circle of orthodox speculation, and like them forced to mark time and discuss only those ideas which had been conceived and consecrated by the Fathers of the Church, and then further developed by the great preachers, he managed to pull off a clever trick, he succeeded in rejuvenating, almost in modifying those ideas by means of a more personal, more lively style. Here and there, in his *Conférences de Notre-Dame*, one comes across stylistic gems, daring choices of words, loving cadences, frolicsome language, cries of joy, and ecstatic effusions that made the time-honoured style smoke under his pen. Then, over and above the oratorical gifts that were his, this clever, gentle monk, whose skills and energies were exhausted in the impossible task of reconciling the liberal ideas of society with the authoritative dogmas of the Church, possessed a temperament rich in fervent brotherly love, in tactful tenderness. Thus, the letters which he wrote to young men contained the fond exhortations of a father to his sons, smiling reprimands, kindly words of counsel, indulgent pardons. Some of these letters, in which he confessed all his craving for affection, were charming; others, in which he supported courage and dissipated doubts, were imbued with a kind of grandeur by the unshakable conviction of his faith. In short, those paternal feelings which took on, under his pen, a delicate, feminine quality, bestowed on his prose an accent which is unique in all the literature of the Church.

After him, few and far between were the ecclesiastics and monks who displayed any individuality whatsoever. At most, a handful of pages written by his pupil Abbé Perreyve* were worth reading. This abbé had left some touching biographical essays on his master, written some appealing letters, composed one or two articles couched in a sonorous oratorical style, and pronounced a few panegyrics, in which the declamatory tone was too much in evidence. It is clear that the Abbé Perreyve was endowed neither with Lacordaire's feelings nor with his fire. There was too much of the priest in him and too little of the man; but, here and there, the rhetoric of his sermons was nevertheless illuminated by fascinating analogies, ample, well-constructed phrases, and an almost majestic elevation of thought.

But one had to turn to writers who were not ordained, to laymen advocates of the Church devoted to its cause, to again find prose writers worthy of attention. The episcopal style, which the prelates had handled with such banality, was filled with new life and in a sense reinfused with male vigour by the Comte de Falloux.* Beneath his moderate exterior this Academician positively exuded venom; his speeches made to the Parliament in 1848 were diffuse and life-less, but his articles published in the *Correspondant* and later collected together in books were, beneath their exaggeratedly deferential form, mordant and scathing. Conceived as formal homilies, they were characterized by a certain bitter zest and by the surprising intolerance of the beliefs they expressed.

A dangerous polemicist by virtue of his skill at ensnaring adversaries, a wily logician who preferred the devious approach and the surprise attack, the Comte de Falloux also wrote some penetrating pages on the death of Madame Swetchine, whose works he had collected and whom he revered as a saint.

But where the writer's temperament really showed itself was in two pamphlets which appeared in 1846 and 1880 respectively, the later one entitled *L'Unité nationale*. Here, filled with an icy rage, the implacable Legitimist—atypically preferring, on this occasion, a frontal assault—launched an attack upon unbelievers, concluding with this violent denunciation:

'And you, you doctrinaire Utopians who take no account of human nature, you advocates of atheism who flourish on hatred and delusion, you emancipators of women and destroyers of the family, you genealogists of the simian race, you whose name was once tantamount to an insult, may you be satisfied: you will have been the prophets, and your disciples will be the high priests, of an abominable future!'

The other tract, entitled *Le Parti catholique*, was aimed both against the despotism of *L'Univers*, and against Veuillot,* whose name it nowhere deigned to mention. The devious attacks were resumed in this pamphlet, where poison oozed from every one of the lines in which the badly bruised gentleman responded with disdainful sarcasm to his opponent's kicks.

Between them, this pair represented to perfection the two parties in the Church whose disagreements have always developed into intractable animosities; de Falloux, the more arrogant and wily of the two, belonged to that liberal sect which already included de Montalembert and Cochin, Lacordaire and de Broglie;* he fully supported the ideas of the *Correspondant*, a review which attempted to conceal the dictatorial doctrines of the Church under a varnish of tolerance; Veuillot, less hidebound and more outspoken, spurned such pretences, unhesitatingly admitted the tyranny of Ultramontane directives, and openly acknowledged and invoked the inflexible yoke of Catholic dogma.

The latter had fashioned himself a special language for the fight, a language which owed something to La Bruyère* and something to the speech of the common low-class worker. This style—half-formal, half-vulgar—took on, when wielded by that brutal personality, the formidable heft of a cudgel. Extraordinarily obstinate and bold, he had used this terrible weapon to belabour free-thinkers and bishops alike, hitting out with might and main, striking his enemies with powerful blows regardless of which party they belonged to. Distrusted by the Church, which disapproved both of his contraband language and of his roughneck posturing, this religious blackguard did none the less command respect on account of his prodigious talent, goading all the newspapers, flaying them in his *Odeurs de Paris* until he drew blood, holding firm against all attacks, and kicking himself free from all the base pen-pushers who tried to snap at his heels.

Unfortunately, his undeniable talent only revealed itself in the ring; Veuillot, when he was not fighting, was simply a mediocre writer; his poetry and novels were pitiful; without the heat of passion, his language fell flat, missing its mark; at rest, the strong man of Catholicism turned into a petulant valetudinarian wheezing out banal litanies and mumbling infantile canticles.

More affected, more stilted, and more solemn was that beloved apologist of the Church, that Grand Inquisitor of the Christian language, Ozanam. Although he was not easily surprised, Des Esseintes never ceased to be astonished at the self-assurance of this author who wrote about God's inscrutable purposes instead of producing the necessary evidence for the incredible assertions he was making; Ozanam would, with the most admirable sang-froid, misrepresent the events and (with even greater impudence than the panegyrists of the other parties) deny the acknowledged events of history, asserting that the Church had never concealed the esteem in which it held science, describing heresies as noxious miasmas, and expressing such contempt for Buddhism and other religions that he even apologized for sullying Catholic prose by so much as attacking their doctrines.

Occasionally, religious passion communicated a certain ardour to his oratory, beneath whose icy surface there seethed a current of suppressed violence; in his numerous works on Dante, on St Francis, on the author of the *Stabat*, on the Franciscan poets, on Socialism, on commercial law, on any subject one can name, this man pleaded the cause of the Vatican which he held to be indefectible, and indiscriminately judged every cause according to how nearly it corresponded with or how far it differed from his own.

This habit of considering issues from only a single standpoint was also a characteristic of that wretched pen-pusher Nettement,* whom some regarded as his rival. Not so strait-laced, Nettement was less arrogant and more worldly in his pretensions; on a number of occasions he had emerged from the literary cloister in which Ozanam chose to immure himself, to glance through some secular works so that he could pronounce judgement on them. He had groped his way through them like a child in a dark cellar, seeing only shadows all around him and discerning nothing, in the midst of this blackness, save the gleam of the candle as it lit his way ahead for a few steps.

In this totally unfamiliar terrain, in this obscurity, he had tripped up at every turn, referring to Murger's* style as 'carefully sculpted and meticulously polished', to Hugo (with whom he dared to compare M. de Laprade*) as seeking out filth and obscenity, to Delacroix as scorning the rules, to Paul Delaroche* and the poet Reboul* with fulsome praise because, in his view, their faith was strong. Des Esseintes could only shrug his shoulders at these unfortunate views that were framed in indigent prose, the threadbare fabric of which would catch and tear on every awkward turn of phrase.

In another area, the works of Poujoulat and Genoude, Montalembert, Nicolas, and Carné* did not arouse his interest to any greater degree; nor did he much appreciate the careful, scholarly historical writing, couched in irreproachable language, of the Duc de Broglie,* or feel drawn to the social and religious questions pursued by Henry Cochin*—who had, however, shown his true colours in a letter describing a touching taking of the veil at Sacré-Cœur. It was years since he had opened these books, and it was even longer since he had thrown away the puerile disquisitions of the lugubrious Pontmartin* or the pathetic Féval,* or had handed over to the servants, to be put to a lowly domestic use, the little tales penned by such as Aubineau and Lasserre,* those contemptible hagiographers of the miracles performed by M. Dupont of Tours,* and by the Blessed Virgin.

In short, this literature did not offer Des Esseintes even a fleeting diversion from his boredom; he therefore stowed away, in the dimmest corners of his library, those piles of volumes which he had perused in years gone by, upon leaving the Jesuit college. 'I really should have left them behind in Paris,' he said to himself, removing from behind other books some which he found particularly unbearable, those of the Abbé Lamennais,* as well as those by that inflexible bigot, that overbearing, pompous, empty-headed bore, Comte Joseph de Maistre.*

One single volume remained in its place on the shelf, within reach of his hand, Ernest Hello's *L'Homme*.* This writer was the absolute antithesis of his colleagues in religion. Virtually isolated within the pious group which found his ideas alarming, Ernest Hello had eventually abandoned that broad highway which leads directly from earth to heaven; disgusted, no doubt, by the banality of this highway, and by the herd of literary pilgrims who for centuries had been following one another in single file along the same road, stopping at the same spots to exchange the same commonplaces about religion, about the Church Fathers, about the same beliefs and the same teachers, he had taken short-cuts, emerging into Pascal's desolate clearing where he had paused for some time to catch his breath, then he had continued on his way, penetrating further than the Jansenist (whom incidentally he despised) into the depths of human thought.

Devious and affected, pompous and complicated, Hello, with his incisive, hair-splitting analyses, reminded Des Esseintes of the acutely probing studies produced by some of the atheistic psychologists of the preceding and present centuries. There was something of a Catholic Duranty* in him, only more dogmatic and more penetrating, an experienced wielder of the magnifying glass, a clever engineer of the soul, a skilful watchmaker of the brain, who took pleasure in studying the mechanism of a passion and explaining it by giving a minutely detailed description of its wheels.

That strangely constituted mind of his harboured unexpected associations, correspondences, and contrasts of thought, as well as a whole peculiar procedure whereby the etymology of words became the springboard for new ideas which, albeit inspired at times by rather tenuous associations, were almost invariably ingenious and vivid.

Thus, despite the imperfect equilibrium of his constructions, he had with extraordinary perspicacity revealed the inner workings of 'the miser,' of 'the average man', analysed the nature of 'the taste for society' and 'the passion for suffering', and pointed out the interesting comparisons which can be established between the processes of photography and those of memory.

But his skill in handling that highly refined tool of analysis, which he had appropriated from the enemies of the Church, represented only one side of this man's temperament. There was yet another being in him; his was a dual spirit, including not simply the verso but also the recto: the religious fanatic and the biblical prophet.

Like Hugo, of whose dislocations of thought and style he occasionally reminded Des Esseintes, Ernest Hello had enjoyed posing as a little St John on Patmos; but he pontificated and vaticinated from the top of a rock made by the manufacturers of pious trash in the shops of the Rue Saint-Sulpice, haranguing the reader in an apocalyptic style seasoned here and there with the acerbity of an Isaiah.

He made great claims, on those occasions, to profundity; a handful of sycophants hailed him as a genius, pretending to view him as the great man of his time, as a well of knowledge for the century, and a well he may indeed have been, but one in whose depths one could frequently make out nothing whatsoever.

In his book *Paroles de Dieu*, in which he paraphrased the Scriptures and did his utmost to complicate their fairly straightforward message, in his other book, *L'Homme*, and in his pamphlet *Le Jour du Seigneur*, written in a disjointed, obscure, biblical style, he appeared in different guises—as a proud, vindictive apostle, easily roused to anger, as a deacon suffering from fits of mystical epilepsy, as a De Maistre endowed with genuine talent, and as an ill-tempered, ferocious bigot.

On the other hand, reflected Des Esseintes, that morbid love of excess frequently inhibited the creative visions of the casuist; with an intolerance greater even than Ozanam's, Hello resolutely denied anything that did not come from his own little circle, propounded the most astounding axioms, declared in disconcertingly authoritative tones that 'geology had gone back to Moses', that natural history, chemistry, that all of contemporary science confirmed the scientific accuracy of the Bible; every page bore witness to the Church as the sole source of truth, the fount of superhuman wisdom, the whole being strewn with alarmingly fallacious aphorisms and furious imprecations spewed out by the bucketful and aimed at the art of the preceding century.

To this strange mixture was added a taste for pious sweetmeats, in the form of translations of Angela da Foligno's *Visions*,* a book flowing with unparalleled inanity, and of the selected works of Jan van Ruysbroeck the Blessed, a thirteenth century mystic, whose prose offered an incomprehensible but appealing amalgam of mysterious ecstasy, sentimental effusions, and scathing outbursts.

Hello's pose as an overweeningly conceited pontiff had sprung from an astounding preface written for this latter book. As he himself pointed out, 'extraordinary things can only be described in halting speech', and his speech was indeed halting, when he declared that 'the sacred darkness where Ruysbroeck spreads his eagle's wings is his ocean, his prey, his glory, and for him the four horizons would be too confining a garment'.

Be that as it may, Des Esseintes felt drawn to this unbalanced yet subtle mind; no fusion had been achieved between the skilled psychologist and the pious pedant, and it was these jarring collisions, these very incongruities that formed the essence of Hello's personality.

The little group of writers operating in the front lines of the clerical camp had rallied round his standard. They did not belong to the main body of the army, but functioned rather as outriders for a religion which distrusted talented people like Veuillot, like Hello, for not being sufficiently cowed or dull; essentially, what religion required was soldiers who did not think for themselves, regiments of those sightless warriors, those nonentities of whom Hello wrote with the fury of one who had suffered under their yoke; accordingly the Catholic Church had made haste to deny publication in its official newspapers to one of its own partisans, Léon Bloy,* a fanatical pamphleteer who wrote in language that was simultaneously irate and affected, naïve and fierce, and had banished from its bookshops as plague-ridden and unclean another writer who had nevertheless made himself hoarse with singing its praises, Barbey d'Aurevilly.

It was true that this writer was far too compromising, far too lacking in docility; others bowed their heads in submission on being reprimanded, and came to heel; but he was the unacknowledged *enfant terrible* of the party, he went whoring through literature and brought his half-dressed women into the sanctuary. Indeed it was solely because of the immense contempt with which Catholicism views real talent that an excommunication in due and proper form had not made an outlaw of this strange servant of the Church who, under the pretext of honouring his masters, smashed the chapel windows, juggled with the sacred ciboria, and performed comic dances round the tabernacle.

Two of Barbey d'Aurevilly's books, in particular, stirred Des Esseintes: *Le Prêtre marié* and *Les Diaboliques*.* Others, such as *L'Ensorcelée*, *Le Chevalier des Touches*, and *Une Vieille Maîtresse*, were undoubtedly better balanced and more polished, but they did not excite Des Esseintes to the same degree, for in reality he was only interested in unhealthy works, works that were sapped and inflamed by fever.

In the case of these comparatively wholesome books, Barbey d'Aurevilly had constantly veered back and forth between those two currents of Catholicism which, eventually, merge into one: mysticism and sadism. But in the couple of books that Des Esseintes was now leafing through, Barbey had abandoned all prudence, had given his mount its head, and set off at breakneck speed along routes which he had followed to their farthermost point.

All the mysterious horror of the Middle Ages hung over that improbable story *Le Prêtre marié;** magic was mingled with religion, sorcery with prayer, and, more pitiless, more barbarous than the Devil, the God of original sin subjected the damned but innocent Calixte to unceasing torments, branding her on the brow with a red cross, just as, long ago, he had had one of his angels mark the houses of the unbelievers he planned to kill.

As if conceived by a fasting monk suffering from delirium, these scenes were unfolded in the jerky, disjointed language of a fever victim; unfortunately, among these ravaged creatures who resembled so many Coppelias* galvanized into life by Hoffmann, there were some, the Néel de Néhou for example, who seemed to have been imagined in those periods of prostration which follow hard upon crises, and in that setting of sombre madness they struck an inappropriate note, introducing the kind of unintentional comedy one associates with the sight of a little zinc manikin in soft boots, standing on the pedestal of a clock and blowing his horn.

After these mystical digressions Barbey had experienced a period of calm; then a terrible relapse had occurred. The belief that man is like Buridan's ass,* a being torn between two equally powerful forces, each of which in turn gains or loses control of his soul; the conviction that human life is nothing but an uncertain struggle between hell and heaven; the faith in two antithetical entities, Satan and Christ, must inevitably engender those internal conflicts in which the soul, exalted by an unremitting struggle, and, as it were, aroused by all the promises and threats, eventually gives in and prostitutes itself to whichever of the two contenders has been the more tenacious in its pursuit.

In *Le Prêtre marié*, Barbey d'Aurevilly sang the praises of Christ whose temptations had triumphed, whereas in *Les Diaboliques* it was to Satan that the author had surrendered, and whose praises he sang. This was the point at which the bastard of Catholicism, sadism, made its appearance; sadism, which, in all its guises, the Church has for centuries pursued with its exorcisms and its burnings at the stake.

This condition, so strange and ill-defined, cannot in fact take root in the soul of an unbeliever; it does not simply consist in wallowing in sexual excesses spiced up with sanguinary acts of cruelty, for then it would be no more than a deviant manifestation of the genetic instincts, a case of satyriasis in its most extreme form; it consists, first and foremost, in a sacrilegious deed, a moral rebellion, an act of spiritual debauchery, an aberration which is wholly idealistic, wholly Christian; it consists also in a pleasure tempered with fear, a pleasure analogous to that wicked delight felt by disobedient children who play with forbidden things, for no reason other than their parents' express prohibition.

Indeed, if it did not include sacrilege, sadism would have no *raison d'être*; then again, a sacrilege which depends on the very existence of a religion, cannot be intentionally and appositely committed except by a believer, for a man would experience no delight in profaning a law which he did not care about, or of which he was unaware.

The power of sadism, the attraction it holds, resides entirely, therefore, in the forbidden pleasure of transferring to Satan the homage and prayers one owes to God; it therefore resides in the non-observance of the Catholic precepts which it actually follows in a negative sense, by committing, in order to reject Christ all the more significantly, those very sins which he particularly anathematized: the profanation of religious services, and acts of carnal debauchery.

Essentially, this condition, to which the Marquis de Sade* bequeathed his name, was as old as the Church; it had flourished during the eighteenth century, reviving, through a simple atavistic process, the impious practices of the medieval witches' sabbath, to search no further back in history.

A quick glance at the *Malleus maleficorum,** that terrible compilation of Joseph Sprenger's which enabled the Church to send to the stake thousands of necromancers and sorcerers, was sufficient for Des Esseintes to recognize, in the witches' sabbath, all of sadism's obscenities and blasphemies. In addition to the unspeakably foul scenes dear to Satan—nights dedicated, in turn, to licit and unnatural copulation, nights steeped in the blood of bestial orgies—he found the same parodies of religious processions, the same unchanging insults and threats aimed at God, the same devotion to his Rival, as when the Black Mass was celebrated (with the celebrant cursing the bread and wine) on the back of a woman on all fours whose naked and repeatedly defiled rump served as altar, while the participants derisively took communion in the form of a black host stamped with the image of a he-goat.

This outpouring of foul mockery and degrading vilification was evident in the writing of the Marquis de Sade, who spiced up his terrifying sensualities with heinous acts of sacrilege. He would hurl insults at Heaven, invoke Lucifer, call God despicable, villainous, imbecilic, spit on the sacraments of communion, do his utmost to desecrate and defile a Divinity which he hoped would be willing to damn him, while yet declaring, as a further act of defiance, that this Divinity did not exist.

Barbey d'Aurevilly came very close to sharing this same psychic condition. If he did not go as far as Sade in uttering abominable imprecations against the Saviour, if (either out of greater prudence or greater timidity) he always made a show of honouring the Church, he nevertheless addressed his prayers to the Devil just as people did in the Middle Ages, and he too, in his need to insult God, gravitated towards demonic erotomania, creating monstrosities of sensuality, and even borrowing, from *La Philosophie dans le boudoir*, a particular episode which he seasoned with new condiments when he composed the short story entitled *Le Dîner d'un athée*.*

This excessive work delighted Des Esseintes; consequently he had had printed, in ink of episcopal violet, inside a border of cardinal scarlet, on genuine parchment blessed by the Auditors of the Rota,* a copy of *Les Diaboliques* set in those *lettres de civilité* of which the weirdly shaped loops and coiled and hooked flourishes take on a Satanic appearance.

Setting aside certain works by Baudelaire which, in imitation of those chants intoned on the nights of witches' sabbaths, consisted of infernal litanies of praise, this volume was unique among all the works of contemporary apostolic literature, being the only one manifesting that spiritual state, at once devout and blasphemous, to which Des Esseintes, impelled by the nostalgic appeal of Catholicism which his attacks of neurosis brought on, had so often felt drawn.

With Barbey d'Aurevilly the series of religious writers came to a close; truth to tell, that pariah more clearly belonged, from every point of view, to secular literature rather than to that other literature in which he claimed a place that was denied him; his wildly romantic language, full of contorted locutions, unheard-of expressions, and far-fetched comparisons, whipped up his sentences into a stampede that thundered through the text, jangling its noisy cattle-bells. In brief, Barbey looked like a stallion, among all those geldings that crowd the Ultramontane stables.

Such were Des Esseintes's thoughts as he reread a few random passages of this book and, as he compared that virile, varied style with the phlegmatic, conventional style of Barbey's fellow-writers, he thought also of that evolution of language so accurately described by Darwin.

Living in the secular world, brought up in the heart of the Romantic movement, well informed about recent literary works and accustomed to reading the latest publications, Barbey inevitably found himself in possession of an idiom which had, since the seventeenth century, undergone numerous and profound modifications, which had regenerated itself.

Restricted, by contrast, to their own territory, confined within a prison of identical, antiquated reading, knowing nothing of the literary developments which had taken place over the years and quite determined, if necessary, to blind themselves rather than take note of those developments, ecclesiastical writers inevitably employed an unchanging language, like that eighteenth-century idiom which the descendants of the first French settlers in Canada still speak and write today, since no choice of expressions or vocabulary has been made available for their language, isolated as it is from its mother country and surrounded on all sides by the English tongue.

At this point, the silvery tinkle of a bell ringing a little angelus informed Des Esseintes that luncheon was ready. He put down his books, wiped his forehead, and went into the dining-room, reflecting that, of all the works he had just been sorting, those of Barbey d'Aurevilly were still the only ones where both ideas and style presented that high, gamey condition, those tainted patches, that bruised skin and overripe flavour which he so much relished in the decadent writers, whether Latin or monastic, of olden times.

13

The weather was becoming very unsettled; that year, the seasons were all mixed up; after the squalls and the fogs, blazing hot skies, like sheets of metal, appeared from over the horizon. In two days, without any transition whatever, the damp, chilly fogs and the streaming rains were followed by torrid heat and atrociously heavy air. As though stirred into life by fierce pokers, the sun opened like the mouth of a furnace, shooting down an almost white light which burned the eyes; a fiery dust rose up from the sun-baked roads, roasting the dry trees, scorching the yellowed lawns; the glare from the whitewashed walls, the light flaming on the zinc roofs and the window panes was blinding; heat like that of a foundry working at full blast hung oppressively over Des Esseintes's house.

Half naked, he opened a window, and received a gust of scorching air full in the face; the dining-room, where he sought refuge, was sweltering, its rarefied air boiling hot. He sat down, feeling miserable, for the intense excitement which had sustained him while he was sorting his books and day-dreaming had now disappeared.

Like all those who suffer from neuroses, he found heat devastating; his anaemia, kept under control by the cold weather, was regaining its hold over him, further weakening his body which had been debilitated by excessive sweating.

With his shirt sticking to his soaking back, his perineum damp, his arms and legs wet, his forehead drenched, salt tears streaming down his cheeks, Des Esseintes lay back exhausted in his chair; the sight of the meat which had just then been placed on the table made his gorge rise; he had it removed, ordered boiled eggs, attempted to eat some fingers of bread dipped in egg but they stuck in his throat; waves of nausea kept coming over him; he drank a few drops of wine which stung his stomach like red-hot needles. He wiped his face; sweat, which a moment earlier had been warm, now flowed icily down his temples; he tried sucking a lump or two of ice to soothe his nausea, but to no avail.

In a state of utter prostration, he remained slumped over the table; then, finding himself unable to breathe, he got to his feet, but the fingers of bread had swollen and were slowly coming back up his gullet and choking him. Never had he felt so apprehensive, so unwell, so ill at ease; on top of everything else, his vision became blurred; he was seeing things double, as though they were revolving; soon he lost his sense of distance; his glass seemed a league away; he kept telling himself he was suffering from sensory illusions and yet he could not shake them off. He went and lay down on the drawing-room sofa, but then a pitching as of a vessel at sea rocked him and his nausea worsened; he stood up, determined to take a liqueur to settle those eggs which were suffocating him.

He returned to the dining-room, gloomily comparing himself, in that cabin, to passengers suffering from sea-sickness; he stumbled over to the cupboard and examined the mouth organ but did not open it, taking off the shelf, further up, a bottle of Benedictine which he kept because of its shape, which inspired thoughts at once sweetly voluptuous and vaguely mystical.

But now he stood there apathetically, gazing with lack-lustre eyes at that squat, dark green bottle, which at other moments reminded him of the priors of medieval days, with its traditional monastic pot-belly, its head and neck garbed in a parchment cowl, its red wax seal quartered by three silver mitres on a blue field and its stopper sealed, like a papal bull, by strips of lead, and with its label, written in resounding Latin on paper yellowed and as though faded by the years: 'Liquor Monachorum Benedictinorum Abbatiae Fiscanensis'.

Beneath that typically abbatial habit, stamped with a cross and the ecclesiastical initials, D.O.M.,* wrapped in its parchments and its bindings just like a genuine charter, there slumbered a saffron-coloured liqueur of an exquisite delicacy. It exuded a quintessential aroma of angelica and hyssop, mingled with seaweed smelling of iodines and brome grasses diluted with syrups, and it stimulated the palate with a volatile fire concealed beneath a completely virginal, completely inexperienced sweetness, delighting the nose with its hint of corruption wrapped in a caress that was at once childish and devout.

This hypocrisy arising out of the extraordinary discrepancy between the container and the contents, between the sacerdotal con-tours of the bottle and its utterly feminine, utterly modern soul, had in the past set him day-dreaming; and his thoughts, in the presence of this bottle, had also often turned to those same monks who sold it, to the Benedictines of the Fécamp Abbey who, belonging to that

Congregation of Saint-Maur which is famous for its historical studies, supported the Rule of St Benedict, but did not follow the observances of the white monks of Cîteaux or the black monks of Cluny. Inevitably he imagined them as they were in the Middle Ages, growing medicinal herbs, heating retorts, distilling sovereign panaceas and infallible cure-alls in their alembics.

He drank a drop of the liqueur and for a few moments experienced some relief; but before long this fire, which a mere drop of wine had kindled in his gut, grew fiercer. Throwing down his napkin, he returned to his dressing-room, where he paced to and fro; he felt as if he was under a bell-jar in which the vacuum each moment was becoming more powerful, and he was conscious of a dreadfully pleasurable faintness flowing from his brain through all his limbs. Bracing himself, unable to endure any more, he took refuge for perhaps the first time since his arrival at Fontenay in his garden, and sought shelter under a tree which cast a small circle of shade. Seated on the lawn, he stared in bewilderment at the vegetable beds the servants had planted. He stared at them, but only after the passage of an hour did he actually observe them, for there was a greenish mist floating before his eyes which prevented him from seeing anything but indistinct images of ever-changing appearance and colour, such as one sees under water.

Eventually, however, he regained his composure, and could clearly distinguish onions and cabbages; farther away was a patch of lettuces, while beyond, along the hedge, stood a row of white lilies, immobile in the heavy air.

His lips curled up in a smile, as he suddenly recollected the strange comparison drawn by the ancient writer Nicander* who, thinking of their similarity of shape, likened the pistil of a lily to the testicles of an ass; he also remembered a statement made by 'Grand Albert',* in which that thaumaturge gives details of an exceedingly odd method of determining, by using a lettuce, whether a girl is still a virgin.

He was a little cheered by these recollections; he studied the garden, his attention drawn by the plants wilting in the heat and by the burning-hot soil which steamed in the scorching pulverescence of the air; then, over the top of the hedge dividing the garden from the road that ran above it up to the fort, he noticed some young lads tumbling about out there in the bright sunlight.

He was watching them intently when another, smaller boy

appeared; he was a squalid sight, with hair like very sandy seaweed, two green bubbles hanging from his nose, disgusting lips edged with white scum from eating a piece of bread that was plastered with herb cheese and sprinkled with chopped green scallions.

Des Esseintes sniffed the air; a perverted craving* overpowered him; that foul slice of bread and cheese made his mouth water. It seemed to him that his stomach, which refused to accept any nourishment, would digest that horrible dish and that his palate would relish it as if it were a feast.

He sprang to his feet, ran to the kitchen, and ordered them to go to the village for a cob-loaf, cream-cheese, and green scallions, instructing them to prepare him an open sandwich exactly like the one the child was gnawing; then he went back and sat down again under his tree.

Now the brats were fighting. They were tearing off bits of bread, stuffing them into their cheeks, licking their fingers. Knocked to the ground by the deluge of kicks and punches, the smaller fry were lashing out and crying, their behinds scraping on the pebbles of the road.

This spectacle revived Des Esseintes; the interest he took in the fight distracted him from his malady; on seeing the ferocity of these nasty brats, he reflected on the cruel, abominable law of the struggle for survival, and although these children were of ignoble stock, he could not stop himself from feeling concern over their fate, and from believing that it would have been better for them if their mothers had never borne them.

And indeed, what was there, from earliest infancy, but impetigo, colics and fevers, measles and slaps; kicks from booted feet and stupefying labour by thirteen or so; faithless mistresses, disease, and cuckoldry, once manhood was attained; and then, with old age, came infirmity and death, in a workhouse or almshouse.

And on the whole the future was the same for every man, and neither the rich nor the poor, if he possessed a modicum of common sense, had any cause to envy his fellow. For the rich it was—albeit in a different milieu—the same passions, the same worries, the same sorrows, the same illnesses, and also the same mediocre pleasures, whether they be alcoholic, literary, or carnal. There was even a vague compensation for all their suffering, a kind of justice which restored the balance of unhappiness between the classes, by more readily exempting the poor from the physical suffering which so relentlessly prostrated the weaker, less muscular bodies of the rich.

'What folly it is to produce youngsters!' reflected Des Esseintes. 'And to think that priests who had taken a vow of sterility were so wildly inconsistent as to canonize St Vincent de Paul,* because he saved innocent babes for a life of pointless torment!

'Thanks to his odious zeal he postponed, for a matter of years, the death of unintelligent, insensate creatures, so that later, when they had become almost rational, and capable, at any rate, of feeling pain, they could foresee their future, expect and dread that death of whose very name they had until recently never heard, and even, in some cases, invoke death, out of loathing for that existence to which they were condemned in the name of an absurd theological ethic!

'And, after that old man's death, his theories gained general acceptance; foundlings were taken into care, instead of being left to die in peaceful tranquillity; yet this life which was being preserved for them became, as the years passed, ever grimmer and more barren! Using the pretext of freedom and progress, Society had hit on the way to make the miserable condition of man even worse, by dragging him from his home, and dressing him up in a ridiculous outfit, and giving him weapons of his own, and stupefying him by a servitude exactly like that from which, in days gone by, negroes were freed out of compassion; all this in order to enable him to assassinate his fellow man, without risking the scaffold as do ordinary murderers, who operate independently, without uniforms, with less noisy, less efficient weapons.

'What an extraordinary age this is,' thought Des Esseintes, 'which, in the interests of humanity, is attempting to perfect anaesthetics so as to eliminate physical suffering, while at the same time devising such goads to intensify moral suffering!

'Ah! If ever, in the name of pity, useless procreation should be abolished, that time is now! But in this case, once again, there are cruel and bizarre laws, enacted by the Portalis* and the Homais of this world. The Law considers methods of cheating the reproductive process perfectly natural; it is an acknowledged, admitted fact; there is no couple, however wealthy, who does not consign its seed to the laundry or use artificial devices, which can be bought openly and which in any case no one would dream of condemning. And yet, if these expedients or these contrivances should prove inadequate, if the device were to fail and, in order to remedy the situation, they resort to some more efficacious method, why then indeed there are not enough prisons, not enough gaols and houses of correction to incarcerate those individuals who are condemned (in perfect good faith, furthermore) by other individuals who, that very night, in the conjugal bed, use every trick they know of to avoid begetting brats!

'It follows that the fraud itself is not a crime, but any measure to correct its failure is one. In brief, Society holds that the act of killing a being endowed with life is a crime; and yet, in expelling a foetus, what was destroyed was an animal that was less developed, less alive, and, unquestionably, less intelligent and uglier than a dog or a cat, which one could with impunity strangle at birth!

'And,' reflected Des Esseintes, 'one should also remember that, to make things even more equitable, it is not the inept male—who usually disappears as fast as he can—but the female, the victim of the incompetence, who pays the penalty for the heinous crime of having saved an innocent creature from this life! Society must surely be riddled with prejudice to want to suppress practices so natural that primitive man, that the Polynesian savage, is induced, purely by instinct, to follow them!'

Des Esseintes was pondering these charitable thoughts when he was interrupted by the servant bringing him, on a silver-gilt platter, the slice of bread and cheese he had asked for. A wave of nausea gripped him; he could not bring himself to bite into this piece of bread, for the unhealthy excitation of his stomach had gone, giving way to a terrible sensation of physical prostration; he felt he must stand up; the sun was gradually moving round to his spot; the heat was becoming at once more oppressive and more intense.

'Throw that bread', he told the servant, 'to those children murdering each other over there on the road; may the weaker ones get knocked about, and get no share of it and, furthermore, be soundly thrashed by their families when they return home with torn pants and black eyes; that will give them a taste of what life holds in store for them!' And, going back into the house, he collapsed, almost fainting, into a chair.

'But I must make an effort to eat something,' he told himself. And he tried soaking a biscuit in an old Constantia* of J.-P. Cloete, a few bottles of which still remained in his cellar.

This wine, the colour of a slightly burnt onion skin, was not unlike a well-balanced Malaga or a Port, but it had a sweet, distinctive bouquet, and an after-taste of juices condensed and purified by blazing suns; he had, at times, found it restorative, and on several occasions it had even infused fresh energy into his stomach weakened by the fasts he was forced to undergo; but this cordial, normally so reliable, brought him no relief. Next, hoping that an emollient might perhaps moderate the red-hot irons that were burning him, he tried Nalifka, a Russian liqueur, contained in a bottle with a dull gold glaze; but that unctuous, raspberry-flavoured syrup had likewise no effect. Long gone, alas, were the days when, in his own home, in the heat of high summer, a perfectly healthy Des Esseintes would climb into a sled and, wrapped in fur rugs, would pull them up to his chest, forcing himself to shiver, and would tell himself, deliberately making his teeth chatter: 'Ah! What an icy wind, it's freezing here, it's freezing!' so that he almost succeeded in convincing himself that it really was cold!

Unfortunately, now that his ailments were genuine, these remedies were no longer efficacious. Nor was he able, either, to resort to laudanum; instead of soothing him, that sedative agitated him to the point of depriving him of sleep. In the past he had tried using opium and hashish to generate mental fantasies, but these two substances had brought on vomiting and intense nervous disturbances; he had been obliged to stop using them immediately, and to ask his brain alone to carry him, without the aid of these crude stimulants, far from real life into the world of dreams.

'What a day!' he said to himself now, mopping his neck and feeling what little strength he still possessed dissolve away in a fresh access of sweating; a feverish excitation still prevented him from remaining in one place; again he roamed through his different rooms, trying every chair in turn. Finally, giving up the struggle, and slumping into the chair at his desk, he stayed leaning on the writing-table, his mind quite empty, automatically running his fingers over an astrolabe which lay, in place of a paperweight, on top of a pile of books and notes.

This instrument, made of engraved and gilded copper, was German in origin, and dated from the seventeenth century. He had bought it from a Paris second-hand dealer following a visit to the Cluny Museum, where he had spent hours gazing rapturously at a marvellous carved ivory astrolabe whose cabbalistic character he had found enchanting.

The paperweight aroused a host of recollections in him. Prompted by the sight of this ornament, his thoughts left Fontenay for Paris, returning to the dealer who had sold it, then travelled further back to the Cluny Museum, and in his mind he again saw the ivory astrolabe, while his eyes continued to contemplate, though without seeing it, the copper astrolabe that lay on his table.

Then, leaving the Museum—though not the city—he sauntered through the streets, strolled down the Rue du Sommerard and the Boulevard Saint-Michel, turned off into adjacent thoroughfares and paused in front of certain establishments, the number and highly distinctive appearance of which had frequently attracted his attention. Inspired, initially, by an astrolabe, this spiritual journey finally led to the dives of the Latin Quarter.

He recalled how many there were of these establishments, the whole way down the Rue Monsieur-le-Prince and that part of the Rue de Vaugirard which leads to the Odéon; sometimes they followed hard one upon the other, like the old *riddecks** of the Rue du Canal-aux-Harengs in Antwerp, that stretch out in an uninterrupted line, their almost identical façades dominating the pavement.

He remembered having glimpsed, through half-open doors and windows inadequately screened by curtains or panes of coloured glass, women who walked with dragging gait and out-thrust head, the way geese do; others who lounged around on benches, roughening their elbows on the marble table-tops as they brooded, head in hands, humming softly; yet others who were wriggling about in front of mirrors, patting with their fingertips at hair-pieces spruced up by the coiffeur; and then there were still others who were extracting, from purses with broken catches, handfuls of coins and small change which they stacked methodically into little piles. Most of these women had coarse features, husky voices, flabby jowls, and painted eyes, and every one of them, like automata who were all being wound up at the same time by the same key, proffered the same invitations in the same tone of voice and, smiling in the same way, uttered the same bizarre remarks, the same outlandish reflections.

Now that he was able to conjure up, in memory, a bird's-eye view of that mass of bars and streets, Des Esseintes found that associations of ideas were forming in his mind and that he was reaching a conclusion. He understood the significance of those cafés which reflected the mood of an entire generation, and from them he deduced the synthesis of that period.

And indeed the symptoms were clear and unmistakable; the brothels were disappearing, and as soon as one of them closed, a low-class bar would open. This diminution of licensed prostitution* in favour of secret love affairs was obviously a consequence of the incomprehensible illusions of men in matters relating to carnal love.

Monstrous though the idea might appear, the low-class bar satisfied an ideal.

Although the utilitarian tendencies passed on by heredity, and fostered by the precocious disrespect and unremitting brutalities of the schools, had made present-day youth singularly ill-mannered as well as singularly matter-of-fact and cold, they had none the less preserved, deep in their hearts, a romantic blossom* from earlier times, an ancient ideal of a musty, vague attachment.

But nowadays, when tormented by their physical urges, the young could not bring themselves to go in, enjoy, pay, and leave; they saw this as a kind of bestiality, like the rutting of a dog who without preamble covers a bitch; besides, vanity fled those brothels unsatisfied, finding in them no semblance of resistance, nor pretence of victory, nor hoped-for preference, nor even any liberality on the part of the vendor, who measured out her caresses according to their market value. The wooing of a barmaid, by contrast, spared every susceptibility of love, every delicacy of sentiment. There were competitors for a barmaid's favours, and those to whom she consented to grant an assignation (in return for generous payment) sincerely imagined they had triumphed over a rival, been granted a great honour, an exceptional favour.

However, those girls working in bars were as stupid, as self-seeking, as base, and as self-indulgent as the women who worked in brothels. Like the prostitutes, they drank without being thirsty, laughed without being amused, went into raptures over the caresses of a common labourer, maligned one another, and scrapped with one another without the slightest provocation; in spite of that, the youth of Paris had never yet observed that, as regards beauty of form, skill of technique, and desirable attire, barmaids were clearly inferior to the women cooped up in the luxurious salons of brothels. 'My God,' thought Des Esseintes, 'what fools these fellows are who hang round bars! Quite apart from their idiotic illusions, they even manage to forget the risks associated with damaged or dubious merchandise, to no longer take into account the money spent on a lot of drinks the landlady charges for in advance, or the time wasted in waiting for goods whose delivery is deferred so as to enhance their value, or the endless shilly-shallying used to prompt and to promote the sport of tipping!'

This inane sentimentalism, combined with a fierce practicality, epitomized the dominant thinking of the century; those same individuals who would have blinded their neighbour for the sake of ten sous lost all their rationality, all their shrewdness when confronted by those shifty tavern girls who harrassed them without mercy and extorted money from them without remission. Business enterprises laboured and families swindled one another in the name of commerce, so that their money could be filched by their sons; they in their turn let themselves be cheated by these women who, in the final analysis, were robbed of everything by their fancy men.

Throughout the whole of Paris, from east to west, from north to south, there existed an uninterrupted sequence of frauds, a pile-up of organized thefts each of which occasioned the next; and all this because, instead of customers being satisfied on the spot, they were persuaded to exercise their patience, they were kept waiting. Essentially, the sum total of human wisdom consisted in dragging things out, in saying 'no' then, eventually, 'yes'; for the most effective way of controlling the younger generation was by constantly putting them off!

'Ah, if only that was true of one's stomach,' sighed Des Esseintes, racked by a cramp which brought his straying thoughts sharply back to Fontenay.

14

Des Esseintes managed to struggle along for several days, thanks to various ruses with which he successfully deluded his distrustful stomach, but there came a morning when he could no longer tolerate the marinades that masked the odour of fat and the smell of blood on the meat, and he wondered anxiously whether his weakness, already quite advanced, might not be going to worsen and force him to remain in bed. Suddenly a gleam of light pierced his distress: he remembered that some time ago a friend of his who was seriously ill had managed, by using a device for making beef essence, to control his anaemia, to arrest the decline of his health, and to conserve what little strength he still possessed.

He dispatched his servant to Paris in search of this precious piece of equipment and, following the manufacturer's instructions, he himself showed the cook how to chop the sirloin into tiny pieces, put these without any liquid into the metal pot with a slice of leek and one of carrot, then screw down the lid and set the whole thing cooking in a double-boiler for four hours.

At the end of this time you squeezed the shreds of meat and drank a spoonful of the cloudy, salty juice which lay in the bottom of the pot. As you did so you felt something like warm bone-marrow, like a velvety caress, slide down your throat.

This nourishing extract put a stop to the gnawing pangs and nausea of emptiness, and even tempted the stomach into accepting a few spoonfuls of soup.

Thanks to this device, the progress of his neurosis was arrested, and Des Esseintes told himself: 'So far so good; perhaps the temperature will drop, perhaps the heavens will cast a little greyness over this odious sun which is so exhausting, and then I shall, without too much difficulty, be able to last out until the first fogs and the first cold spells.'

Sunk as he was into this state of torpor and bored inactivity, his library, which he had still not finished rearranging, got on his nerves. As he never budged from his armchair, his collection of secular works remained constantly within his view, lying askew on the shelves, overlapping one another, leaning against one another or toppled over flat on their backs like toy soldiers; this disarray plagued him all the more because of the contrast it formed with the perfectly balanced arrangement of the volumes on religion, which were carefully aligned, as if on parade, along the walls.

He tried to remedy this confusion but after ten minutes of work he was drenched in sweat; the effort exhausted him; quite worn out, he went and lay down on a sofa and rang for his servant.

Under his instructions, the old man set to work, bringing books over to him one by one; he examined them and indicated where they should be placed.

This task took but little time, for Des Esseintes's library contained remarkably few contemporary secular works. By dint of having subjected them, in his mind, to a process similar to that whereby metal strips are passed through a steel drawing plate, from which they emerge as very thin and light in weight, reduced almost to invisible threads, he had ended up owning only books which could survive that kind of treatment and were sufficiently tough to withstand the additional test of rereading; in attempting to refine his collection in this manner, he had curbed and almost destroyed any pleasure it might afford, by further emphasizing the irreconcilable conflict between his ideas and the world into which fate had decreed he should be born. He had now reached a point where he could no longer find any written work that satisfied his secret desires; and he was even withdrawing his admiration from books which had unquestionably contributed to sharpening his mind, to making it as wary and as subtle as it was.

And yet the point of view from which his ideas on art had sprung was a simple one: for him, literary schools did not exist; the only thing that mattered was the temperament of the artist; the only thing of interest was the way his brain worked, regardless of the subject he was treating. Unfortunately, this forthright approach, worthy of La Palisse,* was more or less inapplicable, for the simple reason that while trying to free himself from prejudice and eschew all passion, every reader turns first to those works which correspond most intimately with his own personality, and ends up rejecting all the rest.

This process of selection had slowly taken place in him; in the past, he had adored the great Balzac,* but at the same time as his constitution had become unbalanced and his nerves had gained the upper hand, his tastes had altered and the objects of his admiration had changed.

Indeed, before long, and although he realized how unfair he was being to the prodigious author of the *Comédie humaine*, he reached the point of no longer opening his books, for he found Balzac's vigorous art irksome; different aspirations excited him now, aspirations which were becoming in a sense indefinable.

However, by delving into his own mind, he first of all grasped that, to appeal to him, a work must possess that aura of strangeness which Edgar Allan Poe required; but he readily ventured further along that path, demanding over-subtle creations of the intellect and complex deliquescences* of language; what he wanted was a disturbing ambivalence he could muse about, until he chose to make it either vaguer or more precise, according to his state of mind at that particular moment. In a word, he wanted a work of art both for what it intrinsically was and for what it potentially allowed him to impart to it; he wanted to go forward with it and because of it, as if aided by an acolyte, as if transported in a vehicle, into a sphere where sublimated feelings would induce in him a state of turmoil which was unexpected, and the causes of which he would, over a long period, try—though quite in vain—to analyse.

In brief, since leaving Paris, he was moving further and further away from reality, and especially from the contemporary world which inspired an ever-growing disgust in him; this aversion had necessarily affected his literary and artistic tastes, and he distanced himself as much as possible from pictures and books whose limited subjects related to modern life.

Consequently, having lost the capacity to admire all beauty impartially, without regard to the form it might take, he preferred Flaubert's *Tentation de saint Antoine* to his *Éducation sentimentale*, Goncourt's *Faustin* to *Germinie Lacerteux*, Zola's *Faute de l'abbé Mouret* to *L'Assommoir*.*

This point of view seemed logical to him; these works, less topical but fully as vibrant and as human, enabled him to penetrate more profoundly into the personalities of their creators, who revealed with greater spontaneity the most mysterious flights of their being, and in their company he too could soar up, more so than with other books, high above this petty existence of which he was so weary.

Furthermore, in reading them, he entered into complete intellectual communion with the writers who had engendered them, because they had then been in a spiritual state analogous to his own. Indeed, when the period in which a man of talent is condemned to live is dull and stupid, the artist is haunted, unknowingly perhaps, by a yearning for a different era. Unable to attune himself—except at rare intervals—to the environment in which he moves; no longer finding, in the study of this environment and of the creatures who endure it, that the pleasures of observation and analysis are adequate distractions, he becomes conscious that certain phenomena are developing and maturing in him. Confused cravings for change arise, and with reflection and study these grow clearer. Inherited instincts, feelings, and propensities are aroused, become increasingly specific, and assert themselves with peremptory boldness. He recalls memories of beings and things which he personally has never known, and the time comes when he breaks violently out of the prison of his century and wanders in complete freedom in a different period with which—as an ultimate self-deception—he imagines he would have been more in harmony.

Some writers take the reader back to past ages, to vanished civilizations, to periods dead and gone; others take a leap into the fantastic and the world of dreams, their vision portraying, with greater or lesser intensity, a time as yet unborn, in which, by an atavistic reaction, the writer unwittingly reproduces the image of past epochs.

In the case of Flaubert we were given vast and majestic scenes, grandiose displays with barbaric, splendid settings peopled by quiveringly sensitive, delicate creatures, mysterious and aloof, women burdened, because of their flawless beauty, with tormented souls, in the depths of which he could already discern horrifying delusions and insane longings, born of their anguish at the daunting mediocrity of those pleasures that might lie ahead.

The entire personality of the great artist sparkled in those incomparable pages of *La Tentation de saint Antoine* and of *Salammbô*,* where, far from our mean-spirited existence, he evoked the oriental brilliance of past centuries, with their mystical exaltation and despair, their aberrations born of idleness, their savagery prompted by that oppressive boredom which is produced—even before these have been experienced to the full—by opulence and by prayer.

In the case of Goncourt, it was a craving for the preceding century, for a return to the elegance of a society lost for ever. The colossal settings where seas battered at breakwaters, where deserts stretched to infinity under torrid skies, had no place in his nostalgic world which confined itself to a boudoir beside a formal garden, warmed by the voluptuous fragrance of a woman with a weary smile, a perversely pouting expression, and unresigned, pensive eyes. The soul with which he gave life to his characters was no longer that with which Flaubert chose to animate his creations, a soul already repelled by the grim certainty that no fresh happiness was possible; it was a soul revolted after the fact, by the experience of all its futile efforts to create less hackneyed spiritual relationships, and to enhance that immemorial sexual pleasure which is passed on down the centuries in the more or less inventively achieved erotic satisfaction of couples.

Although she lived among us and belonged both in mind and body to our own time, La Faustin was, through the influence of her heritage, a creature of the past century, endowed with its ribald spirit, its intellectual indolence, and its penchant for sexual excess.

This novel of Edmond de Goncourt's was one of Des Esseintes's favourites, and in fact that enticement to dream which he craved overflowed from the book, where, beneath the printed line, one could detect another line, visible only to the mind, signalled by a qualifier offering glimpses of passion, by an understatement hinting at depths of the soul which no words could satisfy; and then, too, the language was no longer Flaubert's, that language of unparalleled magnificence, it was a style at once shrewd and vitiated, terse and cunning, painstaking in recording the intangible impression which affects the senses and determines feeling, a style expert at measuring every complicated nuance of an age which was itself extraordinarily complex. In brief, it was the indispensable medium for decaying civilizations which, regardless of their period, require, for the expression of their needs, fresh meanings, fresh stylistic structures, and fresh forms for both words and phrases.

Paganism, in its dying days in Rome, had modified its prosody and transformed its language through Ausonius, through Claudian, and through Rutilius, whose style, careful and precise, sensuous and resounding, provided, particularly in those passages that describe light and shade and subtle tones, an inevitable analogy with the style of the Goncourt brothers.

In Paris, something unique in the history of literature had taken place; that doomed society of the eighteenth century, which had engendered painters, sculptors, musicians, and architects who were deeply influenced by its tastes and imbued with its doctrines, had been unable to produce a genuine writer to do justice to its moribund elegance and to express the essence of its feverish pleasures, for which it paid so extreme a price. Literature had had to await the arrival of Goncourt, whose personality was formed by recollections and regrets which the bitter spectacle of his own age's intellectual poverty and base aspirations further intensified, so that, not only in his historical works but also in a nostalgic work like *La Faustin*, he might revive the very soul of that period, and embody its nervous sensitivities in this actress who felt such a tormenting compulsion to importune her heart and torture her brain, in order to savour, to the point of exhaustion, the painful counter-irritants of love and of art!

For Zola, the yearning for what lies beyond reality was different. There was in him no desire to journey back to regimes that have vanished or worlds that are lost in the mists of time; his nature, powerful, staunch, attracted to the luxuriance of life, to full-blooded vigour and moral health, made him dislike the artificial charms and rouged pallor of the last century, just as he disliked the hieratic rituals, the brutal ferocity, and the effeminate, ambiguous dreams of the ancient Orient. When he too in his turn became obsessed by this nostalgia, by this urge (which is, in essence, poetry itself) to escape far from the modern world which he was studying, he had plunged headlong into an idealized countryside where the sap bubbled up under a hot sun; he had dreamt fantastic dreams of heavenly copulations and of an earth fainting from desire, of fecundating rains of pollen falling into the throbbing genitals of flowers; ultimately his visions had led to a gigantic pantheism and, with this Edenic setting where he placed his Adam and Eve,* he had—perhaps unconsciously—created a marvellous Hindu poem, and, in a style whose bold strokes of colour, daubed on uncompromisingly, had the strange brilliance of an Indian painting, he had sung a hymn to the glory of the flesh, and to living, breathing matter, which by its generative frenzy reveals to the human creature the forbidden fruit of love, its overpowering emotions, its instinctive caresses, its natural poses.

With Baudelaire, these three were the masters of modern, secular French literature who had the most intimately penetrated and shaped

Des Esseintes's mind, but by dint of rereading them, of immersing himself in their works, of knowing them by heart from beginning to end, he had been forced, so as to be able to absorb them afresh, to try to forget them, and to leave them for a while unopened on his shelves.

So now, as the manservant handed them to him, he barely glanced into them. He confined himself to indicating where they should be placed, making sure that they were shelved in the correct order and with appropriate spacing.

The manservant brought him another set of books; these were more of a problem; they were books for which he had gradually developed a liking, books which he found—by virtue of their very faults—a refreshing change from the perfection of writers of greater stature; in this case, again, in seeking to refine his pleasure, Des Esseintes had gone so far as to search through pages of mediocre writing for sentences emitting a kind of electricity that would startle him, even though they discharged into a medium which appeared at first to be unpromising.

Imperfection itself pleased him, provided it was neither parasitic nor ignoble, and there may perhaps have been a grain of truth in his theory that the decadent period's minor writers—those who, while still personal, were not consummate artists—distil a balm more irritant, more stimulating, more acid, than the artist of the same period who is truly great, truly perfect. In his view, it was among their disorderly unfinished drafts that one could see the most extreme transports of sensibility, the most morbid vagaries of psychology, the most outrageous perversions of a style pushed, beyond its ultimate limits, into containing and coating the effervescent salts of sensations and ideas.

It was therefore inevitable that, after the great masters, he should turn to a few writers whom he valued and cherished the more, because of the scorn in which they were held by a public incapable of understanding them.

One of these, Paul Verlaine,* had begun, some years before, with a volume of verse, the *Poèmes saturniens*, an almost anaemic work, where pastiches of Leconte de Lisle* stood shoulder to shoulder with exercises in romantic rhetoric; but where one could already discern, filtering through certain poems like the sonnet entitled 'Rêve familier', the true personality of the poet.

Seeking Verlaine's antecedents, Des Esseintes recognized, beneath the uncertainties of early drafts, a talent already profoundly imbued with Baudelaire, whose influence subsequently grew more pronounced, although the gifts bestowed by the indefectible master never seemed flagrantly obvious. Indeed, some of his later volumes, *La Bonne Chanson*, *Les Fêtes galantes*, *Romances sans paroles*, and his last, *Sagesse*, contained poems which revealed an original artist, who stood out from among the multitude of his fellow-writers.

Using rhymes supplied by verbal tenses, sometimes, even, by long adverbs preceded by a monosyllable from which they poured like a heavy waterfall cascading over a ledge of rock, his verses, bisected by unlikely caesuras, often became extraordinarily abstruse, with their daring ellipses and bizarre solecisms which were not, however, devoid of charm.

An unparalleled master of prosody, he had tried to rejuvenate the conventional poetic forms, the sonnet for example, which he turned upside down with its tail in the air, like those Japanese polychrome clay fish which stand on their base with their gills pointing down; or else he had distorted them, coupling together only masculine rhymes, for which he seemed to have a fondness; he had also often used a very strange form, a stanza of three lines with the second left unrhymed, and a monorhyming tercet followed by a single line added as a refrain that echoes itself like 'Dansons la Gigue' in 'Streets';* he had used still other types of rhyme, with an almost imperceptible timbre which could be distinguished only in distant stanzas, like the muffled ringing of a bell.

But his personality was above all evident in the way he could impart vague, delicious confidences in a whisper, in the twilight. He alone had known how to hint at certain troubling, ineffable mysteries of the soul, thoughts breathed so softly, confessions whispered so faintly and haltingly that the ear which perceived them was left in doubt, communicating to the soul a languor intensified by that mysterious susurration which was inferred rather than heard. Every modulation of Verlaine's voice was audible in these wonderful lines from *Les Fêtes galantes*:

> Le soir tombait, un soir équivoque d'automne:
> Les belles se pendant rêveuses à nos bras,
> Dirent alors des mots si spécieux, tout bas,
> Que notre âme depuis ce temps tremble et s'étonne.*

No longer was this the immense horizon revealed through Baudelaire's unforgettable portals, this was a partial view—glimpsed by moonlight—of a more limited, more intimate scene, in short, a scene peculiar to Verlaine who had, moreover, formulated his poetic system in lines which Des Esseintes found delectable:

> Car nous voulons la nuance encore,
> Pas la couleur, rien que la nuance
>
> .   .   .   .   .   .
>
> Et tout le reste est littérature.*

Des Esseintes had happily kept him company through all of his wide-ranging works. After his *Romances sans paroles*, published by a newspaper press in Sens,* Verlaine had remained silent for quite a time, and then returned in some charming verses where one could hear the sweet and piercing tones of Villon, singing the praises of the Virgin 'loin de nos jours d'esprit charnel et de chair triste'.* Des Esseintes often reread that volume, *Sagesse*, and its poems inspired him to create secret fantasies, fictions about a covert love for a Byzantine madonna capable at any given moment of changing into a Cydalisa* who had strayed into our century, a creature so mysterious and disturbing that one could not tell whether she yearned for depravities so monstrous that they would become irresistible the instant they were realized, or whether she herself was about to soar off into a dream, a dream of immaculate purity where she would be enveloped in a cloud of spiritual adoration that remained forever undeclared, forever pure.

There were yet other poets who inspired his trust: Tristan Corbière,* for example, had, in 1873, in the face of widespread indifference, produced a work of the utmost eccentricity entitled *Les Amours jaunes*. Des Esseintes, who, out of a loathing for the banal and the commonplace, would have welcomed the most laboured literary follies, the most flamboyant extravaganzas, passed many light-hearted hours with this book, in which the comic was intermingled with a chaotic energy, where single disconcerting lines would shine forth brilliantly from totally unintelligible poems like the litanies of his 'Sommeil', where at a certain point he described sleep as: 'Obscène confesseur des dévotes mort-nées.'*

It was barely French; the author was using 'pidgin'* and telegraphese, suppressing far too many verbs, affecting a bantering tone, indulging in dreadful commercial-traveller jokes; then, out of the blue, from this jumbled mess squirming with grotesque conceits and dubious, smirk-provoking remarks, there would burst forth a sudden piercing cry of pain, like a violin string breaking. Furthermore, that harsh, dry, capriciously bare style, bristling with unusual words and unexpected neologisms, would be suddenly illuminated by the flash of some superb stylistic gem or stray fragment of verse shorn of its rhyme; then again, quite apart from his *Poèmes parisiens*, in which this profound definition of woman particularly struck Des Esseintes: 'Éternel féminin de l'éternel jocrisse',* Tristan Corbière had, in a style of almost powerful conciseness, sung the praises of the Britanny seas, the mariners' seraglios, the Pardon of Sainte-Anne, and had even raised himself up to the eloquence of loathing in the invective, referring to the Conlie camp,* which he heaped upon those individuals he called 'the charlatans of the Fourth of September.'

That strong, gamey flavour which Des Esseintes relished and which this poet, with his convoluted epithets and his always faintly suspect stylistic charms, offered him, he also found in another poet he read, Théodore Hannon,* a disciple of Baudelaire and of Gautier, an artist stirred by a very particular sense of studied elegances and factitious pleasures.

By contrast with Verlaine, who was a direct descendant of Baudelaire's, especially in his psychology, his sophistical refinement of thought, and the scholarly essence of his consciousness, Théodore Hannon was above all a follower of the master in the plastic aspect of his work, in his outer vision of beings and things.

His corrupt charm inevitably corresponded with the proclivities of Des Esseintes who, on days of fog or rain, would shut himself up in the retreat of this poet's imagination and intoxicate his eyes with the shimmering of his fabrics, with the scintillations of his precious stones, with his exclusively materialistic luxuries which combined to stimulate the brain, rising up like cantharides in a cloud of warm incense towards an exotic idol with a painted face and a belly tanned by perfumes.

With the exception of these poets and of Stéphane Mallarmé, whom he instructed his servant to put on one side, in order to classify him separately, Des Esseintes was only very moderately drawn to the poets.

Despite his magnificent style, despite the imposing effect of his verse which was so brilliant that even Hugo's hexameters seem by comparison dreary and dull, Leconte de Lisle could now no longer satisfy him. In his hands, the ancient world so marvellously re-created by Flaubert remained cold and lifeless. No heart beat in his poetry which was all façade, and for the most part lacked any ideas to support it; nothing lived in those barren poems whose sterile mythologies now left him unmoved. Similarly, after cherishing him for years, Des Esseintes was also losing interest in Gautier's work;* his admiration for the incomparable painter that this man was had been lessening with every passing day, and now he was more amazed than entranced by those descriptions of his which for some reason seemed uninteresting. Gautier's highly perceptive eye retained a firm impression of an object but this impression was localized, it did not penetrate further into his brain and his flesh; like some extraordinary reflecting mirror, he had always restricted himself to reproducing, with impersonal precision, images of his surroundings.

Des Esseintes did of course still take pleasure in the works of these two poets, just as he took pleasure in rare gemstones and in precious minerals, but no longer could any of the variations of those con-summate instrumentalists fill him with rapture, for none lent itself to dreaming, none gave access, at any rate for him, to one of those vivid experiences which enabled him to speed up the slow passage of the hours.

Reading their poems would leave him deeply unsatisfied, and the same was true when he read Hugo; the oriental and patriarchal side of Hugo was too conventional, too hollow, to hold his interest, while the side that simultaneously evoked the nursemaid and the grand-father exasperated him; it was not until he read *Les Chansons des rues et des bois** that he could whinny admiringly at the impeccable jug-glery of his prosody, but, when all was said and done, with what eagerness would he not have exchanged those feats for a new work by Baudelaire that equalled those already in existence! For undoubt-edly Baudelaire was almost the only poet whose verses, beneath the splendour of their outer bark, contained an aromatic and nutritious pith!

In making the leap from one extreme to the other, from form bereft of ideas to ideas bereft of form, Des Esseintes remained just as cir-cumspect and dispassionate. He was fascinated by Stendhal's psychological labyrinths and Duranty's* analytical divagations, but their bureaucratic, arid, colourless language, their hireling prose, suited— at best—to the ignoble activity of the theatre, repelled him. And besides, to put it in a nutshell, the interesting operations of their perceptive analyses were carried out on minds fired by passions which he no longer shared. He cared little for commonly experienced emotions, for everyday associations of ideas, now that the closing of his mind had grown more pronounced, and he allowed access only to the most highly refined sensations, to crises of faith and to violent disorders of the senses.

In order to enjoy a work that united (as his own tastes dictated) an incisive style with a penetrating and supple analytical approach, he had had to turn to the master of Induction, that strange, profound Edgar Allan Poe, for whom, since the moment he had begun rereading him, his attachment had never wavered.

He, perhaps more than anyone else, conformed, by virtue of deeply personal affinities, with the requirements postulated by Des Esseintes's meditations.

While Baudelaire, in deciphering the hieroglyphics of the soul, studied emotions and ideas at the point of crisis, Poe, working within the sphere of morbid psychology, subjected the domain of the will to particular scrutiny. In literature, he, under the emblematic title of 'The Imp of the Perverse', was the first to explore those irresistible impulses to which the will is subject without recognizing them and for which the pathology of the brain now provides a fairly definitive explanation; he was also the first, if not to emphasize, at any rate to reveal the depressant influence of fear on the will, just as anaesthetics paralyse the senses and curare destroys the motor impulses of the nerves; it was on this point, on this torpor of the will, that his studies all converged, analysing the effects of this moral poison, indicating the symptoms of its progress and the disorders it occasions, beginning with anxiety, moving on to anguish, and ultimately exploding into a terror which numbs the will without prostrating the intellect, badly shaken though this may be.

In his hands, death—a subject so inordinately abused by every dramatist—was, as it were, given a keener edge, made other, by his introduction of an algebraic, superhuman element; but it was, in fact, less the actual physical agony of the dying that he described, than the moral agony of the survivor who, watching beside the awful deathbed, is haunted by the monstrous hallucinations that distress and fatigue engender. He would dwell with a dreadful kind of fascination on acts inspired by terror, on the fracturing of the will, dispassionately rationalizing these, gradually gripping the reader in a stranglehold that leaves him dry-mouthed and breathless in the presence of these mechanically induced, delirium-ridden nightmares.

Violently agitated by hereditary neuroses, maddened by convulsive moral disturbances, his creatures lived solely on their nerves; his women, his Morellas and Ligeias, possessed a vast erudition that was steeped in the fogs of German philosophy and the cabbalistic mysteries of the ancient Orient; all of them had the mannish, inert breasts of angels, they were all, so to speak, asexual.

Baudelaire and Poe, those two minds which had often been coupled together on account of their similar poetics, their mutual interest in the study of mental illness, differed radically in the emotional concepts which played so important a part in their writings. Baudelaire portrayed a bloodthirsty, malevolent passion, reminiscent, in its cruel disillusionments, of the retributions of the Inquisition; Poe, a chaste, incorporeal love, in which the senses played no part but only the brain was aroused, without any correspondence to organs which, supposing they even existed, remained in a perpetual state of frigid virginity.

This mental hospital where Poe, the surgeon of the psyche, performed vivisections in a stifling atmosphere, becoming, the instant his attention flagged, victim of his own imagination (which would conjure up somnambulistic, angelic apparitions like so many delightful miasmas) was, for Des Esseintes, a source of untiring conjectures; however, now that his neurosis had been exacerbated, there were days when he found reading Poe utterly exhausting, days when he was left with trembling hands and ears on the alert, feeling himself, like the wretched Usher,* filled with an irrational terror, with a secret dread.

He was therefore compelled to exercise great moderation, barely touching these dangerous elixirs, just as he could no longer with impunity visit his red vestibule and regale his eyes with the dark visions of Odilon Redon, or with Jan Luyken's portrayals of torture.

And yet, when he was in this frame of mind, all literature seemed insipid to him after those terrible potions imported from America. He would then turn to Villiers de l'Isle-Adam,* in whose sporadic works he found remarks equally seditious, vibrations equally convulsive, but which no longer—except in the case of his 'Claire Lenoir'*—projected such a devastating horror.

Appearing in 1867 in the *Revue des lettres et des arts*, this 'Claire Lenoir' opened a series of short stories published under the generic title of *Histories moroses*. Against a background of obscure speculations taken from the later works of Hegel, we find some unhinged characters bustling about: a puerile, self-important doctor Tribulat Bonhomet, and a Claire Lenoir, comic yet sinister, with round blue spectacles as large as five-franc pieces covering her almost lifeless eyes.

This tale, which centred on a simple case of adultery, came to an inexpressibly terrifying conclusion when Bonhomet, uncovering the pupils of Claire's eyes after her death, and piercing them with monstrous probes, saw clearly reflected therein the image of her husband, flourishing at arm's length the decapitated head of the lover and bellowing out a war-song like some South Sea Island savage.

Based upon the reasonably correct observation that the eyes of certain animals, for example oxen, retain right up to the point of decomposition (as do photographic plates) the image of beings and things upon which their final glance rested at the moment of death, this story was obviously modelled on those of Edgar Allan Poe, the meticulous analyses and terrifying effects of which it adopted for its own.

The same was true of 'L'Intersigne,' later published with the *Contes cruels*, a collection of indisputable talent containing 'Véra',* a work which Des Esseintes considered a minor masterpiece. Here, the hallucination was characterized by an exquisite tenderness; no longer was this one of those gloomy apparitions typical of the American author, but a warm and fluctuating vision that was almost heavenly; the opposite (though identical in kind) of the Beatrices and the Ligeias, those pale and dismal ghosts engendered by the inexorable nightmare of the demon opium. This story likewise involved the operations of the will, but no longer did it describe its failures and defeats under the influence of fear; on the contrary, it studied its moments of exaltation under the impetus of a conviction which had grown into an obsession; it demonstrated the power of the will which could even permeate the atmosphere, and impose its beliefs on its environment.

Another of Villiers's books, *Isis*, struck him as interesting for different reasons. This too was cluttered up with the jumble of philosophical thought we find in 'Claire Lenoir', and offered the reader an incredible hotch-potch of verbose, confused observations and memories of old melodramas—oubliettes, daggers, rope ladders—of all those enduring romantic devices that Villiers was unable to restore to life in his *Elën* and his *Morgane*, plays now forgotten, published by a certain Francisque Guyon, an obscure printer in Saint-Brieuc.

The heroine of *Isis*, a Marquise Tullia Fabriana,* who was supposed to have assimilated the Chaldean science of Edgar Allan Poe's female characters and the diplomatic acumen of Stendhal's Duchess Sanseverina-Taxis,* had in addition assumed the enigmatic countenance of a Bradamante* crossed with a Circe from antiquity. These incompatible elements produced, in combination, a murky vapour in which philosophic and literary influences jostled one another, having been unable to sort themselves out in the author's mind when he was composing the prolegomena to this work, which was to consist of no fewer than seven volumes.

But there was another side to Villiers's personality, a much sharper, more clearly defined side, characterized by black humour and savage mockery; this inspired not paradoxical mystifications like those of Poe but a bitter and lugubrious raillery of the kind Swift relished. A series of works, *Les Demoiselles de Bienfilâtre*, *L'Affichage céleste*, *La Machine à gloire*, *Le Plus beau dîner du monde*, revealed a facetious turn of mind that was extraordinarily inventive and caustic. All the vileness of contemporary utilitarian notions, all the shameful commercialism of the age were immortalized in plays whose poignant irony filled Des Esseintes with intense delight.

No other work in France embodied this type of serious, acerbic ridicule;* the nearest thing was a story by Charles Cros, 'La Science de l'amour',* published long ago in *La Revue du Monde Nouveau*, which might surprise the reader with its scientific absurdities, its wry humour, and its coldly comic observations, but the pleasure it gave was only relative, for its execution was fatally flawed. The firm, colourful, often original style of Villiers had vanished, replaced by a brawn made from scrapings off the workbench of the nearest literary hack.

'My God! How few books there are that are worth rereading,'

sighed Des Esseintes, watching the servant come down from his perch on a three-legged stool and move to one side, so that his master could see all the shelves at a glance.

Des Esseintes gave a nod of approval. There remained on the table only two slim booklets. Dismissing the old man with a gesture, he glanced through a number of sheets bound in onager skin which had been glazed under a hydraulic press, dappled with water-coloured silver clouds, and supplied with endpapers of Chinese flowered silk, on which the slightly faded flower sprays possessed that etiolated charm which Mallarmé* praised in such an enchanting poem. These pages, nine in all, had been taken from unique copies of the first two *Parnasses*,* printed on parchment, and were preceded by the title: *Quelques vers de Mallarmé*, penned by an amazing calligrapher in coloured uncial characters picked out, like those of old manuscripts, with flecks of gold.

Among the eleven poems collected between these covers, there were some—'Les Fenêtres', 'L'Épilogue', 'Azur'—that greatly appealed to him, but one of them, a fragment of 'L'Hérodiade',* bewitched him, at certain times, like a spell.

How many evenings, beneath the lamp that lit the silent room with its dim glow, had he not sensed the gossamer touch of that Herodias who, in Gustave Moreau's painting—now sunk in shadow—was fading into something ever more faint, leaving only an indistinct glimpse of a white statue amid the dying embers of a brazier of jewels! The darkness hid the blood, deadened the colours and the gold, plunged the far reaches of the temple into shadow, engulfed the accomplices of the crime where they stood wrapped in their sombre hues and, sparing only the pale tones of water-colour, drew out the woman from the sheath of her jewels, enhancing her nakedness.

He would turn his eyes compulsively towards her, picking her out by the well-remembered lines of her body, and she would live once more, evoking for him these strange, sweet verses that Mallarmé puts in her lips:

> . . . O miroir!
> Eau froide par l'ennui dans ton cadre gelée
> Que de fois et pendant des heures, désolée
> Des songes et cherchant mes souvenirs qui sont
> Comme des feuilles sous ta glace au trou profond,

Je m'apparus en toi comme une ombre lointaine,
Mais, horreur! des soirs, dans ta sévère fontaine,
J'ai de mon rêve épars connu la nudité!*

He loved these lines, as he loved all the works of this poet who, in an age of universal suffrage and a period when money reigned supreme, lived apart from the world of letters, protected by his contempt from the stupidity surrounding him, taking pleasure, far from society, in the revelations of the intellect, in the fantasies of his brain, further refining already specious ideas, grafting on to them thoughts of exaggerated subtlety, perpetuating them in deductions barely hinted at and tenuously linked by an imperceptible thread. He tied this braid of convoluted, euphuistic ideas with a stylistic knot that was tenacious, solitary, and secret, full of contracted phrases, of elliptical expressions, of daring tropes.

Alert to the most remote analogies, he would often employ a single term simultaneously giving, by association, the form, scent, colour, quality, and brilliancy of the object or being for which a host of different epithets would have been needed to reveal all its aspects, all its nuances, if it had simply been given its technical name. Mallarmé thus contrived to eliminate the terms of the comparison which arose of its own accord in the reader's mind, by analogy, as soon as he had penetrated the symbol, and, avoiding the diffusion of the reader's attention on to each quality individually suggested by a sequence of adjectives, he concentrated it on one single word, on a totality, and produced, as in the case of a painting, an effect that was unique and comprehensive, a whole.

The result was a literary distillate, a concentrated essence, a sublimate of art. This technique, used sparingly in his early works, Mallarmé had paraded boldly in a piece on Théophile Gautier,* and in 'L'Après-midi d'un faune', an eclogue where the subtleties of sensual pleasure were unfolded in mysterious, caressing verses, abruptly rent by this wild, ecstatic cry of the faun:

Alors m'éveillerai-je à la ferveur première,
Droit et seul sous un flot antique de lumière,
Lys! et l'un de vous tous pour l'ingénuité.*

This final line which, by the enjambment of the monosyllable 'lys!' evoked the image of something rigid, slender, white, an image which the rhyming noun 'ingénuité' further emphasized, expressed allegorically, in a single word, the passion, the exhilaration, the transitory excitement of the virgin faun, maddened with sexual desire by the sight of the nymphs.

Every line of this extraordinary poem abounded in surprises, in fresh, previously unimagined images, as the poet described the longings and regrets of the satyr as he gazed from the marsh's edge at the clumps of reeds, which still preserved, in evanescent imprints, the rounded shapes of the naiads who had lain there.

Des Esseintes also derived a specious pleasure from handling this minuscule booklet, with its covers of Japanese felt as white as milk curds, fastened by two silk cords, one Chinese pink, the other black. Concealed behind the binding, the black braid met the pink braid which, like some licentious handmaid, added a whisper of powder, a suggestion of modern Japanese rouge, to the antique whiteness, the artless flesh-tints of the book; it wound itself round the pink, intertwining its sombre colour with the light one in a dainty bow, and introducing a discreet hint of that regret, a vague threat of that sadness which follow in the wake of burnt-out passion and satiated sensual frenzy.

Replacing 'L'Après-midi d'un faune' on the table, Des Esseintes leafed through another little volume which he had had printed for his own use, an anthology of prose poems, a tiny chapel dedicated to Baudelaire and opening on to the parvis of his poems.

This anthology contained a selection from *Le Gaspard de la nuit** by that strange Aloysius Bertrand, who transposed Leonardo da Vinci's methods to prose and with his metallic oxides painted little pictures whose vivid colours sparkled like clear enamels. Des Esseintes had added Villiers's *Vox populi*,* a piece superbly worked in a style of gold, in the manner of Leconte de Lisle and Flaubert, and some extracts from that delicate *Livre de Jade** in which the exotic perfumes of ginseng and tea blend with the fresh fragrance of the babbling water that flows in the moonlight right through the book.

But, in addition, this collection included certain poems rescued from defunct reviews: 'Le Démon de l'analogie',* 'La Pipe', 'Le Pauvre Enfant pâle', 'Le Spectacle interrompu', 'Le Phénomène futur', and most especially 'Plainte d'automne' and 'Frisson d'hiver', Mallarmé's masterpieces, which also ranked among the masterpieces of prose poems, for their style was so magnificently controlled that, in itself, it lulled one like a melancholy incantation, like an intoxicating melody. This style was linked to thoughts of irresistible suggestive power, to the throbbing of the soul of a sensitive being, whose wrought-up nerves pulsate with a keenness that pierces you to the point of ecstasy, to the point of pain.

Of all literary forms, the prose poem was the one which Des Esseintes preferred. In the hands of an alchemist of genius, it should, he believed, contain within its small compass, like beef essence, the power of a novel, while eliminating its tedious analyses and superfluous descriptions. Many times had Des Esseintes reflected upon the thorny problem of how to condense a novel into a few sentences, which would contain the quintessence of the hundreds of pages always required to establish the setting, sketch the characters, and provide a mass of observations and minor facts in corroboration. The words chosen would then be so inevitable that they would render all other words superfluous; the adjective, positioned in so ingenious and so definitive a manner that it could not legitimately be displaced, would open up such vistas that for days on end the reader would ponder over its meaning, at once precise and manifold, would know the present, reconstruct the past, and make conjectures about the future of the souls of the characters, as these were revealed by the light of that single epithet.

Conceived thus, and thus condensed into one or two pages, the novel would become a communion of thought between a magical writer and an ideal reader, a spiritual collaboration of a handful of superior beings scattered throughout the universe, a treat for literary epicures, accessible to them alone.

In a word, the prose poem represented, for Des Esseintes, the physical essence, the osmazome* of literature, the essential oil of art.

This succulent extract already existed, well matured and reduced to a single drop, in the work of Baudelaire, as well as in these poems of Mallarmé's which he was savouring with such intense delight. Closing his anthology, Des Esseintes told himself that, with this final book completing his library, he would probably never again add anything to his collection.

Indeed, the decay of a literature whose organism has received a mortal wound, which is enervated by old ideas and exhausted by a surfeit of syntax, which responds solely to the peculiar interests that exacerbate the sick and yet, in its decline, feels impelled to give expression to everything, and on its deathbed desperately longs to compensate for all the pleasures it has missed and to leave behind a legacy of the subtlest memories of pain—this decay was embodied in Mallarmé in the most consummate, the most exquisite fashion. Here, carried to their most extreme form, were the quintessences of Baudelaire and of Poe; here were their subtlest, most powerful substances distilled even further, giving off new bouquets, fresh intoxicants. Here were the death pangs of the old language which, after being adulterated again and again with the passing centuries, was finally disintegrating, finally arriving at that eclipse which the Latin language attained with the mysterious concepts and enigmatic expressions of St Boniface and St Aldhelm.

The breakdown of the French language, however, took place all at once. In the case of Latin, a lengthy period of transition, a gap of four hundred years existed between the variegated, magnificent styles of Claudian and Rutilius, and the decadent language of the eighth century. In the case of French, there was no lapse of time, no passing of successive ages; the variegated, magnificent style of the Goncourt brothers and the decadent language of Verlaine and of Mallarmé lived side by side in Paris, occurring at the same moment, in the same period, in the same century.

And Des Esseintes smiled to himself, glancing at one of the folio volumes open on his chapel lectern, and reflecting that the time would come when a scholar would produce, for the decadent period of the French language, a glossary* similar to that in which the erudite du Cange noted down the last babblings, the last paroxysms, the last inspired gleams of the Latin language as it lay dying of old age in the furthermost recesses of a monastery.

15

After blazing up like dry straw, his enthusiasm for the digester died away just as rapidly. His nervous dyspepsia, which had, initially, been pacified, returned; and then, that concentrated nourishment was so binding and caused such an irritation of the bowel that Des Esseintes was obliged to discontinue its use forthwith.

His malady resumed its progress, accompanied by entirely new symptoms. The nightmares, the olfactory hallucinations, the visual disturbances, the harsh cough as regular as clockwork, the thudding of the arteries and heart and the cold sweats were succeeded by auditory delusions, those disorders which occur only in the final stages of the disease.

Des Esseintes, consumed by a raging fever, suddenly heard the babbling of water, the buzzing of wasps, then these sounds blended into one which resembled the whirring of a lathe; this whirring grew higher and softer, gradually changing into the silvery tone of a bell. Then he felt his delirious brain being wafted away on waves of music* and enveloped in the swirling mysticism of his adolescence. The songs learnt from the Jesuit Fathers came back to him, re-creating, on their own, the college and the chapel where they had reverberated, and communicating these hallucinations to the olfactory and visual organs, mantling them in fumes of incense and in shadows lit by the glow of stained-glass windows beneath lofty arches.

Under the Fathers, religious ceremonies were performed with great splendour and solemnity; an excellent organist and an outstanding choir made these spiritual exercises an artistic delight profitable to the service of religion. The organist was devoted to the old masters, and on Church feast days would mark the occasion with a mass of Palestrina's or Orlando Lasso's, a psalm by Marcello, an oratorio of Handel's, a Bach motet; in preference to Father Lambillotte's* languid, facile compilations (so favoured by the priests), he would play some sixteenth-century *Laudi spirituali* whose hieratic beauty had many times enthralled Des Esseintes.

But above all else he had experienced ineffable pleasure from listening to plainsong, to which the organist, in defiance of current fashion, had remained faithful. This type of music, now seen as a decadent and barbarous form of the Christian liturgy, as an archeological curiosity, as a relic of the remote past, was the very language of the ancient Church, the soul of the Middle Ages; it was the eternal prayer in song, modulated in accordance with the movements of the soul, the everlasting hymn offered up for centuries past to the Most High.

This traditional melody, with its powerful unison, its harmonies as majestic and massive as blocks of hewn stone, was the only one that could truly blend with the ancient basilicas and fill their Romanesque vaults, of which it seemed to be the very emanation and living voice.

Time without number Des Esseintes had been overpowered with awe and reverence by the sense of an irresistible presence, when the *Christus factus est* of the Gregorian chant went soaring up into the nave amid the pillars that trembled in the swirling clouds of incense, or when the faux-bourdon of the *De profundis* groaned forth, mournful as a stifled sob, poignant as a despairing cry of mankind lamenting its mortal destiny and imploring the tender mercy of its Saviour!

Compared with this magnificent plainsong, created by the genius of the Church, as impersonal and anonymous as the organ (whose inventor is unknown), all religious music seemed to him profane. Essentially, in all the works of Jomelli and Porpora, Carissimi and Durante, in the finest conceptions of Handel and of Bach, there was no renunciation of popular acclaim, no sacrifice of artistic effect, no abdication of human pride listening to itself pray; at most, with those impressive masses by Lesueur* which were celebrated at Saint-Roch, the religious style had reasserted itself, solemn and august, and had, in its uncompromising starkness, drawn closer to the austere majesty of the ancient plainsong.

Since that time, utterly disgusted by those fake *Stabat Maters* dreamt up by a Pergolesi or a Rossini, by all that encroachment of secular art into liturgical art, Des Esseintes had kept well away from those questionable works which are countenanced by an indulgent Church.

Furthermore this permissiveness, tolerated under the guise of attracting the faithful but actually aimed at filling the collection plate, had immediately produced a harvest of arias taken from Italian operas, of contemptible cavatinas and indecorous quadrilles, played *con brio* by full orchestras in churches converted into boudoirs and turned over to second-rate performers who bellowed away up in the clerestory, while down below fashionably dressed ladies examined one another's finery with a jealous eye and swooned at the cries of the ham actors, whose impure voices were defiling the sacred tones of the organ!

For years now he had firmly refused to take part in these pious diversions, remaining faithful to his childhood memories and even regretting having heard some *Te Deums* composed by great masters, for he remembered that admirable *Te Deum* of plainsong, that hymn of such awe-inspiring simplicity, created by some saint or other, a St Ambrose or a St Hilary, who, without the complicated resources of an orchestra, without the musical techniques of modern science, proclaimed a passionate faith, a frenzied joy which burst forth—expressing the feelings of all humanity—in earnest, assured, almost celestial tones!

It must be added that Des Esseintes's ideas on music were in flagrant contradiction with the theories he professed on the other arts. In the sphere of religious music he really only approved of the monastic music of the Middle Ages, that austere music which provoked in him an instinctive nervous reaction, as did certain pages of old Christian Latin texts; and besides, as he himself admitted, he was incapable of appreciating whatever ingenious devices contemporary masters might have introduced into the art of Catholic music. In the first place, he had not studied music with that same passion which had attracted him to painting and to literature. He played the piano as well as the next man, and was, after much initial stumbling, capable of more or less deciphering a score, but he knew nothing of harmony, the technique essential for truly grasping a nuance, for appreciating a subtle point, for savouring, with genuine understanding, a musical refinement.

Furthermore, secular music is a promiscuous art, since you cannot experience it on your own, at home, the way you can read a book;* to enjoy it, he would have been forced to mingle with the unvarying audience that fills the theatres to overflowing and haunts that Cirque d'Hiver* where, under a broiling sun and in a stifling atmosphere, you can watch a hulking brute beating time as though he were beating a sauce, and massacring disconnected excerpts of Wagner to the intense delight of an ignorant crowd!

He had never felt up to plunging into this mob in order to hear

Berlioz, even though some fragments of his compositions had enthralled him with their passionate exaltation and vaulting fire, and he was also only too conscious that not one scene, not so much as one single phrase in any of the mighty Wagner's operas could with impunity be divorced from its context.

Portions sliced off and served up in a concert's bill of fare lost all their significance, were deprived of all their sense, for, just as the chapters of a book complement one another and all lead to the same conclusion, to the same objective, Wagner used his melodies to depict the characters of his dramatis personae, embody their thoughts, and express their motives whether visible or hidden, and these ingenious and recurrent repetitions were only comprehensible to those listeners who had followed the subject from its exposition and watched the characters gradually take shape and grow, in a setting from which they could not be removed without causing them to wither, like branches cut from a tree.

Consequently Des Esseintes believed that in this rabble of melomaniacs who every Sunday went into ecstasies on the benches of the Cirque, there were scarcely twenty who, when the attendants kindly stopped chatting and allowed the orchestra to be heard, recognized the score that was being massacred.

In view also of the further fact that the intelligent patriotism of the French prevented any of their theatres from putting on a Wagner opera, devotees of music who were not versed in its arcana, and either could not or would not travel to Bayreuth, had no option but to remain at home, and this was the reasonable course adopted by Des Esseintes.

On a different level, music of the more popular, less demanding kind, and excerpts from old-fashioned operas, held almost no appeal for him; the cheap little airs of Auber and Boïeldieu, Adam and Flotow,* and the rhetorical banalities turned out by composers like Ambroise Thomas and Bazin* repelled him in the same way as did the outdated affectations and vulgar charms of the Italians. He had therefore kept resolutely away from the musical arts, and, from the many years that this abstinence had continued, the only pleasant memories he retained were of a few performances of chamber music when he had heard some Beethoven and, especially, some Schumann and Schubert, which had wrung his nerves in the same way as did the most deeply felt, most anguished poems of Poe.

Certain of Schumann's parts for the cello had left him actually gasping and choking, in the grip of hysteria; but it was above all Schubert's Lieder that uplifted and carried him away, leaving him afterwards as prostrated as though from a great outpouring of nervous energy, during an extreme mystical experience. Schubert's penetrating music thrilled him to the marrow, forcing a multitude of forgotten griefs and ancient discontents to surface in a heart astonished at containing so much confused misery and ill-defined pain. This desolate music, this lament coming from the furthermost depths of the soul, both terrified and enchanted him. Never had he been able to hum 'Des Mädchens Klage'* to himself without tears of nervous agitation filling his eyes, for there was in that mournful song something more than grief, there was something wrenching that tore at his heart-strings, something that evoked a dying love-affair set in a forlorn landscape.

And whenever they came back to his lips, these exquisite, funereal laments conjured up, in his mind, a place on the outskirts of a city, a mean and voiceless place where silently, in the distance, lines of men and women, wearied and bowed down by life, were disappearing into the twilight, while he himself, surfeited with bitterness and replete with disgust, felt himself alone, utterly alone, in the midst of a tearful Nature, overwhelmed by an inexpressible melancholy, by a relentless anguish, the mysterious intensity of which precluded all consolation, all pity, all repose. Like the tolling of a death-knell, this despairing melody haunted him now that he lay in his bed, prostrated by fever and agitated by a feeling of apprehension which was all the more implacable in that he could no longer determine its cause. Finally he just let himself drift, swept hither and yon in the flood of anguish released by this music which, for a brief moment, would be blocked by the low, soft notes of psalms singing in his head, while his battered temples felt as if they were being pounded by the clappers of tolling bells.

One morning, however, these noises died away; feeling more in command of himself, he asked the servant to give him a mirror; it immediately slipped from his grasp; he scarcely recognized himself, his face was mud-colour, his lips dry and swollen, his tongue furrowed, his skin rough; his hair and his beard, which his manservant had not trimmed since he fell ill, added to the horror of the cadaverous face and the huge, watery eyes which burned with a feverish glitter in that skeletal head covered with bristling hair. He was more frightened by this alteration in his looks than he was by his physical weakness, by the uncontrollable vomiting which rejected all attempts at nourishment, or by the depression into which he was sinking. He believed he was done for; then, despite his overwhelming state of prostration, the energy of a desperate man made him sit up, and gave him the strength to write to his Paris doctor and to order the servant to set off immediately, find this doctor, and bring him back, no matter at what cost, that very day.

All at once he went from a mood of the most complete despair to one of the most bracing optimism; this physician was a famous specialist, a doctor renowned for his cures of nervous disorders; 'he must have cured cases that are more difficult and dangerous than mine,' Des Esseintes told himself; 'I'm sure to be up and about in a day or two'; but then this feeling of confidence was followed by one of utter disillusion: 'however learned and intuitive they may be, doctors don't know a thing about neuroses, they don't even know what causes them.' This doctor, like the others, would prescribe the eternal zinc oxide and quinine, potassium bromide and valerian. 'But who knows,' he continued, clutching at straws; 'if these medicines have done me no good up to now, it's probably because I didn't take them in the proper doses.'

In spite of everything, this prospect of relief was putting new life into him, when he was assailed by fresh misgivings: 'as long as the doctor actually is in Paris, as long as he does agree to come'; and he was immediately beset by the fear of his servant's not being able to find him. His spirits began to sink again, swinging, with every passing moment, between the most irrational hope and the wildest foreboding, exaggerating, in his own mind, both his chances of a rapid cure and his fears of imminent danger; the hours passed and the moment came when, in despair, at the end of his tether, convinced that the doctor would certainly not come, he told himself furiously that if help had reached him in time he would undoubtedly have been saved; then his anger at the servant, at the doctor whom he accused of letting him die, vanished, and he became angry at himself, reproaching himself for having waited so long to ask for help, convincing himself that he would now be cured if he had, even as recently as yesterday, insisted on effective medicines and suitable nursing.

These alternating surges of alarm and hope that were jostling about in his otherwise unoccupied head gradually died away, but the shocks had finally depleted his remaining strength; he fell into an exhausted sleep broken by incoherent dreams, a kind of faint punctuated by periods of insentient wakefulness; in the end he had so completely lost any awareness of his own desires and fears, that when the doctor suddenly entered his room he seemed bewildered, evincing neither astonishment nor joy.

The servant had undoubtedly informed him of Des Esseintes's way of life, and of the various symptoms which he himself had been able to observe, since the day when he had picked up his master from where he was lying beside the window, overcome by the potency of the perfumes, for the doctor asked few questions of the patient, with whose early history he had, in any case, long been familiar; but he examined him, listened to his chest, and carefully scrutinized his urine, in which certain white streaks identified for him one of the main determining causes of the neurosis. He wrote out a prescription and, after saying he would be back soon, departed without another word.

This visit comforted Des Esseintes, although he found the doctor's silence alarming, and entreated his manservant not to conceal the truth from him any longer. The latter asserted that the doctor had not shown any anxiety, and Des Esseintes, notwithstanding his suspicions, could not detect anything whatever about the old man's tranquil face that suggested the demurrals of prevarication.

His thoughts now became more cheerful; his aches and pains had in any case abated and the weakness that he had been feeling in every limb had taken on a certain sweet, comforting quality that was at once indefinable and languid; furthermore he was astonished and pleased not to be encumbered with drugs and medicine bottles, and a feeble smile came to his lips when the servant brought him a nourishing peptone enema, warning him that this procedure was to be repeated three times each day.

The operation was successful, and Des Esseintes could not forbear from tacitly congratulating himself on the event, which was in a sense the crowning achievement of the life he had created for himself; his predilection for the artificial had now—without his even desiring it—achieved its supreme fulfilment; one could go no further; to take nourishment in this manner was unquestionably the ultimate deviation from the norm that anyone could realize.

'How delightful it would be,' he said to himself, 'to continue on this simple diet once your health was fully restored! What a saving of time, what a radical deliverance from the dislike that meat inspires in people who have no appetite! What a complete release from the tediousness that invariably accompanies the necessarily limited choice of dishes! What a spirited protest against the vile sin of gluttony! And finally, what a decided slap in the face for that old Mother Nature whose unvarying demands would be permanently silenced!'

And he went on murmuring to himself: 'It would be a simple matter to sharpen your appetite by swallowing a powerful aperient, then when you could truthfully say: "Whatever can be the time? Surely the dinner must be ready by now, I'm as hungry as a hunter," the table would be laid by placing the august instrument on the table-cloth and then, in just the time it takes to say grace, you would have eliminated the tiresome, vulgar chore of eating.'

A few days later, the servant presented him with an enema the colour and smell of which differed entirely from those of the peptone concoction. 'But this isn't the same!' exclaimed Des Esseintes, staring uneasily at the liquid in the instrument. He asked for the menu, just as though he were in a restaurant, and, unfolding the doctor's prescription, read:

Cod–liver oil:	20 g.
Beef tea:	200 g.
Burgundy:	200 g.
Yolk of egg:	1

This made him wonder. Because of the ruined condition of his stomach, he had been unable to take any serious interest in the art of cooking, and now he suddenly found himself pondering over recipes of inverted epicurism; then a bizarre idea crossed his mind. Perhaps the doctor had supposed that his patient's strange palate was already weary of the taste of the peptone, perhaps, like a clever chef, he had meant to vary the flavour of the food, and forestall the possibility that the monotony of the dishes would bring on a total loss of appetite. Once launched on these reflections, Des Esseintes drew up some novel recipes, designing meatless dinners for Fridays, increasing the dose of cod-liver oil and of wine and striking out the beef tea, since meat was expressly forbidden by the Church; but soon there was no longer any point to his thinking about these nourishing liquids, for very gradually the doctor succeeded in controlling the vomiting and in getting him to swallow, by the normal route, a syrupy punch containing powdered meat, which had a vague aroma of cocoa that pleased his actual palate.

Weeks went by, and finally the stomach consented to function; occasionally, he would still experience bouts of nausea, but these were relieved by ginger beer and by Rivière's anti-emetic draught.

Finally, little by little, the organs recovered, and with the help of pepsins actual meat was digested; Des Esseintes regained his strength and was able to stand up and try to walk about his room, leaning on a stick and holding on to the corners of the furniture; instead of rejoicing at this success, he forgot about his former suffering, grew annoyed at the length of the convalescence, and berated the doctor for dragging things out in this leisurely manner. Some unsuccessful experiments had, it was true, slowed down his cure; his stomach could not tolerate iron, even when it was mixed with laudanum, any more than it could tolerate quinquina; these had to be replaced by arsenates, after two weeks wasted in futile attempts, as Des Esseintes impatiently pointed out.

Eventually, the moment came when he could stay up for the whole afternoon and walk unaided round his rooms. Then his study began to irritate him; the defects to which habit had accustomed him struck him forcibly when he returned to it after this long absence. It seemed to him that the colours he had chosen to be viewed by lamplight did not look well together in the daylight; he considered changing them, and spent hours devising subversive harmonies of hues, hybrid matings of fabrics and of leathers.

'I'm certainly well on the way to recovery,' he said to himself, registering the return of his former preoccupations, his former tastes.

One morning, as he was gazing at his orange and blue walls, musing about ideal hangings made out of Greek Orthodox church stoles, dreaming of gold-embroidered Russian dalmatics, of brocade copes decorated with Slavonic lettering worked in precious stones from the Urals and rows of pearls, the doctor came in and, observing the direction of his patient's eyes, questioned him.

Des Esseintes told him about his unrealizable dreams; and he was beginning to scheme about fresh experimentations with colours, to speak of new couplings and contrasts of tones that he proposed to set up, when the doctor poured cold water on his plans by assuring him in a peremptory manner that at any rate he would not be putting his plans into effect in *that* house.

And, without giving him time to draw breath, he declared that he had set about restoring the digestive functions as rapidly as possible, and it was now essential to tackle the neurosis which was not in any sense cured, and would require years of diet and medical care. He then added that before trying any kind of medication, before embarking on any hydropathic therapy (which would in any case be impossible to carry out at Fontenay), he must abandon this solitary existence, return to Paris, get back into ordinary life, and try to enjoy himself, in short, like other people.

'But I don't enjoy the things other people enjoy!' protested Des Esseintes indignantly.

Ignoring this observation, the doctor simply assured him that this radical change of life-style which he was stipulating was, in his opinion, a matter of life and death, a matter either of a return to health, or of insanity rapidly followed by tuberculosis.

'Then it's death or deportation!' exclaimed an infuriated Des Esseintes.

The doctor, who was imbued with all the prejudices of a man of the world, smiled and made for the door without answering him.

16

Des Esseintes shut himself up in his bedroom, turning a deaf ear to the banging of the hammers as the servants nailed down the crates they had packed; each blow struck him in the heart, sending an excruciating pang through his flesh. The sentence passed by the doctor was being carried out: the fear of once again suffering those torments he had already endured, the dread of an agonizing death, had influenced Des Esseintes more powerfully than did his loathing of the detestable existence to which medical authority was condemning him.

'And yet,' he reflected, 'there are people who live alone, never speaking to a soul, who lead a wholly inward life, isolated from society, for example prisoners in solitary confinement and Trappist monks, and there's no evidence to suggest that those poor devils and those saints ever become lunatics or consumptives.' He had mentioned these examples to the doctor, but to no avail; the latter had simply repeated, in a curt tone which admitted of no argument, that his verdict—which incidentally was confirmed by the opinion of all the specialists in nervous diseases—was that distractions, amusement, pleasure, were the only means of influencing this malady, the psychological side of which lay beyond the chemical efficacy of medicines; and, irritated by his patient's recriminations, he had declared once and for all that he refused to continue treating him if he did not agree to a change of air, and to following a different regimen of health.

Des Esseintes had immediately taken himself off to Paris, where he had consulted other specialists, impartially describing his case to them, and, when all of them, without hesitation, supported their colleague's prescriptions, he had rented a vacant apartment in a new building, returned to Fontenay, and, white with rage, ordered his servants to pack the trunks.

Sunk into his armchair, he now sat brooding over this categorical injunction which overturned his plans, broke the ties with his present life, and buried all his dreams for the future. So, his perfect happiness was at an end! This haven in which he had found shelter must

be abandoned, he must sail right out again into that tempest of stupidity that had battered him in years gone by!

The doctors spoke of amusements and distractions; but with
whom, and with what, could they possibly suppose that he might
amuse or enjoy himself? Had he not outlawed himself from society?
Did he know one man capable of trying to lead a life such as his own,
a life entirely confined to contemplation and to dreams? Did he know
one man capable of appreciating the delicacy of a phrase, the subtlety of a painting, the quintessence of an idea, one man whose soul
was sufficiently finely crafted to understand Mallarmé and to love
Verlaine?

Where, when, in which social group should he make soundings in
order to discover a twin soul, a mind freed from the commonplace,
a mind that blessed silence as a boon, ingratitude as a comfort, suspicion as a haven, a sanctuary? Should he search in the circles he had
moved in before his departure for Fontenay? But most of the well-
born nonentities he had frequented must, since those days, have
become even more stultified by their drawing-room existence, grown
even stupider at the gaming-tables, or ruined themselves in the arms
of prostitutes; most of them must even be married; after having
enjoyed, all their life, the leavings of hoodlums, it was now their
wives who possessed the leavings of the street-walkers, for the first-
fruits belong by right to the masses, the commonalty alone refuses
to accept other people's rejects!

'What a delightful general post, what a fine series of substitutions,
this custom adopted by a society which still believes itself prudish!'
Des Esseintes told himself. And then, the decayed nobility was
finished, the aristocracy growing feeble-minded or vicious. It was
dying away; its members were either senile, their faculties degenerating further with each successive generation, so that eventually they
possessed the instincts of gorillas fermented in the skulls of stable
boys and jockeys, or else—like the houses of Choiseul-Praslin,
Polignac, and Chevreuse*—it was wallowing in the filth of litigation,
which brought it down to the same level of turpitude as the other
classes.

The very mansions, the immemorial coats of arms, the heraldic
uniforms, the pomp and ceremony of this ancient caste had vanished.
The estates, now no longer profitable, had been put up for auction
together with the chateaux, for there was no money to buy the evil

pleasures of the flesh sought by the befuddled descendants of the old families!

The least scrupulous, the least obtuse, threw aside all shame; they dabbled in dubious intrigue, sifted through the muck of money deals, and appeared, like common swindlers, at the bar of the lawcourt, where they slightly raised the tone of human justice which, unable to remain always impartial, solved matters by making them librarians in the penitentiaries.

This craving for profit, this itch for filthy lucre, had also affected that other class which had always turned for support to the nobility, namely the clergy. You now noticed, on the back page of a newspaper, advertisements about corns of the foot that had been cured by a priest. The monasteries had transformed themselves into places of manufacture for apothecaries and liqueur makers. They sold recipes or themselves made the products: the Cistercians, chocolate; the Trappists, semolina and tincture of arnica; the Marists, bisulphate of medicinal chalk and vulnerary water; the Dominicans, anti-apoplectic elixir; the disciples of St Benedict, Benedictine; the monks of St Bruno, Chartreuse.

Trade had invaded the cloister where, instead of antiphonaries, thick ledgers rested on the lecterns. Like a leprous infection, the greed of the century was ravaging the church, keeping monks bowed over inventories and bills, transforming the Fathers Superior into confectioners and quacks, the lay brothers into common packers and pharmacy workers.

Yet even so, in spite of everything, it was still only among ecclesiastics that Des Esseintes could hope to find relationships that to some extent corresponded to his tastes; in the company of canons—generally learned and well-bred men—he might have passed some congenial, cosy evenings; but to do so he would have needed to share their beliefs, and not be torn between his sceptical ideas and the surges of conviction which surfaced from time to time, buoyed up by memories from his childhood.

He would have needed to hold opinions identical with theirs, and not accept (as he was wont to do in his moments of enthusiasm) a Catholicism gingered up with a little magic, as occurred under Henri III, and a touch of sadism, as happened at the end of the last century. This special brand of clericalism, this depraved, artfully perverse mysticism towards which, at certain times of day, he was drawn, could not even be discussed with a priest, who would not have understood it, or who would have promptly, and with horror, rejected it.

For the twentieth time, he wrestled with this same insoluble problem. He would have liked to see an end to that distrustful state of mind with which, at Fontenay, he had struggled in vain; now that he was going to make a completely fresh start, he would have liked to force himself to possess faith, and, once he possessed it, to make of it a protective crust, to fasten it with clamps to his soul, to place it beyond the reach of all those ideas that undermine and uproot it; but the more he desired it, the less was the emptiness of his soul filled, the longer did the Saviour delay his coming. At the same time as his hunger for religion grew, at the same time as, with all the strength he could muster, he summoned, like a ransom paid against the future, like a subsidy for his new life, this faith which he could glimpse, but from which he was divided by a distance he found terrifying, ideas came beating at his ever-restless brain, brushing aside the infirm purposes of his will, rejecting, on grounds of common sense and mathematical proof, the mysteries and dogmas of religion!

'One ought to be able to prevent these arguments with oneself,' he thought miserably; 'one ought to be able to close one's eyes, and let oneself go with the current, forget those accursed discoveries that, for the past two centuries, have rent the structure of religion from top to bottom. And yet,' he sighed, 'it's neither the physiologists nor the sceptics who are destroying Catholicism, it's the priests themselves, whose blundering compositions would totally destroy the most tenaciously held convictions.'

Had not a Dominican, a Doctor of Theology, one Reverend Father Rouard de Card,* a preaching friar, written a pamphlet entitled *On the Adulteration of the Sacramental Substances* in which he categorically demonstrated that the majority of Masses were null and void, due to the fact that the substances used in the rites were adulterated by the tradesmen? For years now, the holy oils had been mixed with poultry grease; the candle-wax, with calcinated bones; the incense, with common resin and old benzoin. But what was worse, was that the indispensable materials for the holy sacrifice, the two substances without which no offering is possible, had likewise been rendered impure: the wine, by repeated diluting, by illicit additions of Pernambuco wood, elderberries, alcohol, alum, salicylate, litharge; the bread, that bread of the Eucharist which must be kneaded from the finest of wheat flour, by haricot-bean flour, potash, and pipe-clay!

And now they had gone even further: they had dared to eliminate wheat entirely, and shameless merchants were manufacturing almost all the Eucharistic hosts out of potato starch! However, God refused to manifest himself in potato starch. This was an undeniable, indisputable fact; in the second volume of his *Moral Theology*, his Eminence Cardinal Gousset had himself also discussed, at some length, this question of fraud, from the divine point of view; and, according to the unquestionable authority of this expert, the priest celebrating Mass could not consecrate bread made from the flour of oats, buckwheat, or barley, and although the matter was unclear in the case of rye-bread, there was no room for any discussion or debate when it came to potato starch, which, to use the ecclesiastical wording, was in no sense a competent substance for the Holy Sacrament.

Because this potato starch can be kneaded quickly and because of the attractive appearance of the unleavened bread it produces, this shameful deception was so widespread that the mystery of the transubstantiation now hardly ever took place, and priest and faithful alike communicated, all unawares, with neutral substances!

Ah! Long gone were the days when Radegonde,* Queen of France, would with her own hands prepare the bread destined for the altars, the days when (as the custom of Cluny required) three priests or three deacons, fasting, wearing the alb and the amice, would wash their face and their fingers, pick through the wheat grain by grain, crush it under the grinder, knead the dough with a water that was cold and pure, and then bake it over a bright fire, singing psalms all the while!

'But the fact remains,' thought Des Esseintes, 'that this idea of always being cheated, even at the Lord's Table, is hardly such as to reinforce a faith that is already wavering; and then, how can one believe in an omnipotence that is hindered by a pinch of potato starch or a drop of alcohol?' These thoughts further darkened the prospect of his future existence, making his horizon appear more threatening, blacker.

It was obvious, there remained no haven, no shore where he might shelter. What was to become of him, in this Paris where he had neither family nor friends? No longer did any tie bind him to the

Faubourg Saint-Germain, to those quavering dotards who were decaying into dusty obsolescence, who lay like so many broken, empty husks, surrounded by a new society! And what point of contact could exist between him and that bourgeoisie which, little by little, had moved up, using every disaster to enrich itself, fomenting every catastrophe so that its own crimes and thievery might be cloaked in respectability?

After the aristocracy of birth, it was now the aristocracy of money; it was the caliphate of the counter, the rule of the Rue du Sentier,* the tyranny of commerce with its venal, narrow ideas, its vain and deceitful instincts.

More villainous, more vile than the despoiled nobility and the clergy in its decline, the bourgeoisie was borrowing their pointless ostentation and their obsolete arrogance, which it debased with its lack of good breeding; it was stealing their faults and converting them into hypocritical vices; overbearing and sly, mean and cowardly, it was pitilessly gunning down its eternal, inevitable dupe, the common people, whom it had with its own hand unmuzzled and set at the throats of the ancient castes!

The battle was now over. The masses, their task accomplished, had, in the interests of public health, been bled white; the bourgeois, confident and jovial, was lording it through the power of his money and the contagion of his stupidity. The consequence of his rise had been the crushing of all intelligence, the negation of all probity, the death of all art; and indeed the artists in their degradation were down on their knees, showering ardent kisses on the foul-smelling feet of the high-placed chisellers and low-born despots on whose charity they lived!

Painting was now a flood of vapid futilities; literature, a riot of stylistic insipidity and timid ideas, for honesty was demanded by the shady speculator, integrity by the swindler who, while pursuing a dowry for his son, refused to provide one for his daughter, chastity by the anticlericalist who accused the clergy of rape and—stupid hypocrite that he was, entirely devoid of true artistic depravity—went sniffing about in dubious bedchambers at basins filled with greasy water, and at warm, pungently dirty petticoats!

It was the vast whorehouse of America* transported on to our continent; it was, in short, the widespread, entrenched, immeasurable boorishness of the financier and the self-made man blazing, like some ignoble sun, over the idolatrous city which grovelled as it chanted vile canticles of praise before the ungodly tabernacle of the Bank!

'May you crumble into dust, Society; old world, may you expire!'* exclaimed Des Esseintes, filled with indignation at the ignominious spectacle he was conjuring up; his protest shattered the nightmare that oppressed him. 'Ah!' he said; 'to think that all this is not a dream! To think that I shall be rejoining the depraved and servile rabble of this age!' He turned for help and comfort to Schopenhauer's consoling precepts; he repeated to himself the painful axiom of Pascal's: 'The soul sees nothing that, upon reflection, it does not find distressing,'* but these words echoed in his mind like meaningless noise; his ennui broke them up, stripping them of all significance, all consolatory power, all gentle, effective potency.

He finally realized that the arguments of pessimism were incapable of giving him comfort, that only the impossible belief in a future life would give him peace.

A fit of rage, like a fierce gale, swept away his efforts at resignation, his attempts at indifference. He could no longer deceive himself, there was nothing, nothing left, everything had been brought down; the bourgeoisie sat about on the ground, as though on a Sunday outing, stuffing themselves from paper bags, amid the majestic ruins of the Church which had become a place of assignation, a pile of débris, defiled by contemptible gibes and infamous jokes. Surely, in order to prove their existence beyond any doubt, surely the terrible God of Genesis and the pale Crucified Christ would revive the cataclysms of the past, reignite the rain of fire that once consumed those cities of the damned, those abodes of death of long ago? Was it possible that this filth would continue to flow and with its pestilence swamp this old world in which nothing now grew save seeds of iniquity and harvests of shame?

The door opened suddenly; in the distance, framed by the doorway, appeared men dressed in cocked hats, with clean-shaven cheeks and little tufts of hair on their chins, heaving packing cases and moving furniture; then the door closed again behind the servant, who was carrying out some parcels of books.

Exhausted, Des Esseintes collapsed into a chair. 'In two days' time I shall be in Paris,' he exclaimed; 'it really is all over; the waters of human mediocrity, like a tidal wave, are rising up to the sky and will engulf this haven whose sea-walls I have with my own hands most unwillingly breached. Ah! My courage fails me and I am sick at heart! Lord, take pity on the Christian who doubts, on the unbeliever who longs to believe, on the galley-slave of life who is setting sail alone, at night, under a sky no longer lit, now, by the consoling beacons of the ancient hope!'

APPENDIX

PREFACE, 'WRITTEN TWENTY YEARS AFTER THE NOVEL'

I believe that all men of letters are like me, that once their works have been published, they never reread them. Indeed nothing is more disillusioning or more painful than to take another look at one's sentences after an interval of years. They have, so to speak, been decanted and settled to the bottom of the book; and, as a rule, books are not like wines, which improve with age; once they have been settled by time, the chapters lose their sparkle and their bouquet fades.

I had that feeling about certain bottles stowed away in the *Against Nature* bin, when I came to uncork them. And, somewhat sadly, I am trying to recall, as I leaf through these pages, my probable state of mind at the time when I wrote them. Naturalism was then in full swing; but this school, which was to accomplish the invaluable service of placing real characters in precisely described settings, was fated to go on endlessly repeating itself and marking time on the spot.

Naturalism refused, at least in theory, to recognize exceptions; it therefore confined itself to the portrayal of existence as it is commonly experienced, and sought, under the pretext of being true to life, to create beings who were as similar as possible to the average. This ideal was embodied, within the genre of the novel, in a masterpiece which has been (to a much greater degree than *L'Assommoir**) the paradigm of Naturalism, Gustave Flaubert's *L'Éducation sentimentale;** that novel was, for all of us who were part of the 'Soirées de Médan',* a veritable bible; but it brought us little profit. It was perfect down to the last detail, and even Flaubert himself could not write another such; we were therefore all reduced, in those days, to beating about and roaming along parallel tracks that had for the most part already been explored.

Since it must be admitted that virtue is the exception in this world, it is thereby excluded from the Naturalist plan. Not understanding the Catholic concept of the fall from grace and of temptation, we were unaware of the struggles and the suffering from which virtue is born; the heroism of the soul that triumphs over life's pitfalls eluded us. It would not have occurred to us to describe this struggle, with its ups and downs, its cunning assaults and feints, and indeed its resourceful allies, who often prepare for the fight in the depths of a cloister, far from the person under attack by the Evil One. Virtue seemed to us to be the attribute of individuals who were lacking in curiosity or devoid of sense, who were in any event of little emotional interest, from the artistic point of view, as subjects to be treated.

Then there were the vices; but in terms of artistic yield this field was limited. It was restricted to the domain of the Seven Deadly Sins, and even there one only, the Sin against the Sixth Commandment, was more or less a possibility.

The others had been cruelly over-harvested; hardly a single bunch of grapes remained to be gathered. Avarice, for example, had had its last drop of juice pressed out by Balzac and by Hello. Pride, Anger, and Envy could be found littering every Romantic publication, and these theatrical themes had been so violently distorted by their overuse in drama that it would have required a veritable genius to rejuvenate them in a novel. As for Gluttony and Sloth, they seemed to be easier to embody in minor characters and better suited to supporting roles, than to the leading men or the prima donnas of the novel of manners.

The truth is that Pride would have been the most splendid of sins to study, in its diabolical ramifications of cruelty towards others and of false humility, that Gluttony, dragging in its wake Lust, Sloth, and Covetousness, would have provided material for astonishing investigations, if these sins had been scrutinized by a Believer, using the lamp and torch of the Church; but not one of us was equipped for such a task; we were therefore forced to re-examine, in all its manifestations, the offence which is the easiest of all to strip of its covering, the sin of Lust; and God knows, we did re-examine it; but this type of replication was short-lived. However inventive one might be, the novel could be summarized in a few lines: why did Monsieur Such-and-such commit (or not commit) adultery with Madame So-and-so; if you wished to be distinguished and to reveal yourself as such, like a novelist of the highest class, you made this transaction of the flesh take place between a marquise and a count; if, on the other hand, you wished to present yourself as a popular novelist, as a writer who knows the ropes, you set it up between a low-class lover and some common little working girl; only the setting differed. It seems to me that the distinguished tone is the one favoured by today's reader, for I observe that at present he does not enjoy stories of plebeian or bourgeois love affairs, but continues to relish the marquise's hesitations as she goes to meet her seducer in a small apartment, the appearance of which varies in accordance with the current fashion in interior decoration. Will she? Won't she? This is known as a psychological study. Personally, I have nothing against it.

However, I must confess that when I open a book and come upon the inevitable seduction and the equally inevitable adultery, I hasten to close it, having no desire to discover how the promised idyll will conclude. Any book which contains no authentic material, any book from which I learn nothing, no longer interests me.

At the time when *Against Nature* was published, that is to say in 1884, this then was the situation: Naturalism was becoming exhausted from endlessly working over the same ground. The supply of observations that each writer had stored up, by watching himself and others, was running out. Zola, that fine painter of theatrical scenery, got along by producing bold canvases that were more or less accurate; he was very good at suggesting the illusion of movement and life; his heroes had no soul, being governed purely by impulses and instincts, which simplified the task of analysis. They moved about, performing a few summary actions, their quite bold silhouettes peopling settings which became the principal characters in his dramas. In this manner he celebrated the Paris markets, the modern department stores, the railways, the mines; the human beings wandering about in these settings had only small or walk-on parts to play; but Zola was Zola, that is to say, a somewhat ponderous artist, but one endowed with powerful lungs and heavy fists. The rest of us, less robustly built, and preoccupied with an art that was subtler and more true, found ourselves wondering whether Naturalism was not heading into a blind alley, in which we would soon find ourselves up against the back wall.

To be truthful, these thoughts only came to me much later. I was vaguely searching for a way out from a cul-de-sac where I was suffocating, but I had no definite plan; *Against Nature*, which gave me air and rescued me from a kind of literature which led nowhere,

is a completely unconscious work, generated without any preconceived ideas, without any pre-determined plans, without anything
at all.

I saw it first as a brief fantasy, in the form of a strange short story;
I thought of it as a kind of companion piece to *A vau-l'eau** trans-
ferred into a different world; I imagined a Monsieur Folantin who
was more cultured, more refined, richer, and who discovered in
artifice a relief from the disgust he felt for the irksome burdens of
life and the American-style manners of his day; I saw him flying
swiftly away into dreams, taking refuge in the illusions of fairyland
extravaganzas, living alone, far from society, in memories conjured
up of more congenial periods, of less sordid environments.

And, as I thought about it, the subject grew, requiring painstaking research: each chapter contained the concentrate of a specialized
subject, the sublimate of a different art; each chapter condensed itself
into a 'meat essence' of precious stones, of perfumes, of flowers, of
religious or secular literature, of profane music or of plainsong.

The odd thing was that, without my realizing it at first, I was led
by the very nature of my work to study the Church from many different points of view. It was, in fact, impossible to go back to the only
unblemished centuries that humanity has experienced, to the Middle
Ages, without realizing that the Church was at the centre of everything, that Art did not exist except in her and through her. Being
outside the faith, I looked at the Church somewhat suspiciously, surprised by her grandeur and her glory, wondering how a religion
which seemed to me designed for children could have inspired such
marvellous works.

For a while I prowled about Her, groping my way, guessing more
than I could see, and, from the odds and ends I found in museums
and in books, re-creating a whole for myself. And today, when,
after more extensive and more reliable investigations, I skim the
pages of *Against Nature* which relate to Catholicism and religious art,
I observe that that miniature survey, sketched on the sheets of a
notepad, is accurate. What I described then was concise, it lacked
development, but it was true. Since then I have merely enlarged and
elaborated my drafts.

Today I could certainly sign my name to the pages on the Church
in *Against Nature*, for they do indeed seem to have been written by
a Catholic. And yet I imagined myself at such a distance from reli-

gion! I never dreamt that from Schopenhauer (whom I admired more than was reasonable) to Ecclesiastes and the Book of Job was but a step. The hypotheses about pessimism are the same, only, when it is time to reach a conclusion, the philosopher makes himself scarce. I liked his ideas on the horror of existence, on the absurdity of the world, on the cruelty of destiny; I also like them in the Holy Scriptures; but Schopenhauer's remarks lead nowhere; he leaves you, so to speak, in the lurch; in a word, his aphorisms are nothing but a herbarium of barren plaints; the Church, on the other hand, elucidates origins and causes, points to conclusions, offers remedies; not satisfied with simply providing a spiritual consultation, she treats you and cures you, whereas the German quack, after having proved to you beyond any question that the condition afflicting you is incurable, turns his back on you with a sneer.

His pessimism is no different from that of the Scriptures, from which he took it. He says no more than Solomon, no more than Job, no more, indeed, than the 'Imitation' which, long before his time, summarized his entire philosophy in one sentence: 'In truth it is a wretched thing to live on this earth!'

From a distance, these similarities and differences are clearly evident, but at that period, if I noticed them, I did not dwell on them; the urge to conclude did not tempt me; it was possible to travel the route marked out by Schopenhauer, and its scenery was full of variety; I drove calmly along it, without wanting to know where it might lead; in those days I had no real awareness of accountability, no dread of final outcomes; the enigmas of the catechism struck me as childish; besides, like all Catholics, I was totally ignorant about my religion; I did not grasp that everything is a mystery, that we live only in mystery, that if chance existed, it would be even more mysterious than Providence. I refused to acknowledge the idea of suffering inflicted by a God, I deluded myself that pessimism could be the solace of superior minds. What stupidity! That certainly was not confirmed by experience, that had nothing of the 'human document'—to use an expression dear to Naturalism—about it. Never has pessimism consoled those who are sick in body or in soul!

I smile on rereading, after all these years, the pages where these resolutely false ideas are proclaimed. But, as I reread, what strikes me most is this: all the novels I wrote after *Against Nature* are contained, in embryo, in this work. Its chapters are, in fact, nothing but the starting points of the volumes that followed.

The chapter on the Latin literature of the Decadent period was, if not actually developed, at any rate more thoroughly explored when I wrote about the liturgy in *En route* and *L'Oblat**. I would republish this chapter today without making any changes, except as regards Saint Ambrose, whose wishy-washy prose and turgid style I still dislike. I still think of him as I did then, as a 'boring Christian Cicero'; but, by contrast, he is charming as a poet; the hymns he and his followers composed which appear in the Breviary are among the most beautiful that the Church has preserved. I also think that the admittedly rather particular literature of the hymnal could well have been included in the special section of this chapter.

Nowadays I like the classical Latin of Maro* and of 'Chick-pea' no more than I did in 1884; I prefer, just as I did when I wrote *Against Nature*, the language of the Vulgate to the language of the Augustan Age, and even to that of the Decadent period, for all that the latter, with its feral redolence and its marbled gamey tints, may be more singular. After disinfecting and rejuvenating the language, the Church, in order to express a category of hitherto unknown ideas, invented some grandiloquent expressions and exquisitely tender diminutives; it seems to me that by so doing she created for herself a medium far superior to the dialect of paganism, and on this point Durtal* still holds the same views as did Des Esseintes.

In *La Cathédrale** I reworked the chapter on precious stones, but from the point of view of their symbolism. I gave new life to the lifeless gems of *Against Nature*. Of course, I do not deny that a beautiful emerald may be admired for the flashes which glitter in the fire of her green waters, but, if one is not versed in her symbolic language, is the stone not an unknown quantity, a stranger with whom one cannot converse and who herself remains silent because people do not understand her speech? But she is more, and better, than that.

Without believing, with Estienne de Claves, an old writer of the sixteenth century, that precious stones, like human beings, propagate their species by means of seed scattered in the womb of the earth, one can perfectly well agree that they are minerals that signify, substances that speak; that they are, in a word, symbols. They have been seen as such since the very earliest times, and the tropology of gems is one branch of that Christian symbolism which has been completely ignored by both priests and laymen today, and which I attempted to reconstitute, in its very broad outlines, in my book on the basilica of Chartres.

The chapter in *Against Nature* is, therefore, only superficial, the simplest of gem settings. It is not what it ought to be, a display of gems from the world beyond reality. It is composed of matched jewellery that is quite well described, quite well displayed in a showcase; but that is all, and it is not enough.

The paintings of Gustave Moreau, the engravings of Luyken, the lithographs of Bresdin and Redon are described exactly as I still think of them. I have nothing to change in the arrangement of that little museum.

As for the terrible Chapter 6, the number of which corresponds, without any preconceived intention, with the Commandment it sins against, and for certain sections of 9 which may be associated with it, obviously I would not write them again in the same manner. At the very least they should have been more thoroughly explained in terms of that diabolical perversity which insinuates itself— particularly in the context of sexual vice—into exhausted minds. Indeed it does seem to be the case that nervous disorders and neuroses create fissures in the soul through which Evil may penetrate. That is an enigma which remains unexplained: the word hysteria solves nothing; it may suffice to define a physical condition, to denote an uncontrollable turmoil of the senses, it does not account for the spiritual consequences associated with it, particularly the sins of dissimulation and falsehood which almost invariably implant themselves therein. What are all the details and characteristics of this sinful malady, to what extent is there a diminution of responsibility for the individual whose soul is besieged by a sort of evil possession which has taken root in the disorder of his wretched body? No one can say; on this topic, medicine talks nonsense and theology remains silent.

In the absence of a solution which he was obviously unable to provide, Des Esseintes should have considered the matter from the perspective of the sin involved, and at least expressed some regret; he refrained from blaming himself, and he was wrong; but despite his education at the hands of the Jesuits, whose praises he sings more loudly than does Durtal, he subsequently grew so defiant of the divine constraints, so obstinately determined to wallow in the slough of his carnal degradation!

In any event, these chapters seem like milestones unconsciously set up to indicate the path *Là-bas** was to follow. It is moreover worth noting that Des Esseintes's library contained a certain number of books on magic, and that the ideas on sacrilege propounded in Chapter 7 of *Against Nature* form the basis for a future work dealing more thoroughly with this subject.

As for *Là-bas*, a work which dismayed so many people, now that I am once more a Catholic I should not write that in the same way either. Certainly the theme of wickedness and sensuality elaborated in it is reprehensible, and yet I must state that I glossed over things, I did not really say anything; the documents that it contains are, by comparison with those I omitted and which I still have in my files, confections without any flavour whatsoever, trifles utterly devoid of any piquancy!

I do nevertheless believe that this novel, its cerebral aberrations and alvine follies notwithstanding, rendered a service by virtue of the very subject it treated. It revived an awareness of the machinations of Satan, who had succeeded in getting men to deny his existence; it was the starting point for all those recently renewed explorations of the Devil's never-changing techniques; by exposing the odious practices of necromancy, it helped to put an end to them, and, in short, the novel aligned itself with, and fought resolutely for, the Church against the Devil.

To return to *Against Nature*, for which *Là-bas* simply served as a succedaneum, I can repeat, on the subject of the flower chapter, what I said about the chapter on gems. *Against Nature* discusses them solely from the perspective of their shape and their colour, and not at all from the perspective of their significance; Des Esseintes selected only orchids that were bizarre in appearance, but silent. It is only fair to add that it would have been difficult, in that novel, to endow an aphonic flower, a mute flower, with speech, for the symbolic language of plants died with the Middle Ages, and the exotic flora dear to Des Esseintes were not known to the allegorists of that age.

Since then, I wrote the companion piece to that botanical study in *La Cathédrale*, in connection with the liturgical horticulture which inspired such strange passages in St Hildegard, St Meliton, and St Eucher.*

The question of odours is quite different and, in the same book,

I talk about their mystical and emblematic meaning. Des Esseintes was interested only in secular perfumes, some of them simple scents or extracts, and some, compound or mixed essences. He might also have experimented with the aromas of the Church, with incense, myrrh, and that strange Thymiama mentioned in the Bible and which the printed ritual still refers to as appropriate for burning, along with incense, under the mouths of Church bells when they are baptized, after the Bishop has washed them with holy water and made the sign of the cross on them with the holy chrism and the oil used in extreme unction; but this fragrance seems to have been forgotten even by the Church herself, and I imagine that it would astonish a parish priest to be asked for Thymiama.

The recipe, nevertheless, is recorded in Exodus. Thymiama was made from a mixture of storax, galbanum, incense, and onycha, this last substance being simply the operculum of a certain kind of shellfish of the 'purple' variety, which is dredged up in the marshes of India. Now it is difficult, not to say impossible, in view of the incomplete description of the shellfish and of the place where it is found, to prepare an authentic Thymiama; which is a pity, for had it been otherwise, the lost perfume would certainly have inspired, in Des Esseintes's imagination, sumptuous evocations of the ceremonial festivals and liturgical rites of the Orient.

As for the chapters on contemporary secular and religious literature, to my mind they, like the chapter on Latin literature, are still true today. The chapter devoted to secular writing helped to draw attention to some poets who were completely unknown to the public of the day: Corbière, Mallarmé, Verlaine. I have nothing to retract from what I wrote nineteen years ago: my admiration for these writers is unchanged; in the case of Verlaine it has even increased. Arthur Rimbaud and Jules Laforgue* would have merited inclusion in Des Esseintes's florilegium, but at that period they had not yet published anything, and it was only much later that their works appeared.

I do not imagine, on the other hand, that I shall ever come to appreciate the modern religious writers excoriated in *Against Nature*. No one will change my opinion that the criticism of the late lamented Nettement is inane and that Mme Augustus Craven and Mlle Eugénie de Guérin are a couple of totally apathetic blue-stockings and ineffectual goody-goodies. Their syrupy concoctions strike me as very insipid; Des Esseintes communicated his taste for spices to Durtal, and I believe that they would still understand one another sufficiently well to prepare, in place of these soothing emulsions, a distinctively flavoured essence of art.

Nor have I changed my mind about the literature produced by the Poujoulat and Genoude fraternity, but nowadays I would be less severe on Father Chocarne, who is named among a bunch of pious cacographers, for he did at least compose several pithy pages on mysticism in his Introduction to the works of St John of the Cross, and I would also be kinder to De Montalembert who, though wanting in talent, provided us with a work about monks which, while uneven and incoherent, is nevertheless moving; above all I would not, nowadays, call the *Visions* of Angela da Foligno silly and effusive, for the truth is just the opposite; but I must state in my defence that I had only read them in Hello's translation. The latter was obsessed by the urge to prune, to edulcorate, to soften the mystics, for fear of offending the sham modesty of Catholics. He put under the press a work full of passion and vigour and extracted from it nothing but a cold and colourless juice that gained but little warmth when heated over the meagre flame of his style. That said, although as a translator Hello showed himself to be a pernickety fuss-pot and a pious bigot, it is fair to state that when he was working purely on his own material, he proved himself to be an originator of new ideas, a shrewd exegete, and an analyst of genuine power. He was even, among the writers of his class, the only thinker; I supported d'Aurevilly* in praising the work of this writer who was at once so uneven yet so interesting, and *Against Nature* did, I believe, help secure the modest success which his best work, *L'Homme*, enjoyed after his death.

The chapter on modern ecclesiastical literature concluded that among all those geldings of religious art, there was but a single stallion, Barbey d'Aurevilly, a view which today still remains unquestionably correct. He was the sole artist, in the true sense of the word, produced by the Catholicism of that period; he was a great prose writer, a fine novelist whose audacity made all of beadledom bray in agitation at the explosive vehemence of his expressions.

Finally, if ever a chapter can be seen as a starting point for other books, then that chapter is the one on plainsong, which I subsequently developed in all my books, in *En Route* and most especially in *L'Oblat*. After this brief survey of each of the specialties displayed in the show-cases of *Against Nature*, the obvious conclusion is this: that novel was the starting point for my Catholic writing, which can be seen there, in embryo, in its entirety.

And, once again, I find the obtuseness and stupidity of some of the priesthood's bigots and hotheads unfathomable. For years on end they demanded the destruction of this novel—the copyright of which, by the way, I do not own—without grasping the fact that the mystical works that succeeded it are not comprehensible without *Against Nature*, which is, I repeat, the stock from which they all sprang. Besides, how can one appreciate the work of a writer in its entirety if one does not study it from its beginnings and follow it step by step; more particularly, how is one to understand the progress of Grace within a soul if one suppresses the evidence of its passage, and erases the earliest footprints it left behind?

What is, in any event, certain, is that *Against Nature* broke with its predecessors, with *Les Sœurs Vatard* and *En ménage** and *A vau-l'eau*, and that with it I embarked on a journey whose ultimate destination I did not even suspect. Zola, shrewder than the Catholics, was well aware of this. I recall that, after the publication of *Against Nature*, I spent a few days at Médan. One afternoon, as the two of us were going for a country walk, he suddenly stopped and with lowered brow reproached me for the book, declaring that I had dealt Naturalism a terrible blow, that I was leading the school astray, and that furthermore I was burning my boats with such a book, inasmuch as I had exhausted the genre in one volume and so made further literary works of that kind impossible; and, in a friendly fashion—for he was the best of men—he urged me to return to the beaten track and get back into harness by writing a novel of manners.

I listened to him, thinking that he was at one and the same time right and wrong—right, in accusing me of undermining Naturalism and blocking my own future progress—wrong, in the sense that the novel as he conceived it seemed to me moribund, ruined by repetition, and whether he liked it or not, entirely devoid of interest for me.

There were many things that Zola could not understand; in the first place, the compulsion I felt to open windows, to escape from an atmosphere in which I was stifling; then, the urge that seized me to shake off prejudices, to break the boundaries of the novel, to introduce into it art, and science, and history, in a word to no longer use this form except as a frame in which one could incorporate work of a more serious nature. As for me, what seemed to me especially important at that period was to get rid of the traditional plot, to get rid even of love, of woman, to concentrate the beam of light on one single character, to do something new regardless of the cost.

Zola made no reply to the arguments with which I was attempting to convince him, but went on endlessly reiterating his statement: 'I cannot accept people changing their style and their opinions; I cannot accept people destroying what they once adored.'

But just a moment! Did not he too, at one time, play the part of the good Sicambrian?* As a matter of fact, if he did not actually modify his method of composition and writing, he at any rate altered his way of conceiving humanity and explaining life. After the black pessimism of his first books, have we not had, under the cloak of socialism, the complacent optimism of his later works?

One has to admit that no one understood the human soul less than these Naturalists who took it upon themselves to observe it. They saw existence as a seamless whole; they only accepted it as conditioned by the probable, whereas I have since learnt, through experience, that the improbable is not always the exception in this world, that the adventures of a Rocambole* are sometimes as true to nature as those of a Gervaise and a Coupeau.* But the idea that Des Esseintes could be as true as his own characters disconcerted and almost angered Zola.

In these few pages I have, up to now, been discussing *Against Nature* mainly from the point of view of literature and of art. At this point it behoves me to consider it from the perspective of Grace, and to show how the unknown, how the projection of a soul devoid of self-knowledge, may often play their part in the making of a book.

I must confess that this clear and obvious Catholic orientation of *Against Nature* remains incomprehensible to me. I was not educated in a school run by a religious order, but instead in a lycée; in my youth I was never pious, and the element of childhood memories, of a First Communion, of schooling, which often plays so significant a part in a conversion, played no part whatsoever in mine. And—which further complicates the problem and confuses any analysis—the fact is that when I was writing *Against Nature* I never used to set foot inside churches, I did not know a single practising Catholic, nor a single priest, I felt no divine hand urging me towards the Church, I was living peacefully in my rut; in seemed to me to be quite natural to gratify the bidding of my senses, and it never even entered my head that encounters of that nature were prohibited.

Against Nature was published in 1884, and I entered a Trappist monastery for my conversion in 1892;* close on eight years passed before the seeds of this book germinated. Allowing two years, or even three, for the operation of Grace—a secret, unremitting, only occasionally perceptible process—there would still remain at least five years during which I do not recall experiencing any urge of a Catholic nature, any remorse for the life I was leading, any desire to change it. Why, by what means, was I shifted on to a track which at that time was hidden from my eyes by the darkness of night? I am quite unable to explain this; nothing, save an ancestry of pilgrimages and monasteries and the prayers of an intensely devout Dutch family (which, however, I barely knew) can explain the total unconsciousness of that final entreaty, that plea for Divine help of the last page of *Against Nature*.

Yes, I am well aware that there are people of great moral strength who draw up plans, who plot, in advance, the course of their existence and follow it; it is even an understood thing, if I am not mistaken, that one can achieve anything through will-power; I fully believe it, but for my part, I confess that I have never been tenacious as a man or far-seeing as a writer. There is, in my life and my literary output, an undeniable element of passivity, of unawareness, of control from outside myself.

Providence was merciful to me, and the Virgin kind. I merely refrained from thwarting them when they revealed their intentions; I simply obeyed; I was led by what are called 'mysterious ways'. If any man can be certain of his nothingness without the help of God, I am that man.

Those outside the Faith will object that such ideas come close to fatalism and to the negation of all psychology. But that is not so, for Faith in our Lord is not the same as fatalism. Free will is untouched. I could, if I so desired, continue to yield to lustful desires and remain in Paris, instead of mortifying myself in a Trappist monastery. Doubtless God would not have insisted; but, while asseverating that the will remains intact, it must nevertheless be admitted that the Saviour is deeply involved, that he harries you, that he hunts you down, that he 'sweats' you, to use a vulgar but forceful police term; but, I say again, you can, at your own risk, send him about his business.

As for psychology, that is another matter. If we consider it, as I am doing, from the perspective of a conversion, it is, in the preliminary stages, impossible to understand; a few points may be discernible, but not others; the subterranean workings of the soul elude us. At the time when I was writing *Against Nature* there must undoubtedly have been a shifting of the soil, a drilling of the ground, to put in the foundations, of which I was not conscious. God was digging holes to lay his wires, and he worked only in the dark reaches of the soul, in the night. There was nothing to be seen; it was not until many years later that the spark began to run along the wires. Then I would feel my soul stirred by these shocks; they were not yet either very painful or very distinct: the liturgy, the mysticism, the art of religion were the vehicles and the means; it generally happened in churches, particularly in Saint Séverin, where I would go out of curiosity and because I had nothing better to do. At the services I would experience only an inward tremor, that tiny shiver one feels on seeing, hearing, or reading a beautiful work, but there was no specific attack, no formal summons to make a decision.

Only I was freeing myself, little by little, from my shell of corruption; I was beginning to be disgusted with myself, but I rebelled, nevertheless, against the articles of Faith. The objections I raised in my mind seemed unanswerable; and on waking one fine morning, they were resolved, without my ever knowing how. I prayed for the first time, and the explosion occurred.

All this seems mad to those who do not believe in Grace. For those who have experienced its effects, no surprise is possible; and if there were any, it could only relate to the period of incubation, the one in which one sees nothing and notices nothing, the period when the ground is cleared and a foundation laid whose existence one did not even suspect.

In a word, I understand, up to a point, what happened between the years 1891 and 1895, between *Là-bas* and *En route*, but nothing at all of what happened between the years 1884 and 1891, between *Against Nature* and *Là-bas*.

If I myself failed to understand them, *a fortiori* others did not understand the impulses that drove Des Esseintes. *Against Nature*

fell like an meteorite into the literary fairgrounds, exciting both stupefaction and anger; the press were thrown into total confusion; such
ramblings and ravings had never been seen; after describing me as a
misanthropic impressionist and calling Des Esseintes a maniac and
an imbecile of a complex kind, the Academics like M. Lemaître*
waxed indignant because I did not sing the praises of Virgil, declaring in peremptory tones that the Decadent school of Latin writers
in the Middle Ages was composed exclusively of 'dotards and
cretins'. Other so-called critics were kind enough to inform me that
I would profit from undergoing, in a thermal penitentiary, a disci-
plinary course of needle shower-baths; and then the public lecturers
joined in the fun. In the Salle des Capucines, the archon Sarcey* was
exclaiming in bewilderment: 'I'll be hanged if I understand one
single blessed word of this novel!' Finally, to complete the picture,
the serious journals like the *Revue des Deux Mondes** deputed their
leader, M. Brunetière, to compare this novel to the vaudevilles of
Waflard and Fulgence.*

In all this hurly-burly only one writer saw clearly, Barbey
d'Aurevilly, who, incidentally, did not know me at all. In an article
published in the *Constitutionnel* of 28 July 1884, which has been
reprinted in his 1902 collection entitled *Le Roman contemporain*, he
wrote:

'After such a book, the only thing left for the author is to choose
between the muzzle of a pistol and the foot of the cross.'*

The choice is made.

EXPLANATORY NOTES

1 *Ruysbroeck the Admirable*: fourteenth-century Flemish mystic, referred to again in Chapter 12 of *Against Nature* for a prose style which 'offered an incomprehensible but appealing amalgam of mysterious ecstasy, sentimental effusions, and scathing outbursts'. Thus not unlike Huysmans's own. Huysmans borrowed the epigraph from the opening line of the second of the canticles which close Ernest Hello's 1869 translation, *Rusbrock* (sic) *l'Admirable*. Not in the manuscript of *Against Nature*.

3 *the Château de Lourps*: six kilometres from Provins, in Seine-et-Marne, south-west of Longueville and north-west of Jutigny. Also evoked in his novel *En rade* (1887); Huysmans spent several days there in 1881, and subsequently the summers of 1884 and 1885.

Duc d'Épernon and the Marquis d'O: Jean-Louis de Nogaret, Duc d'Épernon (1554–1642), was one of Henri III's favourites and played a key role in his rapprochement with Henri de Navarre. François, Marquis d'O (1535–94), was Henri III's superintendent of finance, important in the latter's conversion to Catholicism, and yet a noted *débauché* himself. Huysmans's misleading depiction of these favourites' 'debilitated constitution' reflects a commonplace of romantic versions of history which were ill-disposed towards Henri III. See Dumas *père*'s play *Henri III et sa cour* (1829).

5 *the Voulzie*: a small river in the Seine-et-Marne region, running from close to Plessis-la-Tour via Provins into the Seine near Brey. It was celebrated in a song by Hégésippe Moreau.

Saint-Ruf: arrived in Provence in the fourth century, where he is said to have become the first bishop of Avignon. From the eleventh to the sixteenth centuries a religious congregation bore his name.

6 *Rue de la Chaise*: this was one of the plushest locations in the Saint-Germain district of Paris. Huysmans would often dine at *La Petite Chaise* where this road meets the Rue de Grenelle.

7 *Nicole*: in fact Huysmans makes use here of a description of the seventeenth-century moralist and theologian, Pierre Nicole, by poet, novelist, and critic Charles-Augustin Sainte-Beuve (1804–69), which is found in the latter's *Port-Royal* (1840–59).

9 *Fontenay-aux-Roses*: Huysmans himself had been sent there on medical grounds in 1881 and returned to edit *Against Nature*. His residence was at 3 Rue des Écoles (demolished in 1955).

11 *dandyism*: initially an aristocratic mode of dress and manners exemplified by Beau Brummel and designed to express superiority over the utilitarian values of the rising bourgeoisie, it acquired from Baudelaire and

Barbey d'Aurevilly the philosophical status of social and aesthetic revolt as a cult of artificiality, detachment, and self-control.

12 *dinner to mark . . . host's virility*: an idea borrowed from Grimod de la Reynière (1758–1838), author of the pioneering *Almanach des gourmands, servant de guide dans les moyens de faire grand chère* (1803–12), and related in his *Correspondance* and Bachaumont's *Mémoires secrets*, though Huysmans may have come across the description in Monselet's *Les Oubliés et les dédaignés* (1857).

13 *santonin*: or *santonica herba*, produced from santonica, the dried unexpanded flowerheads of a species of *Artemisia*, produced in Turkestan and used as an anthelmintic.

14 *orange*: in his *Journal* entry for 16 May 1884 Edmond de Goncourt complains that it was in fact he who uncovered the properties of this colour in *La Maison d'un artiste*. The latter account shares with *Against Nature* an obsessive concern with the aestheticization of domestic space.

15 *Weavers' Guild of Cologne*: this association was very powerful throughout the Middle Ages until the revolt of 1618 which led to the migration of workers to Aix-la-Chapelle and other northern towns.

blues: as in Renoir's paintings, for instance, we can see in this particular example of blue and orange the influence of Chevreul's theory of complementary colours.

'Glossarium' . . . of Du Cange: Charles du Fresne du Cange (1610–88) was an eminent author of studies of Byzantine history and of two dictionaries of medieval Latin and Greek, including the three-volume *Glossarium ad scriptores mediae et infimae latinitatis* of 1678. Successive revised editions appeared throughout the eighteenth century.

Abbaye-au-Bois of Bièvre: founded in the eleventh century by the Benedictines and reformed in 1513 as the Val-de-Grâce, this abbey was destroyed by the Huguenots in 1562 and by flooding in 1573. By dropping the 's' from the name of the village where the abbey was located Huysmans evokes (consciously or otherwise) the name of the river which runs through it. As Christopher Prendergast reminds us, 'There was, of course, always an alternative river, that anti-Seine, the Bièvre, whose seedy charms were praised . . . by Huysmans (in both the *Croquis parisiens* and *Le Drageoir aux épices*), and, in more sentimentally affectionate register, by Delvau' (*Paris and the Nineteenth Century* (Oxford: Blackwell, 1995), 203).

'La Mort des Amants' and 'L'Ennemi': Huysmans refers here to two poems from Baudelaire's *Les Fleurs du mal* (1857), the former ('The Death of the Lovers') evoking the theme of decaying desire elucidated in this chapter; and 'The Enemy'.

'Anywhere out of the World': one of Baudelaire's *Petits poèmes en prose (Le Spleen de Paris)*, whose English title was borrowed from Thomas Hood's 'The Bridge of Sighs'. The poems were published posthumously in 1869

and served as a model for Huysmans's own attempts at this hybrid genre. The latter's sense that the prose poem might provide an ideal mixture of freedom and constraint at the level of form is theorized towards the end of Chapter 14 of *Against Nature*.

16 *the lay sisters . . . in Ghent*: the Beguine convent at Ghent dates back to the seventeenth century.

18 *Lloyd's . . . Valéry Companies*: these commercial references are in large part authentic: for instance, Lloyd's Rhine Westphalia, maritime insurers, 13 Rue de Rougemont; and the Royal Mail Steam Packet Company, 38 Avenue de l'Opéra and 26 Rue d'Hauteville.

'The Adventures of Arthur Gordon Pym': Edgar Allan Poe's work, translated by Baudelaire, features a journey towards an hallucinatory Antarctic.

19 *M. Pasteur*: Louis Pasteur (1822–95), the famous French chemist who proved that micro-organisms caused fermentation and found ways of saving the beer, wine, and silk industries when they were threatened by such organisms. Author of *Études sur le vin* (1866) and *Études sur la bière* (1876).

Vigier baths . . . the Seine: named after the attendant on this boat near the Pont-Neuf who became its owner after marrying the widow of its creator, Poitevin.

'Guide Joanne': series of travel guides (including the 21-volume *Itinéraire général de la France*) founded in the nineteenth century by the man of letters, Adolphe-Laurent Joanne, and developed by his son Paul-Béninge Joanne, a geographer.

bateaux-mouches: large riverboats for sightseeing.

20 *the Crampton*: a separate tender locomotive for fast trains, built by Coil between 1848 and 1859, designed by Thomas Russell Crampton and used by the Chemins de fer du Nord, the Chemins de fer de l'Est, and the PLM.

21 *the Engerth*: a tender locomotive for goods trains invented by the Austrian Wilhelm d'Engerth for a competition in 1851 for the Semmering mountain line.

the Verrières woods: the home-town of the romantic hero of Stendhal's *Le Rouge et le noir*, Julien Sorel, whom we first encounter absorbed in reading when he should be working on his father's sawmill.

23 *'The Decadent Period'*: Huysmans borrows this term from Désiré Nisard's *Études de mœurs et de critique sur les poètes latins de la décadence* (Hachette, 1834), but the two authors differ in that Huysmans uses the term 'decadent' in a positive light. In the chapter on Lucan in volume 2 of his study Nisard associates decadent writing with excessive description and also argues that modern literature 'has fallen into its descriptive period. Not for sixty years [i.e. since 1775] has there been so much description.' This process will, of course, be extended in a 'decadent' novel such as *Against*

Nature where descriptions and details threaten to displace events and plotting, though there is still a recognizable beginning, middle, and end, even if they are not those of the traditional novel. The major 'classical' author to entice Des Esseintes is Petronius, whereas his tastes were inclined towards the later 'decadent' authors. He finds Virgil pedantic and plagiaristic (from Homer, Theocritus, Ennius, Lucretius, and in particular Pisander as exposed by Macrobius' commentary on Virgil, *Saturnales*, v. ii. 4). His admiration for Ovid is limited and he loathes Horace. Neither Cicero, Caesar, Sallust, Livy, Seneca, Suetonius, Tacitus, Tibullus, Propertius, Quintilian, the Plinys, Statius, Martial, Terence, nor Plautus find favour.

the colleges of the Sorbonne: this plural also refers to the University of Leipzig where Adolphe Ebert (see note to p. 27 below) worked. The literary choices made in this chapter were influenced in no small degree by the latter's *Allgemeine Geschichte der Literatur des Mittelalters*, translated into French by Joseph Aymeric and James Condamin as *Histoire générale de la littérature de Moyen Âge en Occident*, vol. 1, *Histoire de la littérature latine chrétienne depuis les origines jusqu'à Charlemagne* (Paris: E. Lerroux, 1883). This is pointed out in the retrospective 'Souvenirs sur Huysmans' published in Rémy de Gourmont's *Promenades littéraires*.

the swan of Mantua: Virgil (70–19 BC), author of the *Aeneid*, was so nicknamed because he was born in Andes near Mantua.

Orpheus . . . Aristaeus snivelling over some bees: the rendition of the Orpheus myth in the form in which it came to be known appears in Book IV of the *Georgics*. In the contrast between the farmer Aristaeus and the singer Orpheus we see the opposition between economic man and artistic man. Des Esseintes, of course, uses his economic means (which Folantin does not enjoy) in order to satisfy his artistic sensibilities. Aristaeus actually learns how to regain his bees after losing them to nymphs who were angered by his role in the death of Orpheus' wife, Eurydice.

24 *'Chickpea'*: the name of the Roman statesman Cicero (106–43 BC) means 'chickpea' in Latin.

25 *an interest in the Latin language*: it is only from Latin authors of the first century AD that Des Esseintes begins to take genuine literary pleasure: in particular from the *Pharsalia*, an epic poem by Lucan about the civil war between Pompey and Julius Caesar, and the *Satyricon*, the long picaresque novel by the satirist Petronius. The latter, 'this realistic work, this slice carved from the flesh of Roman daily life', is of particular importance as a model for Huysmans's conception of the modern novel, even though only parts of books 14, 15, and 16 survive. They describe the disreputable adventures of two young men, Encolpius (the narrator) and his friend Ascyltus, and of the sexually promiscuous boy Giton who plays one off against the other. Although Huysmans represents an extreme moment in the history of the nineteenth-century novel, Tony Tanner argues in

his *Adultery in the Novel* (Baltimore: Johns Hopkins University Press, 1979) that Petronius has a more general relevance as a model for the bourgeois novel: 'Of course there is no nineteenth-century novel in any way like it, but in an extreme form the *Satyricon* demonstrates the kind of collapse and perversion or inversion of patterns and systems of relationship that, in a more indirect way, the novelist of bourgeois society was also discovering' (p. 52). It is also invoked in the preface to Balzac's *Une fille d'Ève*.

26 *Trimalchio*: reference to the so-called 'dinner of Trimalchio', an ostentatious banquet given by a wealthy ex-slave, which occupies a third of the extant text of the *Satyricon*.

26-7 *the second century of the Christian era*: after Petronius the highlight of Des Esseintes's Latin library is *Metamorphoses*, a romance in eleven books, more commonly known in English as *The Golden Ass*, by Lucius Apuleius. In the only Latin novel that survives complete we follow the first-person narrator, Lucius, a Greek fascinated by black magic whose adventures culminate in his initiation into the mysteries of the Egyptian gods, Isis and Osiris. This puts in the shade Marcus Cornelius Fronto, foremost orator of his day, much of whose correspondence with Marcus Aurelius survives intact, and Aulius Gellius, author of *Noctes Atticae*, itself a mine of information about other Greek and Latin authors.

27 *Minucius Felix*: early Christian apologist. From this point onwards in this chapter Huysmans makes much use of Adolphe Ebert's *Allgemeine Geschichte der Literatur des Mittelalters* (see above, note to p. 23, *the colleges of the Sorbonne*). Other literary sources included J.-J. Ampère, *Histoire littéraire de la France avant le XIIe siècle* (Hachette, 1839), Dom Rivet de la Grange, *Histoire littéraire de la France*, vols. I (1735) to VI (1742), Chateaubriand, *Études historiques* (1831), and Frédéric Ozanam, *La Civilisation au Ve siècle* (1855). These can be pursued in Jean Céard, 'Des Esseintes et la décadence latine, Huysmans lecteur de Dom Rivet, de Chateaubriand et d'Ozanam', *Studi Francesi*, 65-6 (May–Dec. 1978), 297–310. Ebert finds Minucius Felix's *Octavius*, a dialogue between two converts and an educated pagan, 'extremely original', and devotes to this author the first chapter of his *Allgemeine Geschichte*. Tertullian was known as the Father of Latin theology. What particularly draws Des Esseintes to this author is the way in which he abstracted himself from the slings and arrows of the historical process, continuing to write as Caracalla (nickname of Emperor Aurelius Antoninus) was assassinated in AD 217 by Macrinus, who ruled until he was defeated the following year by Elagabalus (priest of the sun-god of Emesa, Elah-Gabal, from whom he took his name), remembered for his effeminacy and indulgence in gems, perfumes, and fine foods. Less appealing than Tertullian are St Cyprian, Arnobius, and Lactantius with whom Huysmans dispenses rapidly, though Ebert devotes an entire chapter to each of them, calling Lactantius 'beyond doubt the most elegant prose writer of his time'.

28 *The art of the third century*: the period from the third century AD to the middle of the fifth (after which, we are told, Rome and Gaul are sacked by Visigoths and Barbarians) appears to be dominated, according to Des Esseintes, by a few select individuals and works. In the third century there is Commodian of Gaza's *Carmen apologeticum* (written, according to Ebert, in 249 and not 259 as Huysmans asserts, and preferred to writers such as Ammianus Marcellinus, sometimes described as the last great Roman historian to write in Latin). In the fourth century we find the 'last great poet' of paganism, Claudian (praised by Ozanam). What follows is a wave of Christian-inspired writing: Paulinus, Juvencus, Victorinus, Sanctus Burdigalensis, Hilary of Poitiers, Ambrosius, Damasus, and Jerome's *Liber contra Vigilantium* which criticizes Vigilantius' cult of martyrs and practice of vigils and monastic celibacy. Finally, in the fifth century there is St Augustine, though Des Esseintes now actually prefers Prudentius' polemical and didactic poem *Psychomachia* (highlighted by Ozanam), Sidonius Apollinaris, Merobaudes (invoked in Ozanam's *Les Germains avant le christianisme*), Sedulius, the author of *Carmen paschale* and *Opus paschale*, Marius Victor's satire on sexual licence *Epistula de perversis suae aetatis moribus ad Salmonem abbatem*, and Paulinus of Pella's autobiographical narrative poem *Eucharisticon Deo sub ephemeridis meae textu* and Orientius' *Commonitorium*.

32 *Latin . . . remained confined to the convents*: the rest of Des Esseintes's Latin library basically covers the period up to the tenth century. This begins with a variety of authors such as Dracontius, Claudius Mamertus, Avitus of Vienne, Eugippus, Veranius of Gevaudan, the bishops Ennodius of Pavia, Aurelian of Arles, and Ferreolus of Uzes, and Rotherius of Agde (praised by Dom Rivet). His sixth-century authors include Boethius, Gregory of Tours, Jornandes, as well as the *Vexilla regis*, a lexically and figuratively abstruse hymn of the Passion by Fortunatus to which Léon Bloy also returns in *Le Désespéré* (1886). From the seventh and eighth centuries there are chroniclers such as Fredegarius and Paul the Deacon (or Paulus Wernefried), deacon of Aquileia, secretary to Didier, last king of the Lombards, and prisoner of Charlemagne, who fled to Monte Cassino until the end of his life; the seventh-century antiphony in honour of St Comgill from the Irish abbey at Bangor (which produced St Columba); and the biography of St Columba by the seventh-century Italian monk Jonas, the Venerable Bede's *De vita et miraculis S. Cuthberti, episcopi Lindisfarnensis*, the lives of St Radegunde by Baudonivia, and of St Rusticula, seventh-century abbess of Saint-Césair at Arles, written (according to Dom Rivet) by Florent, priest of the Trois-Châteaux, but strangely attributed to Defensor, Synodite of Ligugé, by Huysmans. The Anglo-Saxon authors of Latin texts which he particularly enjoyed, though, include St Aldhelm, composer of riddles dedicated to his son Acircius and of *De laudibus virginatis sive de virginitate sanctorum*; his successors in the art of writing riddles, Tatwine (Archbishop of Canterbury) and Eusebius, and above all St Boniface's acrostic riddles. What remains

includes chronicles by Fréculf, Bishop of Lisieux, and Regino; the tenth-century poem *De bellis parisiacae urbis* on the Norman siege of Paris by the Saint-Germain monk Abbo le Courbé (Huysmans uses *courbé* to translate Dom Rivet's Latin *cernuus*, stooping or bowing forwards); and Macer Floridus' poem *De viribus herbarum* ('On the properties of plants'), an imitation of Walafrid Strabo's *Hortulus* which may well have been read by Huysmans.

33 *volumes that were modern or undated*: in spite of the 'prodigious leap over the centuries' from the tenth century 'to the French of the present day' in Des Esseintes's library, he does own a handful of miscellaneous items. Abbé Jacques-Paul Migne (1800–75), French editor and printer, founded the newspaper *L'Univers religieux* (1833) which was to become Louis Veuillot's Ultramontane organ, and opened at Montrouge near Paris the publishing house which brought out in rapid succession numerous religious works at popular prices, including the *Patrologia* (the Latin series in 221 vols., 1844–55; the Greek collection first published in Latin in 85 vols., 1856–61; and then the Greek texts with Latin translations in 165 vols., 1857–66), of which Des Esseintes owns 'a few odd tomes'. He also possesses Johann Christian Wernsdorf's *Poetae latini minores* (1780–98); work by the Dutch scholar Johannes Meursius, author of *Roma luxurians sive de luxu Romanorum, liber singularis* (1631), on the luxury and refinement of the Roman Empire; Friedrich-Karl Forberg's *Manual of Classical Erotology* (*De figuris veneris*) (re-edited in 1882); the *Moechialogy* (from the Greek *moïcheia*, adultery), an account of sexual morality by doctor and trappist, P. Debreyne (1786–1867), published in Paris by Poussielgue-Rusand in 1846; and the *Diaconals*, an ecclesiastical term for the supplementary sections reserved for the reading of deacons in texts on moral theology, especially those treating the breaches of the Sixth Commandment (which can be traced back to volume 3 of Alphonse de Ligouri's *Theologia moralis* of 1718).

35 *tortoise*: an idea based on the jewel-encrusted tortoise in which the *fin-de-siècle* dandy (and partial model for Des Esseintes) Robert de Montesquiou, delights. The latter writes in his collection *Les Hortensias bleus* of 'ma tortue au dos d'or ou caillouté de turquoise' ('my gold-backed tortoise metalled with turquoise').

37 *almandine*: corruption of 'alabandine', a dark red quartz whose name comes from the town of Alabanda in Asia Minor.

ouvarovite: green emerald garnet found in Bissersk in the Urals (from the proper noun Ouvarof).

sapphirines: gems already highlighted by Huysmans in his description of the passage des Panoramas in Paris in *Croquis et eaux-fortes. Effet du soir* (1876).

38 *Si-a-Fayoune, Moyou-tann, and de Khansky*: rather than choosing actual varieties of tea Huysmans invents names apparently on the basis of their euphony.

39 *mouth organ*: an idea revealed to Huysmans by père Polycarpe Poncelet's *Chimie du goût et de l'odorat, ou principes pour composer facilement et à peu de frais les liqueurs à boire et les eaux de senteur* (*Chemistry of Tastes and Odours, or principles for the simple and inexpensive composition of drinks and perfumes* Paris: Lemercier, 1755). This notion of *correspondances* between different senses echoes not only Baudelaire's famous poem of that name but also Zola's 'symphony' of cheeses in *Le Ventre de Paris* (*The Belly of Paris*, 1873), as Fortassier observes.

40 *'Ballads of Estelle'*: allusion to Jean-Pierre-Claris de Florian's pastoral idyll, *Estelle et Némorin* (1787), invoked by Berlioz's account of youthful passion in his *Mémoires*. Florian's tale of shepherd and shepherdess set in the time of Louis XII was a successful chapbook. Fortassier cites a review of Hervé's staging of the tale in 1876.

'Ah! mother, shall I tell you?': an anonymous eighteenth-century pastoral romance in which a shepherdess confesses her weakness for her beloved shepherd, Silvandre. It inspired several variations for piano by Mozart and appeared in the mid-nineteenth century in *Chants et chansons populaires de la France*.

44 *Gustave Moreau*: (1826–98), painter of mythological and religious scenes, brought to prominence in symbolist and Decadent circles by Huysmans's account here.

Salome: an oil-painting displayed at the Salon of 1876, then at the Universal Exhibition of 1878, now in the Armand Hammer Collection in Los Angeles. Huysmans worked on his depiction of this biblical tale from a Goupil photograph bought for three francs at Baschet's on the Boulevard Saint-Germain. See Introduction, p. xvii.

45 *University of Louvain*: the Department of Theology at the University of Louvain was famous for Catholic vernacular translations of the Bible, first printed in September 1550. The 1578 version (actually revised on the basis of rival Protestant Genevan versions) was frequently reprinted. Pierre Variquet would appear to be a seventeenth-century Parisian printer who also produced works by Dancel and Paulus Courtois, for instance.

47 *Salammbô*: Carthaginian priestess in Flaubert's eponymous novel of 1862. See note to p. 147 below.

'The Apparition': an important watercolour displayed along with *Salome* at the Salon of 1876 and owned by the Cabinet des Dessins du Louvre. It proved to be particularly influential on Redon.

49 *Mantegna*: Andrea Mantegna (*c*.1431–1506), pre-eminent amongst Italian painters of the fifteenth century. In addition to its antiquarian content, his art is characterized by brilliant compositional solutions and an innovative use of perspective and foreshortening. Painted a number of pictures on the theme of *Judith with the Head of Holofernes*.

Jacopo de Barbarino: or Barbarii, was a fifteenth-century Venetian engraver who had just been rediscovered by Émile Galichon (1829–75), founder of the *Chronique des arts et de la curiosité* in 1861 which he edited until 1872, along with the *Gazette des Beaux-Arts* (1861–72).

49 *Da Vinci and . . . Delacroix*: Moreau copied Da Vinci from museums especially during his visits to Italy (1857 to 1859), and had professional links with Eugène Delacroix (1798–1863), one of the greatest painters of the first half of the nineteenth century, the last major history painter and the embodiment of Romanticism in the visual arts.

50 *enameller*: Huysmans's French text refers here to 'l'art du Limosin', the latter being the name of a family of enamellers from Limoges, most notably Léonard I (1505–77), whose series of forty-six enamels of the royal family and their ancestors is to be found in the Louvre.

Jan Luyken: (1649–1712) was an engraver and writer from Amsterdam who illustrated pietist works of martyrology, including the *Theatre of Martyrs from the Death of Christ until the Present* (1685). His support for Calvinist piety is 'perverted' by Huysmans's sadistic impulses.

51 *Callot's*: Jacques Callot (1592–1635), French etcher, engraver, and draughtsman, one of the major exponents of the Mannerist style in the early seventeenth century. His compositions were in turns fantastic, grotesque, and elegant.

dragonnades: campaigns of persecution against the Protestants, led by Louis XIV, in which dragoons (named after their muskets, so called because they 'breathed fire like a dragon') were quartered upon the persecuted.

Comedy of Death: published by *La Revue fantaisiste* in 1854 (Théophile Gautier wrote a poem with the same title). Rodolphe Bresdin (1822–85) was a remarkable engraver and lithographer whose humble origins are evoked in Champfleury's *Chien-Caillou*. He was introduced to Gautier by Baudelaire and is discussed by Robert de Montesquiou in *Rodolphe Bresdin* (1912) and *L'Inextricable Graveur, Rodolphe Bresdin* (1913).

52 *The Good Samaritan*: composed by Bresdin in 1861 during his stay in Paris.

Odilon Redon: (1840–1916), another artist propelled to eminence amongst the Decadents by *Against Nature*. His work is noted for its interpretations of Baudelaire, Flaubert, and Poe, and the charcoals and lithographs which examine fantastic subjects and illuminate the links between natural and human forms.

53 *Proverbs*: (1816–24), an incomplete set of twenty-two prints by Goya, eventually published in 1864. At once enigmatic, mystifying and resistant, they were initially entitled *Disparates* but were subsequently associated with Spanish proverbs. See note to p. 83 below.

Edgar Allan Poe: (1809–49), more influential in France than in his native America; disseminated via Baudelaire's translations and introductions to his work (1848–65), his depictions of sensations on the edge of normal psychic life are characterized by a sense of the macabre which proved highly stimulating for Surrealists and Decadents alike. In 1882 Redon produced in limited edition a set of six lithographs *A Edgar Poe*.

Théotocopuli: name used in the nineteenth century to refer to the sixteenth-century painter El Greco (whose real name was Domenikos Theotokopoulos). This reference anticipates the eulogy in Maurice Barrès's *Gréco ou le secret de Tolède* (1911).

54 *Greuze's*: Jean-Baptiste Greuze (1725–1805), French painter, notably of genre scenes, portraits, and studies of expressive heads. His reputation was revived after 1850 when critics such as the Goncourt brothers returned with enthusiasm to eighteenth-century painting. By the end of the century his work, especially his many variations on the *Head of a Girl*, fetched record prices. The theme of virginity (and its loss) was highlighted in Diderot's famous interpretation of his *Girl Weeping over her Dead Bird* (1765).

61 *'De laude castitatis'*: (*The Praise of Chastity*). Des Esseintes returns here to the section of his library inventoried in Chapter 3 of the novel. The full title of Avitus' work is *De consolatoria laude castitatis ad Fuscinam sororem*.

63 *Lacordaire*: Jean-Baptiste-Henri Lacordaire (1802–61), friend of Lamennais and collaborator on *L'Avenir*, organ of liberal Catholicism; noted for his Lenten sermons at Notre-Dame (1836) and for trying to reconstitute the order of the Frères Prêcheurs de saint Dominique. Politically active, he was a member of the Assemblée Constituante in 1848.

Sorrèze: or Sorèze, a famous ecclesiastical college founded in the Tarn in 1682. After 1840 it fell from Jesuit control into the Dominican hands of Lacordaire.

65 *the Cluny Museum*: the Musée de Cluny in Paris, a museum of national antiquities stored in the former Hôtel de Cluny, built *c.*1490 as a town residence for the abbots of the Benedictine Abbey of Cluny.

67 *Father Labbé's . . . Synods*: Labbé (1607–67), began the *Collection des conciles* (Collection of the Church Councils) (1672, 18 vols., completed by père Gabriel Cossart).

'Nothing is incorporeal . . . own': cited in Flaubert's *La Tentation de saint Antoine*.

68 *De Quincey*: his *Confessions of an Opium-Eater*, translated by Alfred de Musset in 1828 and adapted by Baudelaire, proved deeply influential on Huysmans.

69 *Schopenhauer*: Arthur Schopenhauer (1788–1860), German philosopher whose version of world-weary pessimism proved highly seductive in the atmosphere of self-conscious decline which characterized late-nineteenth-century France. Made fashionable in France by Elme Caro's *Le Pessimisme au XIXe siècle: Léopardi, Schopenhauer, Hartmann* (1878).

'Imitation of Christ': devotional work by Thomas à Kempis (1380–1471).

70 *hydrotherapy*: a water cure for neurosis described in the Goncourts' journal.

71 *asafoetida . . . valerian*: cures used by Huysmans himself (see letter to Zola of 16 April 1882).

72 *plants . . . of exotic origin*: the fashion for rare plants which grew during the Second Empire was underpinned by its literary treatment in the Goncourts' *Renée Mauperin* (1864), Flaubert's *L'Éducation sentimentale* (1869), and Zola's *La Curée* (1871).

75 *monstrosities*: Huysmans may have found these symbols of 'the unnaturalness of nature' in the Jardin des Plantes or in specialist catalogues. Several of the species cited by Des Esseintes appear, as Fumaroli notes, in *L'Album de clichés électrotypes*.

76 *Cattleya*: used to embody the symbolic erotic charge of flowers, as readers of Proust will recall, in the passion of Swann and Odette depicted in *Un amour de Swann*.

77 *It all comes down to syphilis*: an echo of Flaubert's *Dictionnaire des idées reçues* (*Dictionary of Received Ideas*), which tells us that 'everybody is affected by it'.

83 *sorted his Goyas*: Francisco de Goya (1746–1828), the most important Spanish artist of the last quarter of the eighteenth and the first quarter of the nineteenth centuries. Stylistically his work spans the period from late Rococo to Romanticism. His *Caprichos* print series (publised in February 1799) satirized the follies of contemporary Spanish society and brought him international attention. For details of the *Proverbs*, see n. to p. 53 above. During the Peninsular War Goya was called to a besieged Saragossa to paint its citizens' 'glorious deeds' against the French army; he recorded the atrocities and horrors he saw in drawings and small paintings which formed the basis of the print series *Disasters of War* (1810–20, unpublished until 1863). Earlier, in the late 1770s, he had etched *The Garrotted Man*, a powerful image whose technique resembles the work of Tiepolo. Though subsequently many nineteenth-century commentators viewed his works as repugnant and as the products of a 'diseased' mind, in 'Quelques caricaturistes français: Goya' (published in *Le Présent*, 1857), Baudelaire saw that Goya obtained beauty from ugliness.

84 *literary opiates*: Huysmans's French text refers here to 'solanées' (from *solari*, to relieve), the family of plants to which tobacco belongs.

85 *Siraudin*: a famous confectioner, also patronized by the heroine of Edmond de Goncourt's *La Faustin* (1882). He set up his shop on the Boulevard des Capucines after co-authoring, with Labiche and Lubize, the play *Le Misanthrope et l'Auvergnat*. His sweets called 'Perles des Pyrénées' are mentioned on various occasions in the Goncourts' journal and contain sarcanthus, a plant from the orchid family found above all in China.

Miss Urania: Baldick sees her as an echo of Tompkins in the Goncourts' *Les Frères Zemganno* (1879). For images of circus performers as objects of desire, see the paintings of Degas (*Miss Lola au cirque Fernando*) and Rops (*La Femme au trapèze*).

88 *dialogue of the Chimera and the Sphinx*: a reference to Flaubert's *La Tentation de saint Antoine*, which also enjoys a far wider field of intertextual allusion. The sphinx (famously reproduced in Moreau's *L'Œdipe et le Sphinx*) symbolizes the ineffable mystery of Woman (as construed in a male vision which is both idealizing and misogynist). See Bram Dijkstra's *Idols of Perversity* (New York: Oxford University Press, 1986).

90 *Busembaum, Diana, Ligouri, and Sanchez*: Hermann Busembaum, author of *Medulla theologiae moralis facili ac perpetua methodo resolvens casus conscientiae ex variis probatisque authoribus concinnata* (1657), the classic manual of Catholic moral theology until the end of the eighteenth century. Antonin Diana, seventeenth-century Sicilian theologian, author of *Resolutiones morales* (1629–56), abridged in Rome as *Tabula aurea operum omnium* and *Practicae Resolutiones lectissimorum casuum*. Saint Alphonse-Marie de Ligouri (1696–1787) founded the missionary institute of the Ligouristes and wrote a *Moral Theology* (1755) and *Practical Instruction for Confessors* (1780). Thomas Sanchez (1550–1610), famous Spanish Jesuit, wrote for confessors *Disputationes de sancto matrimonii sacramento*.

91 *Henri III*: (1551–89), King of France who succeeded Charles IX in 1574.

93 *Clapisson's*: Antonin Louis Clapisson (1808–66), author of comic-operas and bland romances.

94 *the Atkinsons . . . the Piesses*: J. & E. Atkinson of London had a shop in Paris in the faubourg Poissonnière. We find Chardin, Lubin, Legrand, and Violet at Rue Auber, Rue Saint-Anne, Rue Saint-Honoré, and Boulevard des Capucines respectively. Huysmans got hold of the catalogue, *Produits spéciaux recommandés de Violet, parfumeur breveté, fournisseur de toutes les Cours étrangères* (around 1874). Septimus Piesse was an olfactory chemist in London, author of *Des odeurs, des parfums, et des cosmétiques* (second French edition, with Chardin, Hadancourt, and Henri Massignon, 1877), which Huysmans used.

Saint-Amand's: a reference to Marc-Antoine de Gérard Saint-Amant (*sic*) (1594–1661), capricious baroque poet of *peinture parlante* in varying modes—pastoral, heroic, comic, burlesque, and satirical—with a zestful, exclamatory style noted by Huysmans. Cited as a precursor of Romanticism by Gautier, who also adds to the notorious stereotype of a life said to be as indulgent and extravagant as his writing.

Bossuet: Jacques-Bénigne Bossuet (1627–1704), noted orator at the court of Louis XIV.

Victor Hugo and Gautier: Huysmans draws a comparison between the 'language of flowers' and the literary orientalism of romantic poetry by Victor Hugo (1802–85; see *Les Orientales*, 1829) and Théophile Gautier (1811–72).

94 *the Malherbes . . . Baour-Lormians*: François de Malherbe (1555–1628), reformer of French poetry who demanded discipline, craftsmanship and rhetorical clarity from his fellow poets. Nicolas Boileau-Despréaux (1636–1711), poet, satirist, and critic, known as the 'régent du Parnasse', most renowned for his *Art poétique* (1674) and as the aesthetician of neo-classicism. François Guillaume Andrieux (1759–1833), dramatist and poet, chair of French literature and ethics at the Collège de France from 1816, who embodied Classical academic resistance to early Romanticism. Pierre François Marie Baour-Lormian (1770–1854), translator, poet, and reactionary supporter of the Classical critique of Romantic originality (notably in his satire *Le Classique et le Romantique*, 1825).

96 *Boucher's*: François Boucher (1703–70), painter, draughtsman, and etcher who dominated eighteenth-century fine and decorative arts in France until the emergence of Neoclassicism. Venus reappeared throughout his mythological painting, from *Venus Asking Vulcan for Arms for Aeneas* (1732) as he tried to establish himself, via his design for the tapestry of *Venus in the Forge of Vulcan* (1757) in his series The Loves of the Gods, to his masterpiece, the *Triumph of Venus* (1740), commissioned by the Swedish Ambassador in Paris, Tessin.

Thémidore: Claude Godard d'Aucour's scurrilous thesis novel *Thémidore* (1715), about a certain abbé Dubois, quite possibly encountered by Huysmans in Kistemaecker's edition of 1882 prefaced by Maupassant.

100 *industry . . . Pantin*: in *L'Art moderne*, Huysmans champions the aesthetics of modern life: 'The factory chimneys which rise up in the distance mark out the North, Pantin for instance, with a stamp of melancholy grandeur that it would not otherwise have had.'

104 *high-lows*: boots fastened in front and reaching over the ankle. Huysmans uses the term *brodequins*.

105 *Galignani's Messenger*: a reference to the location of the major English daily newspaper in Paris, *Galignani's Messenger*, founded in 1814, which carried stories on England and France culled from other papers. Its moderation and impartiality allowed it to survive changes of regime and its supposed accuracy drew a sizeable readership in spite of its price.

Baedeker or Murray: famous nineteenth-century travel guides.

107 *du Maurier or John Leech*: G.-L.-P. Busson du Maurier (1834–96) produced paintings, drawings, and writing, and was known particularly for his work in *Punch*. His humorous verse includes 'The History of the Jack Sprats' and his parody of William Morris's ballads, 'The Legend of Camelot', with mock Pre-Raphaelite illustrations. His novel *Trilby* (1894) was also to gain particular fame. John Leech (1817–64), friend of Thackeray and one of the most noteworthy English caricaturists, did about 3,000 drawings of political cartoons and scenes of everyday middle-class life for *Punch* from 1841 onwards, and illustrated around fifty books, including Dickens's *A Christmas Carol*.

Caldecott's: Randolph Caldecott (1846–86) painted, did drawings for *Punch*, *The Graphic*, and *The Pictorial World*, and illustrated fantastic tales and books for children. Praised alongside Kate Greenaway and Walter Crane in a digression on illustrated children's albums which appeared in Huysmans's collection of art criticism, *L'Art moderne*.

108 *Millais . . . The Eve of St Agnes*: the *Eve of St Agnes* by Sir John Everett Millais (1829–96) was a pre-Raphaelite painting shown at the Royal Academy in 1863, much appreciated by Whistler. It was based on Keats's poem, 'The Eve of St Agnes', quoted in part by Millais in the Academy's catalogue: 'Full on this casement shone the wintry moon . . . her vespers done, | Of all its wreathed pearls her hair she frees . . .'

Watts: George Frederick Watts (1817–1904), a painter of historical frescos and portraits, was particularly well known for *Hope* (1886), inspired by the Pre-Raphaelites. Huysmans saw the *Curse of Cain*, *Ida*, and three versions of *Eve* at a small exhibition in 1883 at the galerie Georges Petit, Rue de Sèze, Paris.

110 *Mr Wickfield*: Miss Trotwood's lawyer in *David Copperfield* (1849–50), who gives lodgings to David and whose daughter David eventually marries.

Mr Tulkinghorn: lawyer in *Bleak House* (1852–53).

Little Dorrit . . . Tom Pinch's sister: characters from Dickens's *Little Dorrit*, *David Copperfield*, and *Martin Chuzzlewit* respectively.

cask of Amontillado: reference to *The Cask of Amontillado* (1846) by E. A. Poe, in which the narrator Montresor lures his enemy Fortunato into a catacomb with an offer of rare sherry and then buries him alive.

111 *Rue d'Amsterdam*: the Austin Bar or English Tavern, situated at what is now 24 Rue d'Amsterdam, enjoys superior literary credentials. Baudelaire took a room above it, the Goncourts lauded its 'authentic roast-beef', Valéry took Mallarmé and Huysmans there, and after its rebirth as the Bar Britannia, Gide dined there with Copeau in 1912.

113 *the Dutch School*: for Huysmans's major analysis of Dutch painterly realism, see his *L'Art moderne*.

114 *Ever since leaving home . . . English life*: this idea can be tracked back to a letter of 1882 to Huysmans's editor in Brussels which notes, 'By dressing up in the style of Old England, reading Dickens and going to drink port at the Bodega, you can easily imagine yourself on a journey visiting that diabolical city of industry praised by Taine and de Amicis.'

115 *Archelaüs . . . Villanova*: Archelaüs, Greek poet and alchemist of the fifth century AD referred to in J. L. Ideler's *Physici et medici Graeci minores* (Berlin, 1842), which quotes the 136 lines of his poem in iambic verse on sacred art. Albert Magnus (1193?/1206?–1280), German philosopher and theologian. One of the first thinkers of his time to regard philosophy and science as 'pure' fields of knowledge in their own right, and to draw upon the long neglected writings of Arab philosophers as well as upon

Aristotle. Raymond Lull (1233–1315), Catalan poet, novelist and the-ologian, whose output included *The Book of Contemplation*, *Blanquerna*, and *Fèlix*. Arnaldus de Villa Nova, (*c.*1235–1313), alchemist, astrologer, and physician, apparently of Spanish origin. Author of many alchemical writings, including *Thesaurorum* and *Speculum Alchimiae*.

115 *Perrin of Lyons*: Louis-Benoît Perrin, printer influenced by Renaissance styles, whose editions were highly prized both during and after his life-time (1799–1865). His reputation began with an important edition of *Inscriptions antiques de Lyon* (1846–54).

116 *Lortic . . . Gruel-Engelmann*: Lortic, bookbinder and gilder; Trautz-Bauzonnet, Chambolle-Duru and Gruel-Engelmann all bookbinders. All listed in the *Annuaire du commerce et de l'industrie ou Almanach des 1 500 000 adresses*.

117 *spleen*: term belonging to the language of bodily humours used to depict the world-weariness of the artist in post-revolutionary society, exempli-fied in Baudelaire's title of contrasts, 'Spleen et idéal'.

118 *Rabelais's*: François Rabelais (d. 1553), author of humanist comedies, most famously *Gargantua* and *Pantagruel*, renowned for their exuberant linguistic inventiveness.

Molière's: Molière (1622–73), pseudonym of Jean-Baptiste Poquelin, great comic playwright of Louis XIV's France, whose output included *Le Malade imaginaire* and *Le Misanthrope*. Des Esseintes's attitude reflects Baudelaire's in *Mon cœur mis à nu*.

119 *Villon*: François Villon (*c.*1431–after 1463), perhaps the most romantic of medieval poets, whose conspicuous life-story and autobiographically resonant verse have given him a reputation as a *poète maudit*.

d'Aubigné: Agrippa d'Aubigné (1552–1630), poet, historian, satirist, and polemicist of the Protestant Reformation, and author of *Les Tragiques*, an account of the French Wars of Religion.

Voltaire or Rousseau: Voltaire (1694–1778), pseudonym of François-Marie Arouet, landmark Enlightenment author, active in virtually every genre, imbued with a vision of a secular, tolerant society. Jean-Jacques Rousseau (1712–78), Swiss writer famed for his polemical contributions to political and social debates during the Enlightenment and his fictional and auto-biographical accounts of the human subject (e.g. *The Confessions*), so influential in the development of Romantic writing.

Salons: nine accounts of the exhibitions of the Académie Royale de Pein-ture et de Sculpture, founded on the classical doctrine of the imitation of nature, composed between 1759 and 1781 by Denis Diderot (1713–84), often seen as the beginning of art criticism in France.

Bourdaloue and Bossuet: Louis Bourdaloue (1623–1704), French Jesuit priest renowned for his sermons on social and personal morality; for Bossuet, see note to p. 94 on Bossuet.

Nicole: see note to p. 7.

Pascal: Blaise Pascal (1623–62), mathematician and theologian of Jansenist persuasion (see his attack on the Jesuits in his *Lettres provinciales*), who offers an apology for his faith in the *Pensées* (published posthumously).

literature of Catholicism: as the Preface of 1903 shows, Chapter 12 is important for Huysmans's own development as he was himself to veer towards Catholicism in the early 1890s. Though during the *ralliement* in the final years of the century there was a mass resurgence of the Catholic Church in response to the social forces of modernization, Huysmans chose to identify with the traditionalist version of the faith reinstated by Vatican I (1870), with its élitist cult of authority and taste for superstition and obscurantism. The conflict between the republican state and the Catholic Church grew during the Dreyfus Affair, and the ties of the post-revolutionary Concordat of 1801 were officially severed in 1905 once Émile Combes had broken the grip of the Church on education. This tension between national and universal affiliations had long been implicit within Catholicism itself. The doctrine of Gallicanism was intended to restrain papal authority in the French Church in favour of the bishops or the king. After the Revolution, ecclesiastical (rather than royal) Gallicanism continued to oppose the rise of Ultramontanism until 1870 when the latter triumphed and the First Vatican Council affirmed papal infallibility in *ex cathedra* statements on morality and faith. Ultramontanism, which looked to the authority of Rome (*ultra montes*— beyond the Alps), had been a minority opinion prior to 1789 but came into its own in the nineteenth century, especially in the writings of de Maistre (in *Du pape* of 1819) and Lamennais (until his break with Rome in 1832–4). It came to be associated in the course of the century with reactionary politics and an anti-intellectual strain in theology supported by Louis Veuillot.

Ozanam: Frédéric Ozanam (1813–53), closely linked with the leaders of liberal Catholicism, founder in 1833 of the Society of St Vincent de Paul, Dante specialist and author of *La Civilisation chrétienne chez les Francs* (1849) and of *Des progrès dans les siècles de décadence* (1852), quite at odds with Huysmans's refutation of such faith in progress.

120 *Madame Swetchine*: (1782–1857), née Anne-Sophie Soymonoff, one of the key voices of liberal and legitimist Catholicism under the July Monarchy.

Madame Augustus Craven: (1820–91), née Pauline de La Ferronays, daughter of one of Chateaubriand's friends and author of *Le Récit d'une sœur* (1868), admired by Barbey d'Aurevilly, which depicts in the figure of Alexandrine de La Ferronays both the spirit of romanticism and the charitable piety of the Catholic aristocracy. Also produced novels, including *Fleurange* (1871) and *Éliane* (1882).

121 *Eugénie de Guérin*: (1805–48): her *Journal intime* dating from 1834 to 1842 was published posthumously in 1862 along with her *Lettres* to her brother,

Maurice (1810–39), to whom she devoted much of her pious life, and his *Journal*. Maurice was befriended by Barbey d'Aurevilly and noted for his prose poetry, *Le Centaure* and *La Bacchante*.

121 *M. de Jouy . . . Lebrun*: Victor Joseph Étienne de Jouy (1764–1846), imitator of Addison and Voltaire, known for the creation of the satirical sketches in the *Hermite de la Chaussée d'Antin*, which was vital in the growth of the literary genre of 'physiologies' of social types which exerted such an influence on so much nineteenth-century writing. Ponce Denis Échouard-Lebrun (1729–1807), mediocre neoclassical lyricist and epigrammatist whose works were edited posthumously by his friend Ginguené in 1811.

122 *Dupanloup . . . Chocarne*: Félix Dupanloup (1802–78), Bishop of Orleans from 1849, member of the Académie française from 1854, and a noteworthy preacher praised by Renan as an 'educator without equal'. J.-B. Landriot (1816–74), Bishop of La Rochelle and Saintes from 1856, of Reims from 1867, also a valued preacher, whose seven-volume *Œuvres* appeared between 1864 and 1874. François-Alexandre La Bouillerie (1810–82), Bishop of Carcassonne from 1855, coadjutor to the Cardinal-Archbishop of Bordeaux from 1872, a moderate Ultramontanist from a legitimist family. Jean-Joseph Gaume (1802–79), vicar-general of Nevers, author of *Ver rongeur des sociétés modernes ou le paganisme dans l'éducation* (1852), which once more triggered the quarrel between liberal Catholics and Ultramontanists. Dom Guéranger (1805–75), restorer of the Benedictine abbey at Solesmes and initiator of the liturgical renaissance. Father Marie-Théodore Ratisbonne (1802–1884), co-founder with his brother of the Congregation of Our Lady of Sion, and author of an *Histoire de saint Bernard et de son siècle* (1840). Charles-Émile Freppel (1827–91), professor of sacred rhetoric at the Sorbonne (1855–69), enemy of Renan's *Vie de Jésus* (1863) and Ferry's policies after his election as the deputy of Brest in 1880. Adolphe-Louis Perraud (1818–1906), Bishop of Autun (1874), member of the Académie française (1882), cardinal (1893), a famous 'liberal' preacher, but a fierce enemy of Combes who drove through the separation of Church and State. Gustave-François Ravignan (1795–1858), Jesuit successor to Lacordaire at Notre-Dame, whose *Conférences* were published with much success in 1860. Auguste-Joseph Gratry (1805–72), 'liberal' professor of moral theology at the Sorbonne (1863), elected to the Académie (1867). Pierre Olivaint (1816–71), Jesuit rector of the collège de Vaugirard (1857–65) whose reputation he greatly enhanced, then superior at the Jesuit Résidence de Paris in the Rue de Sèvres, killed during the Commune. Father Dosithée de Saint-Alexis wrote *La Vie de saint Jean de la Croix* (1727) and was, according to le Moyne des Essarts's *Les Siècles littéraires de la France* (1800–1), a founder of the Carmelite order. Henri-Martin Didon (1840–1900), renowned Dominican preacher exiled to Corsica in 1880 for his excessively liberal opinions, where he was forbidden to preach and offer confession. Bernard Chocarne was a Dominican friend and confidant of

Lacordaire, of whom he wrote an account, *P. Lacordaire, sa vie intime et religieuse* (1866).

Lacordaire: see note to p. 63.

123 *Abbé Perreyve*: Henri Perreyve, liberal disciple of Lacordaire (whose letters to 'young people' he edited) and his successor in his lectures at Notre-Dame. Also linked with Ozanam.

Comte de Falloux: Frédéric Alfred Pierre, Count of Falloux (1811–86), ardent advocate of free education, he became Minister of Public Education on 20 December 1848 until 30 October 1849, but was criticized by Veuillot and the Ultramontanists for the inadequacies of the law which bears his name. Became a champion of liberal Catholicism in *Le Correspondant* under the Second Empire which he so disliked.

124 *Veuillot*: Louis-François Veuillot (1813–83), polemical journalist, director from 1842 of the very populist Ultramontane review *L'Univers*, which quarrelled with the liberal Catholicism of Dupanloup and Montalembert, and author of anti-progressive pamphlets and books such as *Les Odeurs de Paris* (1867). Fumaroli notes Huysmans's lack of sympathy towards such liberalism.

Montalembert . . . Broglie: Count Charles-Forbes-René Montalembert (1810–70), a dogged defender of liberal Catholicism who broke with Lamennais after the papal condemnation of *Paroles d'un croyant* (1834). He saw his influence wane to the advantage of Veuillot under the Second Empire. Augustin Cochin (1823–72), French publicist and administrator, member of the Académie des sciences morales et politiques (1864), who dealt with the issue of poverty in *Les Ouvriers européens* (1856), and wrote *La Révolution sociale en France, résumé critique de l'ouvrage de Le Play* (1865). See note to p. 63 on Lacordaire. Albert de Broglie (1821–1901), collaborator on *Le Correspondant* with Montalembert and Falloux, author of *L'Église et l'Empire romain au IVe siècle* (1856) which echoed Ozanam's lessons at the Sorbonne on fifth-century Christian civilization, director of the monarchical opposition to Thiers after 1871.

La Bruyère: Jean de La Bruyère (1645–96), moralist writer and the last great figure of French classicism. Author of *Les Caractères* (eight considerably augmented editions between 1688 and 1694), comprising maxims, reflections, and individual portraits, which expose the follies of human nature.

125 *Nettement*: Alfred Nettement (1805–69), unyielding legitimist who also wrote an essay on the modern novel, *Le Roman contemporain, ses vicissitudes, ses divers aspects, son influence* (1864).

126 *Murger's*: Henri Murger (1822–61), known principally for his *Scènes de la vie de bohème* (1851) which inspired Puccini's *La Bohème*; his mixture of sentimentality and comic realism depicted the failure of youthful idealism in Parisian artistic and literary circles.

M. de Laprade: Victor Richard de Laprade (1812–87), Catholic critic and poet who combined a Romantic sensibility with classical influences to produce a major poem, *Psyché* (1841), as well as much mediocre verse, and articulated a powerful sense of the force of external nature in his *Histoire du sentiment de la nature* (1883).

126 *Paul Delaroche*: (1797–1856), rival to Delacroix who painted under the July Monarchy grand historical canvases in an academicist style, such as *Les Enfants d'Édouard* (1831) and *L'Assassinat du duc de Guise* (1835).

Reboul: Jean Reboul (1796–1864), nicknamed 'the Baker of Nîmes', author of tragedies and *Poésies* (1836).

Poujoulat . . . Carné: J. J. François Poujoulat (1808–80), editor on *La Quotidienne*, the official organ of orthodox legitimism, and co-author with Michaud of historical *Mémoires*. Antoine Eugène Genoude (1792–1849), author of apologist works deemed 'inexhaustible' by Fumaroli. Amédée Nicolas, specialist on the literature of La Salette. Louis Marcien, Count of Carné (1804–76), fervent Catholic and statesman of the July Monarchy, elected to the Académie française in 1863.

Duc de Broglie: Albert de Broglie (1821–1901), contributed to the *Correspondant* under the Second Empire along with Montalembert and Falloux, wrote *L'Église et l'Empire romain au IVe siècle* (Paris, 1856), which echoes Ozanam's lectures at the Sorbonne, and after 1871 directed royalist opposition against Thiers.

Henry Cochin: son of Augustin Cochin who, along with his brother Denys, defended his liberal Catholic position in their political and academic work.

Pontmartin: Armand de Pontmartin (1811–1890), legitimist novelist, author of the wicked contemporary satire on celebrities, *Jeudis de Madame Charbonneau* (1862).

Féval: Paul Féval (1817–87), exponent of serialized fiction such as *Les Mystères de Londres* (1844) which challenged the supremacy of Dumas, and which shone under the Second Empire, in particular his *Le Bossu* serialized in *Le Siècle* in 1857.

Aubineau and Lasserre: Léon Aubineau, author of numerous hagiographies and of a work on Paray-le-Monial (1873). Paul Lasserre de Monzie (1828–1900), author of the highly successful *Notre-Dame de Lourdes*.

Dupont of Tours: Léon-Papin Dupont (1797–1876), 'the holy man of Tours', who helped to found the St Vincent de Paul lectures and was committed to charity work, particularly for working-class children. Commemorated in the account *Le Saint Homme de Tours* (1878) by the archivist for Indre-et-Loire, Léon Aubineau. From 1851 Dupont promoted a shrine in his home for pilgrims to visit a reproduction of the Veil of Veronica. Supposedly 500,000 pilgrims visited the shrine in twenty-five years, and numerous miracles were attributed to this image.

Abbé Lamennais: Félicité de Lamennais (1782–1854), defender of the social virtues of Christianity (in his *Essai sur l'indifférence en matière de religion* (1817, 1821, 1823)) and an Ultramontane opponent of governmental authority (popularized in his *Paroles d'un croyant* (1834)), who counted amongst his followers many Church intellectuals, including Lacordaire, Ozanam, and Montalembert. Papal condemnation led to a break with the Church and he actually became a republican pamphleteer (hence *Le Livre du peuple* (1837)) until his retirement from public life after Louis-Napoléon's *coup d'état* of December 1851.

Joseph de Maistre: (1755–1821), a conspicuous voice in the authoritarian tradition of the French Right, his counter-revolutionary Catholic royalism is evident in his *Considérations sur la France* (1797).

Ernest Hello's 'L'Homme': Hello (1828–85), converted in 1846, an enemy of Renan, whose chronicles in *Le Croisé* were collected in *L'Homme* (1872).

127 *Duranty*: Edmond Duranty (1833–80), co-editor of the review *Réalisme* (1856–57) and author of novels such as *Le Malheur d'Henriette Gérard* (1860) and *La Cause du beau Guillaume* (1862).

128 *Angela da Foligno's 'Visions'*: Angela da Foligno, Italian nun (d. 1309), who collaborated with Ubertino de Casal on *Arbor vitae crucifixae Jesu* and whose mystical writings, collected as *Theologia crucis* (1538) were translated into French (Cologne, 1696) and praised by François de Sales and Bossuet.

129 *Léon Bloy*: (1846–1917), French writer of prose fiction, journalist, and diarist, whose output includes *Le Désespéré* (1887) and *La Femme pauvre* (1897). His vituperative yet visionary style combines the dual functions of the Catholic writer as both creative artist and defender of the faith.

Les Diaboliques: collection of six short stories (1874) which mix a heady cocktail of crime, pleasure and secrecy. Prosecuted by the police, but a shocking success when reissued with nine plates by the engraver Félicien Rops in 1886.

130 *Le Prêtre marié*: Barbey's story *Un* [sic] *prêtre marié* is described by B. G. Roger as 'a lyrical, even sensual poem of blasphemy, sacrilege and apostasy, . . . of the nightmarish world of a heated, unbalanced imagination' (*The Novels and Stories of Barbey d'Aurevilly* (Geneva: Droz, 1967), 91). It relates the story of the ex-priest Sombreval whose neurotic daughter Calixte resolves to bring her father back to the faith. She dies from an acute attack of tetanus after discovering that her father is merely feigning a conversion in order to cure her neurosis by marrying her off to the young nobleman Néel de Néhou. Sombreval in turn commits suicide by jumping into the pond at Le Quesnay, clutching her body in his arms.

Coppelias: Coppelia, automaton from *Der Sandmann* (1815) by E. T. A. Hoffmann (1776–1822), in which the hero lives in a nightmare of morbid fears, falls in love with this automaton, is subject to the hostile influence of an evil being, and ends his life as a madman.

130 *Buridan's ass*: a reference to the French phrase *être comme l'âne de Buridan* which means to be unable to decide between two alternatives. In a commentary on Aristotle's *De caelo* the French philosopher, logician, and scientist Jean Buridan (1300–58) introduces an investigation of probability with the tale of a dog (and not an ass, *l'âne*) forced to choose at random between two equal amounts of food placed before him. This allegorizes the dilemma of a particular kind of moral choice between two evidently identical items.

131 *Sade*: Donatien-Alphonse-François, Marquis de Sade (1740–1814), infamous figure of literary and erotic extremes whose *La Philosophie dans le boudoir* (1795) includes a plea for licence for the passions rather than political reform.

   Malleus maleficorum: (*The Hammer of the Witches*), a treatise on demonology co-authored by Jacob Sprenger with Henri Institoris (1488) and continually re-edited until the second half of the seventeenth century.

132 *Le Dîner d'un athée*: the fifth of Barbey's *Diaboliques*, a tale of violent misogyny in the face of female promiscuity, set during the war with Spain.

   Auditors of the Rota: the Rota, one of the departments of the medieval papal organization, was the supreme court of Christendom, consisting of twelve members.

135 *D.O.M.*: 'Deo optimo maximo' (to God the best and greatest).

136 *Nicander*: Greek author, probably of the second century BC, whose didactic poems on venomous animals and poisons, the *Theriaca* and the *Alexipharmaka*, were translated into French as *Livre des venins* (1567) by Jacques Grévin.

   Grand Albert: actually a reference to the manual of popular medicine known (after the medieval philosopher Albertus Magnus) as 'Grand Albert', which has appeared in countless editions. Fumaroli offers as an example an eighteenth-century edition, *Les Admirables Secrets du Grand Albert, contenant plusieurs traits sur les conceptions des femmes, et les vertus d'herbes, de pierres précieuses, et des animaux* (1703).

137 *craving*: Huysmans's French text uses the medical term 'pica', i.e. a perversion of taste; an attraction to disgusting dishes.

138 *St Vincent de Paul*: (1576–1660), French divine and founder of the Lazarites, known for his charitable works, in particular the establishment of foundling homes in Paris. He was canonized by Clement XII in 1737. The Society of St Vincent de Paul was founded by Ozanam in 1833 in order to achieve practical social benefits for the community. See note to p. 119.

   Portalis: according to Fumaroli, a reference to Auguste Portalis (1801–55), July Monarchy statesman, associated here with Homais, a political opponent of the Catholics trounced in the previous chapter. Fortassier is wise to question whether we can be so certain as to which member of this famous Portalis family Huysmans is actually referring to here.

139 *Constantia*: a wine-growing district of the Cape, South Africa.

141 *riddecks*: Flemish term for bar or pub.

142 *diminution of licensed prostitution*: Huysmans refers to the distinction between illicit prostitution, or 'amours clandestines' (which he recommends), and licensed prostitution, or 'prostitution soumise', in the state-registered *maisons de tolérance* where prostitutes were kept under surveillance by the police. (Huysmans understands only too well why the latter institutions should prove less popular.) The 'incomprehensible illusions' to which Huysmans refers reflect the fashion for simulating seduction without discussing money up front. This was a characteristic of what Alain Corbin calls the 'venal adultery' of the *maisons de rendez-vous* (which were soon to explode across the sexual scene of *fin-de-siècle* Paris) rather than the lower-ranking *maisons de passe* which Huysmans seems to have in mind here, although he refers only to *caboulots*.

romantic blossom: Huysmans's French text refers to 'une vieille fleur bleue' and thus evokes a famous symbol of the tragic idealism and longing of the Romantic spirit.

145 *La Palisse*: Captain Jacques de Chabannes (1470–1525), lord of La Palisse (or La Palice), was the subject of a popular old song full of axioms, which was rejuvenated in the eighteenth century by Mounoye. According to Larousse's *Grand Dictionnaire Universel du XIXᵉ siècle* only one of the original stanzas remains:

> Monsieur d'La Palice est mort,
>   Mort devant Pavie;
> Un quart d'heure avant sa mort,
>   Il était encore en vie.

(M de la Palice is dead | Dead before Pavia | A quarter of an hour before his death | he was still alive). This gives a flavour of subsequent additions through the ages. In French a *lapalissade* has come to mean a self-evident truth.

Balzac: Honoré de Balzac (1799–50), author of the *Comédie humaine*, the vast series of novels which proved to be so significant in the Realist tradition and which had influenced the younger Huysmans.

146 *deliquescences*: this term is echoed in Gabriel Vicaire and Henri Beauclair's pastiche of Decadent writing, *Les Déliquescences d'André Floupette* (1885).

Flaubert . . . Goncourt . . . 'L'Assommoir': in each of these cases Des Esseintes privileges a less well-known work at the expense of canonical texts. As such he undermines assumptions about the achievements of Realism and Naturalism. Flaubert's account of the metaphysical temptations and visions of a fourth-century hermit in *La Tentation de saint Antoine* (1874) is preferred to *L'Éducation sentimentale*, just as Zola's lyrical religious allegory, *La Faute de l'abbé Mouret* (1875), which depicts the struggle between the Church and Nature, is chosen ahead of

L'Assommoir. In the 1903 Preface it is precisely to these relegated classics that Huysmans returns in his setting out of the cultural context of the early 1880s. Des Esseintes, however, represents a change of perspective from the issue of mimetic perspicacity to that of symbolic vision. Similarly, he opts for Edmond de Goncourt's story of an actress, *La Faustin* (1882), in lieu of the better known *Germinie Lacerteux* (1864), co-authored with his brother, Jules, which tells of the double life of a devoted servant whose sexual dissipation leads only to despair and misery.

147 *'Salammbô'*: Flaubert's historical novel of 1862 about the revolt against Carthage by its unpaid mercenary army, which includes accounts of the cruelty of child sacrifice and slow crucifixions, culminating in the torture of Mâtho, leader of this army. Again, this is far removed from the banal contemporary realities of *L'Éducation sentimentale* and *Madame Bovary*.

149 *his Adam and Eve*: in the wild garden called Le Paradou in *La Faute de l'abbé Mouret* a young girl, Albine, tempts the priest Serge who, guilt-ridden, denies his pregnant lover, thus sending her to an early death.

150 *Paul Verlaine*: (1844–96) creator of a poetry of mood and sensation which anticipated Symbolism's concern for musicality and invited Decadent approval. Author of *Poèmes saturniens*, *Fêtes galantes*, *Bonne chanson*, *Romances sans paroles*, and *Sagesse*.

Leconte de Lisle: Verlaine was elected 'Prince of Poets' by the Decadents on the death of Charles-Marie Leconte de Lisle (1818–94), leading figure in the Parnassian movement of poetry.

151 *Streets*: a section of Verlaine's *Romances sans paroles*.

Le soir tombait . . . s'étonne: a quatrain taken from 'Les Ingénus': 'Night was falling, an uncertain autumnal night; the fair ones leaning dreamily on our arms then softly murmured such specious words, that since that time our soul trembles in amazement.' (All verse quoted in this chapter translated by Margaret Mauldon.)

152 *Car nous voulons . . . littérature*: taken from 'Art poétique' in *Jadis et Naguère*: 'For we desire nuances still, not colour, simply nuances . . . And all the rest is *literature*.'

'Romances sans paroles' . . . Sens: this collection was printed in 1874 by Maurice L'Hermite of Sens, who printed the *Courrier de l'Yonne*. With Verlaine in prison at the time, his friend Edmond Lepelletier took responsibility for getting the *Romances* published.

'loin de . . . chair triste': the final line of Part I, Sonnet X, Stanza I of Verlaine's *Sagesse*. This stanza turns away from the 'Gallican and Jansenist' seventeenth century invoked in the previous sonnet: 'It is towards the vast, delicate Middle Ages | That my broken heart would have to navigate, | Far from our days of carnal thoughts and sorry flesh.'

a Cydalisa: in effect a generic label for the young beauties of the Doyenné who succeeded Cydalisa, whose death inspired Gautier to write several elegies. On 14 January 1877 *La République des lettres* published a poem by Huysmans's friend, Léon Hennique, entitled 'Dans la ruelle de Cydalise'.

Tristan Corbière: (1845–75), a poet sensitive to the rhythms of popular speech and the power of the alexandrine. His *Amours jaunes* of 1873 were only brought to the public's attention by Huysmans and Verlaine's *Les Poètes maudits* (also of 1884).

Obscène . . . mort-nées: 'Lewd confessor of fair bigots still-born.'

'pidgin': as Huysmans's French text puts it, 'l'auteur parlait nègre'. It should be noted that Corbière was obsessed by the novel of maritime adventure, *Le Négrier*, written by his father Édouard Corbière.

153 *Éternel féminin de l'éternel jocrisse*: 'Eternal feminine of the eternal dupe.'

Conlie camp: Aurelle de Paladines started to assemble the Army of the Loire in 1870 at the camp de Conlie in the Sarthe. Huysmans is referring to the final poem in Corbière's *Armor*, 'La Pastorale de Conlie par un mobilisé du Morbihan'.

Théodore Hannon: Belgian poet befriended by Huysmans in 1876 during his visit to Brussels where they were introduced by Camille Lemonnier. Hannon showed Huysmans the delights of the city's *demi-monde* as well as its official cultural treasures. They corresponded until 1883 and Huysmans wrote a preface for his *Rimes de joie* (1881), stressing the Baudelairean legacy. This was removed from the 1887 edition. By the time of *A Rebours* they had already fallen out.

154 *Gautier's work*: Théophile Gautier (1811–72), poet, novelist, and critic at the centre of Parisian cultural life for nearly half a century, most commonly identified with an aggressive version of Art for Art's Sake to be found in his preface to *Mademoiselle de Maupin* (1835–6) and an aestheticism often appreciated by the Decadents.

'Les Chansons des rues et des bois': erotic and pastoral lyrics (1865) by that literary colossus, Victor Hugo, whose death the year after the publication of *Against Nature* proved to be a watershed for the *fin-de-siècle* generation of writers.

155 *Stendhal's . . . Duranty's*: we find this same unusual pairing made by both Zola and Barbey d'Aurevilly, which perhaps reflects nineteenth-century under-interpretations of Stendhal's achievement more than it gives a reason for resurrecting Duranty's prose.

156 *wretched Usher*: a reference to E. A. Poe's story *The Fall of the House of Usher*, published in *Tales of the Grotesque and Arabesque* (1839–40). In this Gothic romance the narrator finds his friend, Roderick Usher, and his twin sister, Madeline, in the last stages of mental and physical decline. Madeline is buried alive while in a trance, arises, and carries her brother to death.

Villiers de l'Isle-Adam: Count Villiers de l'Isle-Adam (1838–89) was a Symbolist writer of the fantastic and the supernatural who was championed by Mallarmé and whose short stories, praised by Des Esseintes, were collected later in *Contes cruels* (1883) and *Nouveaux contes cruels* (1888). Villiers met Huysmans in the offices of *La République des lettres* in 1876 and their friendship blossomed in the final months of the former's life.

157 *'Claire Lenoir'*: short philosophical novel in the supernatural mode which reworks the well-worn model of adultery in narrative fiction.

'Véra': the tale of a dead woman magically revived by her husband just so long as his mind can resist the idea of her demise.

158 *Marquise Tullia Fabriana*: Hegelian heroine introduced in Villiers's *Isis*. Retiring from the realm of earthly desires, she houses books of ancient knowledge in the library at the centre of her concealed palatial domain. She avoids suicide by asking the Spirits for a child, Wilhelm, whom she meets at the end of the novel. It is tempting to view her almost as a female version of Des Esseintes (though different genders produce differing narrative endings).

Duchess Sanseverina-Taxis: or Gina Pietranera, is the worldly-wise but passionate aunt of Fabrice del Dongo, hero of Stendhal's novel *La Chartreuse de Parme* (1839). She saves her beloved Fabrice from poisoning by agreeing to sleep with the young prince of Parma, but Fabrice loves Clélia Conti and when he dies, Gina follows him to the grave.

Bradamante: the sister of Rinaldo, future wife of Ruggiero and illustrious ancestor of the Este family in the great Italian romantic epic *Orlando furioso* (1516) by Ludovico Ariosto (1474–1533). This is a continuation of Boiardo's *Orlando innamorato*. A model of constancy, loyalty, magnanimity, and compassion, when she first appears, disguised as a knight, she is described by the Saracen as 'brave, but more than that, she is beautiful' (i. 69).

ridicule: Huysmans's French term 'fumisterie' refers to a literary mode of mischievous wit, located somewhere between whimsical inventiveness and black humour, which resists the seriousness of received art forms. Maupassant notes, for instance, that Rimbaud is either 'un fou ou un fumiste' (a fool or a *fumiste*).

Cros, 'La Science de l'amour': this 'nouvelle' appeared on 1 April 1874 in *La Revue du Monde-Nouveau*, then in *Le Chat noir* (October–November 1885), and in Stock's 1908 collection, *Le Collier de griffes*. Cros's associations with mock-serious literary groups such as the Hydropathes and the Zutistes led to rebuttal by Leconte de Lisle's *Le Parnasse contemporain*. His *Le Coffret de santal* nevertheless reveals worthy prosodic control.

159 *Mallarmé*: in Malcolm Bowie's phrase, Stéphane Mallarmé (1842–98) was 'a *nec plus ultra* of the self-absorbed literary imagination', who embodied the most challenging achievements of Symbolist poetry. His 'Prose pour des Esseintes' can be seen as a response (however backhanded) to Huysmans's laudatory publicity here.

first two 'Parnasses': collections dated 1866 and 1871 (there was a subsequent volume in 1876) which reflected the dominant poetic ideal of the

Second Empire and the early Third Republic in their rejection of out-dated Romantic theories of inspiration voiced by Musset & Co. in favour of a more disciplined, scientific approach to writing verse.

'l'Hérodiade': dramatic poem which, as Huysmans indicates, reflects Moreau's biblical theme.

160 *Oh miroir! . . . nudité*: . . . Oh mirror! Cool water frozen is your frame by ennui; how often, for long hours—abandoned by dreams and seeking memories (like leaves beneath the icy glass covering your fathomless depths)—have I seen myself appear in you as a distant shadow! But, ah, horror! Those evenings when, in your pitiless waters, I have recognized the barrenness of my fragmented dreams!

a piece on Théophile Gautier: Huysmans refers here to 'Toast funèbre'.

Alors . . . l'ingénuité: Then I shall awaken to the primal ardour, solitary and erect, bathed in an antique light, oh lilies! and one among you all for innocence.

161 *'Le Gaspard de la nuit'*: published posthumously in 1842, this pioneering work reflects the Romantic taste for the medieval, the mysterious, and the bizarre. It was written by Aloysius Bertand (1807–41), the 'petit romantique' at the root of developments in the prose poem.

'Vox populi': part of the *Contes cruels*.

'Livre de Jade': a prose poem by Judith Walter (Judith Gautier), published by A. Lemerre in 1867.

'Le Démon de l'analogie': in a letter to Mallarmé from November 1882 Huysmans calls this poem 'La Mort de l'Antépénultième'.

162 *osmazome*: a reference to this concentrated juice of meat can be found in Brillat-Savarin's *Physiologie du goût* (1825), though Huysmans may have recalled its use in *Madame Bovary*.

163 *glossary*: such a glossary was published by Vanier four years later: *Petit glossaire pour servir à l'intelligence des auteurs décadents et symbolistes*, compiled by Paul Adam and one Jacques Plowert (pseud. Félix Fénéon). Fortassier is understandably shocked that this work makes no mention of Huysmans.

164 *waves of music*: like Des Esseintes, Huysmans seems to have had a greater interest in and knowledge of art and literature than he did in the domain of music, which is discussed in the first part of Chapter 15. However, Huysmans associates with Des Esseintes's upbringing the medieval plain-song which he had himself come to appreciate more than the religious music of Handel, Bach, Pergolesi, and Rossini. The sociability of the concert hall and of orchestral performance is, of course, anathema to Des Esseintes's cult of privacy, and in the popular presentation of excerpts and arias he sees a kind of aesthetic crime against the Wagnerian notion of the *Gesamtkunstwerk*, or total work of art. Huysmans himself did not hear any Wagner until after the publication of *Against Nature*, when the fervent Wagnerian, Édouard Dujardin, took him and Mallarmé to the

festival on Good Friday 1885 at the théâtre du Château-d'Eau, 50 Rue de
Malte, near the place de la République. There he heard the *Tannhäuser*
overture and the prelude to *Parsifal*. Huysmans wrote about the overture
for Dujardin's *Revue wagnérienne*, but historians of music have not been
kind about his knowledge of Wagner (see André Coeuroy, *Wagner et l'esprit romantique* (1965) and Léon Guichard, *La Musique et les Lettres en
France au temps du wagnérisme* (1963)). Though he also dismisses comic
opera, Des Esseintes does have time for the smaller-scale intimacy of
chamber music, and in particular the lieder of Schubert.

164 *Father Lambillotte's*: (1797–1855), composer and musicographer who
undertook the restoration of Gregorian chant. Cited by E. de Goncourt
and Montesquiou.

165 *Lesueur*: the Masses of Jean-François Lesueur (d. 1837) were still being
performed at the church of Saint-Roch where they were created.

166 *the way you can read a book*: De Quincey's opium-eater offers a model of
this privileging of solitude above the crowd scenes of the concert hall.

Cirque d'Hiver: from 1861 the Cirque Napoléon (renamed the Cirque
d'Hiver in 1870), in Rue Amelot, was the venue for Pasdeloup's popular
classical concerts.

167 *Auber . . . Flotow*: these composers represent the tradition of French
comic opera which Huysmans finds so banal. Daniel François Esprit
Auber (1782–1871), associate of the librettist Scribe and composer of
light, vivacious operas such as *La Bergère châtelaine* (1820) and in particular *La Muette de Portici* (1828). François Adrien Boïeldieu (1755–1834),
composer of comic operas including *Le Chapeau rouge* (1818) and *La
Dame blanche* (1825), who also provided the singer P. J. Garat with charming songs for piano accompaniment. Adolphe Charles Adam (1803–56),
composer whose considerable output includes over seventy-five comic
operas such as *Le Châlet* (1834) and *Le Toréador* (1849), and a pianist of
some renown. Described by Dieudonné Denne-Baron as 'the worthy
emulator of Boïeldieu', he was from 1848 professor of composition at the
Conservatoire. Friedrich von Flotow (1812–83) studied composition with
Reicha and piano with Pixis in Paris, to which he returned in 1863.

Thomas and Bazin: Charles Louis Ambroise Thomas (1811–96), French
composer of ephemerally popular operas such as *Psyché* (1857) and
Hamlet (1868), who succeeded Auber as director of the Paris Conservatoire in 1871. François Bazin (1816–78) composed, *inter alia*, comic operas
such as *Maître-Pathelin* (1856) and *Voyage en Chine* (1865). Elected to the
Académie des beaux-arts in 1872.

168 *Des Mädchens Klage*: (The Girl's Lament); the poem was sent by Schiller
to Goethe in 1798, appeared in the *Musen-Almanach für das Jahr 1799*,
Die Piccolomini, and then in the former's *Gedichte* of 1800. It was set to
music three times by Franz Schubert, most famously in 1815.

175 *Choiseul-Praslin, Polignac, and Chevreuse*: one of the scandals and trials
which contributed in some part to the onset of the 1848 Revolution, or
at least to creating an atmosphere in which it was possible, concerned the

Duc de Choiseul-Praslin who was having an affair with his children's tutor and on 18 August 1847 had strangled his wife, the daughter of Maréchal Sébastiani; although Fortassier finds such a reference 'barely conceivable', the most notable member of the second family named was the Count of Polignac (1780–1847), prime minister to Charles X in 1829–30, who was held responsible for the repressive policies which caused the latter's downfall (see his *Études historiques, politiques et morales*); most notable in the third case was Marie de Rohan, Duchess of Chevreuse (1600–79), active in unsuccessful intrigues against Richelieu and Mazarin, including the Fronde.

177 *Reverend Father Rouard de Card*: a reference to *De la falsification des substances sacramentelles par le R. P. Fr. Pie Marie Rouard de Card* (Paris: Poussielgue-Rusand, 1856), which Huysmans had in his library.

178 *Radegonde*: Radegunde (d. 587), a Frankish queen whose piety was so noteworthy that it was said that her husband, Clotaire, had married a nun not a queen. Actually consecrated as a nun after he killed her brother, she founded a monastery in Poitiers.

179 *Rue du Sentier*: a busy commercial thoroughfare in the 2nd arrondissement of Paris.

America: anti-Americanism in the Stendhalian tradition. Huysmans deplores the importation of the ways of what he sees as a culturally and politically shallow and materialistic country.

180 *old world, may you expire!*: associated by Fortassier with the apocalyptic vision which threatens the vision of hope at the end of Zola's *Germinal*, published in the same year as *Against Nature*, both of which seem to reflect a collective fear and fascination at the growth of nihilist politics in *fin-de-siècle* France.

The soul . . . distressing: an earlier version of Blaise Pascal's famous fragment 'Divertissement' (Lafuma 136; Brunschvicg 139) to be found in Bossut's 1779 edition of the *Pensées*.

183 *'L'Assommoir'*: (*The Drunkard*); initially criticized for its Naturalist candour, Émile Zola's (1840–1902) novel of 1877, the seventh in his *Rougon-Macquart* cycle, was a scandalous success which signalled his commercial pre-eminence.

'L'Éducation sentimentale': this landmark novel (1869) of sexual and political disillusionment is a story of adultery *manqué* plotted around the events of 1848 and 1851 by the Realist novelist Gustave Flaubert (1821–80). It anticipates the world-weariness of Huysmans's anti-hero and the undermining of traditional plot structures by the lack of 'development' in *Against Nature*.

'Soirées de Médan': collection of short stories (1880) about the Franco-Prussian War by the major Naturalist writers in France. These include, as well as Alexis, Céard, Hennique, and Maupassant, both Huysmans himself (who contributed *Sac au dos*) and the master he denies, Zola.

186 *'A vau-l'eau'*: (*Downstream*) Huysmans's novel of 1882 focuses on the pessimistic Folantin for whom 'Only the worst happens'. Des Esseintes's

aesthetic and economic superiority over this antecedent allows Huysmans to depict an alternative to the disappointments of the contemporary world from which Folantin cannot escape. This is why it is appropriate for Huysmans to give Des Esseintes paintings by Moreau rather than by Degas.

188 *'En route'* and *'L'Oblat'*: published in 1895 and (*The Oblate*) 1903, both reflect Huysmans's movement in the 1890s towards a reactionary and mystical Catholicism.

Maro: i.e. Virgil (Publius Vergilius Maro).

Durtal: another quasi-autobiographical anti-hero of Huysmans, who appears in *Là-bas, En route, La Cathédrale*, and *L'Oblat*.

'La Cathédrale': (1898), by Huysmans, a fiction woven around his study of the history and symbolism of Chartres cathedral.

190 *'Là-bas'*: (*Down There*) Huysmans's novel of 1891 depicts Durtal's analysis of the medieval sadist and Satanist, Gilles de Rais, in the context of a contemporary Paris gripped by the subterranean forces of black magic.

St Hildegard . . . Eucher: St Hildegard (1098–1179), German abbess and mystic apparently blessed with visionary and prophetic powers, as recorded in her *Scivias, visionum et revelationum libri iii* (completed in 1151). Melito, Christian writer of the second century, Bishop of Sardis, and a champion of orthodoxy and apostolic tradition. Author of *Apologia*, two books on the paschal controversy and a selection from the Old Testament. Fragments appeared in Routh's *Reliquiae sacrae* (1814). St Eucherius (d. 450), Bishop of Lyons, author of *De laude eremi, De contemptu mundi et secularis philosophiae*.

191 *Rimbaud . . . Laforgue*: Arthur Rimbaud (1854–91), a companion and lover of Verlaine. The latter dubbed him a *poète maudit* for his visionary evocations of ecstasy and anguish and had his *Illuminations* published in 1886. Jules Laforgue (1860–87) was an anticipatory voice of modernism and a creator of poetry (*Moralités légendaires* (1887) and *Derniers vers* (1890)) which is by turns playful, facetious, and ironic in the face of a Schopenhauerian universe.

192 *d'Aurevilly*: Jules Barbey d'Aurevilly (1808–89) was a major precursor of the Catholic resurgence (known as the *ralliement*) reflected in French literature towards the end of the century. His reactionary journalism and criticism influenced not only Huysmans but also Péladan and Bloy. See discussion of his work in Chapter 12 of *Against Nature*.

193 *'Les Sœurs Vatard' . . . and 'En ménage'*: (*The Vatard Sisters* and *Living Together*) published in 1879 and 1881 respectively, examples of the early Naturalist fiction of Huysmans.

194 *the good Sicambrian*: from the Latin *sicambri*, a Germanic people, originally from the Rhineland, defeated by Drusus who transported many of them to Belgian Gaul where they mixed with the Francs (with whom they were often confused).

Rocambole: the hero of adventure novels by Ponson du Terrail, published from the late 1850s onwards. Hence the adjective *rocambolesque*, meaning far-fetched or fantastic.

Gervaise and a Coupeau: the couple at the centre of Zola's *L'Assommoir*, whose initially sound intentions are undone by weaknesses of character and twists of fate, not least the perpetual return of Gervaise's first lover, Lantier, who even manages to leave a genetic imprint visible in the couple's daughter, Nana.

195 *I entered a Trappist monastery . . . in 1892*: Huysmans first retreated to the Trappe d'Igny in 1892 and returned in 1893, 1894, and 1896.

197 *M. Lemaître*: Jules Lemaître (1853–1914) was a critic and playwright who gave up teaching to devote himself to writing. His influential journalistic essays are collected in the vast *Les Contemporains* and *Impressions du théâtre*.

Sarcey: Francisque Sarcey (1827–99) was a sceptical and conservative journalist, lecturer, and influential drama critic who attacked *Against Nature* virulently in a lecture in the Salle des Capucines.

'Revue des Deux Mondes': founded in 1829, this somewhat staid review of the arts, culture, politics, and economics was by the 1860s the most widely read of such publications. Contributors included Leconte de Lisle, Hérédia, and Maupassant (among many other famous names of the time).

Waflard and Fulgence: reference to Joseph Désiré Fulgence de Bury's collaboration on *Le Célibataire et l'homme marié* (1824), *Le Voyage à Dieppe* (1821), and *Un moment d'imprudence* (1819) with the French dramatist Alexis-Jacques-Marie Wafflard (*sic*), who specialized in comedy and vaudeville.

'After such a book . . . the cross': famous quotation in which, as Huysmans reminds us, Barbey d'Aurevilly predicts the choice between a suicidal Schopenhauerian vision and a return to religious faith (in line with Barbey's own Catholicism) which the author of *Against Nature* must face. This Preface is itself testament to the fact that Huysmans chose the latter path.

ÉMILE ZOLA

L'Assommoir
The Attack on the Mill
La Bête humaine
La Débâcle
Germinal
The Ladies' Paradise
The Masterpiece
Nana
Pot Luck
Thérèse Raquin

The Oxford World's Classics Website

www.worldsclassics.co.uk

- Information about new titles
- Explore the full range of Oxford World's Classics
- Links to other literary sites and the main OUP webpage
- Imaginative competitions, with bookish prizes
- Peruse the Oxford World's Classics Magazine
- Articles by editors
- Extracts from Introductions
- A forum for discussion and feedback on the series
- Special information for teachers and lecturers

www.worldsclassics.co.uk

American Literature

British and Irish Literature

Children's Literature

Classics and Ancient Literature

Colonial Literature

Eastern Literature

European Literature

History

Medieval Literature

Oxford English Drama

Poetry

Philosophy

Politics

Religion

The Oxford Shakespeare

A complete list of Oxford Paperbacks, including Oxford World's Classics, Oxford Shakespeare, Oxford Drama, and Oxford Paperback Reference, is available in the UK from the Academic Division Publicity Department, Oxford University Press, Great Clarendon Street, Oxford OX2 6DP.

In the USA, complete lists are available from the Paperbacks Marketing Manager, Oxford University Press, 198 Madison Avenue, New York, NY 10016.

Oxford Paperbacks are available from all good bookshops. In case of difficulty, customers in the UK can order direct from Oxford University Press Bookshop, Freepost, 116 High Street, Oxford OX1 4BR, enclosing full payment. Please add 10 per cent of published price for postage and packing.